# DICK
# FRANCIS
## COLLECTION

# DICK FRANCIS

## COLLECTION

The Reader's Digest Association, Inc.
New York, NY/Montreal

# CONTENTS

# NERVE

# CHAPTER I

ART Mathews shot himself, loudly and messily, in the center of the parade ring at Dunstable races.

He had walked out of the changing room ahead of me, his head down on his chest as if he were deep in thought. I noticed him stumble slightly down the two steps from the weighing room to the path; and when someone spoke to him he gave absolutely no sign of having heard. But there was nothing to suggest that when he had stood in the parade ring talking for two or three minutes with the owner and trainer of the horse he was due to ride, he would take off his jerkin, produce from under it a large automatic pistol, place the barrel against his temple and squeeze the trigger. The casualness of his movement was as shocking as its effect.

He fell forward to the ground, his face hitting the grass with an audible thud and his helmet rolling off. The bullet had passed straight through his skull, and the exit wound lay open to the sky.

The crack of the gunshot echoed round the paddock. Heads turned and the busy hum of conversation from the three-deep railside racegoers grew hushed and finally silent as they took in the appalling sight.

Mr. John Brewar, the owner of Art's prospective mount, stood with his mouth open, his eyes glazed with surprise. And Corin

Kellar, the trainer for whom both Art and I had been about to ride, went down on one knee beside Art.

The stewards hurried over and stood staring in horror. It was part of their responsibility at a meeting to stand in the parade ring while the horses were led round before each race, so that they would be both witnesses and adjudicators if anything irregular should occur. Nothing as irregular as a public suicide of a top-notch steeplechase jockey had ever, I imagined, required their attention before.

The elder of them, Lord Tirrold, a tall, thin man, bent over Art. I saw the muscles bunch along his jaw, and he looked up at me across Art's body and said quietly, "Finn . . . fetch a rug."

I walked a little way down the parade ring. The trainer of one of the horses due to run in the race took the rug off his horse and held it out to me. I thanked him and went back with it.

The other steward, a sour-tempered hulk named Ballerton, was, I was meanly pleased to see, losing his cherished dignity by vomiting up his lunch.

Lord Tirrold helped me open the rug and we spread it gently over the dead man. Lord Tirrold then went over and spoke to one or two of the little silent groups of people who had runners in the race; presently the stable lads led all the horses out from the parade ring and back to the saddling boxes.

I stood looking down at Corin Kellar and his distress, which I thought he thoroughly deserved. I wondered how it felt to know one had driven a man to kill himself.

There was a click, and a voice announced over the loudspeaker that owing to a serious accident in the parade ring the last two races would be abandoned. I picked up Art's helmet and whip from the grass.

Poor Art. Poor badgered, beleaguered Art, rubbing out his misery with a scrap of lead.

I turned away and walked thoughtfully back to the weighing room. While we changed back from riding kit into our normal clothes the atmosphere down our end of the changing room was one of irreverence covering shock. Art, occupying by general consent the position of elder statesman among jockeys, had been much deferred to and respected. His one noticeable weakness was his conviction that a lost race was always due to some deficiency in his horse or its training, and never to a mistake on his own part. We all knew perfectly well that Art was no exception to the rule that every jockey misjudges things once in a while.

"Thank the Lord," said Tick-Tock Ingersoll, stripping off his blue-and-black-checked jersey, "that Art was considerate enough to let us all weigh out before bumping himself off. If he'd done it an hour ago we'd all have been ten quid out of pocket."

He was right. Our fees for each race were technically earned once we had sat on the scales and been checked out, and they would be automatically paid whether we ran the race or not.

"In that case," said Peter Cloony, "we should put half of it into a fund for his widow." He was a quiet young man prone to overemotional bouts of pity both for others and for himself.

"Not ruddy likely," said Tick-Tock. "Ten quid's ten quid to me, and Mrs. Art's rolling in it."

I sympathized with Tick-Tock. I needed the money, too. Besides, Mrs. Art had treated all of us rank-and-file jockeys icily. Giving her a fiver in Art's memory wouldn't thaw her.

"Let's just buy Art a wreath," I said, "and perhaps a useful memorial, like some hot showers in the washroom here."

Peter Cloony bent on me a look of sorrowful reproof. But from Tick-Tock and the others came nods of agreement.

Grant Oldfield, a dark, thickset man of thirty, said violently, "Besides, that woman probably drove him to it."

There was a curious little silence. A year ago, I reflected, Grant Oldfield would have said the same thing amusingly, not with this unsmiling venom. Lately he could scarcely make the most commonplace remark without giving vent to some inner rage. It was caused, we thought, by the fact that he was going down the ladder again without ever having got to the top. At the vital point in his career when he had had a string of successes and had begun to ride regularly for James Axminster, one of the very top trainers, something had happened to spoil it. He had lost the Axminster job;

other trainers booked him less and less, and his thunderous moods and vile temper increased.

A racecourse official threaded his way down the changing room, spotted me, and shouted, "Finn, the stewards want you."

I finished dressing quickly, walked through the weighing room, and knocked on the stewards' door.

Both stewards were there with the clerk of the course and Corin Kellar. Lord Tirrold said, "Come along in and close the door."

I did as he said and he went on: "Did you actually see Mathews take the pistol out and aim it, or did you look at him when you heard the shot?"

"I saw him take out the pistol and aim it, sir," I said.

"In that case the police may wish a statement; please do not leave the weighing-room building until they have seen you." When I had my hand on the doorknob he said, "Finn, do you know of any reason why Mathews should have wished to end his life?"

I turned and looked at Corin Kellar, who was busy studying his fingernails. "Mr. Kellar might know," I said noncommittally.

The stewards exchanged glances. Mr. Ballerton said, "You're not asking us to believe that Mathews killed himself merely because Kellar was dissatisfied with his riding?" He turned to Lord Tirrold. "Really," he added forcefully, "to suggest that Mathews killed himself because of a few hard words is irresponsible mischief."

Lord Tirrold regarded me with speculation. "That will be all, Finn," he said.

I went out, but before I had crossed the weighing room the door opened again and I heard Corin call me. I turned round and waited for him.

"Thanks very much for tossing that little bomb into my lap," he said sarcastically.

His thin face was deeply lined with worry. He was an exceptionally clever trainer but a nervous, undependable man, who offered you lifelong friendship one day and cut you dead the next.

He said, "Surely you and the other jockeys don't believe Art killed himself because . . . er . . . I had decided to employ him less? He must have had another reason."

"Today was supposed to be his last as your jockey in any case, wasn't it?" I said. "If you want my opinion, he killed himself because you gave him the sack, and he did it in front of you to cause you the maximum amount of remorse."

"He must have been mad," he said, with a tinge of exasperation. "He'd have had to retire sometime. He was getting too old. . . ."

I left him standing there, trying to convince himself that he was in no way responsible for Art's death.

Back in the changing room most of the jockeys had gone home. Tick-Tock, whistling the latest hit tune between his teeth, sat on a bench and pulled on a pair of very fancy yellow socks. On top of those went smooth, slim-toed ankle boots. He shook down the slender legs of his trousers, and grinned at me across the room. *"Tailor and Cutter's* dream boy."

"My father," I said blandly, "was a Twelve Best Dressed man."

"My grandfather had vicuna linings in his raincoats."

"My mother," I said, dredging for it, "has a Pucci shirt."

"Mine," he said carefully, "cooks in hers."

He waved at me, adjusted his Tyrolean trilby, said, "See you tomorrow," and was gone.

Surely, I thought, nothing could be really wrong in the racing world while young Ingersoll ticked so gaily.

But all the same there *was* something wrong. Very wrong. I didn't know what; I could see only the symptoms, and see them all the more clearly, perhaps, since I had been only two years in the game. Between trainers and jockeys there seemed to be an edginess, an undercurrent of resentment and distrust. There was more to it, I thought, than the usual jungle beneath the surface of any fiercely competitive business.

I drank a cup of sugarless tea and eyed the pieces of fruitcake. As usual it took a good deal of resolution not to eat one. Being constantly hungry was the one thing I did not enjoy about race riding. It was the end of September—always a bad time of year, with the remains of the summer's fat to be starved off. I sighed, and tried to console myself that in another month my appetite would have shrunk back to its winter level.

Young Mike, one of the valets, shouted down the room from the doorway, "Rob, there's a copper here to see you."

I went out into the weighing room. A middle-aged policeman in a peaked cap was waiting for me with a notebook in his hand.

"Robert Finn?" he asked.

"Yes," I said.

"I understand from Lord Tirrold that you saw Arthur Mathews put the pistol against his temple and pull the trigger?"

"Yes," I agreed.

He made a note; then he said, "It's a straightforward case of suicide. I don't think we will need to trouble you any further. The only thing for the coroner to decide is the wording of his verdict."

"Unsound mind and so on?" I said.

"Yes," he said. "Thank you for waiting. Good afternoon."

I collected my hat and binoculars and walked down to the racecourse station.

# CHAPTER II

THE large, top-floor flat in Kensington was empty. As usual, it looked as if it had been hit by a minor tornado. Running a practiced eye over the chaos I diagnosed the recent presence of my parents, two uncles and a cousin. In the sitting room my mother's grand piano lay inches deep in piano scores; a violin was propped up in an armchair; a cello and a music stand rested side by side along the length of the sofa. An oboe and two clarinets lay on a table, and music stands leaned at drunken angles against the wall.

The talents with which both my parents' families had been lavishly endowed had not descended to me. By the time I was five they had reluctantly faced the fact that their child was unmusical. I had thereafter been shuffled off from London between school terms to a succession of long holidays on farms, to free my parents for their complicated and lengthy concert tours.

They disapproved of my venture into jockeyship for no other reason than that racing had nothing to do with music. It was no use my pointing out that the one thing I had learned on the various holiday farms was how to ride, and that my present occupation was directly due to their actions in the past.

Thankful to have come in on an intermission, I opened a letter I found waiting for me. I was smiling complacently, which just shows how often life can get up and slap you when you least expect it. In a familiar childish hand the letter said:

> Dearest Rob,
>
> I am afraid this may come as a surprise to you, but I am getting married. He is Sir Morton Henge, and he is very sweet and kind and no cracks from you about him being old enough to be my father, etc. I don't think I had better ask you to the reception, do you? Morton doesn't know about us, and you will be a great dear not to let on. I shall never forget you, dearest Rob. Thank you for everything, and good-bye.
>
> Your loving Paulina

Sir Morton Henge, middle-aged widower and canning tycoon. Well, well. In the eighteen months since I had first met Paulina she had progressed from mousy-haired obscurity to blond blossoming on the cover of at least one glossy magazine a week. I had known that it was inevitable that one day she would forsake me if she struck gold, but all of a sudden a future without her seemed bleak.

I went through to my little bedroom and changed into jeans and an old checked shirt. My stomach gave an extra twist, which was the effect of not having eaten for twenty-three hours. I made for the kitchen. Before I reached it, however, the front door of the flat banged open and in trooped my parents, uncles and cousin.

"Hello, darling," said my mother, presenting a smooth sweet-smelling cheek for a kiss. It was her usual greeting to everyone.

My father, an oboist of international reputation who treated me with polite friendliness, asked as always, "Did you have a good day?" I usually answered briefly yes or no, knowing that he was not really interested.

I said, "I saw a man kill himself. No, it wasn't a good day."

Five heads turned. My mother said, "Darling! *What?*"

"A jockey shot himself at the races. He was only six feet away from me. It was a mess." All five of them stood there looking at me. But they were unaffected. The cello uncle shrugged, and went on into the sitting room, saying over his shoulder, "Well, if you will go in for these peculiar pursuits . . ." The others drifted after him.

I listened to them retuning. The flat was suddenly intolerable. I went out and began to walk. There was only one place to go if I wanted a certain kind of peace, and I didn't care to go there too often for fear of wearing out my welcome. But it was a full month since I had seen my cousin Joanna, and I needed her company.

She was a singer, well on her way to amassing a fair-sized reputation on the concert stage, but when she opened the door with her usual air of good-humored invitation she greeted me in a pair of jeans as old as my own and a black sweater streaked with paint.

"I'm trying my hand at oils," she said, gesturing at an easel on which stood a half-finished portrait. "It's not going very well, damn it." She made a tentative dab at the picture, then, without looking at me, she said, "What's the matter?"

I didn't answer. She said, "There's some steak in the kitchen."

A mind reader, my cousin Joanna. I found a thick steak and grilled it with a couple of tomatoes and made some French dressing for a lettuce I found already prepared in a wooden bowl. The steak smelled wonderful. Joanna and I ate every scrap. I finished first, and sat back and watched her. She had a fascinating face, full of strength and character, with straight dark eyebrows and her short black hair tucked in a no-nonsense style behind her ears.

My cousin Joanna was the reason I was still a bachelor at twenty-six. I had been in love with her from the cradle and had several times asked her to marry me, but she had always said first cousins were too closely related; besides which, I didn't stir her blood.

She pushed away her empty plate and said, "Now, what's the matter?"

I told her about Art and when I had finished she said, "The poor man. Why did he do it, do you know?"

"I think it was because Art was such a perfectionist he simply couldn't face everyone's knowing he'd been given the sack. But the odd thing is that he looked as good as ever to me. He and Corin Kellar, the trainer who retained him, were always having rows when their horses didn't win, but someone else would have employed him, even if not one of the top stables like Corin's."

"And there you have it, I should think," she said. "Death was preferable to decline. I hope that when your time comes to retire you will do it less drastically." I smiled, and she added, "And just what will you do when you retire?"

"Retire? I have only just started," I said.

"And in fourteen years' time you'll be a second-rate, battered forty with nothing to live on but horsy memories."

"And you," I said, "will be a middle-aged contralto's understudy, with your vocal cords growing less flexible every year."

She laughed. "How gloomy. But I see your point. From now on I'll try not to disapprove of your job because it lacks a future."

"But you'll go on disapproving for other reasons?"

"Certainly. It's basically frivolous, unproductive, escapist, and it encourages people to waste time and money on unessentials."

"Like music," I said.

She glared at me. "For that you shall do the washing up."

I did penance for my heresy and then I brought in a peace offering of some freshly made coffee. "Do you mind if I turn the television on?" I asked. "It's a racing program."

"Oh, very well. If you must." But she smiled.

I switched it on, and we saw a batch of advertisements and then a series of speeded-up superimposed views of horses racing, announcing the weekly fifteen minutes of "Turf Talk."

The well-known face of Maurice Kemp-Lore came on the screen, smiling and casual. He began in his easy charming way to introduce his guest of the evening, a prominent bookmaker, and his topic of the evening, the mathematics involved in making a book.

"But first," he said, "I would like to pay tribute to the steeple-chase jockey, Art Mathews, who died today by his own hand at Dunstable races. Although never actually a champion jockey, Art was acknowledged to be one of the six best steeplechase riders in the country, a splendid example to young jockeys. . . ."

He finished off Art's glowing obituary neatly and reintroduced the bookmaker, who gave a clear and fascinating demonstration of how to come out on the winning side. It was well up to the high standard of all the Kemp-Lore programs.

After his "See you all next week at the same time," I switched off the set and Joanna said, "Do you watch that every week?"

"It's a racing must," I said. "Full of things one ought not to miss, and quite often his guest is someone I've met."

"Mr. Kemp-Lore knows his onions, then?"

"He was brought up to it. His father rode a Grand National winner back in the thirties and is now a big noise on the National Hunt Committee; which," I went on, seeing her blank look, "is the ruling body of steeplechasing."

"Has Mr. Kemp-Lore ridden any Grand National winners himself?"

"No," I said. "I don't think he rides much at all. Horses give him asthma, or something like that."

Joanna's interest in racing, never very strong, subsided entirely at this point, and for an hour or so we talked amicably and aimlessly about how the world wagged. Finally, I said good night.

Joanna came with me to the door. "Come again," she said, and then as an afterthought added, "How is Paulina?"

"She is going to marry," I said, "Sir Morton Henge."

I am not sure what I expected in the way of sympathy, but I should have known. Joanna laughed.

# CHAPTER III

Two weeks after Art died I stayed a night at Peter Cloony's. It was the first Cheltenham meeting of the season, and I went down as usual on the race train, carrying some overnight things in a small suitcase. I had one race on each day and intended to spend the night at a pub. But Peter kindly offered me a bed and I accepted.

My ride the first day was a novice hurdler revoltingly called Neddikins. His past form was a sorry record of falls and unfinished races. He had no chance of winning, but I managed to wake him up slightly, so that although we finished last, we finished. A triumph, I considered it, to have got round at all, and to my surprise this was also the opinion of his trainer. Neddikins was the first horse I rode for James Axminster, and I knew I had been asked because he had not wanted to risk injury to his usual jockey. Many such rides came my way, but I counted them good experience.

At the end of the afternoon Peter drove me to the small village in the Cotswolds where he lived. About twenty miles from Cheltenham, we turned off the main road into a narrow secondary road bordered on each side by thick hedges that led to the village. Peter's house was modern, brick-built, with neatly edged flower beds. His wife opened the door. She was, I saw, very soon to have a child. "Do come in," she said shyly, shaking my hand.

The bungalow was sparsely furnished, but neat and clean and smelled of furniture polish. In the sitting room there were only a sofa, a television set, and a dining table with four chairs.

Peter and his wife were clearly devoted to each other; it showed in every glance, every word, every touch.

"How long have you two been married?" I asked.

Peter said, "Nine months," and his wife blushed beguilingly.

After we had had dinner, we washed the dishes and spent the evening watching television and talking about racing.

I slept well. In the morning, after breakfast, Peter did some household jobs and insisted on fetching a loaf of bread from the village to save his wife the walk. As a result we started out for the Cheltenham racecourse later than we had intended. We streaked along the narrow roads and were about to turn into the main road when we first saw the army trailer truck. It was slewed across the road diagonally, completely blocking the way.

Peter's urgent tooting produced one soldier, who ambled over, said they'd been lost, tried to turn round, got stuck, and now his mate was telephoning HQ for instructions.

We both got out of the car to have a look. The great unwieldy trailer truck was solidly jammed across the lane.

Pale and grim, Peter climbed back into his seat with me beside him. He had to back up for a quarter of a mile before we came to a gateway he could turn the car in; then we back-tracked through the village and out onto a road on the far side. We had to make a long detour to get back to the right direction, and altogether the truck put at least twelve miles on to our journey.

Several times Peter said despairingly, "I'll be late." He was due to ride in the first race, and the trainer for whom he rode liked him to report to him an hour early. Trainers had to state jockeys' names at least three quarters of an hour before the event. Peter rode for a man who found a substitute if his jockey was not there an hour before the race.

We reached the racecourse just forty-three minutes before the first race. Peter sprinted toward the weighing room but as I followed him I heard the loudspeaker announce the runners and riders of the first race. P. Cloony was not among them.

I found him in the changing room, sitting on the bench with his head in his hands. "He didn't wait," he said miserably. "He's put Ingersoll up instead."

Tick-Tock caught my eye and grimaced in sympathy. But it was not his fault he had been given the ride.

The worst of it was that Tick-Tock won. I was standing beside Peter when his replacement skated by the winning post, and he made a choking sound as if he were about to burst into tears.

"Never mind," I said awkwardly. "It's not the end of the world."

But all that day Peter couldn't stop boring everyone in the weighing room by harping on the trailer truck over and over again.

For myself, things went slightly better. The young hurdler I was to ride in my second ride for James Axminster had as vile a reputation as his stablemate the previous day. But for some reason the wayward animal and I got on very well together from the start, and to my surprise we came over the last hurdle in second place and passed the leading horse on the stretch to the winning post. The odds-on favorite finished fourth. It was my second win of the season, and it was greeted with dead silence.

I found myself trying to explain it away to James Axminster in the winner's unsaddling enclosure. I knew he hadn't had a penny on it. "I'm very sorry, sir," I said. "I couldn't help it."

He looked at me broodingly without answering, and I thought that there was one trainer who would not employ me again in a hurry. Sometimes it is as bad to win unexpectedly as to lose on a certainty. I stood waiting for the storm to break.

"Well, go along and weigh in," he said abruptly. "And when you're dressed I want to talk to you."

When I came out of the changing room he was talking to Lord Tirrold, whose horses he trained. They turned toward me. "What stable do you ride for most?" James Axminster asked.

I said, "I ride mainly for farmers who train their own horses. I haven't a steady job with a public trainer."

"You know you have made me look a proper fool," Axminster said. "I've told the owner often that his horse is pretty useless."

"I'm sorry, sir," I said again. And I meant it.

"Don't look so glum about it. I'll give you another chance. There's a slow old plug you can ride for me on Saturday—Geranium, in the handicap chase at Hereford—if you're not booked already, and two or three others next week. After that . . . we'll see."

"Thank you," I said dazedly. "Thank you very much." It was as if he had handed me a gold brick when I had expected a scorpion. If I acquitted myself at all well on his horses, he might use me regularly as a second-string jockey. That would be a giant step up.

"Can you do the weight? Ten stone?" One hundred forty pounds.

"Yes," I said. I'd need to lose another three pounds in the two days, but starvation had never seemed so attractive.

"Very well. I'll see you there." I watched him and Lord Tirrold go out of the weighing room together. Between them they had won almost every important event in the National Hunt calendar.

James Axminster was a big man in every sense. Six foot four and solidly bulky, he moved and spoke and made decisions with easy assurance. His training stable was one of the six largest in the country. To have been offered a toehold in this setup was almost as frightening as it was miraculous.

I spent most of the next day running round Hyde Park in three sweaters and a windcheater. At about six o'clock I boiled three eggs and ate them without salt or bread. After that I went to the Turkish baths in Jermyn Street and spent the whole night there. In the morning I went back to the flat and ate three more boiled eggs, and at last made my way to Hereford.

The needle quivered when I sat on the scales with the lightest possible saddle and boots. It pendulumed above and below the ten-stone mark, finally settling a hairsbreadth on the right side.

"Ten stone," said the clerk of the scales in a surprised voice.

In the parade ring James Axminster beckoned the lad who was leading round the slow old plug I was to ride and said, "You'll have to kick this old mare along a bit. She's lazy. A good jumper, but that's about all."

I was used to kicking lazy horses. I kicked, and the mare jumped; and we finished third.

"Hm," said Axminster as I unbuckled the girths. When I had changed into the colors of the other horse I had been engaged to ride that afternoon, Axminster was waiting for me at the changing-room door. He handed me a paper without a word. It was a list of four horses running the following week. "Well?" he said. "Can you ride them?"

I said, "Thank you, sir. I'd be glad to." He turned away, and I folded up the precious list and put it in my pocket.

Tick-Tock and I went out together to the parade ring. We were both riding that afternoon for Corin Kellar.

"Paste on a toothy leer," Tick-Tock said. "The eye of the world has swiveled our way."

I glanced up to a platform where a television camera swung toward us as it followed the progress of a gray horse round the ring.

"The great man himself is here somewhere too," said Tick-Tock, "the one and only Mr. Kemp-Lore no less."

We joined Corin and he began to give us our instructions. Tick-Tock's mount was a good one, but I was as usual riding a horse of whom little was expected, and quite rightly, as it turned out. We trailed in a long way behind, and I saw from the numbers going up in the frame that Corin's other horse had won.

Corin and Tick-Tock and the horse's owner were in the winner's enclosure when I walked back to the weighing room, but Corin caught me by the arm as I went past and asked me to come straight out again, to tell him how the horse had run. When I rejoined him he was talking to a man whom I recognized as Maurice Kemp-Lore. Corin introduced us.

It never ceases to be disconcerting, meeting for the first time in the flesh a man whose face is as familiar to you as a brother's. Kemp-Lore was, I judged, in his early thirties. Of average height and slim build, with firm, sun-tanned features and light hair. His charm was instantly compelling. The effect was calculated, his stock-in-trade. All good interviewers know how to give people confidence and Kemp-Lore was a master of his art.

"I see you were last in that race," he said. "Bad luck."

"Bad horse," said Corin.

"I've been wanting to do a program on—if you'll forgive me—

an unsuccessful jockey." His warm smile took the sting out of his words. "Perhaps it would be fairer to say a jockey who is not yet successful." His blue eyes twinkled. "Would you consider telling my viewers what sort of life you lead—your financial position, reliance on chance rides . . . that sort of thing? Just to give the public the reverse side of the coin. They know all about jockeys who win important races." He smiled. "Will you do it?"

"Yes," I said, "certainly. But I'm not really typical. I . . ."

He interrupted me. "Don't tell me anything now," he said. "I always prefer not to know the answers to my specific questions until we are actually on the air. It makes the whole thing more spontaneous. I will send you a list of the sort of questions I will be asking, and you can think out your replies. Okay?"

"Yes," I said. "All right."

"Good. Next Friday then. The program goes on at nine o'clock. Get to the studios by seven thirty, will you? That gives time for seeing to lighting, makeup, and so on, and perhaps for a drink beforehand. Oh, and by the way, there will be a fee, of course, and your expenses." He smiled sympathetically.

"Thank you." I smiled back. "I'll be there."

He strolled away and Corin said in a smug, self-satisfied voice, "I know Maurice quite well. A grand fellow. Good family. His father won the National and his sister is the best lady point-to-point rider there has been for years. Poor old Maurice, though, he hardly rides at all. Horses give him the most ghastly asthma, you know."

Back in the changing room I was annoyed to see Grant Oldfield standing by my peg, holding the list of horses James Axminster had given me. Grant had been going through my pockets.

My protest was never uttered. Without a word, without warning, Grant swung his fist and punched me heavily in the nose.

Blood splashed in a scarlet stain down the front of my silk shirt and made big uneven blotches on the white breeches.

"For heaven's sake, lay him down on his back," said one of the valets, hurrying over. I was already lying propped up by the leg of the bench. Young Mike, my valet, thrust a saddle under my shoulders and pushed my head backward over it. A second later he was piling a cold, wet towel across the bridge of my nose; and gradually the bleeding lessened and stopped.

Grant scowled down at me, then turned without saying a word and pushed his way out of the changing room as the jockeys returned from the last race. The list of Axminster horses fluttered to the floor in his wake.

Tick-Tock dumped his saddle on the bench. "What have we here? A blood bath?" he said.

"Grant socked him," said one of the jockeys who had been there. "Why?"

"Ask me another," I said. "Or ask Grant." I lifted the towel off my face and stood up gingerly.

I cleaned myself up and changed, and walked down to the station with Tick-Tock. "You must know why he hit you," he said.

I handed him Axminster's list. He read it and gave it back. "Yes, I see. Hatred and jealousy. You're stepping into the shoes he couldn't fill himself. He had his chance there, and he muffed it."

"What happened?" I asked. "Why did Axminster drop him?"

"I don't honestly know," Tick-Tock said. "You'd better ask Grant and find out what mistakes not to make."

THE flat was empty. I made myself an ice bag and lay down on the bed with it balanced on my forehead. I shut my eyes and thought about Grant and Art; two disintegrated people. One had been driven to violence against himself, and the other had turned violent against the world. Poor things, I thought rather too complacently, they were not stable enough to deal with whatever had undermined them; and I remembered that easy pity later on.

On the following Wednesday Peter Cloony came to the races bubbling over with happiness. The baby was a boy, his wife was fine, everything was rosy. The horse he rode that afternoon started favorite and ran badly, but it didn't damp his spirits.

The next day he was due to ride in the first race, and he was twenty minutes late. I heard fragments of his trainer's angry remarks. "Second time in a week . . . irresponsible . . . I've had to get another jockey. . . ."

When I went into the changing room a short time later he was sitting on a bench, white and trembling. "What happened this time?" I asked.

He stood up. "You'll never believe it but there was something else stuck across the lane, and I had to go miles round again." His voice trailed off as I looked at him in disbelief.

"Not another trailer truck?" I asked incredulously.

"No, a car. One of those decrepit old Jaguars. It had its nose in the hedge and it was jammed tight, right across the lane. The doors were locked, and the hand brake was full on."

"It's very bad luck," I said inadequately.

"Bad luck!" he repeated explosively. "It's more than bad luck, it's—it's awful. I can't afford . . . I need the money. . . ."

Peter had not been booked for any other ride that afternoon; he spent the day mooching about the weighing room so as to be under the eye of any trainers looking hurriedly for a jockey. He wore a desperate, hunted look, and I knew that that alone would have discouraged me had I been a trainer. He left, unemployed and disconsolate, just before the fifth race. As I watched him go I felt a surge of irritation. Why didn't he leave himself a margin for error on his journeys? And what a dismal coincidence, I reflected, that the lane should have been blocked twice in a week.

In the parade ring James Axminster introduced me to the owner of the horse I was to ride and we made the usual desultory prerace conversation. In the two earlier races that week I had been riding the stable's second string while Pip Pankhurst, Axminster's top jockey, took his usual place on the better horses. Thursday's handicap hurdle, however, was all my own because Pip could not do the weight.

"Anything under ten stone six, and it's yours," he told me cheerfully, when he found I was riding some of his stable's horses.

By eating and drinking very little I had managed to keep my

riding weight down to ten stone for a whole week. This meant a body weight of nine stone eight, which was a strain, but with Pip in such an ungrudging frame of mind it was well worth it.

Axminster gestured toward the middle-aged handicap hurdler plodding sleepily round the ring. "At the fourth hurdle, you want to be somewhere in the middle. About three from home, you want to lie about fourth. Start him moving going into the second last. Try to come up to the leader at the last. He's a great jumper, but has no finishing speed. See what you can do, anyway."

He had not given me such detailed instructions before. I felt a quiver of excitement. At last I was about to ride a horse whose trainer would not be thoroughly surprised if he won.

I followed my instructions to the letter, and coming into the last hurdle level with two other horses I kicked my old mount hard. He responded with a zipping leap which sped him clean past the other horses in midair and landed us a good two lengths clear of them. It was true that the old hurdler could not quicken, but he held on gamely, and still had half a length in hand when we passed the post. It was a gorgeous moment.

"Well done," said Axminster matter-of-factly. Winners were nothing out of the ordinary to him. But the owner was delighted. "Well done, well done," he said to the horse, Axminster and me indiscriminately.

Axminster's piercing blue eyes were regarding me quizzically. "Do you want the job?" he asked. "Second to Pip, regular?"

I nodded and dragged in a deep breath, and croaked, "Yes."

The owner laughed. "It's Finn's lucky week. Ballerton tells me Maurice is interviewing him tomorrow evening."

"Really?" Axminster said. "I'll try and watch it."

I TELEPHONED to Joanna. "How about having dinner with me? I want to celebrate."

"What?" she asked economically.

"A winner. A new job. All's right with the world," I said.

"All right. Where?"

"Hennibert's," I said. It was a small restaurant in St. James's Street with a standard of cooking to match its address, and prices to match both.

"I'm sold," she said. "I'll be there at eight."

She wore a dress I had not seen before, a slender affair made of a deep-blue shimmering material. Her dark hair curved neatly down onto the nape of her neck, and the tapering lines she had drawn on her eyelids made her black eyes look bigger and deep-set and mysterious. Every male head turned to look at her as we walked down the room.

We ate avocados with French dressing and *boeuf stroganoff* with spinach, and late-crop strawberries and cream. For me, after so many bird-sized meals, it was a feast. We took a long time eating and drank a bottle of wine, and sat over our coffee talking with the ease of a friendship which stretched back to childhood.

Joanna seemed genuinely pleased about the James Axminster job. Even though racing didn't interest her, she saw what it meant to me. My first elation had settled down to a warm cozy glow of satisfaction. I told her about the television program.

"Tomorrow?" she said. "Good. I'll watch you. You don't do things by halves, do you?"

"This is just the start." I grinned. I almost believed it.

We walked back to Joanna's studio. It was a clear crisp night with the stars blazing coldly in the black sky. We stopped in the dark mews outside Joanna's door. I looked at her. It was a mistake. Her uptilted face with starlight reflected in the shadowy eyes swept me into the turmoil I had been suppressing all evening. "Thank you for coming," I said abruptly. "Good night, Joanna."

She put her hand for a moment on my shoulder in a friendly fashion. "A lovely dinner, Rob," she said, and smiled good night. When she had shut her door, I turned and started back down the mews. I swore violently, aloud. It wasn't much relief.

# CHAPTER IV

ON MY arrival at the Universal Telecast Studios I asked the girl at the reception desk where I should go. She smiled kindly. Would I sit down, she said. She spoke into the telephone: "Mr. Finn is here, Gordon."

Within ten seconds a young man with freckles and a rising-young-executive, navy-blue pin-striped suit appeared. "Mr. Finn?" he said expansively, holding out a hand. "Glad to have you here. I am Gordon Kildare, associate producer. Maurice is up in the studio running over last-minute details, so I suggest we go along and have a drink and a sandwich first."

He led the way to a small room where, on a table, stood bottles and glasses and four plates of appetizing-looking sandwiches. "What will you have?" he asked hospitably.

"Nothing, thank you," I said.

"Perhaps afterward, then?" He poured himself a drink and raised it to me smiling. "Good luck," he said. "The great thing is to be natural." He picked up a sandwich and took a squelchy bite.

In a few minutes Maurice Kemp-Lore strode briskly in.

"My dear chap," he greeted me, shaking me warmly by the hand. "Has Gordon been looking after you? You got the list of questions all right and thought out some answers?"

"Yes," I said.

"Good, good. That's fine," he said.

The telephone rang. Gordon answered it, listened briefly and said, "He's here, Maurice."

Kemp-Lore went out, followed by his assistants. His voice could soon be heard coming back along the corridor talking with someone who spoke with a nasal twang. I wondered who the other guest would be. At the doorway Kemp-Lore stood respectfully back to let his guest precede him. My spirits sank. Paunch and horn-rims well to the fore, Mr. John Ballerton was ushered in.

"You know Rob Finn, of course," Kemp-Lore said.

Ballerton nodded coldly in my direction and Kemp-Lore said, "It's time we went up to the studio, I think."

The studio held a tangle of cameras trailing their thick cables over the floor. To one side there was a carpet-covered platform on which stood three low-slung chairs and a coffee table. Three coffee cups on a tray shared the table with three empty balloon brandy glasses, a silver cigarette box and two large glass ashtrays. "We want to look as informal as possible," Kemp-Lore said pleasantly. "As if we were talking over coffee and brandy after dinner."

He took his place between us. Set in front and slightly to one side stood a monitor set. A battery of cameras faced us.

Gordon and his assistants started checking their lights, and testing for sound. Kemp-Lore said, "I'll just run through the order of the program. I am going to talk to you first, John, along the lines we discussed. After that, Rob will tell us what his sort of life entails. We're using some film of a race you rode in, Rob. Now, the great thing is to talk naturally. I've explained that too much rehearsal spoils the spontaneity of a program like this, but it means that a lot of the success of the next quarter of an hour depends on you. I'm sure you will both do splendidly." He finished his pep talk with a cheerful grin.

One of the assistants poured hot black coffee into the three cups. Then he uncorked a bottle of brandy and wet the bottom of the balloon glasses.

"Two minutes," shouted a voice. The spotlights flashed on, dazzling us and blacking out everything in the studio. The monitor set showed an animated cartoon advertising petrol.

"Thirty seconds. Quiet, please," said Gordon.

A hush fell over the studio. Everyone waited. Kemp-Lore beside me arranged his features in the well-known smile, looking straight ahead at the round black lens of the camera.

On the monitor set the superimposed horses galloped and faded. Gordon's hand swept down briskly. The camera in front of Kemp-Lore developed a shining red eye and he began to speak, pleasantly, intimately, straight into a million sitting rooms.

"Good evening . . . tonight I am going to introduce you to two people who are both deeply involved with National Hunt racing, but who look at it, so to speak, from opposite poles. First, here is Mr. John Ballerton." He gave him a fulsome buildup, and skillfully guided by Kemp-Lore, Ballerton talked about his duties as one of the stewards at a race meeting. It involved, he said, hearing both sides if there was an objection to a winner, and summoning jockeys and trainers for minor infringements of the rules.

I watched him on the monitor set. I had to admit he looked a solid, sober, responsible citizen with right on his side. No one watching the performance Kemp-Lore coaxed out of him would suspect him to be the bigoted, pompous bully we knew on the racecourse.

Before I expected it, Kemp-Lore was turning round to me. I swallowed convulsively. He smiled at the camera and said, with the air of one producing a treat, "Now here is Rob Finn, a young steeplechase jockey just scratching the surface of his career. Few of you will have heard of him. He has won no big races, nor ridden any well-known horses, and I have invited him here tonight to give us all a glimpse of what it is like to try to break into a highly competitive sport. . . ."

The red light was burning on the camera pointing at me. I smiled at it faintly. My tongue stuck to the roof of my mouth.

"First," he went on, "here is a piece of film which shows Finn in action. He is the rider with the white cap, fourth from last."

We watched on the monitor set. It was one of the first races I ever rode in, and my inexperience showed sorely. During the few seconds the film lasted the white cap lost two places.

The film faded out and Kemp-Lore said, smiling, "How did you set about starting to be a jockey, once you had decided on it?"

I said, "I knew three farmers who owned and trained their own horses, and I asked them to let me try my hand in a race."

"Usually," Kemp-Lore said, "jumping jockeys either start as

amateur steeplechase riders or as apprentices on the flat, but I understand that you did neither of these things, Rob?"

"No," I said. "I started too old to be an apprentice and I couldn't be an amateur because I had earned my living riding horses."

"As a stable lad?" He clearly expected me to say yes. It was, after all, by far the commonest background of jockeys.

"No," I said.

He raised his eyebrows a fraction.

I said, "I was away from England for some years, wandering round the world, mainly in Australia and South America. I got jobs as a stockman, and spent a year in New South Wales working in a traveling rodeo. Ten seconds on the bucking bronc: that sort of thing."

"Oh." The eyebrows rose another fraction, and there was a perceptible pause before he said, "How very interesting. I wish we had more time to hear about your experiences, but I want to show viewers how a jockey in your position makes a living . . . on a race or two a week. Now, your fee is ten guineas a time . . ."

He took me at some length through my finances, which didn't sound too good when dissected into traveling expenses, valets' fees, replacement of kit and so on. He then turned deferentially to Ballerton. "John, have you any comment to make on what we have been hearing from Rob?"

A trace of malicious pleasure crept into Ballerton's smile. "All these young jockeys complain too much," he stated harshly, ignoring the fact that I had not complained at all. "If they aren't very good at their job they shouldn't expect to be highly paid."

"Eh . . . of course," said Kemp-Lore. "But surely every jockey has to make a start? And there must always be some jockeys who never quite reach the top grade, but who have a living to make."

"They'd be better off in a factory, earning a fair wage on a production line," said Ballerton, with heavy, reasonable-sounding humor. "But they like wearing those bright silks," he added. "People turn to look at them, and it flatters their little egos."

There was a gasp out in the dark studio at this ungentlemanly blow below the belt, and I saw that the red spot on the camera pointing at me was glowing. I raised a smile for Mr. Ballerton then, as sweet and forgiving a smile as ever turned the other cheek.

Kemp-Lore turned to me. "And what do you say to that, Rob?"

I spoke vehemently, and straight from the heart. "Give me a horse and a race to ride it in, and I don't care if I wear silks or . . . or . . . pajamas. I don't care if I don't earn much money, or if I break my bones, or if I have to starve to keep my weight down. All I care about is racing . . . and winning, if I can."

There was a small silence. Both of them were staring at me. John Ballerton looked as if a wasp had stung him, and Kemp-Lore's expression I could not read at all. Then he turned smoothly back to his camera and slid the familiar smile into place, but I felt irrationally that something important had taken place, though I had not the slightest clue to what it was.

Kemp-Lore was very soon closing the program and the hot spotlight flicked off. Kemp-Lore stood up and stretched and grinned round at us all. "Well, John. Well, Rob. Thank you both very much."

I reflected again how superlative he was at his job. By encouraging Ballerton to needle me he had drawn from me, for the ears of a few million strangers, a more soul-baring statement than I would ever have made privately to a close friend.

A good deal of backslapping followed before I left the television building. I wondered why it was that I felt more apprehensive than I had before the show started.

# CHAPTER V

THREE weeks and a day after the broadcast, Pip Pankhurst broke his leg. His horse, falling on him in the second race on a drizzly mid-November Saturday, made a thorough job of putting the champion jockey out of action for the bulk of the chasing season.

I had been watching from the stands and it would be untrue to say that I went down the stairs to the weighing room with a calm heart. However sincere my pity for Pip's plight might be, the faint chance that I might take his place in the following race was playing hop, skip and jump with my pulse.

It was the big race of the week, a three-mile chase with a substantial prize. Pip's mount, which belonged to Lord Tirrold, was the rising star of the Axminster stable: a six-year-old brown gelding called Template, intelligent, fast, and a battler.

As I went into the weighing room I saw James Axminster talking to another jockey. The jockey shook his head. Axminster turned slowly round until he saw me. He looked at me steadily, pondering, unsmiling. Then his eyes focused on someone to my left. He came to a decision and walked briskly past me.

Well, what did I expect? I had ridden for him for only four weeks. Three winners. A dozen also-rans. I was still the new boy, the unsuccessful jockey of the television program. I began to walk disconsolately over to the changing-room door.

Axminster had come up behind me. "Rob," he said in my ear, "Lord Tirrold says you can ride his horse."

The two men were looking at me appraisingly, knowing they were giving me the chance of a lifetime, not sure that I was up to it.

"Yes, sir," I said. I went on into the changing room, queerly steadied by having believed that I had been passed over.

I rode better than I ever had before, but that was probably because Template was the best horse I had ever ridden. He was smooth and steely, and his rocketing spring over the first fence had me gasping; but by the second I was ready for it, exulting in it; as the chase went on I knew I had entered a new dimension of racing.

Axminster had given me no orders on how to shape the race. He said only, "Do the best you can, Rob."

As the pattern of the race shifted, I concentrated on keeping Template lying in about fourth position in the field, where I could see how everyone else was going. Template jumped himself into third place at the second last fence, and was still not under pressure. Coming toward the last I brought him to the outside, to give him a clear view, and urged him on. His stride quickened. He took off so far in front of the fence that for a heartbreaking second I was sure he would land squarely on top of it, but I had underestimated his power. He landed yards out on the far side, passing one horse in midair, collected himself without faltering and surged ahead.

There remained only a chestnut to be beaten. Only. Only the favorite. No disgrace, I fleetingly thought, to be beaten only by him. But I dug my knees into Template's sides and gave him two taps with the whip down his shoulder. He needed only this signal, I found, to put every ounce into getting to the front. He stretched his neck out and flattened his stride, and I knelt on his withers and squeezed him, moving with his rhythm, keeping my whip still for fear of disturbing him. He put his head in front of the chestnut's five strides from the winning post, and kept it there.

There was a cheer as we went into the unsaddling enclosure, and some complimentary things were said, but I felt too weak and breathless to enjoy them. No race had ever before taken so much out of me. Nor given me so much, either.

Surprisingly Lord Tirrold and Axminster were almost subdued.

"That was all right, then," said Axminster, smiling.

"He's a wonderful horse," I said fervently.

"Yes, he is," said Lord Tirrold, patting the dark sweating neck.

Axminster said, "Don't hang about then, Rob. Go and weigh in. You're riding in the next race. And the one after." I stared at him. "You're standing in for Pip until he comes back," he said.

"WHAT a nerve!" Tick-Tock said.

He was waiting for me to change at the end of the afternoon.

"Six weeks ago you were scrounging rides. Then you get yourself on television as a failure and make it obvious you aren't one. Newspapers write columns about your version of the creed. Now you do the understudy-into-star routine, and all that jazz. Three winners in one afternoon!"

I grinned at him. "What goes up must come down." I tied my tie and looked in the mirror at the fatuous smile I could not remove from my face. Days like this don't happen very often, I thought.

"Let's go and see Pip," I said abruptly.

I THINK Axminster had trouble persuading some of his owners that I was capable of taking Pip's place, because I didn't ride all of the stable's horses at first. But as the weeks went by, fewer and fewer other jockeys were engaged. I became used to riding three or four races a day, to going back to my digs contentedly tired in body and mind and waking the next morning with eagerness. I even became used to winning. It was no longer a rarity for me.

While the gods heaped good fortune on my head, others fared badly. Grant Oldfield had offered neither explanation nor apology for hitting me. He withdrew more and more into himself. Oddly enough his riding skill had not degenerated with his character. He rode the same rough, tough race; but he had begun to take out his anger on his mounts, and twice during November he was called before the stewards for "excessive use of the whip."

The Oldfield volcano erupted, as far as I was concerned, one cold afternoon in the parking lot at Warwick. Tick-Tock had gone to a different meeting, and I had the Mini Cooper which he and I had bought together. I was late leaving the meetings as I had won the last race and by the time I got there the lot was empty except for our car and another next to it.

I went toward the Mini still smiling to myself with the pleasure of this latest win, and I did not see Grant until I was quite close to him. A rear wheel lay on the grass and he was kneeling beside his car with a spare. He saw me coming, and he saw me smiling, and he thought I was laughing at him. I could see the uncontrollable fury rise in his face. He got to his feet and then bent forward and picked up a tire iron.

"I'll help you with your tire, if you like," I said mildly.

For answer he took a step sideways, swung his arm in a sort of backward chop, and smashed the tire iron through the back window of the Mini Cooper.

My anger rose quick and hot and I took a step toward Grant. He turned to face me squarely and lifted the tire iron again.

"Don't be an ass, Grant," I said reasonably. "Put that thing down and let's get on with changing your tire."

"You ——" he said, "you took my job."

"No," I said. But before I could add more he slashed forward and downward at my head.

I think that at that moment he must have been truly insane, for had the blow connected he would surely have killed me. I ducked, and the iron whistled past my right ear. His arm returned in a backhand. I ducked again and this time, as he swung wide, I stepped close and hit him hard just below his breastbone. He grunted and the arm with the iron dropped. I hit him on the side of the neck with the edge of my hand. He went down on his hands and knees, and then sprawled on the grass.

He was breathing heavily and moaning. I squatted and said close to his ear, "Grant, why did you get the sack from Axminster?"

He mumbled something I could not hear. I repeated my question. He said distinctly, "He said I passed on the message."

"What message?"

His lips moved but he said nothing more.

I decided that I could not just drive off and leave him lying there. I put the spare wheel on, and slung the jack and the punctured wheel into the trunk of his car. I shook him and called his name. He opened his eyes. I propped him up against his car. He looked utterly worn out.

"Oh God," he said, "Oh God." It sounded like a true prayer.

"If you went to see a psychiatrist," I said gently, "you could get some help."

He didn't answer; but neither did he resist when I helped him into the Mini Cooper. I asked him where he lived, and he told me.

Luckily it was only thirty miles away, and I drew up where he directed outside a semidetached featureless house on the outskirts of a small town. There were no lights in the windows.

"Isn't your wife in?" I asked.

"She left me," he said absently. Then his jaw tensed and he said, "Mind your own —— business." He jerked the door open, climbed out and slammed it noisily. He shouted, "Take your bloody do-gooding off. I don't want your help!"

I drove off but I had only started down the road when I reluctantly decided that he shouldn't be left alone.

In the center of the little town I stopped and asked where a doctor lived. I was directed to a house where a youngish, capable-looking man answered the door.

"Are you by any chance Grant Oldfield's doctor?" I asked.

He said at once, "I'm Parnell. Yes, I'm his doctor."

I introduced myself and said, "Could you please come and take a look at him. He . . . er . . . he was knocked out at the races."

"Half a mo," he said. He came back with his medical bag. We got in the Mini Cooper and I told him how Grant had smashed the back window and explained how I had come to bring him home.

He listened in silence. Then he said, "Why did he attack you?"

"He seems to believe I took his job. I didn't. He lost it months before it was offered to me."

When we reached Grant's house it was still in darkness. There was no answer when we rang the bell.

Then a faint rustle in the dark front garden caught our attention, and with the aid of the doctor's flashlight we found Grant huddling in the bordering privet hedge.

"Come along, old chap," said the doctor, and pulled him to his feet. He found a bunch of keys in Grant's pockets, and handed them to me. I unlocked the front door and turned on the lights. The doctor guided Grant into the first room we came to, the dining room. Grant collapsed on a chair and laid his head down on the table. Parnell felt his pulse, lifted up his eyelid and ran both hands round the base of his skull. Grant moved irritably when Parnell's fingers touched the place where I had hit him.

Parnell stepped back a pace. "There's nothing physically wrong with him as far as I can see, except for what is going to be a stiff neck. We'd better get him to bed and I'll give him a sedative. In the morning I'll arrange for him to see someone who can sort out his troubles for him. You'd better give me a ring during the night if there's any change in his condition."

"I?" I said. "I'm not staying here all night . . ."

"Oh yes, I think so, don't you?" he said cheerfully. "Who else? After all, you hit him, and you cared enough to bring him home."

Put like that, it was difficult to refuse. We took Grant upstairs. His bedroom was filthy. Tangled sheets and blankets were piled on the unmade bed and dirty clothes were scattered about.

I made up the bed with clean sheets I found in the linen cupboard, while Parnell undressed Grant as far as his underpants and made him get into bed. Then, opening his case, he shook out two capsules and made Grant swallow them. "Those pills ought to keep him quiet for a bit," he said. "Give him two more when he wakes up. Have a good night," he added with a callous grin.

I spent a miserable evening and dined off a pint of milk I found on the back doorstep. Several times in the night I went softly in to see how Grant was doing, but he slept peacefully. Eventually I fell uneasily asleep myself.

Dr. Parnell arrived with a nurse at seven. He had also brought eggs, bacon, bread, milk and coffee, and an electric razor.

"All modern conveniences," he said cheerfully.

So I went back to the races washed, shaved and fed. But, thinking of Grant as I had left him, not in a happy frame of mind.

# CHAPTER VI

"THERE's a shortage of jockeys just now," said Axminster.

We were on our way to Sandown, discussing who should ride for him the following week.

"You'd almost think there was a hoodoo on the whole tribe," he said. "Art shot himself, Pip's broken his leg, Grant's had a breakdown. There's Peter Cloony . . . but I've heard he's unreliable, and Danny Higgs bets too much, they say, and Ingersoll doesn't always try, so I've been told. . . ."

In the weeks since Pip broke his leg I had come to like the trainer better every day. Not only was he superb at his job, but he was never moody and always said directly what he thought. He had quite soon told me to drop the "sir" and stick to "James." Once as we drove back from Birmingham races, we passed some posters advertising a concert.

"Conductor, Sir Trelawny Finn," he read aloud. "No relation, I suppose," he said jokingly.

"Well, yes, as a matter of fact, he's my uncle," I said.

There was a dead silence. Then he said, "And Caspar Finn?"

"My father." A pause. "And Dame Olivia Cottin is my mother," I added, matter-of-factly.

"Well," he said, "you keep it very quiet."

"It's really the other way round," I said cheerfully. "They like to keep me quiet."

"All the same," he said thoughtfully, "it explains quite a lot about you. Your air of confidence . . . and why you've said so little about yourself."

I said, "I'd be very glad . . . James . . . if you'd not let my parentage loose in the weighing room, as a favor to them."

He had not, and he had accepted me more firmly as a friend from then on. So when he ran through the reported shortcomings of the other jockeys, it was with some confidence that I said, "Do you know all these things for a fact?"

"Well, Peter Cloony was late for two races a few weeks back."

I told him about Peter's bad luck in twice being delayed by a vehicle stuck across the lane. "As far as I know," I said, "he hasn't been late since. Who told you he was unreliable?"

"Oh, I don't know. Corin Kellar for one. Ballerton too. It's common knowledge."

"How about Danny Higgs, then?" I said.

"He bets too heavily," James said positively. "Corin says he never puts him up because of it."

"And Tick-Tock Ingersoll?" I said. "Who says he doesn't always try?"

He didn't answer at once. Then he said, "Why shouldn't I believe Corin? He depends as we all do on good jockeys. He wouldn't deny himself the use of people like Cloony or Higgs if he didn't have a good reason."

I thought for a few moments, and then said, "I know it's really none of my business, but would you mind very much telling me why you dropped Grant Oldfield? He told me himself that it was something to do with a message, but he didn't explain."

"A message? Oh yes, he passed on the message. You know, if we had a fancied runner he would tip off a professional bettor. Then the owner didn't get good odds on his money because the professional was there before him and spoiled the market. Grant had to go. It was a pity."

"How did you discover it was Grant passing on the information?"

"Kemp-Lore found out more or less by accident while he was working on one of his programs. He told me very apologetically, and just said it would be wiser not to let Grant know too much. But you can't work with a jockey and keep secrets from him."

"What did Grant say when you sacked him?" I asked.

"He denied the whole thing very indignantly, of course."

"Did you talk to the professional bettor in question?" I asked.

"I did. You see, I didn't want to believe it. But Lubbock, the professional, did admit that he had been paying Grant for tips."

It seemed conclusive enough, but I had a feeling that I had missed something, somewhere. I changed the subject. "Going back to Art," I said, "why was he always having rows with Corin?"

"I don't know," James said reflectively. "I heard Corin say once or twice that Art didn't ride to orders. Perhaps it was that."

He glanced at me. "What are you getting at?"

"It seems to me sometimes that there is too much of a pattern," I said. "Too many jockeys are affected by rumors. You said yourself that there seems to be a hoodoo on the whole tribe."

"I didn't mean it seriously," he protested. "You're imagining things. And as for rumors, let me remind you that Ingersoll was called in before the stewards last week for easing his mount out of third place. John Ballerton owned the horse and he was very annoyed about it, he told me so himself."

I sighed. Tick-Tock's version was that since Corin had told him not to overwork the horse, which was not fully fit, he had decided that he ought not to drive the horse just for the sake of finishing third. After the inquiry, changing with the wind as usual, Corin had been heard condemning Tick-Tock's action.

"I hope I am quite wrong about it all," I said slowly. "But if you ever hear any rumors about me, will you remember what I think and make quite sure they're true before you believe them?"

"All right," he said, humoring me. "I think it's nonsense, but I'll agree to it." He drove in silence for a while, and then said with an impatient shake of his big head, "No one stands to gain anything by trying to ruin jockeys. It's pointless."

"I know," I said. "Pointless."

During the week before Christmas, when there was no racing, I spent several days with my parents. They greeted me with their usual friendly detachment and left me to my own devices.

Joanna's time was tangled inextricably with several performances in different places of the "Christmas Oratorio." I managed to hook her only for one chilly morning's walk in the park, and a Christmasy lunch at the Savoy afterward.

She was less serene than usual, and there was a sort of brittleness in her manner which I couldn't understand. I waited until the coffee came, and then said casually, "What's up, Joanna?"

She was silent. Finally she said, "Brian wants to marry me."

I knew she had been seeing a man named Brian, but I did not know what their relationship was.

"I don't know what to do," she said. "He says it's irresponsible not to want to marry at my age, and I say I'll gladly marry him if he lets me keep on with my work and come and go as I please. But he sees me as the complete housewife. He wants me to be respectable and conventional and . . . and stuffy." The last word came out explosively, steeped in contempt.

"How much do you love him?" I asked painfully.

"I don't know," she said unhappily. Then seeing the movement in my face, she said, "Oh hell . . . Rob, I'm sorry. It's so long since you said anything . . . I thought you didn't still . . ."

"Never mind," I said. "It can't be helped."

"What . . . what do you think I should do?"

"It's quite clear," I said, "that you should not marry Brian if you can't bear the prospect of the life he intends you to lead."

But no advice I could give her would be unbiased, and she must have known it. She left presently to go to a rehearsal, and I walked slowly back to the flat. The sort of marriage which Joanna had offered Brian, and which he spurned, was what I most wanted in the world. Why, I wondered disconsolately, was life so ruddy unfair.

ON THE day after Christmas Template won the King Chase, one of the ten top races of the year. It put him conclusively into the star class, and it didn't do me any harm either.

The race had been televised, and afterward, as was his custom, Maurice Kemp-Lore interviewed me as the winning jockey; on the following day a number of trainers I had not yet ridden for of-

fered me mounts and I began to feel at last as though I were being
accepted as a jockey in my own right.

I had, of course, my share of falls during this period. The worst
one happened one Saturday afternoon in January, when the hurdler I was riding tripped over a flight of hurdles and flung me off
onto my head. I woke up dizzily as the First Aid men lifted me into
the ambulance on a stretcher, and for a moment or two could not
remember where I was. James's face looming over me as they carried me into the First Aid room brought me back to earth with a
click, and I asked him if his horse was all right.

"Yes," he said, "how about you?"

"Fine," I said cheerfully. Actually I felt dizzy and shivery, but
concealing one's true state of health from trainers was an occupa-
tional habit, and I knew I would be fit again to ride on Monday.

The only person who was openly annoyed at my run of good
luck was John Ballerton. I had heard that he said to Corin and
Maurice Kemp-Lore in the members' bar at Kempton, "Finn isn't
worth all this fuss; he'll come down just as quickly as he's gone up,
you'll see."

In view of this I was astonished when Corin telephoned to say,
"Ballerton wants you to ride Shantytown at Dunstable tomorrow.
I must say, I don't understand why, as he's been so set against you.
But he was quite definite."

My first instinct was to refuse to ride the horse, but I couldn't
think of a reasonable excuse, as Corin had found out I was free before he told me whose the horse was. A point-blank refusal would
give Ballerton a genuine grievance against me.

Shantytown was no Template. His uncertain manner and unreliable jumping were described to me in unreassuring terms by
Tick-Tock on the way to Dunstable the following morning.

"Dogmeat on the hoof," he said cheerfully. "Anytime he's won or
placed it's because he's dragged his jockey's arms out of the sockets
by a blast-off start and kept right on going."

We were both aware that a few weeks ago riding Shantytown
would have been Tick-Tock's doubtful pleasure, not mine. Since his

parade before the stewards for not pushing his horse all out into third place, he had been ignored by Corin Kellar.

When it came to the race, on a raw January afternoon, Shanty-town was not what I had been led to expect. Far from pulling my arms out of their sockets, he seemed to me to be in danger of fall-ing asleep. The start caught him flat-footed, and I had to boot him into the first fence. He rose to it fairly well, but was slow in his recovery, and it was the same at every jump. We finished inglori-ously last.

A hostile reception met us. John Ballerton glowered like a thun-derstorm. Corin, wearing an anxious, placatory expression, was obviously going to use me as the scapegoat for the horse's failure.

"What the hell do you think you were doing?" Ballerton said as I slid to the ground and began to unbuckle the girths.

"I'm sorry, sir," I said. "He wouldn't go any faster."

"Don't talk such bloody rubbish," he said. "Were you afraid to let him go, or something? If you can't ride a decent race on a horse that pulls, why do you try?"

I said, "The horse didn't pull. There was no life in him."

"Kellar," Ballerton shouted, "isn't my horse a puller?"

"He is," said Corin, not meeting my eyes. "I thought he'd win."

They looked at me accusingly. Corin must have seen that the horse had run listlessly, but he was not going to admit it.

Ballerton narrowed his eyes and said, "I asked you to ride Shan-tytown against my better judgment and only because Maurice Kemp-Lore insisted I had been misjudging you. Well, you'll never ride another horse of mine, I promise you that." He turned on his heel and stalked off, followed by Corin.

By the end of the afternoon the puzzlement I had felt over Shan-tytown's dead running had changed to a vague uneasiness, for nei-ther of the other two horses I rode afterward did anything like as well as had been expected. Both finished nearly last, and although their owners were a great deal nicer about it than Ballerton had been, their disappointment was obvious.

On the following day the run of flops continued. All three horses

I rode ran badly. Runs of bad luck are commoner in racing than good ones, and the fact that six of my mounts in a row had made a showing far below their usual capabilities would not have attracted much notice had it not been for John Ballerton.

After the fifth race I found him standing close by the weighing room with some cronies. Their heads turned toward me and Ballerton said something and the word "disgrace" floated across clearly. I gave no sign of having heard but I wondered what effect Ballerton's complaints would have on the number of horses I was asked to ride. He was not a man to keep his grudges to himself.

I went up to the stands to watch the last race and Maurice Kemp-Lore came across to talk to me. "Bad luck, Rob," he said cheerfully. "I hear the good word I put in for you with John Ballerton has gone awry."

"You can say that again," I agreed. "But thanks for trying."

I could hear a high-pitched wheeze as he drew breath into his lungs, and I realized it was the first time I had encountered him in an asthmatic attack. I felt sorry for him.

"Are James's plans fixed for the Midwinter Cup?" he continued casually, his eyes on the horses. I smiled. But he had his job to do, I supposed, and there was no harm in telling him.

"Template runs, all being well," I said.

"And you ride him?"

"Yes," I agreed.

"How is Pip getting along?" he asked, wheezing quietly.

"They think his leg is mending well. He might be ready for Cheltenham, but of course he won't be fit for the Midwinter."

"What chance do you give Template in that race?" Maurice asked, watching the start through his race glasses.

"Oh, I hope he'll win," I said grinning. "You can quote me."

"I probably will," he agreed. We watched the race together, and such was the effect of his charm and personality that I left Dunstable cheerfully, the dismal two days' results temporarily forgotten.

# CHAPTER VII

It was a false security. My run of good luck had ended with a vengeance, and Dunstable proved to be only the fringe of the whirlpool. During the next two weeks I rode seventeen horses. Fifteen of them finished in the rear of the field, and in only two cases was this a fair result. I couldn't understand it. As far as I knew there was no difference in my riding, and it was unbelievable that my mounts should all lose their form simultaneously. I could feel my confidence oozing away as each day passed.

There was one gray mare I particularly liked riding because of the speed of her reactions. She was sweet-tempered and silken-mouthed, and jumped magnificently. While we watched her walk round the parade ring her owner, a jolly Norfolk farmer, commiserated with me on my bad luck and said, "Never mind, lad. The mare will not fail you. You'll do all right on her, never fear."

I believed I would do all right on her, too, but that day she might have been another horse. Same color, same size, same pretty head. But no zip. It was like driving a car with four flat tires. The jolly farmer looked less jolly and more pensive when I brought her back. "She's not been last ever before, lad," he said reproachfully.

We looked her over, but there was nothing wrong with her that we could see. "Are you sure you gave her her head, lad?" the farmer said doubtfully.

"Yes," I said. "But she had no enthusiasm at all today."

The farmer shook his head, doleful and puzzled.

Failures like these were too numerous to escape attention, and as the days passed I noticed a change in the way people spoke to me. I could almost feel the wave of gossip I left in my wake. I didn't know what they were saying, so I asked Tick-Tock.

"Pay no attention," he said. "Ride a couple of winners and they'll be throwing the laurel wreaths again. It's bad-patchville, chum, that's all." And that was all I could get out of him.

One Thursday evening James telephoned and asked me to come up to his house. I walked up, wondering miserably whether he, like two other trainers that day, was going to find an excuse for putting someone else up on his horses. I couldn't blame him.

James showed me into his office, shut the door, and faced me almost aggressively across the familiar room. "I hear," he said without preamble, "that you have lost your nerve."

I stared at James and didn't answer. It was not a surprise. I had guessed what was being said about me.

"You have been showing the classic symptoms," he went on. "Trailing round nearly last, pulling up for no clear reason, never going fast enough to keep warm. A few weeks ago I promised you that if I heard any rumors about you I would make sure they were true before I believed them. Well, I heard this rumor last Saturday. Several people sympathized with me because my jockey had lost his nerve. I didn't believe it. I have watched you closely ever since."

I waited dumbly for the axe. During the week I had been last five times out of seven. He sat down heavily and said, "Oh, sit down, Rob. Don't just stand there like a stricken ox, saying nothing. I expected you to deny it. Is it true, then?"

I sat down. "No," I said.

"It isn't enough to say no, Rob. You owe me an explanation."

"I can't explain," I said despairingly. "Every horse I've ridden in the last three weeks seems to have had its feet dipped in treacle. The difference is in the horses . . . I am the same." It sounded futile and incredible, even to me.

"You have certainly lost your touch," he said slowly. "Perhaps Ballerton is right . . ."

"Ballerton?" I said sharply.

"He's always said you were not as good as you were made out to be, and that I'd given you a top job when you weren't ready for it."

"I'm sorry, James," I said.

"They say the fall you had three weeks ago frightened you."

"I didn't give that fall another thought," I said.

"Then why, Rob, why?"

But I shook my head. I didn't know why.

He stood up and opened a cupboard which contained bottles and glasses, poured out two whiskies, and handed one to me.

"I can't convince myself yet that you've lost your nerve," he said. "Before I took you on, wasn't it your stock in trade to ride all the rough and dangerous horses that trainers didn't want to risk their best jockeys on? That's why I first engaged you. You aren't the sort of man to lose his nerve suddenly and for nothing. I remember the way you rode Template that first time. . . ."

I smiled, realizing how deeply I wanted him not to lose faith in me. "I feel as if I'm fighting a fog," I said. "I tried everything I knew today to get those horses to go faster, but they were all half dead. Or I was. I don't know . . . it's a pretty ghastly mess."

"I'm afraid it is," he said gloomily. "And I'm having owner trouble about it, as you can imagine."

"What rides can I still expect?" I said.

He sighed. "I don't exactly know. Broome's out of touch, on a Mediterranean cruise. You can have all his runners. And my two as well. For the rest, we'll have to wait and see."

I could hardly bring myself to say it, but I had to know. "How about Template?" I asked.

He looked at me steadily. "I haven't heard from George Tirrold," he said. "I think he will agree that he can't chuck you out after you've won so many races for him. Unless something worse happens," he finished judiciously, "I think you can still count on riding Template in the Midwinter a week from Saturday. But if you bring him in last in that . . . it will be the end."

I stood up and said, "I'll win that race. Whatever the cost, I'll win it."

WE WENT silently together to the races the following day, but when we arrived I discovered that two of my three prospective mounts were mine no longer. I stood on the stands and watched both the horses run well.

I went out to ride James's runner in the fourth race absolutely determined to win. I knew him to be a competent jumper and a willing battler in a close finish.

We came in last. It was an effort to go back and face the music. James, his face blank, said, "It can't go on, Rob. I'm very sorry. I'll have to get someone else to ride my horses tomorrow."

I nodded. He gave me a searching, puzzled look, tinged for the first time with pity. I found it unbearable.

I took my saddle back to the weighing room, aware of the glances which followed me. Conversation died when I walked in. I went over to my peg and began to take off my colors. It was surely impossible, I thought confusedly, to be subconsciously afraid. But the shattering fact remained that none of the many horses I had ridden since I had been knocked out in that fall had made any show at all. There were too many of them for it to be a coincidence, especially as those I had been removed from had done well.

I went back to Kensington in a mood of deep despair. There was no one in the flat and no food in the refrigerator.

I took a whisky bottle out of the cupboard and lay down on the sofa in the sitting room. I uncorked the bottle and took two large gulps. The spirit scorched down to my empty stomach. I put the bottle on the floor beside me. Getting drunk wouldn't do any good. Nothing would do any good. Everything was finished.

I spent a long time looking at my hands. Hands. The touch they had for horses had earned me my living all my adult life. I knew no other skill but riding, nor had ever wanted any. I felt more than whole on horseback: more speed, more strength, more courage . . . I winced at the word. A saddle was to me as the sea to a fish: home. Without a racing saddle, I thought bleakly, I am incomplete.

And what of the future? I could return during the next week and race on one or two of James's horses, if he would still let me, and perhaps even on Template in the Midwinter. But I no longer expected to do well. Better to start a new life. But a new life doing what? Whatever I did, I would drag round with me the knowledge that I had totally failed at what I had tried hardest to do.

After a long time I stood up, put the whisky bottle back in the cupboard and went out to a pub where I was sure I was not known by sight. I ordered ham sandwiches but they stuck tastelessly in my mouth.

The fact that it was Friday had meant nothing to me all evening, and the approach of nine o'clock went unnoticed. But just when I had pushed away the sandwiches, someone turned up the volume of the television set; a bunch of racing fans made shooshing noises and Maurice Kemp-Lore's features materialized on the screen.

"Good evening," Kemp-Lore said, the spellbinding smile in place. "This evening we are going to talk about handicapping, and I have here two well-informed men who look at weights and measures from opposing angles. The first is Mr. Charles Jenkinson, an official handicapper. He decides upon the weight each horse must carry in a race." Mr. Jenkinson's face appeared briefly on the screen. "And the other is the well-known trainer, Corin Kellar." Corin's thin face glowed with satisfaction.

"Mr. Jenkinson," said Maurice, "will explain how he builds a handicap. And Mr. Kellar will tell you how he tries to avoid having his horses defeated by their weights."

I listened to Jenkinson with only half my mind, and Corin had been speaking for some moments before I paid much attention to him. ". . . Horses from my stable always do their best to win."

"But surely you don't insist on their being ridden hard at the end when they've no chance at all?" said Maurice.

"As hard as necessary, yes," Corin asserted. "Not long ago I dismissed a jockey for not riding hard enough at the end when he could have come third . . ." His voice droned on, and I thought of Tick-Tock, thrown to the stewards for obeying orders too conscientiously and now having trouble getting other trainers to trust him. I thought of Art, driven to death; and the active dislike I already felt for Corin Kellar sharpened into hatred.

"One is always in the hands of one's jockey," Corin was saying. "You can slave away for weeks preparing a horse for a race and then a jockey can undo it all with one stupid mistake."

"But there is always some explanation for a jockey's not getting the most out of a horse," Maurice interrupted. "Whatever the reason, trivial, like a mistake, or more serious, like a failure of resolution at a crucial point . . ."

"No guts, you mean?" said Corin flatly. "I'd say that that would be as obvious to a handicapper as to everyone else. There's a case in point now . . ." he hesitated, but Maurice did not try to stop him, "a case now where everything a certain jockey rides comes in last. He's lost his nerve, you see. Well, you can't tell me any handicapper thinks those particular horses are not as good as they were. Of course they are. It's just the rider who's going downhill."

I could feel the blood rush to my head.

"What's usual in these cases, Mr. Jenkinson?" Maurice asked.

"I . . . that is . . . they aren't usually as blatant as this. It really isn't a thing I can discuss here."

"Where better?" said Maurice persuasively. "We all know that this poor chap took a toss three weeks ago and has ridden . . . er . . . ineffectively . . . ever since. Surely you'd have to take that into account when you are handicapping those horses?"

While the camera focused on Jenkinson, Corin's voice said, "I'll be interested to know what you decide. One of those horses was mine, you know. It was a shocking exhibition. Finn won't be riding for me again, or for anyone else either, I shouldn't wonder."

Jenkinson said uneasily, "I don't think we should mention names," and Maurice cut in quickly, saying, "No, no. I agree. Better not." But the damage was done.

"Well, thank you both very much for giving us your time this evening," he said, and slid expertly into his closing sentences, but I was no longer listening. Between them, he and Corin had hammered in the nails on the ruins of my career, and watching them at it on the glaring little screen had given me a blinding headache.

I stumbled out into the street, and walked slowly back to the dark, empty flat; without switching on any lights I lay down fully dressed on my bed. My head throbbed. I groaned aloud.

It was a long way down from my window to the street. Five

stories. A long, quick way down. I could hear a chiming clock counting away the quarter hours. It struck ten, eleven, twelve, one, two. Five stories down. But however bad things were, that way wasn't for me. I shut my eyes, and finally, after the long despairing hours, drifted into an exhausted, dream-filled sleep.

I woke less than two hours later, and heard the clock strike four. My headache had gone, and my mind felt sharp and clear. Somewhere between sleeping and waking I found I had regained myself, come back to the lifesaving certainty that I was the person I thought I was, and not the cracked-up mess that everyone else believed. And that being so, I thought in puzzlement, there must be some other explanation of my troubles. All—*all* I had to do was find it. I began, at long last, to use my brain.

In the morning I went to see a psychiatrist.

# CHAPTER VIII

I HAD known the psychiatrist all my life as he was a friend of my father. At eight o'clock I telephoned him and asked urgently to see him. He said to come at once and a quarter of an hour later I was sitting with him in his consulting room.

"Suppose . . ." I began, and stopped. It didn't seem so easy, now that I was there. What had seemed obvious at five in the morning, in the full light of day was going to sound preposterous.

"Yes?" he waited for me calmly.

"Suppose I had a sister," I said, "who was as good a musician as Mother and Father, and I was the only one in the entire family to lack their talent—as you know I am—and I felt they despised me for lacking it, how would you expect me to act?"

"They don't despise you," he protested.

"No . . . but if they did, would there be any way in which I could persuade them—and myself—that I had a very good excuse for not being a musician?"

"Oh, yes," he said instantly, "I'd expect you to do exactly what you have done. Find something you can do, and pursue it fanatically until in your own sphere you reach the standard of your family in theirs."

I felt as if I'd been hit in the solar plexus. So simple an explanation of my compulsion to race had never occurred to me.

"That . . . that isn't what I meant," I said helplessly. "But when I come to think of it, I see it is true." I paused. "What I really meant to ask was, could I, when I was growing up, have developed a physical infirmity to explain away my failure?"

He looked at me intently for a few moments. "You had better stop waltzing round it and ask me your question straight out," he said finally.

"There are two," I said. "Could a boy whose family were all terrific cross-country riders develop asthma to hide a fear of horses?" My mouth was dry. So very much depended on his answers.

He didn't answer at once. He said, "What's the other question?"

"Could that boy, as a man, develop such a loathing for steeplechase jockeys that he would try to smash their careers? Even if, as you said, he had found something else which he could do well?"

"It obviously matters so desperately to you, Robert, that I can't give you an answer without knowing more about it. You must tell me why you ask these questions."

I told him what had happened to my friends and to me. And I told him about Maurice Kemp-Lore. "He comes from a family who ride as soon as they walk, but horses give him asthma, and that, everyone knows, is why he doesn't ride himself."

I paused, but as he made no comment, I went on. "You can't help being drawn to him. You can't imagine the spell of his personality unless you've felt it. He has the ear of everyone from the stewards down . . . and I think he uses his influence to sow seeds of doubt about jockeys' characters."

"Go on," he said, his face showing nothing.

"The men who seem to be especially under his spell are Corin Kellar, a trainer, and John Ballerton, a member of the ruling body. I think Kemp-Lore picked them as friends solely because they had the right sort of mean-mindedness for broadcasting every damaging opinion he insinuated into their heads. I think all the rumors start with Kemp-Lore, and that even the substance behind them is his work. Why isn't he content with what he has? The jockeys he is hurting like him. Why does he need to destroy them?"

He said, "If this were a hypothetical case I would tell you that such a man could both hate and envy his father—and his sister— and have felt both these emotions from early childhood. But because he knows these feelings are wrong he represses them, and the aggression is transferred to people who show the same qualities and abilities that he hates in his father. Such individuals can be helped. They can be understood, and treated, and forgiven."

"I can't forgive him," I said. "And I'm going to stop him."

He considered me. "You must make sure of your facts," he said. "At present you are just guessing. And as I've had no opportunity to talk to him you'll get no more from me than an admission that your suspicions of Kemp-Lore are *possibly* correct. You are making a very serious accusation. You need cast-iron facts. Until you have them, there is always the chance that you have interpreted what has happened to you as malice from outside in order to explain away your own inner failure."

"Don't psychiatrists ever take a simple view?" I said, sighing.

He shook his head. "Few things are simple."

"I'll get the facts," I said and stood up and thanked him.

At the door he said, "Go gently, Robert. If you are right about Kemp-Lore, you must persuade him to ask for treatment."

I said flatly, "I can't look at it from your point of view. I don't think of Kemp-Lore as ill, but as wicked."

"Where illness ends and crime begins . . ." He shrugged. "It has been debated for centuries. But take care, Robert."

OVER a triple order of eggs and bacon in a nearby café, I bent my mind to the problem of how the cast-iron facts were to be dug up. On reflection, there seemed to be precious few of them to work on.

Using the café's telephone, I rang up Tick-Tock. "If you are not using the car this afternoon I want to call at some stables. About six altogether, I think, apart from Axminster's. And Kellar's. I'll have to go there as well."

"You've got a nerve," said Tick-Tock.

"Thanks," I said. "You're about the only person who thinks so."

"Damn it . . . I didn't mean . . . But it's no use going to any stables today. The trainers will all be at the races."

"Yes, I sincerely hope so," I agreed. "I'll come down to Newbury by train and pick the car up."

"What are you up to?" he asked suspiciously.

"Retrieving the fallen fortunes of the House of Finn," I said.

When I stepped off the train at Newbury Tick-Tock was waiting. He opened the car door. "Where to?" he said.

"You're not coming," I said.

"I certainly am. This car is half mine. Where it goes, I go." He was clearly determined. "Where to?"

"Well . . ." I showed him a list I had made on the train. "These are the stables I want to go to."

"Phew," he said, looking at the list, "we'll never cover this lot in one day." He let in the clutch and drove off to his place where we collected some overnight things. Then Tick-Tock pointed the Mini Cooper's blunt nose toward the first stable on the list, Corin Kellar's, in Hampshire.

"Now," he said. "Tell me. The works."

"No," I said. "I'm not going to tell you why we're going. Listen and watch, and then you tell me."

We arrived at Corin's stable while the lads were doing up the horses after the second morning exercise. Arthur, the head lad, was crossing the yard with a bucket of oats when we climbed out of the car, and his usual welcoming smile got halfway to his eyes before he remembered. "The guvnor's gone to the races," he said awkwardly.

"I know," I said. "Can I speak to Davey?" Davey was the lad who looked after Shantytown.

"Fourth box from the end over that side," Arthur said doubt-fully. We found Davey tossing the straw bed round the big chestnut. We leaned over the bottom half of the door, and watched Davey's expression, too, change from warmth to disgust.

I said, "Davey, there's a quid for you if you feel like talking a bit. About the day I rode Shantytown at Dunstable."

"I remember the day," he said offensively.

I ignored his tone, and took a pound note out of my wallet and gave it to him. He shrugged, and thrust it into his pocket. "Now, tell me what happened from the moment you set off from here until I got up on Shantytown in the parade ring."

He shrugged again, but said, "We went in the horse van from here to Dunstable, and unloaded the horses, two of them, in the stables there, and went and got a cuppa in the canteen. Then I went back to the stables and got Shantytown and put on his pad-dock clothing and led him out into the paddock. . . ." His voice was bored as he recited the everyday racing routine of his job.

"Could anyone have given Shantytown anything to eat or drink in the stables, say a bucket of water just before the race?" I asked.

"Don't be stupid. Of course not. Who ever heard of giving a horse anything to eat or drink before a race?"

"How tight is the security on the Dunstable stables?" I asked. "Would anyone but a lad or a trainer get in there?"

"No," he said, "it's as tight as a drum."

"Go on then," I said. "We've got you as far as the paddock."

"Well, I walked the horse round the assembly ring for a bit, waiting for the guvnor to bring the saddle up from the weighing room . . ." he smiled suddenly, as at some pleasant memory, "and then I took Shanty into the saddling box and the guvnor saddled up, and then I took Shanty down into the parade ring and walked him round until they called me over and you got up on him."

"What happened while you were walking round the assembly ring?" I asked. "Something you smile about when you remember it? The quid was for telling everything."

He sniffed. "It's nothing to do with racing. It was that chap on the telly, Maurice Kemp-Lore, he came over and spoke to me and admired Shanty and gave him a few sugar knobs, and he asked me what his chances were, and I said pretty good . . . more fool me. . . ."

Tick-Tock and I got back into the car and drove out of the yard. He flicked a glance at me and drove without speaking.

We reached the next yard on my list shortly before one o'clock, and disturbed the well-to-do farmer, who trained his own horses, just as he was about to sit down to his lunch. I had ridden and disgraced his best horse the previous week. After he had got over the unpleasant shock of finding me on his doorstep, he told me in a friendly enough fashion where I could find the lad who looked after the horse in question.

I gave the lad a pound to describe in detail what had happened on the day I had ridden his horse. He didn't see any sense in it but eventually I got him started, and then there was no stopping him.

Sandwiched between stripping off the paddock clothing and buckling up the saddle came the news that Maurice Kemp-Lore had lounged into the saddling box, said some complimentary things about the horse, meanwhile feeding the animals some lumps of sugar, and had drifted away again leaving behind him the usual feeling of friendliness and pleasure.

"How odd," said Tick-Tock pensively as we sped along the road to the next stable, eighty miles away. "How odd that Maurice Kemp-Lore . . ." But he didn't finish the sentence; nor did I.

Two hours later, in Kent, we listened, for another pound, to a gaunt boy of twenty telling us what a smashing fellow that Maurice Kemp-Lore was, how interested he'd been in the horse, how kind to give him some sugar. Tick-Tock by now had become extremely interested.

"He drugged them," he said flatly, after a long silence, as he drove onto the Maidstone bypass. "He drugged them to make it look as if . . . to make everyone believe you'd lost your nerve."

"Yes," I agreed.

"But it's impossible," he said. "Why on earth should he? It must be a coincidence that he gave sugar to three horses you rode."

"Maybe. We'll see," I said.

And we did see. We went to the stables of every horse (other than Axminster's) that I had ridden since Shantytown, talking to every lad concerned. And in every single case we heard that Maurice Kemp-Lore had made the lad's afternoon memorable by admiring the way the lad had looked after his horse, and by offering those tempting lumps of sugar. It took us the whole of Saturday, and all Sunday morning, and we finished the last stable on my list on the edge of the Yorkshire moors at two o'clock in the afternoon.

On Monday I went alone to the Axminster stables to see James. He had just come in from supervising the morning exercise.

"Come into the office," he said. His tone was neutral. "I can't give you much to ride." His back was to me. "All the owners have cried off, except one. You'd better look at this; it came this morning." He held a letter out to me. It was from Lord Tirrold.

> Dear James,
>
> Since our telephone conversation I have been thinking over our decision to replace Finn on Template next Saturday, and I now consider that we should allow him to ride as originally planned. I do not want it said that I hurried to throw him out at the first possible moment, showing heartless ingratitude after his many wins on my horses. I am prepared for the disappointment of not winning the Midwinter. I would rather lose the race than the respect of the racing fraternity. . . .

I put the letter down. "He doesn't need to worry," I said thickly. "Template will win." I sat down in one of the battered armchairs. "James, there are a few things I'd like you to know. First, however bad it looks, I have not lost my nerve. Second, every single horse I have ridden since that fall three weeks ago has been doped. Not enough to be very noticeable, just enough to make it run like a slug. Third, the dope has been given to all the horses by the same man. Fourth, the dope has been given to the horses on sugar lumps."

James stood looking at me in shocked disbelief.

I said, "Before you conclude that I am out of my mind, do me the favor of calling in one of the lads whose horse I have ridden in the last three weeks, and see what he has to say."

He went to the door and shouted for someone to find Eddie,

the lad who looked after a big chestnut I had ridden last Friday. In a moment the boy arrived. James gave me no chance to do the questioning. He said brusquely to Eddie, "When did you last talk to Rob?"

The boy looked scared. "N-not since l-l-last Friday."

"Very well, then. You remember when the big chestnut ran badly last Wednesday week? Did anyone give the chestnut some sugar before the race?"

"Yes, sir," said Eddie thoughtfully. I breathed a sigh of relief.

"Who was it?"

"Maurice Kemp-Lore, sir. He said how well I looked after my horses, sir. He was leaning over the rails of the assembly ring and he spoke to me as I was going past. So I stopped, and he gave the chestnut some sugar, sir. I didn't think it would matter."

"Thank you, Eddie," said James, rather faintly. "No matter about the sugar . . . run along, now."

He looked at me blankly. The clock ticked.

Presently I said, "I've spent the last two days talking to the lads of all the horses I've ridden for other stables. Every one of them told me that Maurice Kemp-Lore gave the horse some lumps of sugar before I rode it. Tick-Tock came with me. You've only to ask him if you can't believe it from me."

"But Maurice never goes near horses," James protested.

"That's precisely what helped me to understand what was happening," I said. "I talked to Kemp-Lore at Dunstable just after Shantytown and two other horses had run hopelessly for me, and he was wheezing audibly. He had asthma. Which meant that he had recently been very close to horses. I didn't give it a thought at the time, but it means a packet to me now."

"But Maurice . . ." he repeated. "It's just not possible."

"It *is* possible," I said.

There were two things I wanted James to do to help me. I said slowly, persuasively, as if the thought had just occurred to me, "Let me ride a horse for you . . . one of your own, if the owners won't have me . . . and see for yourself if Kemp-Lore tries to give it sugar. Perhaps you could stick with the horse yourself, and if he comes up with his sugar lumps, maybe you could manage to knock them out of his hand. You might pick them up and put them in your pocket, and give the horse some sugar lumps of your own instead? Then we would see how the horse runs."

He said, "That's fantastic. I can't do things like that."

"It's simple," I said mildly. "You've only to bump his arm."

"No," he said, but not obstinately. A hopeful no, to my ears.

I went on, "Aren't you friendly with that man who arranges the regular dope tests at the races?" One or two spot checks were made at every meeting, mainly to deter trainers of doubtful reputation from pepping up or slowing down their horses with drugs. At the beginning of each afternoon the stewards decided which horses to test—for example, the winner of the second race, or the favorite in the fourth race. No one knew in advance which horses would have their saliva taken.

James followed my thoughts. "You mean, will I ask him if any of the horses you have ridden since your fall have been tested for dope in the normal course of events?"

"Yes," I agreed. "Could you possibly do that?"

"Yes," he said. "I will ring him up. But if any of them have been tested and proved negative, you do realize that it will dispose of your wild accusations absolutely?"

"I do," I agreed. "Actually, I've ridden so many beaten favorites that I can't think why such systematic doping has not already been discovered."

"You really do believe it, don't you?" said James, wonderingly.

"Yes," I said, getting up. "And so will you, James."

I left him staring frozen-faced out of the window, the incredible nature of what I had said to him still losing the battle against his own personal knowledge of Kemp-Lore. James liked the man.

# CHAPTER IX

LATE that Monday evening James rang me up at my digs and told me that I could ride his own horse, Turniptop, in the novice chase at Stratford-on-Avon on the following Thursday. "I'm doing you no favor," he went on. "He won't win. He's never been over fences, only hurdles, and all I want is for you to give him an easy race round, getting used to the bigger obstacles. All right?"

"All right," I said. There was no mention of whether he would or would not contemplate juggling with sugar knobs.

On Tuesday, I appropriated the Mini Cooper to make a call at Peter Cloony's. His wife opened the door to me. She no longer looked rosily content, but thin and wispy. "Come in," she said, "but Peter isn't here. He was given a lift to Birmingham races . . . perhaps he'll get a spare ride . . ."

"Of course he will," I said. "He's a good jockey."

"The trainers don't seem to think so," she said despairingly. "Ever since he lost his regular job, he's barely had one ride a week. We can't live on it. If things don't change very soon, he's going to give up racing and try something else. But it will break his heart."

The room was cold—too cold for the baby I saw huddled under blankets, asleep in a crib placed where the television had stood when I first visited there. She insisted on making us a cup of tea, and I had to wait before asking her what I really wanted to know.

I said, "That Jaguar—the one which blocked the lane and made Peter late—who did it belong to?"

"We don't know," she said. "It was very odd. No one came to move it away and it stayed across the lane all that morning. In the end the police arranged for it to be towed away."

"You don't happen to know where the Jaguar is now?" I asked.

"It used to be outside the big garage beside Timberley station."

I thanked her and stood up, and took a sealed envelope out of my pocket and gave it to her. "This is a present for the baby. There's likely to be a lot of cold weather coming, so you must promise to spend most of it on keeping warm."

"I promise," she said faintly.

The battered, elderly Jaguar was where she had said. I went into the garage to ask if I could buy it.

"Sorry, sir, no can do," the man in charge said breezily. "I can't sell it to you because I don't know who it belongs to."

With a bit of prompting he told me all about the Jaguar's being stuck across the lane and how his firm had fetched it.

I said, "But someone must have seen the driver after he left the car?"

"No. The police think he must have got a lift, and then decided the car wasn't worth coming back for."

I parted from the garageman and decided to try the railway station. The one tremendous disadvantage Kemp-Lore had to overcome, I thought, was his own fame. His face was so well known that he could not hope to move about the country inconspicuously, and it should be possible to find someone who had seen him.

But there was nothing to learn from the elderly stationmaster. Maurice Kemp-Lore had never (more's the pity, he said) caught a train at Timberley. Most certainly not the midday train. Passengers for that train were always ladies going shopping in Cheltenham. "Bit of a joke it is round here, see, the midday."

I gave him a hot tip for Birmingham that afternoon and left.

Timberley village pub had never been stirred, they told me regretfully, by the flashing presence of Maurice Kemp-Lore. None of the garages within ten miles had seen him ever. The local taxi service had never driven him. If I hadn't been so utterly sure that it was Kemp-Lore who had abandoned the Jaguar, I would have admitted that if no one had seen him he hadn't been there.

The army trailer truck that had blocked Peter's and my way the first time was there accidentally. But a weapon was put straight

into the hand of Peter's enemy. He had only had to make Peter late
again, and to spread his little rumors, and the deed was done. No
confidence, no rides, no career for Cloony.

I still hoped by perseverance to dig something up, so I booked a
room in a hotel in Cheltenham, and the next morning I went down
to the Cheltenham railway station and found the man who had
collected the tickets from the passengers on the twelve-thirty train
from Timberley on the day the Jaguar was abandoned. He, too, had
never seen Kemp-Lore, except on television; but he hesitated and
said, "Though I think I've seen his sister."

"What was she like?" I asked.

"Very like him, of course, sir, or I wouldn't have known who
she was. And she had on riding clothes. You know—jodhpurs. And
a scarf over her head. Pretty, she looked. I couldn't think who she
was for a bit, and then it came to me. When was it? Ah, sometime
before Christmas, I'd say."

He expertly slipped the pound I gave him into an inner pocket.
"Thank you, sir, thank you indeed," he said.

ON THURSDAY James was so busy with his other runners that I
did not exchange more than a few words with him during the first
part of the afternoon. When I went out into the parade ring to join
him for Turniptop's race, he was standing alone. "Maurice Kemp-
Lore's here," he said abruptly.

"Yes, I know," I said. "I saw him."

"He has given sugar to several horses already."

"What?" I exclaimed.

"I have asked quite a few people . . . Maurice has been feeding
sugar to any number of horses during the past few weeks, not only
to the ones you have ridden. None of the horses you rode were
picked for the regulation dope test, but some of the other horses
Maurice gave sugar to were tested. All negative."

"He only gave doped sugar to my mounts. The rest were camou-
flage," I said. It sounded improbable, but I was sure of it.

James shook his head.

"Did Kemp-Lore try to give Turniptop any sugar?"

But before James could answer one of the stewards came over to talk to him, and then it was time to mount and go out for the race.

I knew by the second fence that Turniptop was not doped. He leaped and surged and I could have shouted aloud with relief. He was eager. He was rash. And my mood matched his exactly. We infected each other with recklessness. We took some indefensible risks and we got away with them.

I began to be afraid we would win. Afraid, because I knew James wanted to sell the horse, and if he had already won a novice chase he would not be as valuable as if he had not. It would disqualify him from entering a string of good novice chases in the following season. It would be far, far better, I knew, to come second.

Coming into the second to the last fence, there was only one other tiring horse alongside, and the disaster of winning seemed unavoidable. Turniptop rose, or rather, fell, to the occasion. In spite of my urging him to put in another stride, he took off far too soon and landed with his hind feet tangled hopelessly in the birch fence. His forelegs buckled and he went down onto his knees, with my hands round his throat. Even then his indomitable sense of balance rescued him, and he staggered back onto his feet, tipping me back into the saddle, and tossing his head as if in disgust, he set off again toward the winning post. The horse which had been alongside was now safely ahead, and two that had been behind me had jumped past, so that we came to the last fence in fourth position.

I had lost my irons and couldn't get my feet into them again in time to jump, so we went over the last with them dangling in the air. I collected him together and squeezed my legs, and Turniptop, game to the end, accelerated past two horses and flashed into second place four strides from the post.

James waited for me to dismount in the unsaddling enclosure. "Don't ever ride a race like that for me again," he said. His eyes gleamed, narrowed and inscrutable. "You proved your point. But you could have killed my horse doing it." He gave me a hard stare. "You'd better come up to the stable this evening," he said. "We can't talk here. There are too many people about."

So I had to weigh in, still without knowing exactly what had happened in the saddling box before the race.

JAMES was waiting for me in the office. He got up and poured drinks when I came in. His strong heavy face looked worried. "I apologize," he said abruptly. "I very nearly let Maurice give Turnip-top that damned sugar."

"What happened in the saddling box?" I asked.

He took a sip from his glass. "I gave Sid instructions that no one, absolutely no one, was to give Turniptop anything to eat or drink before the race. When I reached the box with your saddle, Maurice was in the box next door and I watched him giving the horse there some sugar. Sid said no one had given Turniptop anything. I put on your saddle, and began to do up the girths. Maurice came round from the next box and said hello. That infectious smile of his . . . I found myself thinking you were mad. He was wheezing a bit with asthma . . . and he put his hand in his pocket and brought out three lumps of sugar. He did it naturally, casually, and held them out to Turniptop. I had my hands full of girths and I thought you were wrong . . . but . . . I don't know . . . there was something in the way he was standing. People who are fond of horses stroke them when they give them sugar, they don't stand as far away as possible. Anyway, I did decide suddenly that there would be no harm done if Turniptop didn't eat that sugar, so I dropped the girths and pretended to trip, and grabbed Maurice's arm. The sugar fell onto the straw and I stepped on it as if by accident while I was recovering my balance."

"What did he say?" I asked, fascinated.

"Just for a second he looked absolutely furious. Then he smiled again, and . . ." James's eyes glinted ". . . he said how much he admired me for giving poor Finn this one last chance."

"Dear of him," I said.

"I told him it wasn't exactly your last chance. I said you would be riding Template on Saturday as well. He just said 'Oh really?' and wished me luck and walked away."

"So the sugar was crunched up and swept out with the dirty straw," I said. "Nothing to analyze? No evidence?" A nuisance.

"If I hadn't stepped on it, Maurice could have picked it up and offered it to Turniptop again. I hadn't taken any sugar with me to substitute . . . I didn't believe I would need it."

He hadn't intended to bother, I knew. But he had bothered. I would never stop feeling grateful. We drank our drinks. James said suddenly, "Why? I don't understand why he should have gone to such lengths. What has he got against you?"

"I am a jockey, and he is not," I said flatly. "That's all. It's no coincidence that you and most other trainers have had trouble finding and keeping a jockey. You've all been swayed by Kemp-Lore, either by him directly, or through those two shadows of his, Ballerton and Corin Kellar, who soak up his poison like sponges and drip it out into every receptive ear. They've said it all to you. You repeated it to me yourself, not so long ago. Peter Cloony is always late, Tick-Tock doesn't try, Danny Higgs bets too heavily, Grant sold information, Finn has lost his nerve . . . You believed it all, James, didn't you? It doesn't take much for an owner or a trainer to lose confidence in a jockey. Art killed himself because Corin sacked him. Grant had a mental breakdown. Peter Cloony is stony broke. Tick-Tock makes jokes like Pagliacci . . . And I haven't exactly enjoyed the last three weeks myself."

"No," he said, as if thinking about it from my point of view for the first time. "No, I don't suppose you have."

"It's been so calculated, this destruction of jockeys," I said. "When he had me on the program he introduced me as an unsuccessful rider, and he meant me to stay that way."

James said firmly, "It's a matter for the Hunt Committee."

"No," I said. "His father's a member. Besides, the whole committee's a stronghold of pro-Kemp-Lore feeling and there aren't any facts yet that Kemp-Lore couldn't explain away. But I'm digging. The day will come."

"You sound unexpectedly cheerful," he said.

I stood up abruptly. "James, I wanted to kill myself last week. I'm glad I didn't. It makes me cheerful."

He looked so startled that I laughed. "Never mind," I said, "but you must understand I don't think the National Hunt Committee meets the case at the moment. Too gentlemanly. I favor something stronger for dear Maurice."

But I had as yet no useful plan, and dear Maurice still had his teeth; and they were sharp.

# CHAPTER X

ALTHOUGH neither Tick-Tock nor I had any rides the next day, I pinched the car to go to the meeting at Ascot, and walked round the course to get the feel of the turf. There was a bitterly cold wind blowing and the ground was hard with a touch of frost in the more exposed patches. I finished the circuit, planning the race in my mind as I went. If the ground remained firm it would be a fast run affair, but that suited Template well.

Outside the weighing room Peter Cloony stopped me. "I'll pay you back," he said, almost belligerently. "We don't need charity."

I told him that he was a fool, that he should cheer up, and perhaps what I had given his wife would help him forget his worries and get his mind back on racing.

I walked off, leaving him looking surprised. What Kemp-Lore had pulled down, I could try to rebuild, I thought.

In the weighing room after the fourth race I was handed a telegram. It said: PICK ME UP WHITE BEAR, UXBRIDGE, 6:30 P.M. IMPORTANT. INGERSOLL. I cursed Tick-Tock soundly because Uxbridge was in the opposite direction from home. But the car was half his, after all, and I'd had more than my fair share of it during the past week, so I followed his instructions.

Mine was only the second car in the dark parking space beside the White Bear. The bar held only a droopy-mustached old man pursing his lips to the evening's first half-pint. I ordered a whisky. No Tick-Tock. I looked at my watch. Twenty to seven.

"Are you by any chance Mr. Finn?" the barman asked.

I said I was.

"Then I've a message for you, sir. A Mr. Ingersoll telephoned and said he couldn't get here to meet you but could you pick him up at the railroad station at six fifty-five."

Finishing my drink, I thanked the barman and went out to the car. I climbed into the driving seat and stretched my hand out to turn on the lights. I stretched out my hand . . . but I didn't reach the lights. My neck was gripped violently from behind.

I flung up my hands and clawed but I couldn't reach the face of whoever was behind me, and my nails were useless against his thick leather gloves. The fingers were strong, and what was worse, they knew exactly where to press, each side of the neck, just above the collarbone, where the carotid arteries branched upward.

I hadn't a chance. In a few seconds a roaring blackness took me off.

I COULDN'T have been out very long, but it was long enough. When consciousness slowly returned, I found I could open neither my eyes nor my mouth. Both were covered with adhesive tape. My wrists were tied together, and my ankles, when I tried to move them, would only part a foot or two: they were hobbled together.

I was lying on my side on the floor in the back of a car which, from the size and smell and feel, I knew to be the Mini Cooper. I was very cold and I realized that I was no longer wearing either a jacket or an overcoat. My arms were dragged forward between the two front seats so that I couldn't reach the tape to rip it off. Though I couldn't see who was driving, I didn't need to. There was only one person in the world who could have set such a trap, only one person who had any reason, however mad, to abduct me. Maurice Kemp-Lore did not intend that I should win the Midwinter Cup.

Did he know, I wondered helplessly, that it was no accident that

Turniptop had not eaten the doped sugar? Did he guess that I knew all about his anti-jockey activities?

After some time, the car swung suddenly to the left and bumped onto an unevenly surfaced side road. Soon it rolled to a stop. Kemp-Lore got out, tipped forward the driver's seat, and tugged me out after him by the wrists. I couldn't get my feet under me because of the hobble, and I fell on my back. The ground was hard and gravelly. He pulled me to my feet, and I stood there swaying. He had some sort of lead fixed to my tied wrists, and he began to pull me forward by it. The ground was uneven and the rope joining my ankles was very short. I kept stumbling, and then I fell. He dragged me along the ground on my back for a long way.

At length he paused and let me stand up again. He still didn't speak. There was the sound of a door being opened, and I was tugged on. There was a step up, as I realized a fraction too late to prevent myself falling again. It knocked the wind out of me.

It was a wooden floor, and smelled strongly of dust and faintly of horses. He pulled me to my feet again and I felt my wrists being hauled upward and fastened to something just above my head. When he had finished and stepped away I explored with my fingers to find out what it was; and as soon as I felt the smooth metal hooks, I knew exactly the sort of place I was in.

It was a tack room, the place where saddles and bridles are kept, with the brushes and bandages and rugs that horses need. From the ceiling of every tack room hangs a harness hook, a gadget something like a three-pronged anchor, which is used for hanging bridles on while they are being cleaned. There were no bridles hanging from these particular hooks. Only me.

This tack room was very cold. There were no horses moving in the stalls. The silence took on a new meaning. It was an empty stable. I shivered from something more than cold.

I heard him step out into the gritty yard, and presently there was the sound of a tap being turned on and water splashing into a bucket. Oh no, I thought, oh no, I'm so cold already.

He turned off the tap and came back across the yard into the tack room and stopped behind me, wheezing faintly. The handle of the bucket clanked. I took a deep breath, and waited.

He threw the water. It hit me squarely between the shoulder blades and soaked me from head to foot. It was bitterly, icy cold, and it stung the skinned patches on my back like murder.

After a short pause he went across the yard again and refilled the bucket. You can't be wetter than wet, I thought, and you can't be colder than freezing.

He came back with the bucket, and this time he threw the whole arctic bucketful in my face. My chest hurt and I couldn't get my breath. He was standing close beside me now. His asthma was worse. He pulled my head back by the hair and spoke for the first time. "That should fix *you*," he said in a low unrecognizable voice.

He let go of my hair and went out. I heard him walk away across the yard and after a while the Mini Cooper's engine started, the car drove off, and soon I could hear it no more.

One thing was clear, he wouldn't be back for hours, because it was Friday. From eight o'clock until at least nine thirty he would be occupied with his program.

The first necessity was to get the adhesive tape off my eyes and mouth. After a good deal of rubbing my mouth against my arm, I only succeeded in peeling back one corner of it—enough to let in a precious extra trickle of air, but no good for shouting for help.

My wet trousers clung clammily to my legs, my shoes were full of water. Already my fingers were completely numb, and my feet were going through the stage that precedes loss of feeling.

Harness hooks. I considered their anatomy. A stem with three upward-curving branches at the bottom. At the top a ring, and, attached to the ring, a chain. At the top of the chain, a staple driven firmly into a beam.

Somewhere, I thought, there must be a weak link. Literally a weak link. When they were bought, harness hooks didn't have chains on. Chain was cut to the length needed and added when the hook was installed in the tack room. Therefore, somewhere there was a joining link.

The bottom curve of the hooks brushed my hair, and my wrists were tied some three inches above that. It gave me very little leverage, but it was the only hope I had. I started pivoting, leaning my forearms on the hooks and twisting the chain. In two and a half full turns, as near as I could judge, it locked solid. If I could turn it farther, the weak link would snap.

The theory was simple. Putting it into operation was different. Twisting the chain, I pressed round as hard as I could. Nothing happened. I unwound the chain a fraction, and jerked it tight again. The jolt ran right down my body and threw me off my feet. I stumbled miserably upright again, and did it again. The chain didn't break.

After that I got back to work on the adhesive tape and finally dislodged it entirely from my mouth. It meant that now I could open my mouth and yell.

I yelled—but no one came. My voice echoed round the tack room. I shouted, on and off, for a long while. No results.

It was at this point, perhaps an hour after Kemp-Lore had gone, that I became both very frightened and very angry. The dismal fact had to be faced that if I had to stay where I was all night my hands, which I could no longer feel, might be dead in the morning. Dead. Gangrenous.

Being angry gave me both strength and resolution. I wound the chain up tight again and jerked. It took my breath away. I loosened and jerked, loosened and jerked, pushing against the hooks, trying to twist them round with all my strength. The chain rattled, and held. I started doing it rhythmically. Six jerks and a rest, six jerks and a rest, until I was sobbing.

Six jerks and a rest. Six jerks and a rest. The rests got longer. Time passed. I became giddy as I grew tired. Why—jerk—wouldn't—jerk—the ruddy chain—jerk—jerk—break.

I was quite unprepared for it when it happened. One minute I was screwing up the dregs of willpower for another series of jerks, and the next, after a convulsive, despairing heave, I was collapsing in a tumbled heap on the floor with the harness hook clattering down on top of me, still tied to my wrists.

But after a moment or two, when my head had cleared, I rolled into a kneeling position so that the blood was flowing down my arms at last, and put my hands between my thighs to try to warm them. The relief of having my arms down made me forget how cold I was, and how wet. I felt almost cheerful, as if I had won a major battle; and indeed, looking back on it, I know I had.

KNEELING very soon became uncomfortable, so I shuffled across the floor until I came to a wall, and sat with the bottom of my spine propped against it and my knees bent up.

The adhesive on my eyes was still stuck tight. I tried to scrape it off by rubbing it against the rope on my wrists but the hooks hindered me, and in the end I gave up and concentrated again on warming my hands, alternately cradling them between my thighs and thumping them against my knees to restore the circulation.

After a time I found I could move my fingers. I still couldn't feel them at all, but movement was a tremendous step forward. I put my hands up to my face and tried to scrape the tape off with my thumbnail, but my thumb bent uselessly. I put my right thumb in my mouth, to warm it. Every few minutes I tested the results on the edge of the tape. Eventually, my nail had pushed a flap unstuck which was big enough for me to grip between my wrists, and I finally managed to pull the tape off.

Dazzling moonlight poured through the open door. I stretched out my bound feet. My fingers wouldn't undo the knots. My pockets had been emptied; no knife, no matches. There was nothing in the tack room to cut with. I stood up stiffly, leaning against the wall, and slowly, carefully, shuffled over to the door.

I looked round the moonlit yard. There, beside the tap, was an object I was very glad to see. A boot scraper, a thin metal plate bedded in concrete. With small careful steps I made my way to it.

Leaning against the wall, and with one foot on the ground, I stretched the rope tautly over the boot scraper and began to rub it to and fro, using the other foot as a pendulum. It took a long time to fray through the rope, but it parted in the end. I knelt down and tried to do the same with the strands round my wrists, but the harness hook kept getting in the way. I stood up wearily. It looked as though I'd have to lug that tiresome piece of ironmongery round with me a while longer.

Being able to move my legs, however, gave me a marvelous sense of freedom. Stiffly, shaking with cold, I walked out of the yard round to the house. There were no lights and the downstairs windows were all shuttered. It was as empty as the stable. I continued on down the long drive.

A lane ran past the end of the drive giving no indication as to which way lay civilization. Since it had to be one thing or the other, I turned right. Aching all over, I stumbled on, hanging onto the fact that if I went far enough I was bound to come to a house.

What I came to first was not a house but something much better. A telephone booth. I could call the police, but that would mean unending questions, and like as not I'd end up in the hospital.

They would be racing at Ascot the next day. Template would turn up for the Midwinter, and James didn't know his jockey was wandering around unfit to ride. Unfit . . . I came to the conclusion that the only satisfactory way to cheat Kemp-Lore of his victory was to go and ride the race, and win it if I could, and pretend that tonight's misfortunes had not happened. He was not, I vowed, going to get the better of me anymore.

I dialed O with an effort, gave the operator my telephone credit-card number, and asked to be connected to the one person in the world who would give me the help I needed.

Joanna's voice sounded sleepy. She said, "Is that you, Rob?"

"Yes," I said.

"Well, go back to bed and ring me in the morning," she said.

"Please don't ring off, Joanna," I said urgently. "I need help."

"What's the matter?" I heard her yawn.

"I . . . I . . . Joanna, come and help me. Please."

There was a little silence and she said in a more awake voice, "Where are you, Rob?"

"I don't really know," I said despairingly. "I'm in a telephone booth on a country road miles from anywhere. The telephone exchange is Hampden Row." I gave her the digits. "I don't think it's very far from London, but I can't make it on my own. I've no money and my clothes are wet."

"Oh." A pause. "All right, then. I'll find out where you are and come in a taxi. Anything else?"

"Bring a sweater," I said. "Some dry socks, if you have any, some gloves and a pair of scissors."

"Okay. I'll come as soon as I can."

I fumbled the receiver back onto its rest. However quick she was, she wouldn't arrive for an hour.

I sat down on the floor of the booth and leaned gingerly against the wall. There was a good deal to think about to take my mind off my woes. That adhesive tape for instance. What would have happened differently, I wondered, if I had been able to see and talk? The strip over my mouth had been to stop me shouting for help. But what did it matter if I could see? I would have seen Kemp-Lore . . . that was it! It was himself he had not wanted me to see. He must have believed I did not know who had abducted me. Which meant that he thought James had knocked Turniptop's doped sugar out of his hand by accident, that he hadn't heard about Tick-Tock and me going round to all the stables. It gave me, I thought, a fractional advantage for the future. If he didn't know he was due for destruction himself, he would not be excessively on his guard.

Looking at my bloodless hands and knowing that on top of everything else I still had to face the pain of their return to life, I was aware that all the civilized brakes were off my conscience. Helping to build up what he had broken was not enough. He himself had hammered into me the implacability I had lacked, to avenge myself and all the others, thoroughly and without compunction.

SHE came, in the end.

I heard a car draw up, and her quick tread on the road. The door of the telephone booth opened, letting in an icy blast, and there she was, dressed in slacks and a warm jacket, with the light falling on her dark hair and making hollows of her eyes.

I did my best at a big smile of welcome, but it didn't come off very well. I was shivering too much. She knelt down and took a closer look at me. "Your hands," she said; her face went stiff with shock. She opened her handbag, took out a pair of scissors and cut me free. She carefully peeled the cut pieces of rope from my wrists, exposing big raw patches, dark and deep.

There was a step on the road outside and a big sturdy man's shape loomed up behind Joanna. "Are you all right, miss?" he said.

"Yes, thank you."

He looked at my wrists and hands. "Crikey. You've been done proper, haven't you?" he said.

"Proper," I agreed.

He smiled faintly. "Come on then. No sense in hanging about here." He and Joanna helped me to the cab.

The driver held the door open. "We'd better take him to a doctor," he said. "That's frostbite."

"No," I said. "No doctor. Just cold. Not frostbite."

"What happened to your back?" asked the driver, looking at the tattered bits of shirt sticking to me.

"I . . . fell," I said. "On some gravel."

"There's a lot of dirt in it," said Joanna, sounding worried.

"You wash it," I said. "I need antiseptic, aspirins and sleep."

"I hope you know what you're doing," said Joanna. She looked at me judiciously, and out came the scissors. Some quick snips and the ruins of my shirt lay on the seat beside me. She cut two long strips of it and wound them carefully round my wrists. She then helped my arms into the clothes she had brought, and a pair of mittens. There was a thermos flask full of hot soup too. Joanna held a cup of it to my mouth.

The driver started up and Joanna asked, "Who did it?"

"Tell you later."

"All right." She brought out some fleecy slippers and thick socks from her suitcase and got down on her knees on the floor of the cab and changed my wet socks and shoes. My arms and shoulders ached unceasingly and if I leaned back the raw bits didn't like it.

After a while I slipped to the floor and finished the journey sitting there with my head and my hands in Joanna's lap.

WHEN we finally got back to Joanna's warm room I sat with my elbows on my knees, watching my fingers gradually change color from yellowy white to smudgy charcoal, to patchy purple, and finally to red. Joanna had dug out some aspirins, then she made some black coffee and held it for me to drink. It was stiff with brandy.

It was then that my fingers began to tingle. The tingle increased first to a burning sensation and then to a feeling of being agonizingly squeezed in a vise. When the pulse got going, it felt as though my hands had been taken out of the vise, laid on a bench, and were being rhythmically hammered.

When I looked up Joanna was watching, blinking to disguise the tears in her eyes. "Is it over?" she said.

"More or less."

"I'd better wash those scratches on your back."

"In the morning," I said. "A few more hours won't hurt. I've had four antitetanus injections in the last two years, and there's always penicillin . . . and I'm too tired."

She didn't argue but helped me get into her bed. There was still a dent in her pillow where her head had been. I put mine there, too, with an odd feeling of delight.

She bent down to kiss me good night on the forehead. I couldn't help it; I pulled her down and kissed her. For a moment she seemed to kiss me back, but it was so brief and passing that I thought I had imagined it.

She stood up abruptly, her face scrubbed of any emotion. She turned away without speaking and went across the room to the sofa, where she twisted a blanket round herself and lay down. She stretched out her hand to the table light and switched it off.

Her voice reached me across the dark room, calm, self-controlled. "Good night, Rob."

"Good night, Joanna," I said politely.

I rolled over onto my stomach and put my face in her pillow.

# CHAPTER XI

SOME time after it was light I heard Joanna go into the kitchen where she made some fresh coffee. Saturday morning, I thought. Midwinter Cup day. I turned over slowly onto one side, shutting my eyes against the stiffness which afflicted every muscle.

She came across the room with a mug of steaming coffee and put it on the bedside table. Her face was pale and expressionless.

"How do you feel?" she asked, a little too clinically.

"Alive," I said.

She sat down again on the edge of the bed. I shoved myself up into a sitting position, and brought a hand out from under the bedclothes to reach for the coffee.

As a hand it closely resembled a bunch of sausages.

"Blast," I said. "What's the time?"

"About eight o'clock," she said. "Why?"

Eight o'clock. The race was at two thirty. I began counting backward. I would have to be at Ascot by, at the latest, one thirty, and the journey down would take about fifty minutes. Allow an hour for holdups. That left me precisely four and a half hours in which to get fit enough to ride, and, the way I felt, it was a tall order.

"What's the matter?" asked Joanna.

I told her.

"You aren't seriously thinking of racing today?" she said.

"I am riding Template in the Midwinter Cup," I said. And I told her why. I told her everything, all about Kemp-Lore's anti-jockey obsession and all that had happened the previous evening.

When I had finished she looked at me without speaking for half a minute and then she cleared her throat and said, "Yes, I see. We'd better get you fit, then. What first?"

"Hot bath and breakfast," I said.

Joanna said, "Are you absolutely determined to go?"

"Absolutely."

"Well . . . I'd better tell you . . . I watched 'Turf Talk' last night on television. I sometimes do, since you were on it."

"And?"

"Kemp-Lore talked about the Midwinter Cup—biographies of the horses and trainers, and so on. I was waiting to hear him mention you, but he didn't. He just went on about how superb Template is. But what I thought you'd like to know is that he said he personally would be there today, and that he personally would interview the winning jockey. If only you can win, he'll have to describe you doing it, which would be a bitter enough pill, and then congratulate you publicly in full view of several million people."

I gazed at her, awestruck. "That's a great thought," I said.

I pushed back the bedclothes. "I'd better get going," I said. "What do you have in the way of antiseptic and bandages?"

"Not much," she said apologetically. "But there's a chemist two blocks away. I'll stop at your family's, too, and pick up a shirt and jacket."

She left and I got out of bed and went into the bathroom. Gradually the heat of the bath did its work until I could rotate my shoulders and turn my head from side to side without feeling that I was tearing something adrift.

She had pressed my trousers. I put them on and when Joanna came back she dressed my wounds. She was neat and quick, and her touch was light.

"Most of the dirt came out in the bath," she observed, busy with adhesive tape and scissors. "You've got quite an impressive set of muscles, haven't you? You must be very strong." She slowly unwound the bloodstained bandages on my wrists. What lay underneath was a pretty disturbing sight. "I can't deal with this," she said positively. "You must go to a doctor."

"This evening," I said. "Put some more bandages on, for now."

"It's too deep," she said. "It's too easy to get it infected. You can't ride like this, Rob, really you can't."

"I can," I said. "I'll dunk them in antiseptic for a while, then you wrap them up again. Nice and flat, so they won't show."

She sighed, but did as I asked. When she had finished, the white cuffs looked tidy and narrow, and I knew they would be unnoticeable under racing colors.

The pity about hot baths is that, although they loosen one up beautifully for the time being, the effect does not last; one has to consolidate the position by exercise. I did a few rather halfhearted bend-stretch arm movements while Joanna scrambled us some eggs, and after we had eaten and I had shaved I went back to it with more resolution, knowing that if I didn't get onto Template's back in a reasonably supple condition he had no chance of winning. It wouldn't help anyone if I fell off at the first fence.

After an hour's work I got to the stage where I could lift my arms above shoulder height without wanting to cry out. And after another hour of it I had loosened up from head to foot, with hardly a muscle that wasn't moving reasonably freely.

Joanna had already told me that she would not come to Ascot with me, but would watch on television. "And mind you win," she said, "after all this."

"Can I come back to your place, afterward?" I said.

"Why, yes . . . yes," she said, as if surprised that I had asked.

"Fine," I said. "Well . . . good-bye."

"Good luck, Rob," she said seriously.


# CHAPTER XII


BEFORE starting for Ascot I had the taxi stop at a haberdasher's shop and I bought a pair of gloves. As we proceeded I kept the warmth and flexibility going in my arms by some minor exercises and imaginary piano playing.

The driver announced, when I paid him, that he thought he would stay and have a flutter on the races himself, so I arranged for him to drive me back to London again at the end of the afternoon. "Got any tips?" he said, counting my change.

"How about Template, in the big race?" I said.

"I dunno." He frowned. "They say Finn's all washed up."

"Don't believe all you hear," I said, smiling. "See you later."

I went along to the weighing room. The hands of the clock on the tower pointed to five past one. Sid, James's head traveling lad, was standing outside the weighing-room door when I got there, and he came to meet me, and said, "You're here, then."

"Yes," I said. "Why not?"

"The guvnor posted me here to wait for you. There's a rumor going round that you weren't going to turn up, see?" He bustled off.

I went through the weighing room into the changing room.

"So you came after all," said Peter Cloony.

Tick-Tock said, "Where in hell have you been?"

"Why did everyone believe I wouldn't get here?" I asked.

"I don't know. Some rumor or other. Everyone's been saying you frightened yourself again on Thursday and you'd chucked up the idea of riding anymore. I rang your pad this morning, but they said you hadn't been back all night. I wanted to see if it was okay for me to have the car after racing today."

"The car?" I said. "Oh . . . yes. Certainly. Meet me outside the weighing room after the last race, and I'll show you where it is."

"I say, are you all right? You look a bit night-afterish."

"Of course I'm all right."

"Well, the best of luck on Template, and all that rot."

An official called me out of the changing room. James was waiting in the weighing room. He looked relieved. "I was sure you wouldn't have stayed away without at least letting me know."

"Of course not," I said. Not unless, I thought, I had still been hanging in a deserted tack room, being crippled for life.

"There's a touch of frost in the ground still," he said, "but that's really to our advantage." I could see that for once he was excited.

When I went back into the changing room to put on colors, I

decided to use the washroom. I wanted to change out of sight, so that no one would see the bandages.

The first race was over and the jockeys were beginning to stream in when I went back to my peg. I took my saddle and weight cloth along to the scales to weigh out, and gave my saddle to Sid, who was standing there waiting for it.

He said, "The guvnor says I'm to saddle Template in the stable, and bring him straight down into the parade ring when it's time, and not go into the saddling boxes at all."

"Good," I said emphatically. Evidently James was keeping his word that Template would have no chance to be doped.

The time dragged. The second race was run with me still sitting in the changing room. I flexed my fingers. Most of the swelling had gone, and they seemed to be getting fairly strong again.

Back came the other jockeys and I felt apart from it all, as if I were living in a different dimension. Another slow quarter of an hour crawled by. Then an official put his head in and shouted, "Jockeys out, hurry up there, please."

I fastened my helmet, picked up my whip, and followed the general drift to the door.

Down in the paddock stood cold little bunches of owners and trainers, most of them muffled to the eyes against the wind. Lord Tirrold and James both wore on their faces the same look of excitement. "Well, Rob," said Lord Tirrold, "this is it."

"Yes, sir," I agreed, "this is it."

"What do you think of Emerald?" he asked.

We watched the new Irish mare who had come over with a terrific reputation shamble round the parade ring with the sloppy walk and the low-carried head that so often denotes a champion.

"They say she's another Kerstin," said James, referring to the best steeplechasing mare of the century.

"Template will beat her," said Lord Tirrold.

"I think so," James agreed.

I swallowed. They were too sure. Their very confidence weakened mine. A bell rang: time for the jockeys to mount. The boy brought Template across to us and took off his rug.

Template's eyes were liquid, clear, his muscles quivering to be off: the picture of a taut, tuned racing machine eager to get on with the job he was born for.

James gave me a leg up into the saddle and I gathered the reins and put my feet into the irons. What he read in my face I don't know, but he said suddenly, anxiously, "Is anything wrong?"

"Everything's fine," I said. I smiled, reassuring myself as much as him. I touched my cap to Lord Tirrold and turned Template to take his place in the parade down the course.

There was a television camera on a tower not far down the course from the starting gate, and I found the thought of Kemp-Lore raging at the sight of me on his monitor set a most effective antidote to the freezing wind.

"Line up," called the starter, and we straightened into a row across the course, with Template on the inside, hugging the rails.

I watched the starter's hand. He had a habit of stretching his fingers just before he pulled the lever to let the tapes up. He stretched his fingers. I kicked Template's flanks. He was moving quite fast when we went under the rising tapes, with me lying flat along his withers to avoid being swept off. We were away, securely on the rails and on the inside curve for at least the next two miles.

The first three fences were the worst, as far as my comfort was concerned. By the time we had jumped the fourth—the water—I had felt the thinly healed crusts on my back tear open, had found just how much my wrists and hands had to stand from the tug of the reins. My chief feeling, as we landed over the water, was one of relief. It was all bearable; I could contain it and ignore it.

The pattern of the race was simple, because from the start to finish I saw only three other horses, Emerald and two lightly weighted animals whom I had allowed to go on and set the pace.

My main task was keeping Emerald from cutting across in front of me and being able to take the opening between the front pair and the rails. I left just too little room between me and the front pair for Emerald to get in, forcing the mare to race all the way on my outside. It didn't matter that she was two or three feet in front: I could see her better there.

With the order unchanged we completed the whole of the first circuit and swept out to the country again. Template jumped the four fences down to Swinley Bottom so brilliantly that I kept finding myself crowding the tails of the pacemakers as we landed, and had to ease him back on the flat each time to avoid taking the lead too soon, and yet not ease him so much that Emerald could squeeze into the space between us.

For another half mile the two horses in front kept going splendidly, but one of the jockeys picked up his whip at the third last fence, and the other was already busy with his hands. They were dead ducks, and because of that they swung a little wide going round the last bend into the straight. Emerald's jockey chose that exact moment to go to the front. I saw him spurt forward from beside me and accelerate, but he had to go round on the outside of the two front horses and he was wasting lengths in the process.

After the bend, tackling the straight for the last time, with the second last fence just ahead, Emerald was in the lead on the outside, then the two tiring horses, then me.

There was a three-foot gap then between the innermost pacemaker and the rails. I squeezed Template. He pricked his ears and bunched his colossal muscles and thrust himself forward into the narrow opening. He took off at the second last fence half a length behind and landed a length in front of the tiring pacemaker. With no check in his stride he sped smoothly on, still hugging the rails, with Emerald only a length in front. I urged him a fraction forward to prevent the mare from swinging over to the rails and blocking me at the last fence. She needed two lengths' lead to do it safely, and I had no intention of letting her have it. As we galloped toward the last fence, Emerald was a length ahead and showing no sign of flagging, but I was still holding Template on a tight rein.

Ten yards from the fence, I let him go, and squeezed with my legs and he went over the birch like an angel, smooth, surging, the nearest to flying one can get.

He gained nearly half a length on the mare, but she didn't give up easily. I sat down and rode Template for my life, and he stretched himself into his flat-looking stride. He came level with Emerald halfway along the run in. She hung on grimly for a short distance, but Template floated past her with an incredible increase of speed, and he won, in the end, by two clear lengths.

There are times beyond words, and that was one of them. I patted Template's sweating neck over and over; how does one thank a horse? How could one ever repay him, in terms he would understand, for giving one such a victory?

Axminster and Lord Tirrold stood side by side, waiting for us in the unsaddling enclosure, the same elated expression on both their faces. I smiled at them and slid off onto the ground.

"Rob," said James, shaking his big head. "Rob."

"I knew he'd do it," Lord Tirrold said. "What a horse! What a race!"

An official came over and asked Lord Tirrold not to go away, as the Cup was to be presented to him in a few minutes. To me he said, "Will you come straight out again after you have weighed in? There's a trophy for the winning jockey as well."

I nodded, and went in to sit on the scales. I felt appallingly weak and tired, and the pain in my wrists had increased to the point where I was finding it very difficult to keep it all out of my face.

When I got outside again the horses had been led away and in their place stood a table bearing the Midwinter Cup and other trophies, with a bunch of racecourse directors and stewards beside it.

And Maurice Kemp-Lore as well. It was lucky I saw him before he saw me. I felt a strong shock of revulsion run right down my body. He couldn't have failed to understand it, if he had seen it. I found James at my elbow. He followed my gaze.

"Why are you looking so grim?" he said. "He didn't even try to dope Template. He must have seen there was no chance anymore of persuading anyone you had lost your nerve. Not after the way you rode Turniptop on Thursday."

It was the reckless way I had ridden on Thursday that had

infuriated Kemp-Lore into delivering the packet I had taken on Friday. "Have you told anyone about the sugar?" I asked.

"No, since you asked me not to. But I think something must be done, evidence or not . . ."

"Will you wait," I asked, "until next Saturday? A week today? Then you can tell whoever you like."

"Very well," he said slowly. "But I still think . . ."

He was interrupted by the presentation of the Midwinter Cup to Lord Tirrold, a silver tray to James, and a cigarette box to me.

When the ceremony was over I heard Kemp-Lore's voice behind me and it gave me time to arrange my face before turning slowly round and meeting his eyes. They were piercingly blue and very cold, and they didn't blink or alter in any way as I looked back at them. I relaxed a little, thankful that the first difficult hurdle was crossed. He had searched, but had not read in my face that I knew it was he who had abducted me the evening before.

"Rob Finn is the jockey you just watched being carried to victory by this wonder horse, Template," he said in his charming television voice. Then he turned to me. "I expect you enjoyed being his passenger, Rob?"

"It was marvelous," I said emphatically, smiling a smile to outdazzle his. "It is a great thrill for any jockey to ride a horse as superb as Template. Of course," I went on before he had time to speak, "I am lucky to have had the opportunity. As you know, I have been taking Pip Pankhurst's place while his leg has been mending, and today's win should have been his. He is much better now, and we are all delighted that it won't be long before he is riding again."

A silent chill crept into the corner of Kemp-Lore's mouth. "You haven't been doing as well, lately . . ." he began.

"No," I interrupted warmly. "Aren't they extraordinary, those runs of atrocious luck in racing? Did you know that the great Doug Smith once rode ninety-nine losers in succession? It makes my twenty or so seem quite paltry."

"You weren't worried, then, by . . . er . . . by such a bad patch as you've been going through?" His smile was slipping.

"Well, naturally I wasn't exactly delighted, but these runs of bad luck happen to everyone in racing, and one just has to live through them until another winner comes along. Like today's," I finished with a grin at the camera.

"Most people understood it was more than bad luck," he said sharply, and for an instant I saw a flash of the fury in his eyes.

I said, "People will believe anything when their pockets are touched. I'm afraid a lot of people lost their money backing my mounts . . . it's only natural to blame the jockey when they lose."

He listened to me mending the holes he had torn in my life and he couldn't stop me without giving an impression of being a bad sport. He had been standing with his profile to the camera, but now he took a step toward me and turned so that he stood beside me. As he moved he dropped his arm heavily across my shoulders, with his fingers spread out on my back in a gesture which must have appeared one of genuine friendship on the television screen. I stood still, and turned my head slowly toward him, and smiled. Few efforts have ever cost me more.

"And what are Template's plans for the future?" He strove to be conversational, normal, but there was an expression of puzzlement in his eyes. His arm felt like a ton weight on my aching muscles; I gathered my straying wits. "There's the Gold Cup at Cheltenham in three weeks' time."

"And you hope to ride him again in that?" he asked. There was an edge to his voice which stopped just short of offensiveness.

"It depends," I said, "on whether or not Pip is fit in time. . . . Of course I'd like to, if I get the chance."

"You've never yet managed to ride in the Gold Cup, I believe?" He made it sound as if I had been trying unsuccessfully for years to beg a mount.

"No," I agreed. "But it has only been run twice since I came into racing, so if I get a ride in it so soon in my career I'll count myself very lucky."

His nostrils flared and I thought in satisfaction, That got you squarely in the guts, my friend.

Kemp-Lore was speaking now toward the camera, finishing off his broadcast. He gave me a last, natural-looking little squeezing shake, and let his arm drop away from my shoulders. I silently repeated to myself the ten most obscene words I knew, and after that, Ascot racecourse stopped attempting to whirl round.

Kemp-Lore turned directly to me again and said, "Well, that's it. We're off the air now."

"Thank you, Maurice," I said carefully, constructing one last warm smile. "That was just what I needed to set me back on top of the world. A big race win and a television interview with you to clinch it. Thank you very much."

He gave me a look in which the cultivated habit of charm struggled for supremacy over spite, and still won. Then he turned on his heel and walked away. It is impossible to say which of us loathed the other more.

# CHAPTER XIII

I SPENT most of the next day in Joanna's bed. She gave me a cup of coffee for breakfast, a cozy grin, and instructions to sleep.

I had arrived in a shaky condition on her doorstep the evening before, having first taken Tick-Tock by taxi to the White Bear at Uxbridge where, as I had imagined, the Mini Cooper stood abandoned in the parking space.

My wristwatch and wallet were on the glove shelf, and my jacket and overcoat on the backseat.

"Why the blazes," Tick-Tock said slowly, "did you leave your things here? It's a wonder they weren't pinched. And the car."

He picked up the coats, and transferred them to the waiting taxi. "You may have fooled everyone else today, mate," he said lightly, "but to me you've looked like death warmed over, and it's something to do with your hands . . . the gloves are new . . . you don't usually wear any. What happened?"

"You work on it," I said amiably, getting back into the taxi.

The taxi driver, in a good mood because he had backed three winners, drove me back to Joanna's flat. I paid him and added a fat tip on top.

"Did you back a winner, too, then?" he asked.

"Yes. Template."

"Funny thing that," he said. "I backed him myself, after what you said. You were quite right; that fellow Finn's not washed up at all, not by a long chalk. He rode a hell of a race. I reckon he can carry my money again, any day." He shifted gears, and drove off.

JOANNA was singing quietly at her easel when I surfaced finally at about four o'clock the following afternoon. I sat up in bed. "Joanna, I'm starving," I said.

"All right. I'll cook."

And cook she did: fried chicken with sweet corn and pineapple and bacon. While the preliminary smells wafted tantalizingly out of the kitchen I put my clothes on, and changed her bed, making it fresh and neat for her to get into.

She carried a tray in from the kitchen and saw the bundle of dirty sheets and the smooth bed. "What are you doing?"

"The sofa isn't good for you," I said.

"So you are not sleeping here tonight?"

"No."

"You could try the sofa," she said. "You might as well find out what I have endured for your sake." I didn't answer at once, and she added compulsively, "Stay, Rob. I'd like you to."

I looked at her carefully. Was there the slightest chance, I wondered, that her reluctance to have me leave meant that she was at last finding the fact of our cousinship less troublesome? If so, it was definitely not the time to walk out. "All right," I said smiling. "Thank you. I'll stay."

She became suddenly animated and talkative, and told me in great detail how the race and the interview had appeared on television. "You looked like lifelong buddies standing there with his arm round your shoulders and you smiling at him. How did you manage it?" She stopped in midflow, and in a sober tone of voice she said, "What are you going to do about him?"

I told her. It took some time. Then I asked, "Will you help?" Her help was essential.

She was shaken. "But what you are planning . . . it's cruel and complicated, and expensive. Won't you change your mind and go to the police instead?"

"No. Will you make that one telephone call for me?"

She sighed. "All right," she said. "I'll do it. You can go ahead with . . . with what you plan to do."

On the following morning I hired a drive-yourself car and went to see Grant Oldfield.

When I rang the bell it struck me that the brass bell push was brightly polished. The door opened and a neat, dark-haired young woman looked at me inquiringly.

"I came . . ." I said. "I wanted to see . . . er . . . I wonder if you could tell me where I can find Grant Oldfield?"

"Indoors," she said. "I'm his wife. What name shall I say?"

"Rob Finn," I said.

"Oh," she said, and smiled warmly. "Do come in."

I stepped into the narrow hall and she led the way to the kitchen. Everything was spotless and shining.

Grant was sitting at a table, reading a newspaper. When he saw me his face, too, creased into a smile of welcome. He looked much older and shrunken, but a whole man again.

"How are you, Grant?" I said inadequately.

"I'm much better, thanks. I've been home a fortnight now."

"He was in the hospital," his wife explained. "Dr. Parnell wrote to me and told me Grant was ill and couldn't help being how he was. So I came back." She smiled at Grant. "And everything's going to be all right now. Grant's got a job lined up selling toys. They thought it would be better for him to do something which had nothing to do with horses."

"Grant," I said, "I believe you were telling the truth when you told Axminster you had not sold information to that professional bettor, Lubbock," I said. "But Lubbock did pay for and get information. The question is, who was receiving the money?"

"I went to see Lubbock," Grant said, "and he said that until James Axminster tackled him about it, he hadn't known for sure who he was buying information from. He had only guessed it was me. But he said I had given him the information over the telephone and he had sent the payments to me in the name of Robinson, care of a post office in London."

"Can you give me Lubbock's address?" I asked.

"He lives in Solihull," he said slowly, "I can't remember the exact address."

"I'll find it," I said. "Would it mean anything to you if I proved that you were telling the truth all along?"

His face came suddenly alive. "I'll say it would. You can't imagine what it was like, losing that job for something I didn't do."

I didn't tell him that I knew exactly what it was like, only too well. I said, "I'll do my best, then."

I DROVE the thirty miles to Solihull, looked up Lubbock in the telephone directory, and rang his number. A woman answered. She told me he was lunching at the Queen's Hotel.

Mr. Lubbock proved to be a plumpish, middle-aged man with a gingery mustache. I introduced myself and ordered him a brandy and a cigar. Then I came straight to the point. "I want to know about Grant Oldfield."

He gave me a sharp glance. "Do you want a deal, is that it? Well, for every winner you put me on to, I'll pay you the same as I paid Oldfield."

"Did you pay the money to him personally?" I asked.

"No," he said. "He fixed it up on the telephone. He was very secretive: said his name was Robinson, and asked me to send money orders to a post office for him to collect."

"You didn't know for sure it was Oldfield, did you?" I asked.

"It depends what you mean by know," he said. "Who else could it have been? But I suppose I didn't actually know until Axminster said 'I hear you've been buying information from my jockey.' "

"So you wouldn't have told anyone before that that it was Old-field who was selling you tips?"

"Of course not." He gave me a hard stare. "You don't broadcast things like that in my business. Just what is all this about?"

"Well . . ." I said. "I'm very sorry to have misled you, Mr. Lubbock, but I am not really trying to sell you tips, I'm just trying to unstick a bit of mud that was thrown at Grant Oldfield."

To my surprise he gave a fat chuckle. "Do you know," he said, "if you'd agreed to tip me off I'd have been looking for the catch?" He jabbed his cigar in my direction. "You aren't the type."

"Thanks." I grinned. "Mr. Lubbock," I said, "Oldfield was not Robinson, but his career and his health were broken up because you and Mr. Axminster were led to believe that he was. Oldfield has now given up riding, but it would still mean a great deal to him to have his name cleared. Will you help to do it?"

"How?" he said.

"Would you just write a statement to the effect that you saw no evidence at any time to support your guess that in paying Robinson you were really paying Oldfield, and that at no time before James Axminster approached you did you speak of your suspicions as to Robinson's identity?"

"That can't do any harm," he said. "But I think you're barking up the wrong tree. Only a jockey would go to all that trouble to hide his identity. Still, I'll write what you ask."

He took a sheet of hotel writing paper and wrote and signed the statement. "There you are," he said.

I read what he had written and put it in my wallet. "Thank you very much, Mr. Lubbock, for your help," I said and stood up.

"Anytime." He waved his cigar. "See you at the races."

# CHAPTER XIV

ON TUESDAY morning I bought a copy of *Horse and Hound* and telephoned a farmer who had advertised a hunter for sale. I made an appointment to view the animal in two days' time. Next I rang up one of the farmers I rode for and persuaded him to lend me his Land Rover and trailer on Thursday.

Then, having borrowed a tape measure from Joanna, I drove down to James's stables. I found him sitting in his office. When I entered he stood up and rubbed his hands, and held them out to the fire. "Some of the owners have telephoned," he said. "They're willing to have you back. I told them . . ." and he smiled ". . . that you would be on Template in the Gold Cup."

"What!" I exclaimed. "Do you mean it? What about Pip?"

"I've explained to Pip," he said, "that I can't take you off the horse when you've won both the King Chase and the Midwinter on him. I have arranged with him that he starts again the week after Cheltenham, which will give him time to get a few races in before the Grand National. He'll be riding my runner in that. I've enough horses to keep both Pip and you fairly busy."

"I don't know how to thank you," I said.

"Thank yourself," he said sardonically. "You earned it."

"James," I said, "will you write something for me? That it was Kemp-Lore who told you that Oldfield was selling information about your horses, and that he said he had learned it from Lubbock?"

"I don't see . . ." He gave me an intent look and shrugged. "Oh, very well." He sat down at his desk and wrote what I had asked. "What good will that do?" he said, handing it to me.

I showed him Mr. Lubbock's paper.

"It's incredible," he said. "Suppose I had checked carefully with Lubbock? What a risk Maurice took."

"It wasn't so big a risk," I said. "You wouldn't have thought of questioning what he put forward as a friendly warning."

"I wish there was something I could do about Grant," James said.

"Write him and explain," I suggested. "He would appreciate it more than anything."

"I'll do that," he said.

"On Saturday morning," I said, "these little documents will arrive with a plop on the senior steward's doormat. They should be conclusive enough to kick friend Kemp-Lore off his pedestal."

"I should say you were right." He looked at me gravely, and then said, "Why wait until Saturday?"

"I . . . er . . . I won't be ready until then," I said evasively.

BACK in the hills a mile or so away from his stable, James owned an old deserted caretaker's cottage. After leaving him I drove up there. The cottage was set in a small fenced garden. The neglected grass had been cropped short by sheep. There were two windows facing the front and two the back. The whole place smelled faintly musty, but the walls and floorboards were still in good condition. It could not have been more convenient for my purpose.

I took out Joanna's tape and measured a window frame. Then I counted the number of broken panes of glass and measured one of them. That done, I drove into Newbury, and at a hardware store I ordered ten panes of glass, enough putty to put them in with, several pieces of water pipe cut to a specified length, a bucket, some screws, a stout padlock, a bag of cement, a pot of green paint and various tools. Then I returned to the cottage.

I painted the weather-beaten front door and left it open to dry. I went into one of the back rooms and knocked out the panes of glass which remained. Then I mixed a good quantity of cement, using water from the rain barrel, and fixed six three-foot lengths of pipe upright in a row across the window. That done, I fitted the padlock to the door of the same room. On the inside of the door I unscrewed the handle and removed it.

The final job was replacing the glass in the front windows and when it was done, with its whole windows and fresh green door, the cottage already looked more cheerful and welcoming.

I smiled to myself and drove back to London.

ON WEDNESDAY morning I went to a photographic agency and asked to see a picture of Kemp-Lore's sister Alice. I bought a copy of a photograph which showed her as a striking girl watching some hunter trials, dressed in a riding jacket and head scarf.

Leaving the agency, I went to the offices of my parents' accountants, and talked the manager into letting me use a typewriter and a photocopying machine.

I typed a bald account of Kemp-Lore's actions against Grant Oldfield. I made ten copies of this statement and then on the photocopier printed ten copies each of the statements from Lubbock and James. I then returned to Joanna's and showed her the photograph of Alice Kemp-Lore.

"But," said Joanna, "she isn't a bit like her brother. It can't have been her that the ticket collector saw at Cheltenham."

"No," I said. "It was Kemp-Lore himself. Could you draw me a picture of him wearing a head scarf?"

"I've only seen him on television," she said, but with concentration she made a recognizable likeness. "It isn't very good." She began to sketch in a head scarf over the forehead, then she emphasized the lips so that they looked dark and full.

"Lipstick," she explained. "How about clothes?"

"Jodhpurs and riding jacket," I said. "The only clothes which look equally right on men and women."

She drew in a collar and tie and the shoulders of a jacket. The portrait grew into a likeness of a pretty girl dressed for riding. It made my skin crawl.

I filled ten long envelopes with the various statements. I addressed one to the senior steward and four others to influential people on the National Hunt Committee. One to the chairman of Universal Telecast, one each to John Ballerton and Corin Kellar, to show them their idol's clay feet. One to James. And one to Maurice Kemp-Lore.

I stacked nine of the envelopes on the bookshelf and propped the tenth, the one for Kemp-Lore, up on end behind them.

"We'll post that lot on Friday," I said. "And I'll deliver the other one myself."

AT EIGHT thirty on Thursday morning Joanna made the telephone call upon which so much depended.

I dialed Kemp-Lore's flat for her. We had rehearsed what she was going to say. Joanna looked at me anxiously.

"Oh? Mr. Kemp-Lore?" She could do a beautiful cockney-suburban accent. "You don't know me, but I wondered if I could tell you something that you could use on your program in the newsy bits at the end? I do admire your program. It's ever so good . . ."

His voice clacked, interrupting the flow.

"What information?" repeated Joanna. "Oh, well, you know all the talk there's been about athletes using them pep pills, well I wondered if you wanted to know about jockeys doing it, too . . . one jockey, actually . . . Which jockey? Oh . . . er . . . Robbie Finn, you know, the one you talked to on the telly on Saturday. Pepped to the eyebrows as usual he was, didn't you guess? How do I know? Well, it was me got some stuff for him once. I work in a doctor's dispensary in Newbury . . . he told me what to take and I got it for him. But now look here, I don't want to get into no trouble that . . . I think I'd better ring off . . . Don't ring off? You won't say nothing about it then, you know, me pinching the stuff?

"Why am I telling you? . . . Well, he don't come to see me no more, that's why." Her voice was superbly loaded with jealous spite. "After all I've done for him . . . Check, what do you mean check? . . . You can't take my word for it on the telephone? Well, yes, you can come and see me if you want to . . . no, not today, I'm at work all day . . . yes, all right, tomorrow morning then.

"How do you get there? . . . Well, you go to Newbury and then out toward Hungerford . . ." She went on with the directions slowly while he wrote them down. "And it's the only cottage along there, you can't miss it. About eleven o'clock? All right then. What's my name? . . . Doris Jones . . . Well, ta-ta then."

She put the receiver down slowly, looking at me with a serious face. "Hook, line and sinker," she said.

WHEN the banks opened I drew out one hundred and fifty pounds. As Joanna had said, what I was doing was complicated and expensive; but I grudged the money not at all. What I wanted was to pay Kemp-Lore in his own coin.

I hired a car and drove off to Bedfordshire to collect the Land Rover and trailer from my farmer friend. I bought from him two bales of straw and one of hay, and then I started away to my appointment with the man with the hunter for sale.

My appointment proved to be with an old brown mare, sound in limb but noisy in wind. She was big, but quiet to handle. I got her for eighty-five pounds. Then I loaded the mare, whose name was Buttonhook, into the trailer and turned my face south again to Berkshire.

Three hours later I turned the Land Rover into the lane at the cottage, and bumped Buttonhook to a standstill on the rough ground behind the bushes beyond the building. While she waited in the trailer I spread the straw thickly over the floorboards in the room with the water pipes cemented over the window, filled her a bucket of water out of the rain barrel and carried an armful of hay into a corner of the room.

She was an affectionate old thing. She came docilely out of the trailer, in through the front door of the cottage and into the room prepared for her. I gave her some sugar and rubbed her ears, and she butted her head playfully against my chest. After a while, as she seemed quite content, I padlocked her in.

I dumped the rest of the hay and straw in one of the front rooms of the cottage, shut the front door, and set off to deliver the Land Rover and trailer to their owner. Then I drove the hired car back to Joanna's flat.

When I went in she sprang up from the sofa and kissed me. It was utterly spontaneous, and it was a surprise to both of us. I smiled incredulously into her black eyes, and watched the surprise there turn to confusion. I turned my back on her to give her time, saying casually over my shoulder, "The lodger is installed in the cottage. A big brown mare with a nice nature."

"I was just . . . glad to see you back," she said in a high voice.

"That's fine," I said lightly. "Can we rustle up an egg?"

She made an omelet for me and I told her about Buttonhook, and the difficult moment passed.

Later on she announced that she was coming down to the cottage with me in the morning. "He's expecting Doris Jones to open the door to him. It will be much better if she does."

I couldn't budge her.

"And," she said, "I don't suppose you've thought of putting curtains in the windows? If you want him to walk into your parlor, you'll have to make it look normal. He probably has a keen nose for smelling rats." She collected pins and scissors and some printed cotton material and then rolled up the big rag rug which the easel stood on and took a flower picture off the wall.

"What are those for?" I said.

"To furnish the hall, of course. It's got to look right."

"Okay, genius," I said, giving in. "You can come."

# CHAPTER XV

WE SET off early and got down to the cottage before nine. I hid the car behind the bushes again, and we carried the rug and the other things inside. Buttonhook was delighted to see us. I fetched her some more hay and water, and Joanna cut and pinned up the flowery material so that it hung like curtains. After I had finished with Buttonhook, leaving the door to her room companionably open, and Joanna had put down the rug in the little hall and hung up the picture, we stood back and admired our handiwork. With its freshly painted front door, pretty curtains, and the rug and picture showing through the half-open door, the cottage looked well cared for and homey. My watch said twenty minutes to eleven. "We'd better get ready in case he comes early," I said.

We shut the front door and sat on the remains of the hay bale in the front room, giving ourselves a clear view of the front gate. A minute or two ticked by in silence. Joanna shivered.

"Are you too cold?" I said with concern.

"It's nerves as much as cold," she said, shivering again.

I put my arm round her shoulders. She leaned comfortably against me, and I kissed her cheek. Her eyelids flickered, but she didn't move. I had a sudden feeling that if I lost this time, I had lost forever, and a chill of despair settled in my stomach.

"No one forbids marriage between cousins," I said slowly. "The law allows it and the Church allows it, and you can be sure they wouldn't if there were anything immoral in it. And the medical profession raises no objection either." I paused, but she still said nothing. Without much hope I said, "I don't really understand why you feel the way you do."

"It's instinct," she said. "I've always thought of it as wrong . . . and impossible."

There was a little silence. I said, "I think I'll sleep in my digs tonight, and ride out with the horses tomorrow morning. I've been neglecting my job this week. . . ."

She sat up straight, pulling free of my arm. "No," she said abruptly. "Come back to the flat."

"I can't. I can't anymore," I said. "I can't go on like this if you know beyond any doubt that you'll never change your mind."

"Before last weekend there wasn't any problem as far as I was concerned," she said. "You were just something I couldn't have . . . like oysters, which give me indigestion . . . And now"—

she tried to laugh—"it's as if I've developed a craving for oysters."

"Come here," I said persuasively. She moved close beside me on the hay bale. I took her hand.

"If we weren't cousins, would you marry me?" I held my breath.

"Yes," she said simply. No reservations, no hesitation anymore.

I turned toward her and put my hands on the sides of her head and tilted her face up. I kissed her, gently, and with love. Her lips trembled.

"It will be all right," I said. "Our being cousins won't worry you in a little while."

She looked at me wonderingly for a moment. "I believe you," she said, "because I've never known anyone more determined in all my life. You don't care what trouble you put yourself to to get what you want . . . like riding in the race last Saturday, and fixing up this cottage, and living with me as you have this week . . . so my instinct against blood relatives marrying would have to start getting used to the idea that it isn't wrong. I will try," she finished seriously, "not to keep you waiting very long."

"In that case," I said, "I'll go on sleeping on your sofa as often as possible, so as to be handy when the breakthrough occurs."

She laughed and we went on sitting on the hay bale, talking calmly as if nothing had happened; and nothing had, I thought, except a miracle that one could reliably build a future on.

The minutes ticked away toward eleven o'clock. I closed Buttonhook's door now, leaving the padlock undone.

"I almost hope he doesn't come," she said. "Those letters would be enough by themselves."

"You won't forget to post them when you get back?" I said.

"Of course not. But I wish you'd let me stay."

I shook my head. We sat on, watching the gate. The minute hand passed the hour on my watch.

"He's late," she said.

Five past eleven. Ten past eleven.

"He isn't coming," Joanna murmured.

"He'll come," I said. "He clearly didn't know at the end of that television interview with me last Saturday that I was on to him. If he feels as secure as I am sure he does, he'll never pass up an opportunity to learn about something as damaging as pep pills . . . so he'll come."

A quarter past eleven. Twenty past eleven. Eleven thirty. She said again, "He isn't coming."

I didn't answer.

At eleven thirty-three, the sleek nose of an Aston Martin slid to a stop at the gate and Maurice Kemp-Lore stepped out. He wore a beautifully cut riding jacket and cavalry twill trousers, and there was poise and grace in his every movement.

"Glory, he's handsome," breathed Joanna in my ear. "Television doesn't do him justice."

Kemp-Lore banged the knocker on the front door.

Joanna gave me a half smile, and walked unhurriedly into the hall. I followed her and stood against the wall where I would be hidden when the door opened. She opened the door.

"Doris Jones?" the honey voice said. "I'm so sorry I'm late."

"Won't you come in, Mr. Kemp-Lore," said Joanna in her cockney-suburban accent. "It's ever so nice to see you."

"Thank you," he said, stepping over the threshold. Joanna took two paces backward and Kemp-Lore followed her into the hall.

Slamming the front door with my foot, I seized Kemp-Lore from behind by both elbows, forcing him forward at the same time. Joanna opened the door of Buttonhook's room and I brought my foot up into the small of Kemp-Lore's back and gave him an almighty push. He staggered forward through the door and I had a glimpse of him sprawling face downward in the straw before I had the door shut again and the padlock firmly clicking into place.

"That was easy," I whispered with satisfaction. "Thanks to you."

Kemp-Lore began kicking the door. "Let me out," he shouted. "What do you think you're doing?"

"He didn't see you," said Joanna softly.

"No," I agreed. "I think we'll leave him in ignorance while I take you in to Newbury to catch the train."

Before leaving I moved Kemp-Lore's car until it was hidden in the bushes. Then I took Joanna to the station and drove straight back again.

Walking quietly I went round to the back of the cottage. Kemp-Lore's hands gripped the water-pipe bars in the window. He was shaking them vigorously. He stopped abruptly when he saw me and the anger in his face changed to blank surprise.

"Who did you expect?" I said.

"I don't know what's going on," he said. "Some damn fool of a woman locked me in here nearly an hour ago and went away and left me. You can let me out. Quickly." His breath wheezed sharply in his throat. "There's a horse in here," he said, looking over his shoulder, "and they give me asthma."

"Yes," I said steadily, without moving. "I know."

It hit him then. His eyes widened. "It was you . . . who pushed me . . ."

"Yes," I said.

He stood staring at me through the crisscross of window frame and bars. "You did it on purpose? You put me in here with a horse on purpose?" His voice rose. "Why?"

"I'll give you half an hour to think about it," I said.

"No," he exclaimed. "My asthma's bad. Let me out at once." His breath whistled fiercely, but he had not even loosened his collar and tie. He was in no danger.

"Stand by the window," I said, "and breathe the fresh air."

"It's cold," he objected. "This place is like an icehouse."

I smiled. "Maybe it is," I said. "But then you are fortunate . . . you can move about to keep warm, and you have your jacket on, and I have not poured two bucketfuls of cold water over your head."

He gasped and it was then, I think, that he began to realize that he was not going to escape easily.

When I walked round to the window after listening to him kicking the door for half an hour, I found him fending off Buttonhook, who was putting her muzzle affectionately over his shoulder. He was nearly choking with rage and fear. "Get her away from me," he screamed. "She won't leave me alone. I can't breathe."

He clung onto a bar with one hand, and chopped at Buttonhook with the other. His asthma was much worse. He had unbuttoned his collar and pulled down his tie and I could see his throat heaving.

I put the box of sugar cubes I was carrying on the inner windowsill, withdrawing my hand quickly as he made a grab at it. "Put some sugar on her hay," I said. "Go on," I added, as he hesitated. "This lot isn't doped."

His head jerked up. I looked bitterly into his eyes. "Twenty-eight horses," I said. "Starting with Shantytown. Twenty-eight sleepy horses who all ate some of your sugar before they raced."

"You won't get away with this," he said. "You'll go to jail for it." His breath hissed. "Now, hurry up and say whatever it is you want to say. You'll have to let me out by two thirty at the latest," he said unguardedly. "I've got rehearsals today at five."

I smiled and said, "It's no accident that you are here on Friday."

His jaw literally dropped. "The program . . ." he said.

"Will have to go on without you," I agreed.

"But you can't," he shouted, gasping, "you can't do that. Millions of people are expecting to see the program."

"Then millions of people are going to be disappointed," I said.

He stopped shouting and took three gulping, wheezing breaths. "If you let me go in good time for the rehearsals, I won't report you to the police as I threatened."

"I think you had better keep quiet and listen," I said. "I suppose you find it hard to realize that I don't give a damn for your influence or your dazzling, synthetic personality. You are a fraud, a sick mess of envy and frustration and spite. But I wouldn't have found you out if you hadn't doped twenty-eight horses I rode and told everyone I had lost my nerve. And you can spend this afternoon reflecting that you wouldn't be missing your program tonight if you hadn't tried to stop me from riding Template."

He stood stock-still, his face pallid. "No," he said. A muscle in his cheek twitched. "No. You can't. You did ride Template . . . you must let me do the program."

"You won't be doing any more programs," I said. "Not tonight or any night. I didn't bring you here just for a personal revenge. I brought you here on behalf of Art Mathews and Peter Cloony and Grant Oldfield, Danny Higgs and Ingersoll, and every other jockey you have hit where it hurts. In various ways you saw to it that they lost their jobs; so now you are going to lose yours."

For the first time, he was speechless. His lower jaw hung slack. I took the long envelope addressed to him out of my pocket and handed it to him through the bars. "Open it," I said.

He pulled out the sheets of paper and read them. His face showed from the first that he understood the extent of the disaster.

"As you will see," I said, "those are photostat copies. More like them are in the mail to the senior steward and to your boss at Universal Telecast, and to several other people as well. They will get them tomorrow morning. And they will no longer wonder why you failed to turn up for your program tonight."

He still seemed unable to speak. I passed to him the rolled-up portrait Joanna had drawn of him. He opened it, and it was clearly another blow.

"I brought it to show you," I said, "so that you would realize beyond any doubt that I know exactly what you were doing when you rammed that old Jaguar across Peter Cloony's lane."

His head jerked, as if still surprised that I knew so much.

"Most of your vicious rumors," I said, changing tack, "were spread for you by Corin Kellar and John Ballerton. I hope you know Corin well enough to realize that he never stands by his friends. When the contents of the letter he will receive in the morning sink into that rat-brain of his, and he finds that other people have had letters like it, there won't be anyone spewing out more damaging truth about you than him.

"You see," I finished after a pause, "I think it is only justice that as far as possible you should suffer exactly what you inflicted on other people."

He spoke at last. "How did you find it out?" he wheezed disbelievingly. "You didn't know last Friday, you couldn't see. . . ."

"I did know last Friday," I said. "I knew just how far you had gone to smash Peter Cloony, and I knew you hated me enough to give yourself asthma doping my mounts. I knew all about your curdled, obsessive jealousy of jockeys. I didn't need to see you . . . there wasn't anyone else with any reason to want me out of action."

"You can't have known all that," he said obstinately. "You didn't know the next day when I interviewed you after the race . . ." His voice trailed off in a croak.

"You aren't the only one who can smile and hate at the same time," I said neutrally. "I learned it from you."

I walked away, round the cottage and in at the front door, and sat down on the hay in the front room. I looked at my watch. It was a quarter to two. The afternoon stretched lengthily ahead.

Kemp-Lore had another spell of screaming for help; then he tried the door again, but it was too solidly constructed for him to kick his way through. Buttonhook grew restive from the noise and started pawing the ground, and Kemp-Lore shouted at me furiously to let him out.

The slow hours passed. At about five o'clock he was quiet for a long time. I got up and walked round the outside of the cottage and looked in through the window. He was lying facedown in the straw near the door, not moving.

I watched him for a few minutes and called his name, but as he still did not stir I began to be alarmed, and decided I would have to make sure he was all right. I returned to the hall, and unlocked the padlock on the back room. The door swung inward.

Kemp-Lore was alive, that at least was plain. The sound of his high, squeezed breath rose from his still form. I bent down beside him to see into just how bad a spasm he had been driven, but as soon as I was down on one knee he heaved himself up, knocking me sprawling, and sprang for the door.

I caught his shoe and yanked him back. He fell heavily on top of me and we rolled toward Buttonhook. The mare was frightened.

She cowered back against the wall to get out of our way, but it was a small room and our struggles took us among Buttonhook's feet. She stepped gingerly over us and made for the open door.

Kemp-Lore's left hand was clamped round my right wrist. He couldn't have struck on anything better calculated to cause me inconvenience. I hit him in the face and neck with my left hand, but I was too close to get any weight behind it. He tried lacing his fingers in my hair and banging my head against the wall. He was staggeringly strong, in view of his asthma, and the desperation which fired him blazed in his blue eyes like a furnace. If my hair hadn't been so short he would probably have succeeded in knocking me out, but his fingers kept slipping and I managed at last to wrench my right hand free.

I landed a socking right jab in his ribs, and the air screeched out of his lungs. He went a sick gray-green color and fell off me, gasping and clawing his throat for air. I got to my feet and hauled him up, and staggered with him over to the window, holding him where the fresh cold air blew into his face. After three or four minutes his color improved and the terrifying heaving lessened. I clamped his fingers round the bars in the window and let go of him. He swayed a bit, but his hands held, and I walked dizzily out of the room and padlocked the door shut behind me.

Buttonhook had found her way into the front room and was placidly eating the hay. I leaned weakly against the wall and cursed myself for the foolish way I had nearly got myself locked into my own prison.

There was no sound from the back room. I walked round to the window. He was standing there, holding onto the bars where I had put him, and there were tears running down his cheeks. "Damn you," he said. Another tear spilled over. "Damn you. Damn you."

There wasn't anything to say. I went back to Buttonhook, and put on her halter. Leading her out of the front door and through the gate, I jumped onto her back and rode her along a lane which gave into a field owned by a farmer I had often ridden for. I opened the gate, led her through and turned her loose.

She was so amiable that I was sorry to part with her, but I frankly didn't know what else to do with her. I fed her a handful of sugar. Then I slapped her on the rump and watched my eighty-five quid kick up her heels and canter down the field like a two-year-old. The farmer would no doubt be surprised to find an unclaimed brown mare on his land, but I hadn't any doubt that he would give her a good home.

I turned away and walked back to the cottage. It was beginning to get dark, and I walked softly through the garden to the back window. He was still standing there. When he saw me he said quite quietly, "Let me out."

I shook my head.

I went round into the front room and sat down again on the hay. It was a quarter past six. Still three hours to wait: three hours in which the awful truth would slowly dawn on Kemp-Lore's colleagues in the television studio, three hours of stopgap planning, culminating in the digging out of a bit of old film to fill in the empty fifteen minutes and the smooth announcement, "We regret that owing to the—er—illness of Maurice Kemp-Lore there will be no 'Turf Talk' tonight."

Or ever again, mates, I thought, if you did but know it.

It grew dark. Kemp-Lore began kicking the door again. "I'm cold," he shouted. "Let me out."

I made no reply to him at all, and I heard him slither down the door as if exhausted and begin sobbing with frustration. I listened without emotion; for I had cried, too, in the tack room.

The hands crawled round the face of my watch. At a quarter to nine, when nothing could any longer save his program, I got stiffly to my feet and went out into the front garden. I walked along to the bushes and started Kemp-Lore's car, turning it and driving it back to the gate. Then for the last time I walked round the cottage to talk to him through the window. He was standing there already. "My car," he said hysterically. "I heard the engine. You're going to drive away in my car and leave me."

I laughed. "No. You are going to drive it away yourself. As fast and as far as you like. If I were you, I'd drive to the nearest airport and fly off. No one is going to like you very much when they've read those letters in the morning, and it will be only a day or two before the newspapers get on to it. As far as racing goes, your face is too well known in Britain for you to hide or change your name or get another job."

"You mean . . . I can go? Just go?" He sounded astounded.

"Just go," I said, nodding. "If you go quickly enough, you'll avoid the inquiry the stewards are bound to hold. You can get away to some helpful distant country where they don't know you, and you can start again from scratch."

He moaned and crashed his fists down on the window frame.

I went round into the cottage and unlocked the padlock and pushed open the door. He turned from the window and walked unsteadily through the door, passing me without a glance. He stumbled down the path to his car. I walked behind him.

He paused when he was sitting in his car, and with the door still open looked out at me. "You don't understand," he said, his voice shaking. "When I was a boy I wanted to be a jockey. I wanted to ride in the Grand National, like my father. And then there was this thing about falling off . . . I'd see the ground rushing past under my horse and there would be this terrible sort of pain, and I sweated until I could pull up and get off. And then I'd be sick."

His face twisted. Then he said suddenly, fiercely, "It made me feel good to see jockeys looking worried. I broke them up all right. It made me feel warm inside. Big."

He looked up at me with renewed rage, and his voice thickened venomously. "I hated you more than all the others. You rode too well for a new jockey and you were getting on too quickly. You took your strength for granted, and too many people were saying you'd be champion one day . . .

"I waited for you to have a fall, and then I used the sugar. It worked. I felt ten feet tall, looking at your white face and listening to everyone sniggering about you. I watched you find out how it felt. I wanted to see you writhe when everyone you cared for said . . . like my father said to all his friends . . . that it was a pity about you, a pity you had no nerve . . . no nerve . . ."

His voice died away, and his hollowed eyes were wide, unfocused, as if he were staring back into an unbearable past. I stood looking down at the wreck of what could have been a great man. All that vitality, I thought; all that splendid talent wasted for the sake of hurting people who had not hurt him.

I could understand him in a way, I supposed, because I was myself the changeling in a family. But my father had rejected me kindly, and I felt no need to watch musicians suffer.

Without another word I shut the car door on him and gestured to him to drive away. He gave me one more incredulous glance as if he still found it impossible that I should let him go, and began to fumble with the light switches, the ignition and the gears. The car began to roll, and I caught a last glimpse of the famous profile as he slid away into the dark.

I walked up the path to the quiet cottage, to sweep it clean.

Forgiveness, I thought. That was something else again.

It would take a long time to forgive.

# IN THE FRAME

# CHAPTER ONE

I STOOD on the outside of disaster, looking in.

There were three police cars outside my cousin's house, and an ambulance with its blue turret light revolving ominously, and people bustling in seriously through his open front door. The chill wind of early autumn blew dead brown leaves sadly onto the driveway, and harsh scurrying clouds threatened worse to come. Six o'clock, Friday evening, Shropshire, England.

Intermittent flashes from the windows spoke of photography within. I dumped my shoulder satchel and my suitcase on the grass, and with justifiable foreboding completed my journey to the house.

I had traveled by train to stay for the weekend. No cousin with car to meet me as promised, so I had started to walk the mile and a half of country road, sure he would come tearing along soon in his muddy Peugeot, full of jokes and apologies and plans.

No jokes.

He stood in the hall, dazed and gray. His body inside his neat business suit looked limp, and his arms hung straight down from the shoulders, as if his brain had forgotten they were there. His head was turned slightly toward the sitting room, the source of the flashes, and his eyes were stark with shock.

"Don?" I said. I walked toward him. "Donald!"

He didn't hear me. A policeman, however, did. He came swiftly from the sitting room in his dark blue uniform, took me by the arm, and swung me unceremoniously back toward the door.

"Out of here, sir," he said. "If you please."

Donald's strained eyes slid uncertainly our way. "Charles . . ."

The policeman's grip loosened very slightly. "Do you know this man, sir?" he asked Donald.

"I'm his cousin," I said.

"Oh." He took his hand off, told me to stay where I was and look after Mr. Stuart, and returned to the sitting room.

"What's happened?" I said.

Don was past answering. His head turned toward the white-paneled sitting-room door. I disobeyed the policeman, took ten quiet steps, and looked in.

The room was bare of pictures and ornaments. No Oriental rugs. Just gray walls, chintz-covered sofas, furniture pushed awry, and a great expanse of dusty wood-block flooring.

And, on the floor, my cousin's young wife, bloody and dead.

The big room was scattered with police, measuring, photographing, dusting for fingerprints. But all I saw was Regina, lying on her back. Her eyes were half open, and her lower jaw had fallen open, emphasizing brutally the shape of the skull. There had been no mercy.

I felt sickeningly faint.

The policeman who had grabbed me before saw me swaying in the doorway and strode to my side.

"I told you to wait outside, sir," he said with exasperation.

I nodded dumbly and went back into the hall. Donald was sitting on the stairs, looking at nothing. I sat abruptly on the floor near him and put my head between my knees.

"I . . . f-found . . . her," he said.

I swallowed. The faintness passed slowly, leaving a sour feeling. I leaned back against the wall and wished I could help him.

"She's . . . never . . . home . . . on F-Fridays," he said. "Six o'clock . . . she comes b-back. Always."

"I'll get you some brandy," I said. I pushed myself off the floor and went into the dining room. In that room, too, there were bare walls and shelves, and drawers dumped out on the floor. A jumble of napkins and broken glass.

My cousin's house had been burgled. And Regina—Regina, who was never home on Fridays—had walked in.

I went over to the plundered sideboard, flooding with anger and wanting to smash in the heads of all greedy, callous, vicious people who cynically devastated the lives of total strangers. Compassion was all right for saints. What I felt was plain hatred.

I found two intact glasses, but all the drink had gone. Furiously I stalked into the kitchen and filled the kettle.

In that room, too, the destruction had continued, with stores swept wholesale off the shelves. What valuables, I wondered, did thieves expect to find in kitchens? I jerkily made two mugs of tea and rummaged in Regina's spice cupboard till I found the cooking brandy. They'd missed that, at least.

Donald still sat on the stairs. I pressed the mug into his hands and told him to drink, and he did, mechanically.

"She's never home . . . on Fridays," he said.

"No," I said, and wondered just how many people knew that.

We both slowly finished the tea. I sat near him, as before. Most of the hall furniture had gone. The small Sheraton desk, the studded leather chair, the nineteenth-century carriage clock . . .

"God, Charles," he said.

I glanced at his face. There were tears, and dreadful pain. I could do nothing, nothing, to help him.

THE impossible evening lengthened to midnight. The police were efficient and not unsympathetic, but they left a distinct impression that they felt their job was to catch criminals, not to succor the victims. It seemed to me that there was also, in many of their questions, a faint hovering doubt, as if it were not unknown for householders to arrange their own well-insured burglaries, and for smooth-seeming swindles to go horrifically wrong.

Donald didn't notice. He answered wearily, automatically.

Yes, the missing goods were well insured.

Yes, he had been to his office all day, as usual.

Yes, he had been out to lunch. A sandwich in a pub.

He was a wine shipper. His office was in Shrewsbury.

He was thirty-seven years old.

Yes, his wife was much younger. Twenty-two.

He couldn't speak of Regina without stuttering. "She always s-spends F-Fridays working in a . . . friend's . . . f-flower . . . shop."

"Why?"

Donald looked vaguely across the dining-room table at the detective inspector. The matched antique dining chairs had gone. Donald sat in a garden chair brought from the sunroom. The inspector, a constable, and I sat on kitchen stools.

"Why did she work in a flower shop on Fridays?"

"She . . . she . . . l-likes—"

I interrupted brusquely. "She was a florist before she married Donald. She liked to keep her hand in. She used to spend Fridays making arrangements for dances and weddings and things."

"Thank you, but I'm sure Mr. Stuart can answer for himself."

"And I'm sure he can't. He's too shocked."

"Are you a doctor, sir?" I shook my head impatiently. His gaze wandered briefly over my jeans, faded denim jacket, fawn turtleneck, and desert boots, and returned to my face, unimpressed.

"Very well, sir. Name?"

"Charles Todd."

"Age?"

"Twenty-nine."

"Occupation?"

"Painter."

The constable unemotionally wrote down these details in his pocket notebook.

"Houses or pictures?" asked the inspector.

"Pictures."

"And your movements today, sir?"

"Caught the two thirty from Paddington and walked from the local station."

"Purpose of visit?"

"Nothing special. I come here once or twice a year."

He turned his attention again to Donald. "And what time do you normally reach home on Fridays, sir?"

Don said tonelessly, "Five. About." A spasm twitched the muscles of his face. "I saw . . . the house had been broken into. . . . I telephoned . . ."

"Yes, sir. We received your call at six minutes past five. And after you had telephoned, you went into the sitting room?"

Donald didn't answer.

"Our sergeant found you there, sir, if you remember."

"*Why?*" Don said in anguish. "Why did she come home?"

"I expect we'll find out, sir."

The questions went on and on and, as far as I could see, achieved nothing except to bring Donald ever closer to breakdown.

I, with a certain amount of shame, grew ordinarily hungry. I thought with regret of the dinner I had been looking forward to, with Regina tossing in unmeasured ingredients and herbs and wine and casually producing a gourmet feast. Regina with her cap of dark hair and ready smile, chatty and frivolous. A harmless girl, come to harm.

At some point during the evening her body was driven away in the ambulance. The inspector finally rose. He said he would leave a constable at the house all night and would return himself in the morning. Donald nodded vaguely and, when the police had gone, still sat like an automaton in the chair.

"Come on," I said. "Let's go to bed." I steered him up the stairs. He came in a daze, unprotesting.

His and Regina's bedroom was a shambles, but the twin-bedded room prepared for me was untouched. He flopped full length in his clothes and put his arm up over his eyes, and in appalling distress asked the unanswerable question of all the world's sufferers.

"*Why?* Why did it have to happen to *us?*"

I STAYED with Donald for a week, during which time some questions, but not that one, were answered.

One of the easiest was the reason for Regina's premature return home. She and the flower-shop friend had had a quarrel of enough bitterness to make Regina leave at about two thirty. She had probably driven straight home, as it was considered she had been dead for at least two hours by five o'clock.

This information was given to Donald by the detective inspector on Saturday afternoon. Donald walked out into the garden and wept. The inspector, Frost by name and cool by nature, came into the kitchen and stood beside me, watching Donald, with his head bowed, among the apple trees.

"I would like you to tell me how Mr. and Mrs. Stuart got on."

"Can't you tell for yourself?"

He answered after a pause. "The intensity of grief shown is not always an accurate indication of the intensity of love felt."

"Do you always talk like that?"

A faint smile flickered and died. "I was quoting from a book on psychology."

"Your book is bunk," I said. "And as far as I could see, the honeymoon was by no means over."

"After three years?"

"Why not?"

He shrugged and didn't answer. I turned to him and said, "What are the chances of getting back any of the stuff from this house?"

"Small, I should think. There have been hundreds of similar break-ins, with very little recovered. Antiques are big business."

"Connoisseur thieves?" I said skeptically.

"The prison library service reports that their most requested books are on antiques."

He sounded suddenly quite sensible. I offered him some coffee and he sat on a kitchen stool while I fixed the mugs—a fortyish man with thin sandy hair.

"Are you married?" he asked.

"Nope."

"In love with Mrs. Stuart?"

"You do try it on, don't you?"

"If you don't ask, you can't find out. When did you visit this house last?"

"Last March. Before they went off to Australia."

"Australia?"

"They went to see the vintage there. Donald had some idea of shipping Australian wine over in bulk. They were away for at least three months."

He blew gently across the top of his mug. "What would you all have been doing today? In the normal course of events?"

"Going to the races. We always go to the races when I visit."

"Fond of racing, were they?" The past tense sounded wrong.

"Yes . . . but I think they only go—went—because of me."

"In what way do you mean?" he asked.

"What I paint," I said, "is mostly horses."

Donald came in through the back door and sat down heavily on a stool. "Charles," he said, "if you wouldn't mind, I'd like some soup now."

"Sure," I said, surprised. He had rejected it earlier.

Frost waited while Donald disposed of two bowlfuls of Campbell's condensed and a chunk of brown bread. Then, politely, Frost asked me to take myself off, and when I'd gone, he began what Donald afterward referred to as serious digging.

It was three hours later when the inspector and the constable left. In spite of his long session with the inspector, Donald seemed a lot calmer. He said, "The police want a list of what's gone. Will you help me make it?"

"Of course."

"We did have an inventory, but it was in that desk in the hall. The one they took."

"Damn silly place to keep it," I said.

"That's more or less what *he* said. Inspector Frost."

"What about your insurance company? Haven't they got a list?"

"Only of the more valuable things, like some of the paintings and her jewelry. Everything else was lumped together as contents."

We started on the dining room and made reasonable progress. There had been a good deal of silver tableware, acquired by Donald's family in its affluent past. But instead of being indignant over its loss, Donald seemed decidedly bored.

Faced by the ranks of empty shelves where once had stood a fine collection of early-nineteenth-century porcelain, he balked entirely. "What does it matter?" he said drearily, turning away.

"How about the paintings, then?"

He looked round vaguely at the light oblong patches on the bare walls. In this room there had mostly been works of modern British painters: a Hockney, two Lowrys, and a Spear, for openers.

"You probably remember better than I," he said. "You do it."

"I'd miss some."

"Is there anything to drink?"

"Only the cooking brandy," I said.

"We could have some of the wine." His eyes suddenly opened wide. "Good God, I'd forgotten about the cellar."

"I didn't even know you had one."

He nodded. "Reason I bought the house. Perfect humidity and temperature for long-term storage. There's a small fortune down there in claret and port."

There wasn't, of course. There were three floor-to-ceiling rows of empty racks, and a single cardboard box on a table.

Donald merely shrugged. "Oh, well . . . that's that."

I opened the box and saw the elegant shapes of the wine bottles. "They've left these, anyway," I said. "In their rush."

"Probably on purpose." Don smiled twistedly. "It's Australian. We brought it back. But it's better than most, you know."

I carried the case up to the kitchen and dumped it on the table. The door to the cellar stairs was inconspicuous, and I had always thought it was just another cupboard.

"Do you think the burglars *knew* in advance the wine was there?" I asked. "I would never have found it."

"You're not a burglar, though."

He searched for a corkscrew, opened a bottle, and poured the deep red liquid into two kitchen tumblers. It was a marvelous wine, even to my untrained palate. Wynn's Coonawarra Cabernet Sauvignon. Donald drank his absentmindedly, as if it were water, the glass clattering once against his teeth. His movements were uncertain, as if he could not quite remember how to do things.

The old Donald had been a man of confidence, capably running a middle-sized inherited business. He had a blunt uncompromising face, lightened by amber eyes that smiled easily. The new Donald was a tentative man shattered with shock.

We spent the evening in the kitchen, talking desultorily, eating a scratch meal, and tidying the shelves. Donald made a good show of being busy, but put half the tins back upside down.

We eventually went upstairs to bed, although it seemed likely that Donald would sleep no more than the night before.

"Do you mind," he said, "if I sleep alone tonight? We could make up a bed for you in one of the other rooms."

"Sure."

He pulled open the linen-cupboard door on the upstairs landing and gestured indecisively at the contents. "Could you manage?"

"Of course," I said.

He turned away and seemed struck by one patch of empty wall.

"They took the Munnings," he said. "We bought it in Australia. I hung it just there . . . only a week ago. I wanted you to see it."

"I'm sorry," I said. Inadequate words.

"Everything," he said helplessly. "Everything's gone."

Frost arrived again Sunday morning. He followed me to the kitchen, where Donald and I seemed to have taken up permanent residence. I gestured him to a stool.

"Two pieces of information you might care to have, sir," he said to Donald. "Despite our intensive investigation of this house, we have found no fingerprints for which we cannot account."

"Would you expect to?" I asked.

He flicked me a glance. "No, sir. Professional housebreakers always wear gloves."

Donald waited with a gray patient face, as if he would find whatever Frost said unimportant.

"Second," said Frost, "our investigations reveal that a moving van was parked outside your front door early Friday afternoon."

Donald looked at him blankly.

Frost sighed. "What do you know of a bronze statuette of a horse, sir? A horse rearing up on its hind legs?"

"It's in the hall," Donald said. "I mean, it used to be."

Frost's face was calm. "We found it in the sitting room, near Mrs. Stuart."

Donald understood clearly. "P-poor Regina." The words were quiet, the desolation immense.

Frost said that the sitting room would be kept locked for a few more days, and please would neither of us try to go in there. Apart from that, they had finished their inquiries at the house, and Mr. Stuart was at liberty to have the other rooms cleaned, if he wished, of the grayish white fingerprint dust.

Mr. Stuart gave no sign of having heard.

Had Mr. Stuart completed the list of things stolen?

I passed it over. It still consisted only of silver and what I could remember of the paintings. Frost pursed his lips.

"We'll need more than this, sir."

"We'll try again today," I promised. "There's a lot of wine missing, as well."

"Wine?"

I showed him the empty cellar. He looked thoughtful.

"It must have taken hours to move that lot," I said.

"Very likely, sir," he said primly.

Whatever he was thinking, he wasn't telling. Almost casually he said, "Is your cousin in financial difficulties?"

I knew his catch-them-off-guard technique by now.

"I wouldn't think so," I said. "You'd better ask him."

"I will, sir." He gazed sharply at me. "A great many private companies are going bankrupt these days."

"So I believe."

"Because of cash-flow problems," he added.

"I can't help you. You'll have to look at his company's books."

"We will, sir."

"And even if the firm turns out to be bust, it doesn't follow that Donald would fake a robbery. If he needed money, he could simply have sold the stuff."

"Maybe he had. Some of it. Most of it, maybe."

I took a slow breath and said nothing.

"The wine, sir. As you said yourself, it would have taken a long time to move."

"The firm is a limited company," I said. "If it went bankrupt, Donald's own house and private money would be unaffected."

"You know a good deal about it, don't you?" He peered at me with narrowed eyes, as if trying to work out a way in which I, too, might have conspired to arrange the theft.

I said mildly, "My cousin Donald is an honorable man."

"That's an out-of-date word."

"There's quite a lot of that quality about."

He looked wholly disbelieving. He saw far too much in the way of corruption, day in, day out, all his working life.

We went upstairs and Frost took Donald off to another private session. If his questions to Don were to be as barbed as those he'd asked me, poor Don was in for a rough time. While they talked, I wandered aimlessly round the house.

The burglars had largely ignored the big sunroom, which held few antiques and no paintings. The sunroom was gray and cold, and I ended up sitting there on a bamboo armchair among sprawling potted plants, looking out into the garden. Dead leaves were blowing from the trees, and a few late roses clung to thorny stems.

I hated autumn. The time of melancholy, the time of death. My spirits fell each year with the soggy leaves and revived only with crisp winter frost. Statistics proved that the highest suicide rate occurred in the spring, the time for rebirth and growth. I could not understand it. If ever I jumped over a cliff, it would be in the depressing months of decay.

I went upstairs, fetched my suitcase, and brought it down. Over years of wandering, I had reversed the painter's traditional luggage: my suitcase now contained the tools of my trade, and my satchel, clothes. The suitcase was in fact a sort of portable studio, containing besides paints and brushes a light collapsible metal easel, unbreakable containers of linseed oil and turpentine, and a rack that would hold four wet paintings safely apart.

I untelescoped the easel and set out my palette and began a melancholy landscape—Donald's garden, as I saw it, against a sweep of bare fields and gloomy woods. Not my usual sort of picture, but it gave me something to do. I worked steadily, growing ever colder, until the chillier Frost chose to depart. He went without seeing me again, the front door closing decisively on his purposeful footsteps.

Donald, in the warm kitchen, looked torn to rags. "Do you know what he thinks?" he said.

"More or less."

He stared at me somberly. "I couldn't convince him. He kept asking the same questions over and over. He wants me to meet him in my office tomorrow. He says he'll be bringing colleagues. He says they'll want to see the books."

I said awkwardly, "Don, I'm sorry. I told him the wine was missing. It made him suspicious. . . . It was my fault."

He shook his head tiredly. "I would have told him myself."

"But . . . I even pointed out that it must have taken a fair time to move so many bottles."

"Mmm. Well, he would have worked that out for himself."

"How long, in fact, do you think it would have taken?"

"Depends how many people were doing it," he said, rubbing his hand over his face. "They would have needed proper wine boxes in any case. That means they had to know in advance that the wine was there. And that means—Frost says—that I sold it myself some time ago and am now saying it is stolen so I can make a fraudulent claim for insurance, or, if it was stolen last Friday, that I told the thieves they'd need proper boxes, which means that I set up the whole frightful mess myself."

We thought it over in depressed silence. Eventually I said, "Who *did* know you had the wine there? And who knew the house was always empty on Fridays? And was the prime target the wine, the antiques, or the paintings?"

"God, Charles, you sound like Frost."

"Sorry."

"Every business nowadays," he said defensively, "is going through a cash crisis. Look at the wage rises and the taxes and the inflation. Of *course* we have a cash-flow problem. Whoever hasn't?"

"How bad is yours?" I said.

"Bad enough. But not within sight of liquidation. It's illegal for a limited company to trade if it can't cover its costs."

"But it could . . . if you could raise more capital to prop it up?"

He surveyed me with the ghost of a smile. "It surprises me still that you chose to paint for a living."

"It gives me a good excuse to go racing whenever I like."

"Bloody lazy." He sounded for a second like the old Donald, but the lightness passed. "The absolutely last thing I'd do would be to use my personal assets to prop up a dying business. If my firm was that rocky, I'd wind it up. It would be mad not to."

"I suppose Frost asked if the stolen things were insured for more than their worth?"

"Yes, he did. Several times." He sighed. "They were under-insured, if anything. God knows if they'll pay up for the Munnings. I'd only arranged the insurance by telephone. I hadn't actually sent the premium."

"It should be all right, if you can show proof of purchase."

He shook his head listlessly. "All the papers to do with it were in the hall desk. The receipt from the gallery where I bought it, the letter of provenance, and the customs and excise receipt. All gone."

"Frost won't like that."

"He doesn't."

"Well . . . I hope you pointed out that you would hardly be buy-ing expensive pictures and going on world trips if you were down to your last farthing."

"He said it might be *because* of buying expensive pictures and going on world trips that I might be down to my last farthing."

Frost had built a brick wall of suspicion for Donald to batter his head against. My cousin needed hauling away before he was punch-drunk.

"Have some spaghetti," I said. "It's about all I can cook."

"Oh . . ." He focused unclearly on the kitchen clock. It was half past four and long past feeding time, according to my stomach.

"If you like," he said.

THE police sent a car the following morning to fetch him to his ordeal in the office. He went lifelessly, having made it clear that he wouldn't defend himself. "What does it matter? Without Regina . . . there's no point making money."

"Don, we're not talking about making money, we're talking about suspicion. If you don't defend yourself, they'll assume you can't."

"I'm too tired. They can think what they like."

He was gone all day. I spent it painting.

Not the sad landscape. The sunroom seemed even grayer that morning, and I had no mind anymore to sink into melancholy. I removed myself to the warmth of the kitchen. I painted Regina standing beside the stove, with a wooden spoon in one hand and a bottle of wine in the other. I painted the way she held her head back to smile, and I painted the smile, shiny-eyed and guileless. I painted the kitchen as I saw it in front of my eyes, and I painted Regina herself from the clearest of inner visions. So easily did I see her that I looked up once or twice to say something to her, and was disconcerted to find only empty space.

I knocked off in the late afternoon because of the light. I was cleaning my brushes when the front doorbell rang.

I opened the door. A policeman stood there, holding Donald's arm. My cousin's face looked white, his eyes lifeless.

"Don!" I said, and no doubt looked as appalled as I felt.

He didn't speak. The policeman leaned forward, said, "There we are, sir," and transferred the support of my cousin from himself to me. Then the policeman turned on his heel and drove off in his waiting car.

I helped Donald inside and shut the door. I had never seen anyone in such a frightening state of disintegration. His face was stony, and his voice came out in gasps. "I asked about the funeral. They said . . . no funeral. They said . . . she couldn't be buried until they had finished their inquiries. They said . . . it might be months. They said they will keep her . . . refrigerated. They said . . . the body of a murdered person belongs to the state."

I couldn't hold him. He collapsed at my feet in a deep and total faint.

# CHAPTER TWO

For two days Donald lay in bed, and I grew to understand what was meant by prostration.

He was heavily sedated, his doctor calling morning and evening with injections. No matter that I was a hopeless nurse and a worse cook, I was appointed, for lack of anyone else, to look after him.

I sat with him a good deal when he was awake, seeing him struggle to come to terms with the horrors in his mind. He lost weight visibly, the rounded muscles of his face slackening and the contours changing to the drawn shape of illness. The shadows round his eyes darkened to charcoal, and all his strength seemed to have vanished.

While he slept, I made progress with both paintings. The sad landscape was no longer sad but merely Octoberish, with three horses standing around in a field, one of them eating grass. Pictures of this sort were my bread and butter. They sold quite well, and I normally churned one off the production line every ten days or so, knowing that they were all technique and no soul.

The portrait of Regina, though, was the best work I'd done for months. She laughed out of the canvas, alive and glowing. The emphasis in my mind had shifted, so that the kitchen background was growing darker and Regina herself more luminous.

I hid that picture in my suitcase whenever I wasn't working on it. I didn't want Donald to come face to face with it unawares.

Early Wednesday evening he came shakily down to the kitchen in his dressing gown, trying to smile. He sat at the table, drinking Scotch and watching while I cleaned my brushes.

He waved a limp hand at the horse picture, which stood drying on the easel. "How much does it cost to paint that?"

"In raw materials, about ten quid. In heat, rent, food, Scotch, and general wear and tear on the nervous system, about the amount I'd earn in a week if I chucked it in and went back to selling houses."

"Quite a lot, then," he said seriously.

I grinned. "I don't regret it."

I pinched the brushes into shape and stood them upright in a jar to dry. Good brushes were at least as costly as paint.

"After the digging into the company accounts," Donald said abruptly, "they took me along to the police station and tried to prove that I had actually killed her myself."

"I don't believe it!"

"They said I could have done it at lunchtime."

I poured a decent-sized shot of Scotch into a tumbler. Added ice. "They must be crazy," I said.

"There was another man besides Frost. A superintendent. I think his name was Wall . . . thin, with fierce eyes. He never seemed to blink. Just stared and said over and over I'd killed her because she'd come back and found me supervising the burglary."

"For God's sake!" I said disgustedly. "And anyway, she didn't leave the flower shop until half past two."

"The girl in the flower shop now says she doesn't know to the minute when Regina left. Only that it was soon after lunch. And I didn't get back from the pub until nearly three. I went to lunch late. I was hung up with a client all morning. . . ." He stopped, gripping his tumbler as if it were a support. "They let me come home, but I don't think they've finished."

It was five days since he'd found Regina dead. When I thought of the mental hammerings he'd taken on top, the punishing assault on his emotional reserves, where common humanity would have suggested kindness and consoling help, it seemed marvelous that he had remained as sane as he had.

He drank slowly. "I see no end to it. No end at all."

BY MIDDAY Friday the police had called twice more at the house, but for my cousin the escalation of agony seemed to have slowed. He was still exhausted, apathetic, but it was as if he were saturated with suffering and could absorb little more.

"You're supposed to be painting someone's horse, aren't you?" Donald said suddenly as we shaped up to lunch.

"I told them I'd come later."

He shook his head. "I remember you saying, when I asked you to stay, that it would fit in fine before your next commission." He thought a bit. "You should have gone to Yorkshire on Tuesday."

"I telephoned and explained."

"All the same, you'd better go."

He said he would be all right alone now, and thanks for everything. I could see that the time had indeed come for him to be by himself, so I packed up my things to depart.

"I suppose," he said, as we waited for the taxi to fetch me, "that you never paint portraits? People, that is, not horses."

"Sometimes," I said.

"I just wondered. . . . Could you, one day . . . I mean, I've got quite a good photograph of Regina. . . ."

I looked searchingly at his face. As far as I could see, it could do no harm. I unclipped the suitcase and took out the picture, with its back toward him.

"It's still wet," I warned. "And not framed. But you can have it if you like."

"Let me see."

I turned the canvas round. He stared and stared, but said nothing at all. The taxi drove up to the front door.

"See you," I said, propping Regina against a wall.

He nodded, opened the door for me, and sketched a farewell wave. Speechlessly, because his eyes were full of tears.

I SPENT nearly a week in Yorkshire doing my best to immortalize a patient old steeplechaser, and then went home to my noisy flat near Heathrow airport, taking the picture with me to finish.

Saturday I downed tools and went to the races.

Jump racing at Plumpton, and the familiar swelling of excitement at the liquid movement of racehorses. Paintings could never do justice to them—never. The moment caught on canvas was always second best.

I would love to have ridden in races, but hadn't had enough practice or skill; nor, I daresay, nerve. Like Donald's, my background was of middle-sized private enterprise, with my father an auctioneer in Sussex. I had spent countless hours in my growing years watching the horses train on the downs round Findon, and had painted them from the age of six. Art school later had been fine, but at twenty-two, alone in the world with both parents newly dead, I'd had to face the need to eat. It had been a short meant-to-be-temporary step to the real estate agents across the street, but I'd liked it well enough to stay.

Half the horse painters in England seemed to have turned up at Plumpton, which was not surprising, as the latest Grand National winner was due to make his first appearance of the season. It was a commercial fact that a picture called, for instance, *Nijinsky on Newmarket Heath* stood a much better chance of being sold than one labeled *A Horse on Newmarket Heath*.

"Todd!" said a voice in my ear. "You owe me fifteen smackers."

"I bloody don't," I said.

"You said Seesaw was a certainty for Ascot."

"Never take sweets from a stranger."

Billy Pyle laughed extravagantly and patted me heavily on the shoulder. Billy Pyle was one of those people you met on racecourses who greeted you as a bosom pal, plied you with drinks and bonhomie, and bored you to death. I'd never worked out how to duck him without positive rudeness, and I found it less wearing to get the drink over quickly than dodge him all afternoon.

I waited for him to say, How about a beverage? as he always did.

"How about a beverage?" he said.

"Er . . . sure," I agreed resignedly.

I knew the irritating routine by heart. He would meet his auntie Sal in the bar, as if by accident, and in my turn I would buy them both a drink. A double brandy and ginger for Auntie Sal.

"Why, there's Auntie Sal," Billy said, entering the bar.

Auntie Sal was a compulsive racegoer in her seventies, with a perpetual cigarette dangling from the corner of her mouth and one finger permanently inserted in her form book, keeping her place.

"Know anything for the two thirty?" she demanded.

"Hello," I said.

"What? Oh. Hello. Know anything for the two thirty?"

"Fraid not."

"Huh." She peered into the form book. "Treetops is well in at the weights, but can you trust his leg?" She looked up suddenly and prodded her nephew. "Billy, get a drink for Mrs. Matthews."

"Mrs. who?"

"Matthews. What do you want, Maisie?"

She turned to a large middle-aged woman who had been standing in the shadows behind her.

"Oh . . . gin and tonic, thanks."

"Got that, Billy? And a double brandy and ginger for me."

Maisie Matthews's clothes were new and expensive, and from lacquered hair via crocodile handbag to gold-trimmed shoes she shouted money. The hand that accepted the drink carried a huge opal set in diamonds.

"How do you do?" I said politely.

"Eh?" said Auntie Sal. "Oh, yes, Maisie, this is Charles Todd."

Billy handed round the drinks, and Maisie Matthews said, "Cheers," looking cheerless.

"Maisie's had a bit of bad luck," Auntie Sal said.

Billy grinned. "Backed a loser, then, Mrs. Matthews?"

"Her house burned down."

As a light-conversation stopper, it was a daisy.

"Oh . . . I say . . ." said Billy uncomfortably. "Hard luck."

"Lost everything, didn't you, Maisie?"

"All but what I stand up in," she agreed gloomily.

"Have another gin," I suggested.

"Thanks, dear."

When I returned with the refills, she was in full descriptive flood.

"I wasn't there, of course. I was staying with my sister Betty up in Birmingham, and there was this policeman on the doorstep telling me what a job they'd had finding me. But by that time it was all over, of course. When I got back to Worthing, there was just a heap of cinders with the chimney breast sticking up in the middle. Well, they said it was a flash fire, whatever that is, but they didn't know what started it, because there'd been no one in the house for two days."

She accepted the gin, gave me a brief unseeing smile, and returned to her story.

"Well, I was spitting mad, I'll tell you, over losing everything like that, and I said why hadn't they used seawater, what with the sea being only the other side of the tamarisk hedge, because of course they said they hadn't been able to save a thing because they hadn't enough water, and this fireman said they couldn't use seawater because for one thing it corroded everything and for another the pumps sucked up seaweed and shells, and in any case the tide was out."

I smothered an unseemly desire to laugh. She sensed it, however. "Well, dear, it may seem funny to you, but you haven't lost all your treasures that you'd been collecting since heaven knows when."

"I'm sorry. I don't think it's funny. It was just . . ."

"Yes, well, dear. I suppose you can see the funny side of it, all that water and not a drop to put a fire out with, but I was mad."

"I think I'll have a bit on Treetops," Auntie Sal said.

Maisie Matthews looked at her uncertainly, and Billy Pyle,

who had heard enough of disaster, broke gratefully into geniality, clapped me again on the shoulder, and said yes, it was time to see the next contest.

Duty done, I thought with a sigh, and took myself off to watch the race from the top of the stands, out of sight and earshot.

The afternoon went quickly, as usual. I won a little, lost a little. On the stands for the last race, I found myself approached by Maisie Matthews. No mistaking the bright red coat, the air of gloss, and the big kind-looking worldly face. She drew to a halt on the step below me, looking up.

"Aren't you the young man I had a drink with?"

"Yes, that's right."

"I wasn't sure," she said. "You look older out here."

"Different light," I said, agreeing. She, too, looked older. Fifty-something, I thought. Bar light always flattered.

"They said you were an artist."

"Mmm," I said, watching the runners canter past.

"Not very well paid, is it, dear?"

I grinned. "It depends who you are. Picasso didn't grumble."

"How much would you charge to paint a picture for me?"

"What sort of picture?"

"Well, dear, you may say it sounds morbid and I daresay it is, but I was just thinking this morning when I went over there, that actually it makes a crazy picture, that burned ruin with the chimney sticking up and the burned hedge behind and all that sea, and I was thinking of getting the local photographer to come along and take a color picture, because when it's all cleared away and rebuilt, no one will believe how awful it was."

"But . . ."

"So how much would you charge? Because I daresay you can see I am not short of the next quid, but if it should be hundreds, I might as well get the photographer of course."

"Of course," I said gravely. "How about if I came to see the house, or what's left of it, and gave you an estimate?"

"All right, dear. It will have to be soon, though, because once the insurance people come, I am having the rubble cleared up. So, dear, as you're halfway there, could you come today?"

We discussed it. She said she would drive me in her Jaguar, as I hadn't a car, and I could go home by train. I agreed.

One takes the most momentous steps unaware.

ON THE way to the ruin she talked more or less nonstop about her late husband, Archie, who had looked after her very well, dear. "Well, that's to say, I looked after him, too, dear, because I was a nurse. Private, of course. I nursed his first wife all through her illness, and then I stayed on for a bit to look after him, and, well, he asked me to stay on for life, dear, and I did. Of course he was much older, he's been gone more than ten years now. He looked after me very well, Archie did."

She glanced fondly at the huge opal.

"Since he left me so well-off, dear, it seemed a shame not to get some fun out of it, so I carried on with what we were doing, which was going round to auction sales in big houses, because you pick up such nice things there." She changed gear with a jerk and aggressively passed an inoffensive little van. "And now all those things are cinders, and all the memories of Archie and the places we went together, and I'll tell you, dear, it makes me mad."

"It's really horrid for you."

"Yes, dear, it is."

It was the second time in a fortnight that I'd been cast in the role of comforter, and I felt as inadequate for her as I had for Donald.

She stamped on the brakes outside the remains of her house and rocked us to a standstill. All that was left was a sprawling black heap, with jagged pieces of outside wall defining its former shape, and the thick brick chimney pointing skyward from the center.

I could smell the ash. "How long ago?" I asked.

"Last weekend, dear. Sunday."

While we surveyed the mess, a man walked slowly into view from behind the chimney. He was looking down, poking into the rubble.

Maisie, for all her scarlet-coated bulk, was nimble on her feet.

"Hey," she called, hopping out of the car and advancing purpose-fully. "What do you think you're doing?"

The man straightened up, looking startled. About forty, with a raincoat, a crisp-looking trilby, and a down-turning mustache.

He raised his hat politely. "Insurance, madam."

"I thought you were coming on Monday."

"I happened to be in the district. No time like the present, don't you think?"

"Well, I suppose not," Maisie said. "And I hope there isn't go-ing to be any shilly-shallying over you paying up, though of course nothing is going to get my treasures back and I'd rather have them than any amount of money, as I've got plenty of that in any case."

"Er . . ." he said. "Oh, yes. I see."

"Have you found out what started it?" Maisie demanded.

"No, madam."

"Well, how soon can I get all this cleared away?"

"Anytime you like, madam." He was picking his way toward us through the blackened debris. He had steady grayish eyes, a strong chin, and an overall air of intelligence.

"What's your name?" Maisie asked.

"Greene, madam." He paused slightly and added, "With an *e*."

"Well, Mr. Greene with an *e*," Maisie said good-humoredly, "I'll be glad to have all that in writing."

He inclined his head. "As soon as I report back." He lifted his hat again, wished her good afternoon, and walked to a white Ford parked along the road.

"Now," Maisie said, "how much for that picture?"

"Two hundred, plus two nights' expenses in a local hotel."

"That's a bit steep, dear. *One* hundred, and two nights, and I've got to like the results or I don't pay."

We settled on one fifty if she liked the picture, and fifty if she didn't, and I was to start on Monday unless it was raining.

MONDAY was a bright breezy day with an echo of summer's warmth. I went to Worthing by train and to the house by taxi, and set up my easel where the front gates would have been had they not been unhinged by the firemen. The gates lay flat on the lawn, one of them still pathetically bearing a neat painted nameboard: Treasure Holme. Poor Archie. Poor Maisie.

I worked over the canvas with a coffee-colored underpainting of raw umber thinned with turpentine and linseed oil, and while it was still wet I drew in, with a darker shade of the same color, the shape of the ruined house against the horizontals of hedges, beach, sea, and sky. It was easy with a tissue to wipe out mistakes at that stage and try again: to get the proportions right and the perspective.

That done and drying, I strolled round the garden, looking at the house from different angles, and staring out over the blackened stumps of the tamarisk hedge that had marked the end of the grass and the beginning of the pebble beach. The sea sparkled in the morning sunshine, with the small hurrying cumulus clouds scattering patches of slate-gray shadow. The sea wind chilled my ears. I turned to get back to my task and saw two men in overcoats emerge from a station wagon. I walked back to where they stood by my easel.

One heavy and fiftyish. One lean, in the twenties. Both with firm self-confident faces and an air of purpose.

The elder raised his eyes as I approached. "Do you have permission to be here?" he asked.

"The owner wants her house painted," I said. "And you?"

He raised his eyebrows slightly. "Insurance."

"Same company as Mr. Greene?" I said.

"Mr. who?"

"Greene. With an *e*."

"I don't know who you mean. We are here by arrangement with Mrs. Matthews to inspect the damage to her house, which is insured with us."

"No Greene?" I repeated.

"Neither with nor without an *e*."

I warmed to him. Half an ounce of a sense of humor, as far as I was concerned, achieved results where thumbscrews wouldn't.

"Well . . . Mrs. Matthews is no longer expecting you, because the aforesaid Mr. Greene, who said he was in insurance, told her she could roll in the demolition squad as soon as she liked."

His attention sharpened like a tightened violin string. "Are you serious?"

"I was here. I saw him and heard him."

"Did he show you a card?"

"No, he didn't." I paused. "And . . . er . . . nor have you."

He reached into his pocket and did so.

"Isn't it illegal to insure the same property with two companies?" I asked idly, reading the card.

Foundation Life & Surety
D. J. Lagland, Area Manager

"Fraud." He nodded.

"Unless, of course, Mr. Greene with an *e* had nothing to do with insurance."

"Much more likely."

I put the card in my trouser pocket. He looked at me thoughtfully, his eyes observant but judgment suspended.

"Gary," he said to his younger sidekick, "go and find a telephone and ring the Beach Hotel. Tell Mrs. Matthews we're here."

"Will do," Gary said. He was that sort of man.

While he was away, D. J. Lagland turned his attention to the ruin, and I tagged along at his side.

"What do you look for?" I asked.

"Evidence of arson. Evidence of goods reported destroyed."

"Don't the firemen look for signs of arson?" I asked.

"Yes, and also the police, and we ask them for guidance."

"And what did they say?"

"None of your business, I shouldn't think. Why don't you go over there and paint?"

"What I've done is still wet."

"Then if you stay with me, shut up."

I stayed with him, silent. He was making what appeared to be a preliminary reconnaissance, lifting small pieces of debris, inspecting them closely, and carefully returning them to their former positions.

"Permission to speak?" I asked.

"Well?"

"Mr. Greene was doing much what you are, though in the area behind the chimney breast."

"Did he take anything?" he said.

"Not while we were watching, which was a very short time."

"Wouldn't you think he was a casual sightseer?"

"He hadn't the air."

D.J. frowned. "Then what did he want?"

A rhetorical question. Gary rolled back, and soon after him Maisie. In her Jaguar. In her scarlet coat. In a temper.

"What do you mean," she said, advancing upon D.J. with eyes flashing fortissimo, "the question of arson isn't yet settled? Your man said on Saturday that everything was all right and I could start clearing away, and anyway, even if it had been arson, you would still have to pay up because the insurance covered arson."

D.J. opened and shut his mouth several times and finally found his voice. "Didn't our Mr. Robinson tell you that the man you saw here on Saturday wasn't from us?"

Our Mr. Robinson, in the shape of Gary, nodded vigorously.

"Mr. Greene distinctly said he *was*," Maisie insisted.

"Well . . . what did he look like?"

"Smarmy," said Maisie without hesitation. "Not as young as Charles"—she gestured toward me—"or as old as you." She thought, then shrugged. "He looked like an insurance man, that's all."

D.J. swallowed the implied insult manfully.

"About five feet ten," I said. "Suntanned skin, gray eyes with deep upper eyelids, widish nose, mouth straight under drooping dark mustache, straight brown hair brushed back and retreating from the two top corners of his forehead, brown trilby of smooth felt, shirt, tie, fawn raincoat, gold signet ring on little finger of right hand."

"Good God," D.J. said.

"An artist's eye," said Maisie admiringly. "Well, I never."

D.J. said they had no one like that in their claims department.

"Well," said Maisie with a resurgence of crossness, "I suppose that still means you are looking for arson, though why you think that anyone in his right senses would want to burn down my lovely home and all my treasures is something I'll never understand."

Surely, Maisie, worldly Maisie, could not be so naïve. I caught a deep glimmer of intelligence in the glance she gave me and knew that she certainly wasn't.

"Do you want your picture," I asked, "to be sunny like today, or cloudy and sad?"

She looked up at the bright sky. "A bit more dramatic, dear."

D.J. AND Gary inch-by-inched over the ruin all afternoon. At five o'clock on the dot we all knocked off.

I went by foot and bus along to the Beach Hotel, cleaned my brushes, thought a bit, and at seven met Maisie downstairs in the bar, as arranged.

"Well, dear," she said, sipping her gin and tonic, "did they find anything?"

"Nothing at all, as far as I could see."

"Well, that's good, dear."

I put my draft down carefully. "Not altogether, Maisie."

"Why not?"

"What exactly were your treasures which were burned?"

"I daresay you wouldn't think so much of them, of course, but we had ever such fun buying them. Things like an antique spear collection that used to belong to old Lord Stequers, and a whole wall of beautiful butterflies, and a wrought-iron gate from Lady Tythe's old home, and six warming pans from a castle in Ireland, and two tall vases with eagles on the lids, which once belonged to a cousin of Mata Hari—they really did, dear—and a marble table from Greece, and a silver tea urn which was once used by Queen Victoria, and really, dear, that's just the beginning."

"Did the Foundation insurance company have a full list?"

"Yes, they did, dear, and why do you want to know?"

"Because," I said regretfully, "I don't think many of those things were inside the house when it burned down."

"*What?*" Maisie seemed genuinely astounded. "But they must have been."

"Mr. Lagland as good as said they didn't find any traces of them."

Alternate disbelief and anger kept Maisie going through two more double gins. Disbelief eventually won.

"You got it wrong, dear," she said finally. "Because everything was in its place, dear, when I went off last Friday week to stay with Betty, because of course you can't stay at home forever on the off chance your house is going to catch fire, as you'd never go anywhere and I would have missed my trip to Australia."

She paused for breath. Coincidence, I thought.

"All I can say, dear, is that it's a miracle I took most of my jewelry with me to Betty's."

"Australia?" I said.

"Well, yes, dear. I went out there to visit Archie's sister, who's lived there since heaven knows when and was feeling lonely since she'd been widowed, and I went for a bit of fun, dear, and I was there for six weeks. She wanted me to stay, and of course we got on together like a house on fire. . . . Oh, dear, I didn't mean that exactly. . . . Well, anyway, I said I wanted to come back to my little house by the sea and think it over."

I said idly, "I don't suppose you bought a Munnings while you were there." I didn't know why I'd said it, apart from thinking of Donald in Australia. I was totally unprepared for her reaction.

She knocked over her gin, slid off her barstool, and covered her open mouth with four trembling red-nailed fingers. "How do you know?"

"I don't. . . ."

"Are you from Customs and Excise?"

"Of course not."

"Oh, dear. Oh, dear. . . ."

I led her over to an armchair beside a small bar table.

"Sit down," I said coaxingly, "and tell me."

"Well, dear, I'm not an art expert, as you can probably guess, but there was this picture by Sir Alfred Munnings, signed and everything, dear, and it was such a bargain really, and, well, Archie's sister egged me on a bit, and I felt quite . . . I suppose you might call it *high*, dear, so I bought it." She stopped.

"You brought it into this country without declaring it?"

She sighed. "Yes, dear, I did. Of course it was silly of me, but I never gave customs duty a thought when I bought the painting, not until just before I came home—a week later—and Archie's sister asked if I was going to declare it, and, well, dear, I really *resent* having to pay duty on things, don't you? So anyway, I thought I'd better find out just how much the duty would be, and I found there isn't duty on secondhand pictures being brought in from Australia, but they said I would have to pay value-added tax, a sort of tax on buying things, you know, dear, and I would have to pay eight percent on whatever I had bought the picture for. Well, I ask you! I was that mad, dear, I can tell you. So, well, it was all done up nicely in boards and brown paper, so I just camouflaged it a bit with my best nightie and popped it in my suitcase, and pushed it through the Nothing to Declare lane at Heathrow when I got back, and nobody stopped me."

"How much would you have had to pay?" I said.

"Well, dear, to be precise, just over seven hundred pounds."

I did some mental arithmetic. "So the painting cost about nine thousand?"

"That's right, dear. Nine thousand." She looked anxious. "I wasn't done, was I? I've asked one or two people since I got back and they say lots of Munningses cost fifteen thousand or more."

"So they do," I said absently. And some could be got for fifteen hundred, and others, I dared say, for less.

"Well, anyway, it was only when I began to think about insurance that I wondered if I would be found out—if the insurance people wanted a *receipt* or anything, which they probably would—so I didn't do anything about it, because if I *did* go back to Australia I could just take the picture with me and no harm done."

"Awkward," I agreed.

"So now it's burned, and the nine thousand's gone up in smoke."

"I know it's not my business, Maisie, but how did you happen to have nine thousand handy in Australia? Aren't there rules about exporting that much cash?"

She giggled. "It was all hunky-dory. I just toddled along with Archie's sister to a jeweler's and sold him a brooch I had, a nasty sort of *toad*, dear, with a socking big diamond in the middle of its forehead, and I sold it for nine thousand five, though in Australian dollars of course. You won't *tell* anyone, will you, dear, about the picture?"

"Of course not, Maisie."

"I could get into such trouble, dear."

"No one will find out if you keep quiet." A thought struck me. "Unless you've told anyone already that you'd bought it?"

"No, dear, I didn't, because of thinking I'd better pretend I'd had it for years, and of course I hadn't even hung it on the wall yet, because one of the rings was loose in the frame and I thought it might fall down and be damaged and I couldn't decide who to ask to fix it. So I wrapped it up and hid it."

I was fascinated. "You hid it? Where?"

She laughed. "Nowhere very much, dear. I slipped it behind one of the radiators in the living room, and don't look so horrified, dear, the central heating was turned off."

I PAINTED at the house the next day, but no one else turned up.

In between stints at the easel I poked around on my own. There were a good many recognizable remains, durables like bed frames, kitchen machines, and radiators, all of them twisted and buckled. But of all the things Maisie had described, I found only the wrought-iron gate from Lady Tythe's old home. No warming pans. No marble table. No antique spears. Naturally, no Munnings.

When I went back to the Beach at five o'clock, I found Maisie waiting for me in the lobby. Not the kindly Maisie I had come to know, but a belligerent woman in a full-blown rage.

"I've been waiting for you," she said, fixing me with a furious eye.

"What's the matter?" I asked.

"The bar's shut," she said. "So come upstairs to my room. I'm so *mad* I think I'll absolutely *burst.*"

She did indeed, in the lift, look in danger of it. Her cheeks were bright red. Her blond-rinsed hair, normally lacquered, stuck out in wispy spikes, and for the first time since I'd met her, her generous mouth was not glistening with lipstick.

I followed her into her room.

"You'll never believe it," she said forcefully, turning to face me. "I've had the police here half the day and those insurance men here the other half, and *do you know what they're saying?*"

"Oh, Maisie." I sighed inwardly. It had been inevitable.

" 'What do you think I am?' I asked them. I was so *mad.* There they were, having the nerve to suggest I'd sold all my treasures and overinsured my house and was trying to take the insurance people for a ride. I told them over and over that everything was in its place when I went to Betty's, and if it was overinsured, it was to allow for inflation, and anyway, the brokers had advised me to put up the amount pretty high, but that Mr. Lagland says they won't be paying out until they have investigated further. They were absolutely *beastly,* and I *hate* them all."

She paused to regather momentum. "They made me feel so *dirty,* and maybe I *was* screaming a bit, but they'd no call to be so *rude* and making out I was some sort of criminal, and just what *right* have they to tell me to pull myself together when it is because of *them* and their bullying that I am yelling at the top of my voice?"

It must, I reflected, have been quite an encounter.

"They say it was definitely arson because Lagland couldn't find any of my treasures in the ashes, and they said even if I hadn't sold the things first, I had arranged for them to be stolen and the house burned to cinders while I was at Betty's, and they kept asking who

I'd paid to do it, and I got more and more furious, and if I'd had anything handy I would have *hit* them, I really would."

It struck me after a good deal more diatribe that genuine though Maisie's anger undoubtedly was, she was stoking herself up again every time her temper looked in danger of subsiding. She seemed to need to be in the position of the righteous wronged.

In a breath-catching gap in the flow of hot lava I said, "I don't suppose you told them about the Munnings."

The red spots on her cheeks burned suddenly brighter.

"I'm not *crazy*," she said bitingly. "If they found out about that, there would have been a fat chance of convincing them I'm telling the truth about the rest."

"I've heard," I said tentatively, "that nothing infuriates a crook more than being had up for the one job he didn't do."

It looked for a moment as if I'd just elected myself as the new target for hatred, but suddenly, as she glared at me in rage, her sense of humor reared its battered head. Her eyes softened, and after a second or two she ruefully smiled.

"I daresay you're right, dear, when I come to think of it." The smile slowly grew into a giggle. "How about a gin?"

Little eruptions continued all through dinner, but the red-centered volcano had subsided to manageable heat.

"You didn't seem surprised, dear, when I told you what the police thought I'd done."

"No." I paused. "You see, something very much the same has just happened to my cousin. Too much the same, in too many ways. I'd like to take you to meet him."

"But why, dear?"

I told her why. The anger she felt for herself burned up again fiercely for Donald.

"How *dreadful*. How *selfish* you must think *me*, after all that poor man has suffered."

"I don't think you're selfish at all. In fact, Maisie, I think you're a proper trouper."

She looked pleased and almost kittenish, and I had a vivid impression of what she had been like with Archie.

"There's one thing, though, dear," she said awkwardly. "After today, I don't think I want that picture you're doing. I don't want to remember the house as it is now, only like it used to be. So if I give you just the fifty pounds, do you mind?"

# CHAPTER THREE

WE WENT to Shropshire in Maisie's Jaguar, sharing the driving.

Donald on the telephone had sounded unenthusiastic at my suggested return, but also too lethargic to raise objections. When he opened his front door to us, I was shocked.

It was two weeks since I'd seen him. In that time he had shed at least fourteen pounds and aged ten years. His skin was tinged with bluish shadows, his face was stark, and his hair seemed speckled with gray.

"Come in," he said. "I'm in the dining room now. I expect you'd like a drink."

"That would be very nice, dear," Maisie said.

He waved to me to pour the drinks, as if it would be too much for him, and invited Maisie to sit down. The dining room had been roughly refurnished, now containing a large rug, all the sunroom armchairs, and a couple of small tables. We sat in a close group round one of the tables.

"Don," I said, "I want you to listen to a story."

Maisie, for once, kept it short. When she came to the bit about buying a Munnings in Australia, Donald's head lifted a couple of inches and he looked from her to me with the first stirring of attention. When she stopped, there was a small silence.

"So," I said finally, "you both bought a Munnings in Australia, and soon after your return you both had your houses burgled."

"Coincidence," Donald said.

"Where did you buy your picture, Don? Where exactly, I mean."

"I suppose . . . Melbourne. In the Hilton Hotel."

I looked doubtful. Hotels seldom sold Munningses.

"Fellow met us there," Don added. "Brought it up to our room. From the gallery where we saw it first."

"Which gallery?"

"Might have been something like Fine Arts."

"Would you have it on a check stub or anything?"

"No. The wine firm I was dealing with paid for it for me, and I sent a check to their British office when I got back."

"Which wine firm?"

"Monga Vineyards Proprietory, Limited, of Adelaide and Melbourne."

"What was the picture like? I mean, could you describe it?"

Donald looked tired. "One of those 'going down to the start' things. Typical Munnings."

"So was mine," said Maisie, surprised. "A long row of jockeys in their colors against a darker sort of sky. The nearest jockey in my picture had a purple shirt and green cap, and that was one of the reasons I bought it, because when Archie and I were thinking what fun it would be to buy a horse, we decided we'd like purple with a green cap for our colors, if no one already had that."

"Don?" I said.

"Mmm? Oh . . . three bay horses cantering . . . in profile . . . one in front, two slightly overlapping behind. Bright colors on the jockeys. White racetrack rails and a lot of sunny sky."

"What size?"

"Not very big. About twenty-four inches by eighteen."

"And yours, Maisie?"

"A bit smaller, dear, I should think."

"Look," Donald said. "What are you getting at?"

"Trying to make sure that there are no more coincidences. Don, could you possibly tell us how you came to buy your picture?"

Donald passed a weary hand over his face. "We went into the Victorian Arts Centre for a stroll round. We came to the Munnings they have in the gallery there . . . and while we were looking at it we just drifted into conversation with a woman near us. She said there was another Munnings, not far away, for sale in a small commercial gallery, and it was worth seeing even if one didn't intend to buy it. We had time to spare, so we went."

Maisie's mouth had fallen open. "But, dear," she said, "that was *just* the same as us, my sister-in-law and me, though it was the Sydney art gallery, not Melbourne. We were admiring this marvelous picture there, *The Coming Storm*, when this man sort of drifted up to us and joined in. . . ."

Donald suddenly looked a great deal more exhausted. "Look . . . Charles . . . you aren't going to the police with all this? Because I don't think I could stand . . . a new lot of questions."

"No, I'm not," I said.

Maisie finished her drink and smiled a little too brightly. "Which way to the little girls' room, dear?" she asked, and went out to the powder room.

Donald said faintly, "I'm sorry, Charles, but I can't seem to do anything . . . while they still have Regina . . . *stored*."

Time, far from dulling the agony, seemed to have preserved it. I had been told that the bodies of murdered people could be held by refrigeration in that way for six months or more in unsolved cases. I doubted whether Donald would last that long.

He stood up and walked to the sitting room. I followed.

The room still contained only the chintz-covered sofas and chairs. The floor where Regina had lain was clean and polished. The air was cold. Donald stood in front of the empty fireplace, looking at my picture of Regina, which was propped on the mantelpiece.

"I stay in here with her most of the time," he said. "It's the only place I can bear to be." He sat down, facing the portrait.

"You wouldn't mind seeing yourselves out, would you, Charles?" he said. "I'm really awfully tired."

"Take care of yourself." One could see he wouldn't.

"I'm all right," he said. "Quite all right. Don't you worry."

I looked back from the door. He was sitting immobile, looking at Regina. I didn't know whether it would have been better or worse if I hadn't painted her.

MAISIE and I drove to one of the neighbors who had originally offered refuge, because Donald clearly needed help now.

Mrs. Neighbor shook her head. "Yes, I know he should have company and get away from the house, but he won't. I've called several times. So have lots of people round here. He just tells us he's all right. He won't let anyone help him."

Maisie drove soberly, mile after mile. Eventually she said, "We shouldn't have bothered him. Not so soon after . . ."

Three weeks, I thought. To Donald it must have seemed like three months. You could live a lifetime in three weeks' pain.

"I'm going to Australia," I said.

Maisie turned to me. "You're very fond of him, dear, aren't you?"

"He's eight years older than me, but we've always got on well together. His mother and mine were sisters. They used to visit each other, with me and Donald in tow. He was always pretty patient about having a young kid under his feet."

She drove another ten miles in silence. Then she said, "Are you sure it wouldn't be better to tell the police? About the paintings, I mean? They might find out things more easily than you."

I agreed. "I'm sure they would, Maisie. But you heard what Donald said, that he couldn't stand a new lot of questions. And as for you, it wouldn't just be confessing to a bit of smuggling and paying a fine, but having a conviction against your name for always, and having the customs search your baggage every time you traveled, and all sorts of other humiliations. Once you get on any blacklist nowadays, it is just about impossible to get off."

"I didn't know you cared, dear." She tried a giggle, but it didn't sound right.

We stopped after a while to exchange places. I liked driving her car, particularly as for the last three years, since I'd given up a steady income, I'd owned no wheels myself. The power purred elegantly under the pale blue bonnet and ate up the southward miles.

"Can you afford the fare, dear?" Maisie said. "And hotels?"

"I've a friend out there. Another painter. I'll stay with him."

"You can't get there by hitchhiking, though."

I smiled. "I'll manage."

"Yes, well, dear, I daresay you can, but I've got a great deal of this world's goods, thanks to Archie, and since it's partly because of me having gone in for smuggling that you're going at all, I am insisting that you let me buy your ticket."

"No, Maisie."

"Yes, dear. Now be a good boy, dear, and do as I say."

I didn't like accepting her offer, but the truth was that I would have had to borrow anyway.

"Shall I paint your picture, Maisie, when I get back?"

"That will do very nicely, dear."

I pulled up outside the house near Heathrow whose attic was my home.

"How do you stand all this noise, dear?" she said, wincing as a huge jet climbed steeply overhead.

"I concentrate on the cheap rent."

She smiled, opening her handbag and producing her checkbook. She wrote out a check that was far more than enough for my fare.

"If you're so fussed, dear," she said across my protests, "you can give me back what you don't spend." She gazed at me earnestly with gray-blue eyes. "You will be careful, dear, won't you?"

"Yes, Maisie."

"Because of course, dear, you might turn out to be a nuisance to some really *nasty* people."

I LANDED at Mascot airport, near Sydney, at noon five days later. Jik met me with a huge grin and a bottle of champagne.

"Todd," he said. "Who'd have thought it?" He slapped me on the back with an enthusiastic hand. Jik Cassavetes, longtime friend, my opposite in almost everything.

Bearded, which I was not. Exuberant, extravagant, unpredictable— qualities I envied. Blue eyes and blond hair. Muscles that left mine gasping. An outrageous way with girls. An abrasive tongue, and a wholehearted contempt for the things I painted.

We had met at art school, drawn together by mutual truancy on race trains. Jik compulsively went racing, but strictly to gamble, never to admire the contestants, and certainly not to paint them. Horse painters to him were the lower orders. No *serious* artist, he frequently said, would be seen dead painting horses.

Jik's paintings, mostly abstract, were the dark reverse of the bright mind: fruits of depression, full of despair at the hatred and pollution destroying the fair world. Living with Jik was like a toboggan run, downhill, dangerous, and exhilarating.

At art school we'd shared a studio flat. They would have chucked him out of school except for his prodigious talent, because he'd missed weeks in the summer for his other love, sailing.

I'd been out with him several times in the years afterward. I reckoned he'd often taken us a bit nearer death than was necessary, but the Atlantic and the North Sea had been a nice change from the real estate office where I worked. He was a great sailor. I was sorry when one day he said he was setting off single-handed round the world. We'd had a paralytic farewell party on his last night ashore, and the next day, when he'd gone, I gave the real estate agent my notice.

Jik had brought his car to fetch me: a British MG sports, dark blue. Both sides of him right there, extrovert and introvert, the flamboyant statement in a somber color.

The engine roared to life, and he switched on the windshield wiper. "Welcome to sunny Australia. It rains all the time here."

"But you like it?"

"Love it, mate."

"And how's business?"

"There are thousands of painters in Australia." He glanced at me sideways. "A hell of a lot of competition."

"I haven't come to seek fame and fortune."

"But I scent a purpose," he said.

"How would you feel about harnessing your brawn?"

His eyebrows rose. "What are the risks?"

"Arson and murder, to date."

"God."

The blue car swept gracefully into the center of the city. Sky-scrapers grew like beanstalks.

"I live right out on the other side," Jik said. "Very suburban. What has become of me?"

"Contentment oozing from every pore," I said, smiling.

"Yes. So okay, for the first time in my life I've been actually happy. I daresay you'll soon put that right."

The car nosed onto the expressway, pointing toward the harbor bridge. "To your right," Jik said, "you'll see the triumph of imagination over economics."

I looked. It was the opera house, gray with rain.

"Dead in the day," Jik said. "It's a night bird. Fantastic."

The great arch of the bridge rose above us, intricate as steel lace. "This is the only flat bit of road in Sydney," Jik said, grinning.

The road continued up and down through the city past close-packed red-roofed houses.

"There's one snag," Jik said. "Three weeks ago I got married."

The snag was living with him aboard his boat, which was moored near a headland he called the Spit. You could see why—temporarily—the glooms of the world could take care of themselves.

She was not plain, but not beautiful. Oval-shaped face, brown hair, so-so figure and clothes. I found myself the target of bright brown eyes.

"Sarah," Jik said. "Todd. Todd, Sarah."

We said hi and did I have a good flight and yes, I did. I gathered she would have preferred me to have stayed at home.

Jik's thirty-foot ketch, which had set out from England as a cross between a studio and a chandler's warehouse, now sported curtains and cushions. Jik poured champagne into shining glasses.

"By God," he said. "It's good to see you."

I apologized for gate-crashing the honeymoon.

"Nuts," Jik said. "Too much domestic bliss is bad for the soul."

"It depends," said Sarah neutrally, "on whether you need love or loneliness to get you going."

For Jik, before, it had always been loneliness. I wondered what he had painted recently, but there was no sign in the now comfortable cabin of so much as a brush.

"I walk on air," Jik said. "I could bound up Everest and do a handspring on the summit."

"As far as the galley will do," Sarah said.

Jik in our shared days had been the cook, and times, it seemed, had not changed. He chopped open some crayfish, covered them with cheese and mustard, and set them under the grill. Then he washed the lettuce and assembled crusty bread and butter. We ate the feast round the cabin table, with rain pattering on the portholes. Over coffee I told them why I had come to Australia.

They heard me out in concentrated silence. And then Jik, whose politics had not changed much since his student days, muttered darkly about "pigs," and Sarah looked nakedly apprehensive.

"Don't worry," I told her. "I'm not asking for Jik's help."

"You have it. You have it," he said explosively.

I shook my head. "No."

Sarah said, "What precisely do you plan to do first?"

"Find out where the two Munningses came from."

"And after?"

"Melbourne," Jik said suddenly. "You said one of them came from Melbourne. Well, that settles it. We'll go there at once. Do you know what next Tuesday is?"

"No," I said. "What is it?"

"The day of the Melbourne Cup!"

His voice was triumphant. Sarah stared at me darkly across the table. "I wish you hadn't come," she said.

I SLEPT that night in the converted boathouse that constituted Jik's postal address and studio.

A huge old easel stood in the center, with a table to each side holding neat arrays of paints, brushes, knives, pots of linseed and turpentine, and cleaning fluid—all the usual paraphernalia.

No work in progress. Everything tidy. The palette was small, because he used most colors straight from the tube and got his effects by overpainting. A box of rags stood under one table, ready to wipe clean everything used to apply paint to picture, not just brushes and knives, but fingers, palms, wrists. I smiled to myself. Jik's studio was as identifiable as his pictures.

Along one wall, a two-tiered rack held rows of canvases, which I pulled out one by one. Dark, strong, dramatic colors. Still the troubled vision, the perception of doom. Decay and crucifixions, horrific landscapes, flowers wilting.

Jik hated to sell his paintings, and seldom did, which I thought was just as well, as they were enough to cause depression in a skylark. They had a vigor, though; that couldn't be denied. Those who saw his work remembered it. He was a major artist in a way I would never be.

In the morning I walked down to the boat and found Sarah alone.

"Jik's gone for milk," she said. "I'll get you some breakfast."

"I came to say good-bye."

She looked at me levelly. "Back to England?"

I shook my head.

"*Men,*" she said. "Never happy unless they're risking their necks."

She was right, to a degree. A little healthy danger wasn't a bad feeling, especially in retrospect. "I won't take Jik with me."

She turned her back. "You'll get him killed," she said.

NOTHING looked less dangerous than the small suburban gallery from which Maisie had bought her picture. It was shut for good. The bare premises could be seen through the window.

The little shops on each side shrugged their shoulders.

"They were only open for a month or so. Never seemed to do much business. No surprise they folded."

Did they, I asked, know which real estate agent was handling the letting? No, they didn't.

"End of inquiry," Jik said. "Where now?"

"The Art Gallery?"

"In the Domain," Jik said, which turned out to be a chunk of park in the city center. The Art Gallery had a suitable façade of six pillars outside and the Munnings, when we ran it to earth, inside.

We stood there for a while, with me admiring the absolute mastery that set the two gray ponies in the shaft of prestorm light at the head of the darker herd, and Jik grudgingly admitting that at least the man knew how to handle paint.

Absolutely nothing else happened. No one approached to advise us we could buy another one cheap in a little gallery in an outer suburb. We drove back to the boat.

"What now?" Jik said.

"Telephone work, if I could borrow the one in the boathouse."

It took nearly all afternoon, but alphabetically systematic calls to every real estate agent as far as Holloway & Son produced the goods in the end. The premises in question, said Holloway & Son, had been let to North Sydney Fine Arts on a three-month lease.

No, they did not know the premises were now empty. They could not relet them until December 1, because North Sydney Fine Arts had paid all the rent in advance. I blarneyed a bit, giving the impression of being in the trade myself, with a client for the empty shop. Holloway & Son mentioned a Mr. John Grey, with a post office box number for an address.

How could I recognize Mr. Grey if I met him? They couldn't say; all the negotiations had been done by telephone and post. I could write to him myself if my client wanted the gallery before December 1.

Ta ever so, I thought.

All the same, it couldn't do much harm. I wrote Mr. Grey and asked him if he would sell me the last two weeks of his lease so that I could mount an exhibition of a young friend's *utterly meaningful* watercolors. Yours sincerely, I wrote: Peregrine Smith. I used Jik's box number as a return address.

"He won't answer," Sarah said, "if he's a crook."

"The first principle of fishing," Jik said, "is to dangle a bait."

"This wouldn't attract a starving piranha."

I posted it anyway, though none of us expected it to bring forth any result.

Jik's session on the telephone proved more rewarding. Melbourne was crammed to the rooftops for the richest race of the year, but he had been offered last-minute cancellations.

"Where?" I asked suspiciously.

"In the Hilton," he said.

I COULDN'T afford it, but we went anyway. Jik in his student days had lived on cautious handouts from a family trust, and it appeared that the source of bread was still flowing. The boat, the boathouse, the MG, and the wife were none of them supported by paint.

We flew south to Melbourne the following morning, looking down on the Snowy Mountains and thinking our own chilly thoughts. Sarah's disapproval from the seat behind froze the back of my head, but she refused to stay in Sydney. Jik's natural bent for adventure was being curbed by love, and his reaction to danger might not henceforth be practical. That was, if I could find any dangers for him to react to. The Sydney trail was dead and cold, and maybe Melbourne, too, would yield a gone-away private gallery. And if it did, what then? For Donald the outlook would be bleaker than the puckered ranges sliding away underneath us.

If I could take home enough to show that the plundering of his house had its roots in the sale of a painting in Australia, it should get the police off his neck, and Regina into a decent grave. If.

And I would have to be quick, or it would be too late to matter. Donald, staring hour after hour at a portrait in an empty house. Donald, on the brink.

MELBOURNE was cold and wet and blowing a gale. We checked gratefully into the warm plush Hilton, souls cosseted by rich reds and purples and blues, velvety fabrics, copper and gilt. A long way from the bare boards of home.

I unpacked, which is to say, hung up my one suit, slightly crumpled from the satchel, and then went to work on the telephone.

The Melbourne office of the Monga Vineyards Proprietory, Ltd., cheerfully told me that the person who dealt with Mr. Donald Stuart from England was the managing director, Mr. Hudson Taylor, and he could be found in his office at the vineyard, which was north of Adelaide. Would I like the number?

Thanks very much.

"No sweat," they said, which I gathered was Australian shorthand for "It's no trouble, and you're welcome."

I pulled out the map of Australia I'd acquired on the flight from England. Melbourne, capital of the state of Victoria, lay right down in the southeast corner. Adelaide, capital of South Australia, lay about four hundred and fifty miles northwest.

Hudson Taylor was not in his vineyard office. An equally cheerful voice there told me he'd already left for Melbourne. He had a runner in the Cup. He would be staying with friends. Number supplied. Ring at nine o'clock.

Sighing, I went two floors down to Jik and Sarah's room.

"We've got tickets for the races tomorrow and Tuesday," Jik said, "and a car pass, and a car. And the West Indies play Victoria at cricket on Sunday and we've tickets for that, too."

"Courtesy of the Hilton," Sarah said, looking much happier. "The whole package was on offer with the canceled rooms."

"So what do you want us to do this afternoon?" finished Jik.

"Could you bear the Arts Centre?"

It appeared they could. The National Gallery at the Centre was modern, inventive, and its Great Reception Hall was endowed with the largest stained-glass roof in the world. Jik took deep breaths, as if drawing the living spirit of the place into his lungs, and declaimed at the top of his voice that Australia was the greatest, the only adventurous country left in the corrupt, militant, meanminded, polluted world. Passersby stared in amazement and Sarah showed no surprise at all.

We found the Munnings deep in the maze of galleries. It glowed in the remarkable light that suffused the whole building—the *Departure of the Hop-Pickers*, showing a great wide sky and the dignified gypsies with their ponies and caravans.

A young man sat at an easel nearby, working on a copy. On a table beside him stood pots of linseed oil and turps, paints, and a jar of brushes. Some people stood about, watching him.

Jik and I went behind him to take a look. We saw him squeeze flake white and cadmium yellow onto his palette and mix them together into a nice pale color. On the easel stood his study, barely started. The outlines were there, and a small amount of blue on the sky. Jik and I watched with interest while he applied the pale yellow to the shirt of the nearest figure.

"Hey," Jik said loudly, slapping him on the shoulder. "You're a fraud. If you're an artist, I'm a gas fitter's mate."

Hardly polite, but not a hanging matter. The faces of the scattered onlookers registered embarrassment, not affront.

On the young man, though, the effect was galvanic. He leaped to his feet, overturning the easel and staring at Jik with wild eyes, and Jik, with huge enjoyment, put in the clincher.

"What you're doing is *criminal*," he said.

The young man reacted to that ruthlessly, snatching up the pots of linseed and turps and flinging the liquids at Jik's eyes.

I grabbed his left arm. He scooped up his palette in his right hand and swung round fiercely, aiming at my face. I ducked. The palette missed me and struck Jik, who had his hands to his eyes and was yelling.

The young man tore his arm free and ran for the exit, dodged round two openmouthed spectators, and pushed them violently into my path. By the time I'd disentangled myself, he had vanished.

A fair-sized crowd had surrounded Jik, and Sarah was in a fury. "Do something!" she screamed at me. "Do something, he's going blind. I knew we should never have listened to you!"

"Sarah," I said fiercely. "Jik is *not* going blind. Linseed oil will do no harm. The turps is painful, but that's all."

She glared at me and turned back to Jik, who was rocking around in agony and, being Jik, was exercising his tongue.

"The slimy little bastard . . . wait till I catch him. . . . Sarah, where's that bloody Todd? . . . I'll strangle him. . . . Get an ambulance . . . my eyes are burning out. . . ."

I spoke loudly in his ear. "You know damn well you're not going blind, so stop hamming it up."

"They're not your eyes."

"And you're frightening Sarah," I said.

That message got through. He took his hands away and stopped rolling about.

At the sight of his face, the audience let out a murmur of pleasant horror. Yellow and blue paint streaked his jaw; his eyes were red and pouring with tears, and looked very sore indeed.

"Sorry, Sarah," he said, blinking painfully. "Todd's right. Turps never blinded anybody."

"Not permanently," I said, because to do him justice he obviously couldn't see anything but tears at the moment.

Sarah's animosity was unabated. "Get him an ambulance, then."

I shook my head. "All he needs is water and time."

"He's right, love. Lead me to the nearest gents."

While Sarah solicitously helped him away, I picked up the overturned mess of paints and easel that the young man had left. Artists' quality, not students' cheaper equivalents. None of it new, but not old, either, and none of it marked with the owner's name. The picture itself was on a standard-sized piece of hardboard.

I wiped my hands on a piece of rag and said slowly to the onlookers, "I suppose that no one here was talking to the artist before any of this happened?"

"We were," said one woman, surprised at the question.

"So were we," said another.

"What about?"

"Munnings," said one, and "Munnings," said the other.

"Not about his own work?" I asked.

Both of the ladies and their husbands shook their heads and said they had talked about the pleasure of owning a Munnings.

I smiled slowly. "I suppose," I said, "that he didn't happen to know where you could get one?"

"Well, yeah," they said. "As a matter of fact, he sure did."

"Where?"

"Look here, young fellow," said the elder of the husbands, a seventyish American with the unmistakable stamp of wealth. "You're asking a lot of questions."

"I'll explain," I said. "Would you like some coffee?"

They said, doubtfully, they possibly would.

"There's a coffee shop just down the hall," I said.

THEY were all Americans, all rich, retired, and fond of racing. Mr. and Mrs. Howard K. Petrovitch, of Ridgeville, New Jersey, and Mr. and Mrs. Wyatt L. Minchless, from Carter, Illinois.

Wyatt Minchless, the elder man, called the meeting to order. White-haired, black-framed specs, pompous manner. "Now, young fellow, let's hear it from the top."

"Um," I said. Where exactly was the top? "The artist boy attacked my friend Jik because Jik called him a criminal."

"Yuh." Mrs. Petrovitch nodded. "Why would he do that?"

"It isn't criminal to copy good painting," Mrs. Minchless said knowledgeably. "In the Louvre in Paris, you can't get near the *Mona Lisa* for those irritating students."

She had blue-rinsed puffed-up hair, uncreasable navy and green clothes, and enough diamonds to attract a top-rank thief.

"It depends what you are copying *for*," I said. "If you're going to try to pass your copy off as an original, that *is* a fraud."

Mrs. Petrovitch began, "Do you think the young man was *forging*—" but was interrupted by Wyatt Minchless.

"Are you saying that this young boy was painting a Munnings he later intended to sell as the real thing? Are you saying that the Munnings picture he told us we might be able to buy is a forgery?"

"I don't know," I said. "I just thought I'd like to see it."

"You don't want to buy a Munnings yourself? You are not acting as an agent for anyone else?"

"Absolutely not," I said.

"Well, then." Wyatt looked round the other three, collected silent assents. "He told Ruthie and me there was a good Munnings at a very reasonable price in a little gallery not far away. . . ." He fished into his outer pocket. "Yes, here we are. 'Yarra River Fine Arts. Third turning off Swanston Street.' "

"He told us exactly the same," Mr. Petrovitch said. "He asked where we would be going after Melbourne. We told him Alice Springs, and he said Alice Springs was a mecca for artists and to be sure to visit the Yarra River gallery there, too. Always had good pictures."

Mr. Petrovitch would have misunderstood if I had leaned across and hugged him. I kept my excitement to myself.

"You didn't tell us," Mrs. Petrovitch said, looking puzzled, "why your friend called the young man a criminal."

"My friend Jik," I said, "is an artist himself. The young man was painting with paints which won't really mix. Jik's a perfectionist. He can't stand seeing paint misused."

"What do you mean, won't mix?"

"Paints are chemicals," I said. "Most of them don't have any effect on each other, but you have to be careful. If you mix flake white, which is lead, with cadmium yellow, which contains sulfur, like the young man was doing, you get a nice pale color to start with, but the two minerals react against each other and in time darken the picture."

"And your friend called this criminal?" Wyatt said in disbelief.

"Er . . . my friend," I said, "didn't think much of the young man's effort. He called it criminal. He might just as well have said lousy." The permanence of colors had always been an obsession with Jik.

# CHAPTER FOUR

I FOUND Jik and Sarah in their hotel room. "How are the eyes?" I asked, advancing tentatively.

"Awful." They were bright pink, but dry. Getting better.

Sarah said with tight lips, "This has all gone far enough."

"Todd—" Jik said.

Sarah leaped in fast. "No, Jik. It's not our responsibility. Todd's cousin's troubles are nothing to do with us. We are not getting involved any further."

"Todd will go on with it," Jik said.

"Then he's a fool." She was angry, scornful, biting.

"Sure," I said. "Anyone who tries to right a wrong these days is a fool. Much better not to get involved. I really ought to be painting away safely in my attic at Heathrow—minding my own business and letting Donald rot. The trouble is I simply can't do it. I see the hell he's in. How can I just turn my back?"

I came to a halt. A blank pause.

"Well," I said, raising a smile. "Have fun at the races."

I sketched a farewell and eased myself out. Neither of them said a word. I took the lift up to my room.

A pity about Sarah, I thought. She would have Jik in cotton wool and slippers if he didn't look out; and he'd never paint those magnificent brooding pictures anymore, because they sprang from a torment he would no longer be allowed.

I looked at my watch and decided to try the Yarra River Fine Arts. I wondered, as I walked up Swanston Street, whether the young turps flinger would be there and, if he was, whether he would know me. I'd seen only glimpses of his face, as I'd mostly been standing behind him. All one could swear to was light brown hair, a round jaw, and a full-lipped mouth. Under twenty. Dressed in blue jeans, white T-shirt, and tennis shoes. About five feet eight, a hundred and thirty pounds. And no artist.

The gallery was open, brightly lighted, with a horse painting on display in the window. Not a Munnings. A picture of an Australian horse and jockey, every detail sharp-edged, emphatic, and to my taste overpainted.

The gallery had narrow frontage, with premises stretching back a good way. Two or three people were wandering about inside, looking at the merchandise on the well-lighted walls.

I took a deep breath and stepped over the threshold.

Greeny-gray carpet within, and an antique desk near the door, with a youngish woman handing out catalogues.

"Feel free to look around," she said. "More pictures downstairs."

She handed me a folded white card with several typed sheets clipped into it. I flipped them over. One hundred and sixty-three items, with titles, artists' names, and asking prices. A painting already sold, it said, would have a red spot on the frame.

I thanked her. "Just passing by," I said.

She nodded and smiled professionally, eyes sliding rapidly over my denim clothes. She wore the latest trendy fashion. Australian, assured, too big a personality to be simply a receptionist.

I walked slowly down the long room. Most of the pictures were by Australian artists, and I could see what Jik had meant about the hot competition. The field was just as crowded as at home, and the standard in some respects better.

At the far end of the display was the staircase. I went down. There the gallery was not one straight room, but a series of small rooms off a long corridor. To the rear of the stairs was a comfortably furnished office. Heavily framed pictures adorned the walls, and a substantial man was writing in a ledger at the desk.

He raised his head. "Can I help you?" he said.

"Just looking."

He gave me an uninterested nod and went back to his work. He, like the whole place, had an air of permanence and respectability quite unlike the fly-by-night suburban affair in Sydney. This could not be what I was looking for.

Sighing, I continued down the corridor, thinking I might as well finish taking stock of the competition. In the end room, which was larger than the others, I came across the Munningses. Three of them. They were not in the catalogue, and they hung without ballyhoo in a row of similar subjects. To my eyes they stuck out like Thoroughbreds among hacks.

Prickles began up my spine. It wasn't just the workmanship, but one of the pictures itself. Horses going down to the start. A long line of jockeys, bright against a dark sky. The silks of the nearest rider, purple with a green cap.

Maisie's chatty voice reverberated in my inner ear, describing what I saw. "That was one of the reasons I bought it, because Archie and I . . . decided we'd like purple with a green cap for our colors, if no one already had that."

Munnings had always used a good deal of purple and green. All the same . . . this picture—size, subject, and coloring—was exactly like Maisie's, which had presumably been burned.

The picture in front of me had the right sort of patina for the time since Munnings's death, the excellence of draftsmanship, the indefinable something that separated the great from the good. I gently felt the surface. Nothing there that shouldn't be.

An English voice from behind me said, "Can I help you?"

"Isn't that a Munnings?" I said casually, turning round.

He was standing in the doorway, looking in. I knew him instantly. Brown receding hair combed back, drooping mustache, suntanned skin: all last on view almost two weeks ago beside the sea in Sussex, England, prodding around in a smoky ruin.

Mr. Greene. With an *e*.

It took him only a fraction longer. Puzzlement as he glanced from me to the picture and back, then the shocking realization of where he'd seen me. He took a sharp step backward and raised his hand to the wall outside.

I was on my way to the door, but I wasn't quick enough. A steel gate slid down very fast in the doorway and clicked into a bolt in the floor. Mr. Greene stood outside, disbelief stamped on every feature. I revised all my theories about danger being good for the soul and felt as frightened as I'd ever been in my life.

"What's the matter?" called a voice from up the corridor.

Mr. Greene's tongue was stuck. The man from the office appeared at his shoulder and looked at me through the imprisoning steel.

"A thief?" he asked with irritation.

Mr. Greene shook his head. A third person arrived outside, his young face bright with curiosity.

"Hey," he said. "He was the one at the National Gallery. The one who chased me."

I was standing in the center of a room of about fifteen feet square. No windows. No way out except through the guarded door.

"I say," I said plaintively. "Just what is all this about?" I tapped on the gate. "Open this up, I want to get out."

"What are you doing here?" the office man asked. He was a big man and obviously more senior in the gallery. Dark spectacles over unfriendly eyes, and a blue bow tie with polka dots under a double chin. Small mouth with a full lower lip.

"Looking," I said, trying to sound bewildered. "Just looking at pictures." An innocent at large, I thought, and a bit dim.

"He chased me in the National Gallery," the boy repeated.

"You threw some stuff in that man's eyes," I said indignantly.

"Friend of yours, was he?" the office man said.

"No," I said. "I was just there. Same as I'm here. Just looking at pictures. Nothing wrong in that, is there? I go to galleries all the time."

Mr. Greene got his voice back. "I saw him in England," he said to the office man. Then he pulled him away, up the corridor.

"Open the door," I said to the boy, who still gazed in.

"I don't know how," he said. "And I don't reckon I'd be popular, somehow."

The two other men returned. "Who *are* you?" said the office man.

"Nobody. I mean, I'm just here for the racing."

"Name?"

"Charles Neil." Charles Neil Todd.

"What were you doing in England?"

"I live there!" I said. "Look, I saw this man here"—I nodded to Greene—"at the home of a woman I know slightly in Sussex. She was giving me a lift home from the races, see, and she said she wanted to make a detour to see her house which had lately been burned, and when we got there, this man was there. He said his name was Greene and that he was from an insurance company, and that's all I know about him. So what's going on?"

"It is a coincidence that you should meet here again, so soon."

"It certainly is," I agreed fervently. "But that's no bloody reason to lock me up."

I read indecision on their faces. I shrugged exasperatedly. "Fetch the police, then, if you think I've done anything wrong."

The man from the office put his hand on the outside wall, and the gate slid up out of sight. "Sorry," he said. "But we have to be careful, with so many valuable paintings on the premises."

"Well, I see that," I said, stepping forward and resisting a strong impulse to make a dash for it. "But all the same . . ." I managed an aggrieved tone. "Still, no harm done, I suppose."

They all walked behind me along the corridor and up the stairs, doing my nerves no slightest good. All the other visitors seemed to have left. The receptionist was locking the front door. "I thought everyone had gone," she said in surprise.

"Slight delay," I said with a feeble laugh.

She gave me the professional smile and opened the door.

Six steps. Out in the fresh air. God Almighty, it smelled good. I half turned. All four stood watching me go. I trudged away, feeling as weak as a field mouse dropped by a hawk.

I caught a tram and traveled into unknown regions of the city, anxious to put distance between myself and the gallery.

They were bound to have second thoughts. They would wish they had found out more about me before letting me go. They couldn't be certain it wasn't a coincidence, but the more they thought about it the less they would believe it.

If they wanted to find me, where would they look? Not at the Hilton, I thought in amusement. At the races; I had told them I would be there. I wished I hadn't.

At the end of the tramline, I got off and found myself opposite a small restaurant with B.Y.O. in large letters on the door. I went in and ordered a steak and asked for the wine list.

The waitress looked surprised. "You a stranger? It's B.Y.O. Bring Your Own. We don't sell drinks here, only food. If you want something to drink, there's a drive-in bottle shop down the road. I could hold the steak until you get back."

I settled for a teetotal dinner, grinning all through coffee at a notice on the wall saying WE HAVE AN ARRANGEMENT WITH OUR BANK. THEY DON'T FRY STEAKS AND WE DON'T CASH CHEQUES.

When I set off back to the city center on the tram, I passed the bottle shop, which looked so like a garage that if I hadn't known, I would have thought the cars were queuing for petrol. I could see why Jik liked the Australian imagination: both sense and fun.

I walked the last couple of miles. Thinking of Donald and Maisie and Greene with an *e*. The overall plan had all along seemed fairly simple: to sell pictures in Australia and steal them back in England, together with everything else lying handy. Since I'd met the Petrovitches and the Minchlesses, it seemed I'd been wrong to think of all the robberies taking place in England. Why not in America? Why not anywhere?

Why not a mobile force of thieves shuttling antiques from continent to continent, selling briskly to a ravenous market? As Inspector Frost had said, few antiques were ever recovered. The demand was insatiable and the supply, by definition, limited.

Suppose I were a villain and I didn't want to waste weeks in foreign countries finding out exactly which houses were worth robbing. I could just stay in Melbourne selling paintings to rich visitors. I could chat with them about their pictures back home, and I could shift the conversation easily to their silver and china and *objets d'art*. When they bought my paintings, they would give me their addresses. Nice and easy. Just like that.

I would reckon that if I kept the victims reasonably well scattered, the fact that they had been to Australia within the past year or so would mean nothing to each regional police force, or to insurance companies.

If I were a villain, I thought, with a well-established business, I wouldn't put myself at risk by selling fakes. Forged oil paintings were almost always detectable under a microscope, and a majority of experienced dealers could tell them at a glance. A painter left his signature all over a painting, because the way he held his brush was as individual as handwriting.

Suppose I sold a genuine picture to Maisie in Sydney, and got it back, and started to sell it again in Melbourne. . . . My supposing stopped right there, because it didn't fit.

Maybe Maisie's picture had been stolen like her other things and was right now glowing in the Yarra River Fine Arts, but if so, why had the house been burned, and why had Mr. Greene turned up to search the ruins?

It only made sense if Maisie's picture had been a copy and if the thieves hadn't been able to find it. Rather than leave it around, they'd burned the house. But I'd just decided that I wouldn't risk fakes. Except that . . . would Maisie know an expert copy if she saw one? No, she wouldn't.

I sighed. To fool even Maisie, you'd have to find an accomplished artist willing to copy, instead of pressing on with his own work, and they weren't that thick on the ground.

The hotel rose ahead across a stretch of park. The night air blew cool on my head. I had a vivid feeling of being disconnected, a stranger in a vast continent. The noise and warmth of the Hilton brought the expanding universe down to imaginable size.

Upstairs, I telephoned Hudson Taylor. Nine o'clock on the dot. He sounded mellow, courteous, and vibrantly Australian.

"Donald Stuart's cousin? Is it true about Regina being killed?"

"I'm afraid so."

"It's a real tragedy. A real nice lass, that Regina. Well, what can I do for you? Tickets for the races?"

"Er . . . no," I said. It was just that since the receipt and provenance letter of the Munnings had been stolen along with the picture, Donald would like to get in touch with the people who had sold it to him, for insurance purposes, but he had forgotten their name. And as I was coming to Melbourne for the Cup . . .

"That's easy enough," Hudson Taylor said pleasantly. "I remember the place well. I went there with Donald, and the guy in charge brought the picture along to the hotel afterward, when we arranged the finance. Now, let's see . . ." There was a pause. "I can't remember the name of the place just now. Or the manager. But I've got him on record here in the Melbourne office, so I'll look it up in the morning. You'll be at the races tomorrow?"

"Yes," I said.

"How about meeting for a drink, then? You can tell me about poor Donald and Regina, and I'll have the information he wants."

I said that would be fine, and he told me where I would find him, and when. The spot he described sounded public and exposed. I hoped that it would only be he who found me on it.

"I'll be there," I said.

JIK telephoned at eight next morning. "Come down to the coffee shop and have breakfast."

I met him in the hotel's informal restaurant. He was sitting alone, wearing dark glasses, and making inroads into a mountain of scrambled eggs.

"They bring coffee," he said. "You have to fetch everything else from that buffet." He nodded toward a well-laden table.

"How are the eyes?"

He whipped off the glasses with a theatrical flourish. Still inflamed, but on the definite mend.

"Has Sarah relented?" I asked.

"She says she's got nothing against you personally."

"But," I said.

He put down his knife and fork. "I told her to cheer up and face the fact she hadn't married a marshmallow. Anyway, there's this car we've got. Damned silly if you didn't come with us to the races."

"Would Sarah," I asked carefully, "scowl?"

"She says not."

I accepted this offer and inwardly sighed. It looked as if he wouldn't take the smallest step henceforth without the nod from Sarah. When the wildest ones got married, was it always like that?

"Where did you get to last night?" he asked.

I told him about the gallery, the Munnings, and my brief moment of captivity. I told him what I thought of the burglaries.

His eyes gleamed with excitement. "I'd like to help," he said.

"You'll do what pleases Sarah."

"Don't sound so bloody bossy."

We finished breakfast, amicably trying to build a suitable new relationship on the ruins of the old.

When I met them later in the lobby at setting-off time, it was clear that Sarah, too, had made a reassessment and put her mind to work on her emotions. She greeted me with an attempted smile and an outstretched hand. I shook the hand lightly and gave her a token kiss on the cheek. She took it as it was meant.

Jik the mediator stood around looking smug.

"Take a look at him," he said, flapping a hand in my direction. "The complete stockbroker. Suit, tie, leather shoes. If he isn't careful, they'll have him in the Royal Academy."

"Let's go to the races," Sarah said.

We went slowly, on account of the traffic. The car park at Flemington Racecourse looked like a giant picnic ground, with hundreds of lunch parties going on. Tables, chairs, china, silver, glass. Sun umbrellas raised in defiance of threatening rain clouds. A lot of gaiety. To my mild astonishment, Jik and Sarah whipped out table, chairs, drinks, and food from the rented car's boot. Sarah said it was easy when you knew how, you just ordered the works.

She was really trying, I thought. She was wearing an olive-green linen coat, with a broad-brimmed hat of the same color. Overall, a new Sarah, prettier, more relaxed, less afraid.

"Champagne?" Jik offered. "Steak and oyster pie?"

"How will I go back to cocoa and chips?"

"Fatter."

We demolished the goodies, repacked the boot, and, with a sense of taking part in some vast semireligious ritual, squeezed along with the crowd through the gate.

"It'll be much worse on Tuesday," observed Sarah. "Melbourne Cup Day is a public holiday. The city has three million inhabitants and half of them will try to get here."

We went through the bottleneck and, by virtue of our package tour, through a second gate and round into the calmer waters of the green oblong of the Members' lawn. Much like Derby Day at home, I thought. Same triumph of will over weather. Bright faces under gray skies. Umbrellas at the ready.

My friends were assessing the form of the first race. Sarah, it appeared, had a betting pedigree as long as her husband's.

"I know it was soft going at Randwick last week," she said, "but it's pretty soft here, too, after all this rain, and he likes it hard."

"He was only beaten by Boyblue at Randwick, and Boyblue was out of sight in the Caulfield Cup."

"Please your silly self," Sarah said loftily. "But it's still too soft for Grapevine."

"Want to bet?" Jik asked me.

"Right." I consulted the race card. "Two dollars on Generator."

They both looked him up, and they both said, "Why?"

"If in doubt, back number eleven."

They made clucking and pooh-poohing noises and told me I could make a gift of my two dollars to the bookies.

We paid our money, and Generator won at twenty-five to one.

"Beginner's luck," Sarah said.

They tore up their tickets, set their minds to race two, and placed their bets. I settled for four dollars on number one.

"Why?"

"Double my stake on half of eleven."

"Oh, God," said Sarah. "You're something else."

One of the more aggressive clouds started scattering rain.

"Come on," I said. "Let's go and sit up there in the dry."

"You two go," Sarah said. "Those seats are only for men."

I laughed. I thought she was joking, but it appeared it was no joke. Very unfunny, in fact. About two-thirds of the best seats in the Members' stands were reserved for males.

"What about their wives and girlfriends?" I said.

"They can go up on the roof."

Sarah, being Australian, saw nothing very odd in it. To me, and surely to Jik, it was ludicrous.

We escalated to the roof, which had a proportion of two women to one man and was windy and damp, with bench seating.

"Don't worry about it," Sarah said, amused at my aghastness on behalf of womankind. "I'm used to it."

We could see the whole race superbly from our aerie. Sarah and Jik screamed encouragement to their fancies, but number one finished in front by two lengths, at eight to one.

"It's disgusting," said Sarah, tearing up more tickets. "What number do you fancy for the third?"

"I won't be with you for the third. I've got an appointment to have a drink with someone who knows Donald."

"Yes." She swallowed. "Well . . . good luck."

The Members' lawn was bounded on one long side by the stands and on the opposite side by the path taken by the horses on their way to the parade ring. One short side of the lawn lay alongside part of the parade ring itself, and it was at one of those corners that I was to meet Hudson Taylor.

I reached the appointed spot and waited, admiring the bed full of scarlet flowers that lined the railing between horse walk and lawn. Cadmium red with highlights of orange and white.

"Charles Todd?"

"Yes. . . . Mr. Taylor?"

"Hudson. Glad to know you." We shook hands. Late forties, medium height, comfortable build, with affable, slightly sad eyes sloping downward at the outer corners. He was one of the minority of men in morning dress, and he wore it as comfortably as a sweater.

"Let's find somewhere dry," he said. "Come this way."

He led me up a bank of steps, through an entrance door, down a wide corridor, past a guard and a notice saying COMMITTEE ONLY, and into a comfortable room fitted out as a small bar. A group of four stood chatting with half-filled glasses, and two women in furs were complaining loudly of the cold.

"They love to bring out the sables," Hudson Taylor said, chuckling, as he fetched two glasses of Scotch and gestured me to a seat. "Spoils their fun, the years it's hot for this meeting."

"Is it usually hot?"

"Melbourne's weather can change twenty degrees in an hour."

He sounded proud of it. "Now, then, this business of yours." He delved into an inner breast pocket and surfaced with a folded paper. "Here you are. The gallery was called Yarra River Fine Arts."

I would have been astounded if it hadn't been.

"And the man we dealt with was someone called Ivor Wexford."

"What did he look like?" I asked.

"I don't remember clearly. It was back in April, do you see."

I pulled a small slim sketchbook out of my pocket.

"If I draw him, might you know him?"

He looked amused. "You never know."

I drew a reasonable likeness of Greene. "Was it him?"

Hudson Taylor shook his head. "No, that wasn't him."

"How about this?"

I turned the page and drew the man from the basement office.

"Maybe," he said.

I made the lower lip fuller, added heavy-framed spectacles and a spotted bow tie.

"That's him," said Hudson in surprise. "I remember the bow tie. You don't see many of those these days. How did you know?"

"I walked round a couple of galleries yesterday afternoon."

"That's quite a gift you have there," he said with interest.

"Practice, that's all." Years of seeing people's faces as matters of proportions and planes, and remembering which way the lines slanted. It was a knack I'd had from childhood.

"Sketching is your hobby?" Hudson asked.

"And my work. I mostly paint horses." We talked a little about painting for a living.

"Maybe I can give you a commission, if my horse runs well in the Cup. If he's down the field, I'll feel more like shooting him." He stood up and gestured me to follow. "Time for the next race. Care to watch it with me?"

We emerged into daylight in the prime part of the stands. "Down here," Hudson said, pointing to the front rows of seats, reserved for men.

"May we only go up if accompanied by a lady?" I asked.

He smiled. "You find our ways odd? We'll go up, by all means."

He led the way and settled comfortably among the predominantly female company, greeting several people and introducing me companionably as his friend Charles from England. Instant first names, instant acceptance, Australian-style.

"This division of the sexes has interesting historical roots." He chuckled. "Australia was governed nearly all last century with the help of the British army. The officers and gentlemen left their wives back in England, but such is nature, they all set up liaisons here with women of low repute. They didn't want their fellow officers to see the vulgarity of their choice, so they invented a rule that the officers' enclosures were for men only, which effectively silenced their popsies' pleas to be taken."

I laughed. "Very neat."

"It's easier to establish a tradition than to get rid of it."

"You're establishing a tradition for fine wines, Donald says."

The sad-looking eyes twinkled. "He was most enthusiastic."

The horses for the third race cantered away to the start, led by a fractious chestnut colt with too much white about his head.

"Ugly brute," Hudson said. "But he'll win."

"Are you backing it?"

He smiled. "I've a little bit on."

The race started and the field sprinted, and Hudson's knuckles whitened so much from his grip on his binoculars that I wondered just how big the little bit was. The chestnut colt was beaten into fourth place. Hudson put his race glasses down slowly.

"Oh, well," he said. "Always another day." He shrugged resignedly, cheered up, shook my hand, and asked if I could find my own way out.

"Thank you for your help," I said.

He smiled. "Anytime. Anytime."

Jik and Sarah, when I rejoined them, were arguing about their fancies for the next race.

"Hello, Todd," Sarah said. "Pick a number, for God's sake."

"Ten."

"Why ten?"

"Eleven minus one."

"Lord," Jik said. "You used to have more sense."

We bought our tickets and went back up to the roof, and none of our bets came up. The winner was number twelve.

"You should have *added* eleven and one," Sarah said. "You make such silly mistakes."

"What are you staring at?" Jik said.

I was looking down at the crowd on the Members' lawn.

"Lend me your race glasses."

Jik handed them over. I took a long look and put them down.

"What is it?" Sarah said anxiously. "What's the matter?"

"Do you see those two men . . . about twenty yards along from the parade-ring railing . . . one of them in a gray morning suit?"

"What about them?" Jik said.

"The man in the morning suit is Hudson Taylor, the man I just had a drink with. He's the managing director of a wine-making firm, and he saw a lot of my cousin Donald when he was over here. And the other man is called Ivor Wexford, and he's the manager of the Yarra River Fine Arts gallery."

"So what?" Sarah said.

"So I can just about imagine the conversation that's going on down there," I said. "Something like 'Excuse me, sir, but didn't I sell a picture to you recently?' 'Not to me, Mr. Wexford, but to my friend Donald Stuart.' 'And who was that young man I saw you talking to just now?' 'That was Donald Stuart's cousin, Mr. Wexford.' 'And what do you know about him?' 'That he's a painter by trade and drew a picture of you and asked me for your name.' "

I stopped. "Go on," Jik said.

I watched Wexford and Hudson Taylor stop talking, nod casually to each other, and walk their separate ways.

"Ivor Wexford now knows he made a horrible mistake in letting me out of his gallery last night." I tried a smile. "At the least, he'll be on his guard."

"And at the most," Jik said, "he'll come looking for you."

"Er . . ." I said thoughtfully, "what do either of you feel about a spot of instant travel?"

"Where to?"

"Alice Springs?" I said.

# CHAPTER FIVE

JIK complained all the way to the airport. One, he would be missing the cricket. Two, his Derby clothes would be too hot in Alice. Three, he wasn't missing the Melbourne Cup for any little creep with a bow tie. None of the colorful gripes touched on the fact that he was paying for all our fares with his credit card, as I had left my traveler's checks in the hotel. It had been Sarah's idea not to go back there.

"If we're going to vanish, let's get on with it," she said.

As far as I could tell, no one had followed us from the racecourse to the airport. We traveled on a half-full aircraft to Adelaide and an even emptier one from there to Alice Springs.

The country beneath us from Adelaide north turned gradually from fresh green to gray green, and finally to brick red. The land looked baked, deserted, and older than time, but there were track-like roads here and there, and incredibly isolated homesteads. I watched in fascination until it grew dark, the purple shadows rushing in like a tide as we swept into the central wastelands.

The night air at Alice was hot, as if someone had forgotten to switch off the oven. A taciturn taxi driver took us straight to a new-looking motel, which proved to have air-conditioned rooms.

Jik and Sarah's room was on the ground floor, their door opening directly onto a shady walk that bordered a small garden with a pool. Mine, in an adjacent wing across the car park, was two tall floors up, reached by an outside tree-shaded staircase and a long open balcony. The whole place looked greenly peaceful in the scattered spotlights that shone unobtrusively from palms and gums.

The motel restaurant had closed for the night, so we walked along to another. The main street was macadam, but some of the side roads were not, nor were the footpaths uniformly paved. Often enough we were walking on bright red grit.

"Bull dust," Sarah said. "My aunt swore it got inside her locked trunk once when she and my uncle drove out to Ayers Rock."

"What's Ayers Rock?" I said.

"A chunk of sandstone two miles long and about a quarter of a mile high, left behind by a glacier in the Ice Age."

"Miles out in the desert," Jik added. "A place of ancient magic regularly desecrated by the plastic society."

We reached the restaurant and ate a meal of such excellence as to make one wonder at the organization it took to bring every item of food and clothing and everyday life to an expanding town of thirteen and a half thousand inhabitants surrounded by hundreds of miles of desert.

"It was started here, a hundred years ago, as a relay station for sending cables across Australia," Sarah said. "And now they're bouncing messages off the stars."

We walked back a different way and sought out the Yarra River Fine Arts gallery, Alice Springs variety. It was in a prosperous-looking shopping arcade. From what we could see in the single dim streetlight, the merchandise in the window consisted of two bright orange landscapes of desert scenes.

"Crude," said Jik, whose own colors were not noted for pastel subtlety. "The whole place will be full of local copies of Albert Namatjira. Tourists buy them by the ton."

We strolled back to the motel more companionably than at any time since my arrival. Maybe the desert invoked its own peace. At any rate, when I kissed Sarah's cheek to say good night, it was no longer as a sort of pact, as in the morning, but with affection.

At breakfast she said, "You'll never guess. The main street here is Todd Street. So is the river. Todd River."

"Such is fame," I said modestly.

"And there are eleven art galleries."

"She's been reading the Alice Springs Tourist Promotion Association Inc.'s handout," Jik explained.

The daytime heat was fierce. The radio was cheerfully forecasting a noon temperature of thirty-nine, which was a hundred and two in the old Fahrenheit shade. The walk to the Yarra River gallery, though less than half a mile, was exhausting.

"I suppose one would get used to it if one lived here," Jik said. "Thank God, Sarah's got her hat."

We dodged in and out of the shadows of overhanging trees, and the local inhabitants marched around bareheaded, as if the branding iron in the sky were pointing another way. The Yarra River gallery was quiet and air-conditioned.

As Jik had prophesied, all visible space was knee-deep in the hard clear watercolor paintings typical of the disciples of Namatjira. They were fine if you liked that sort of thing. I preferred the occasional fuzzy outline, indistinct edge, impression, and ambiguity. Namatjira, given his due as the first and greatest of the aboriginal artists, had had a vision as sharp as a diamond. He'd produced about two thousand paintings, and his influence on Alice Springs had been extraordinary. Mecca for artists. Tourists buying pictures by the ton. He had died, a plaque on the wall said, in Alice Springs Hospital on August 8, 1959.

"See anything you fancy?" the gallery keeper asked.

His voice conveyed an utter boredom with tourists. He was small, languid, long-haired, and pale, and had large dark eyes with tired-looking lids. About the same age as Jik and myself.

"Do you have any other pictures?" I asked.

He glanced at our clothes. Jik and I wore the trousers and shirts in which we'd gone to the races, but no ties and no jackets. Without discernible enthusiasm he held back half of a plastic-strip curtain, inviting us to go through. "In here," he said.

The inner room was bright from skylights, and its walls were covered with dozens of pictures. Our eyes opened wide. At first sight we were surrounded by an incredible feast of Dutch interiors, French impressionists, and Gainsborough portraits. At second blink one could see that although they were original oil paintings, they were basically second-rate. The sort sold as "school of" because the artists hadn't bothered to sign them.

"Do you have any pictures of horses?" I asked.

The gallery keeper gave me a long steady gaze. "Yes, we do. They are in racks through there." He pointed to a second plastic-strip curtain directly opposite the first. "Are you looking for anything in particular?"

I murmured the names of some of the Australians whose work I had seen in Melbourne. There was a slight brightening of the lackluster eyes.

"Yes, we do have a few by those artists."

He led us into the third room. Half of it was occupied by tiers of racks. The other half was the office and packing department. Directly ahead, a glass door led out to a garden.

Beside the glass door stood an easel bearing a small canvas with its back toward us. Various signs showed work recently interrupted.

"Your own effort?" asked Jik, walking over for a look.

The pale gallery keeper made a fluttering movement with his hand, as if he would have stopped Jik if he could, and something in Jik's expression attracted me to his side like a magnet.

A chestnut horse, three-quarter view, its elegant head raised, as if listening. In the background, the noble lines of a mansion. The rest, a harmonious composition of trees and meadow. The painting, as far as I could judge, was more or less finished.

"That's great," I said with enthusiasm. "Is that for sale?"

After the briefest hesitation he said, "Sorry. That's commissioned."

"What a pity! Couldn't you sell me that one and paint another?"

He gave me a regretful smile. "I'm afraid not."

"Do tell me your name," I said earnestly.

He was unwillingly flattered. "Harley Renbo."

"Is there anything else of yours here?"

He gestured toward the racks. "One or two."

All three of us pulled out the paintings, making amateur-type comments.

"That's nice," said Sarah, holding a small picture of a fat gray pony with two country boys. "Do you like that?"

Jik and I looked at it. "Very nice," I said kindly.

Jik turned away, as if uninterested. Renbo stood motionless.

"Oh, well," Sarah said, "I just thought it looked nice."

We found one with a flourishing signature: Harley Renbo.

"Ah," I said appreciatively. "Yours."

Jik, Sarah, and I gazed at his work. Derivative Stubbs type. Elongated horses. Composition fair, anatomy poor, execution good, originality nil.

At our urging, he brought out two more examples of his work. Neither was better than the first, but one was a great deal smaller.

"How much is this?" I asked.

He mentioned a sum that had me shaking my head at once.

"Awfully sorry," I said. "I like your work, but . . ."

The haggling continued for a long time, but we came to the usual conclusion, higher than the buyer wanted, lower than the painter hoped. Jik lent his credit card, and we bore our trophy away.

"My God," Jik exploded when we were safely out of earshot. "Why the hell did you want to buy that rubbish?"

"Because," I said contentedly, "Harley Renbo is the copier."

"But this is his own abysmal original work."

"Like fingerprints?" Sarah said. "You can check other things he paints against this?"

"Got brains, my wife," Jik said. "But that picture he wouldn't sell was nothing like any Munnings I've ever seen."

"You never look at horse paintings if you can help it. That picture was a Raoul Millais."

"God."

We walked along the scorching street almost without feeling it.

"I don't know about you two," Sarah said, "but I'm going to buy a bikini and spend the rest of the day in the pool."

We all bought swimming things, changed, splashed around for

ages, and lay on towels to dry. It was peaceful in the shady little garden. We were the only people there.

"That picture of a pony and two boys that you thought was nice," I said to Sarah. "It was a Munnings."

She sat up abruptly on her towel. "Why didn't you say so?"

"I was waiting for our friend Renbo to tell us, but he didn't."

"A real one?" Sarah asked. "Or a copy?"

"Real," Jik said, with his eyes shut against the sun dappling through palm leaves.

I nodded lazily. "I thought so, too. Munnings had that gray pony for years when he was young, and painted it dozens of times."

"You two do know a lot," Sarah said, lying down again.

"Engineers know all about nuts and bolts," Jik said. "Do we get lunch in this place?"

I looked at my watch. Nearly two o'clock. "I'll go and ask."

I put shirt and trousers on over my sun-dried trunks and ambled into the lobby. No lunch, said the reception desk. We could buy lunch nearby at a takeaway and eat in the garden. Drink? Buy your own at a bottle shop. I told Jik and Sarah the food situation. "I'll go and get it," I said. "What do you want?"

Anything, they said. And Cinzano to drink.

I picked up my room key from the grass and set off to collect some cash. Walked along to the tree-shaded outside staircase, went up two stories, and turned onto the blazing-hot balcony. There was a man walking along it toward me, about my own height, build, and age; and I heard someone else coming up the stairs at my back. Thought nothing of it. Motel guests.

I was totally unprepared for the attack and for its ferocity. They reached me together. They sprang into action like cats. They snatched the dangling room key out of my hand, picked me up by my legs and armpits, and threw me over the balcony.

It probably takes a very short time to fall two stories. I found it long enough for thinking that my body, which was still whole, was going to be smashed. That disaster was inevitable.

What I actually hit first was one of the young trees growing round the staircase. Its boughs bent and broke, and I crashed on

through them to the hard driveway beneath. The monstrous impact was like being wiped out. Like fusing electrical circuits. A
flash into chaos. I lay in a semiconscious daze, not knowing if I was
alive or dead. I couldn't move any muscle. I felt like pulp.

It was ten minutes, Jik told me later, before he came looking for
me, and he came only because he wanted to ask me to buy a lemon
to go with the Cinzano, if I had not gone already.

"God Almighty." Jik's voice, low and horrified, near my ear.

I heard him clearly. I'm alive, I thought.

Eventually I opened my eyes. The light was brilliant. Blinding.
There was no one where Jik's voice had been. Perhaps I'd imagined
it. No, I hadn't. The world began coming back fast. I knew also that
I hadn't imagined the fall. I knew, with increasing insistence, that
I hadn't broken my neck. Sensation came flooding back from every
insulted tissue.

After a while I heard Jik's voice returning. "He's alive," he said.
"And that's about all."

"It's impossible for anyone to fall off our balcony." The voice of
the reception desk, sharp with anxiety. "It's more than
waist-high."

"Don't . . . panic," I said. It sounded a bit croaky.

"Todd!" Sarah was kneeling on the ground and looking pale.

"If you give me time . . . I'll fetch . . . the Cinzano."

"You gave us a shocking fright," Jik said, standing at my feet.
He was holding a broken-off branch of tree.

"Sorry."

"Shall I cancel the ambulance?" said the reception desk
hopefully.

"No," I said. "I think I'm bleeding."


ALICE Springs Hospital, even on a Sunday, was as efficient as
one would expect from a Flying Doctor base. They investigated and
x-rayed and stitched, and presented me with a list.

> One broken shoulder blade. (Left.)
> Two broken ribs. (Left side. No lung puncture.)
> Large contusion, left side of head. (No skull fracture.)

Four jagged tears in skin of trunk, thigh, and left leg.
(Stitched.)
Grazes and contusions on practically all of left side of body.

"Thanks," I said, sighing.

"Thank the tree. You'd've been in a mess if you'd missed it."

They suggested I stay there that night.

"Okay," I said resignedly. "Are my friends still here?"

They were. In the waiting room. "Hey," Jik said as I shuffled in.
"He's on his feet."

"Yeah." I perched gingerly on the arm of a chair, feeling a bit
like a mummy, wrapped in bandages from neck to waist, with my
left arm totally immersed, as it were, and anchored firmly inside.

"No one but a raving lunatic would fall off that balcony," Jik
said.

"Mmm," I agreed. "I was pushed."

Their mouths opened like landed fish. I told them exactly what
had happened.

"Who were they?" Jik said.

"I don't know. They didn't introduce themselves."

Sarah said definitely, "You must tell the police."

"Yes," I said. "But I don't know your procedures here, or what the
police are like. I wondered . . . if you would explain to the hospital,
and start things rolling in an orderly and unsensational manner."

"Sure," she said, "if anything about being pushed off a balcony
could be considered orderly and unsensational."

"They took my room key first," I said. "Would you see if they've
pinched my wallet?"

They stared at me in awakening unwelcome awareness.

I nodded. "Or that picture," I said.

Two policemen came, took notes, and departed. Very non-
committal. The locals wouldn't have done it. The town had a constant stream of visitors, so by the law of averages some would be
muggers. Their downbeat attitude suited me fine.

By the time Jik and Sarah came back, I was in bed, feeling absolutely rotten. Shivering. Gripped by the system's aggrieved reaction to injury—or, in other words, shock.

"They took the painting," Jik said. "And your wallet as well."

"And the gallery's shut," Sarah said. "So what do we do now?"

"Well, there's no point in staying here anymore. Tomorrow we'll go back to Melbourne."

"Thank God," she said, smiling widely. "I thought you were going to want us to miss the Cup."

I SPENT a viciously uncomfortable night. Unable to lie flat. Feverishly hot. Throbbing in fifteen places. I counted my blessings until daybreak. It could have been so very much worse.

What was most alarming was not the murderous nature of the attackers, but the speed with which they'd found us. I'd known ever since I'd seen Regina's head that the directing mind was ruthlessly violent.

I had to conclude that it was chiefly this pervading callousness which had led to my being thrown over the balcony. As a positive means of murder, it was too chancy. The men had not, as far as I could remember, bothered to see whether I was alive or dead, and they had not, while I lay half unconscious and immobile, come along to finish the job.

So it had either been simply a shattering way of getting rid of me while they robbed my room, or they'd intended to injure me so badly that I would have to stop poking my nose into their affairs. Or both. And how had they found us?

It seemed most likely that Wexford or Greene had telephoned from Melbourne and told Harley Renbo to be on his guard in case I turned up. But even the panic that would have followed the realization that I'd seen the Munnings and the fresh Millais copy, and actually carried away a specimen of Renbo's work, could not have transported two toughs from Melbourne to Alice Springs in the time available.

Perhaps we had been followed all the way from Flemington

Racecourse, or traced from the airplane passenger lists. But if that were the case, surely Renbo would have been warned we were on our way and would never have let us see what we had.

I gave up. I didn't even know if I would recognize my attackers again if I saw them. They could, though, reasonably believe they had done a good job of putting me out of action; and indeed, if I had any sense, they had.

If they wanted time, what for?

To tighten up their security and cover their tracks, so that any investigation I might persuade the police to make would come up against the most respectable of brick walls.

Even if they knew I'd survived, they would not expect any action from me in the immediate future; therefore, the immediate future was the best time to act.

Right. Easy enough to convince my brain. From the neck down, a different story.

Jik and Sarah didn't turn up until eleven.

"Todd," Sarah said. "You look much worse than yesterday. You're never going to make it to Melbourne."

"Nothing to stop you going," I said.

She stood beside the bed. "Do you expect us just to leave you here—like this—and go and enjoy ourselves?"

Jik sprawled in a visitor's chair. "It isn't our responsibility if he gets himself thrown from heights," he said.

Sarah whirled on him. "How *can* you say such a thing?"

"We don't want to be involved," Jik said.

I grinned. Sarah heard the sardonic echo of what she'd said herself three days ago. She flung out her arms in exasperation.

"You absolutely bloody beast," she said.

Jik smiled like a cream-fed cat. "We went round to the gallery. It's still shut. We looked in through the glass door in the back garden, and you can guess what we saw."

"Nothing."

"Right. No easel with imitation Millais. Everything dodgy carefully hidden out of sight. Everything else normal."

I shifted a bit to relieve one lot of aches, and set up protests from another. "Even if you'd got in, I doubt if you'd've found anything dodgy. I'll bet everything the least bit incriminating disappeared yesterday afternoon."

Sarah said, "We asked the receptionist at the motel if anyone had been asking for us."

"And they had?"

She nodded. "A man telephoned. She thought it was soon after ten o'clock. He wanted to know if a Mr. Charles Todd was staying there with two friends, and when she said yes, he asked for your room number. He said he had something to deliver to you."

"Why didn't she tell us someone had been inquiring for us?"

"She went off for a coffee break and didn't see us when we came back. And after that, she forgot."

"There aren't all that many motels in Alice," Jik said. "It wouldn't have taken long to find us. I suppose the Melbourne lot telephoned Renbo, and that set the bomb ticking."

"I guess."

"They must have been apoplectic when they heard you'd bought that picture."

"I wish I'd hidden it," I said. The words reminded me briefly of Maisie, who had hidden her picture and had her house burned.

Sarah sighed. "Well . . . what are we going to do?"

"Last chance to go home," I said.

"Are you going?" she demanded.

I listened to the fierce plea from my battered shell, and I thought, too, of Donald in his cold house. I didn't answer her.

She listened to my silence. "Quite," she said. "So what do we do next?"

"Well . . ." I said, "first of all, tell the girl at the motel that I'm likely to be in hospital for at least a week."

"No exaggeration," Jik murmured.

"Tell her it's okay to pass on that news, if anyone inquires. Tell her you're leaving for Melbourne, pay our bills, and make a normal exit to the airport on the airport bus."

"But when will you be fit to go?" Sarah asked.

"With you," I said. "If you can think of some way of getting a bandaged mummy onto an airplane without anyone noticing."

Jik looked delighted. "I'll do that."

"Book a seat for me under a different name. Buy me a shirt and some trousers. Mine are in the dustbin. And reckon all the time that you may be watched."

"Put on sad faces, do you mean?" Sarah said.

I grinned. "I'd be honored."

"And after we get to Melbourne, what then?" Jik said.

"We'll have to go back to the Hilton. Our clothes are there, and my passport and money. We don't know if Wexford and Greene ever knew we were staying there, so it may be safe."

"And tomorrow," Sarah said. "What about tomorrow?"

Hesitantly, with a pause or two, I outlined what I had in mind for Cup Day. When I had finished, they were both silent.

"So now," I said, "do you want to go home?"

Sarah stood up. "We'll talk it over," she said soberly. "We'll come back and let you know."

THEY came back at two o'clock lugging a large fruit-shop bag, with a bottle of Scotch and a pineapple sticking out of the top.

"Provisions for hospitalized friend," said Jik, putting them on the end of the bed. "Sarah says we go ahead."

I looked searchingly at her face. Her dark eyes stared steadily back, giving assent without joy. She was committed, but from determination, not conviction.

"Okay," I said.

"Item," said Jik, busy with the bag, "one pair of medium gray trousers. One light blue cotton shirt. You won't be wearing those, though, until you get to Melbourne. For leaving Alice Springs, we bought something else." With rising glee they laid out what they had brought for my unobtrusive exit from Alice Springs.

Which was how I came to stroll around the little airport with the full attention of everyone in the place. Wearing ragged, faded jeans. No socks. Rope-soled sandals. A brilliant orange, red, and magenta poncho over my shoulders like a cape. A sloppy white T-shirt underneath. A large pair of sunglasses. Artificial suntan on every visible bit of skin. And, to top it all, a large straw sun hat with a two-inch raffia fringe round the brim, the sort of hat worn in the bush for keeping flies away. Flies were the torment of Australia. The brushing-away-of-flies movement of the right hand was known as the Great Australian Salute.

On this hat there was a tourist-type hatband, bright and distinctly legible. It said, I CLIMBED AYERS ROCK.

Accompanying all this, I carried the airline bag Sarah had bought on the way up. Inside it, the garments of sanity.

They were both at the airport, sitting down and looking glum, when I arrived. They gave me a flickering glance and gazed thereafter at the floor, both of them, they told me later, fighting off terrible fits of giggles at seeing all that finery on the march.

I walked composedly to the postcard stand and took stock of the room. About fifty prospective passengers. Some airline ground staff. A couple of aborigines with patient black faces. No one remotely threatening.

The flight was called. The passengers, including Jik and Sarah, picked up their hand luggage and straggled to the gate. It was then that I saw him.

The man who had come toward me on the balcony to throw me over.

I was certain. He had been sitting among the waiting passengers, reading a newspaper, which he was now folding up. He watched Jik and Sarah go through to the tarmac. When they'd vanished into the aircraft, he made a beeline in my direction.

My heart lurched painfully. I absolutely could not run.

He looked just the same. Exactly the same. Young, strong, purposeful, as well coordinated as a cat. Coming toward me. He didn't even give me a glance. Three yards away he stopped beside a wall telephone and fished in his pocket for coins.

My feet didn't want to move. I was still sure he would recognize me. I could feel the sweat prickling under the bandages.

"Last call for flight to Adelaide and Melbourne."

I would have to walk past him to get to the door. I unstuck my feet. Walked. Waiting with every awful step to hear the voice shouting after me. Or, even worse, his heavy hand. I got to the door, presented the boarding pass, made it out to the tarmac. Couldn't resist glancing back. I could see him through the glass, earnestly telephoning and not even looking my way.

# CHAPTER SIX

I HAD a seat near the rear of the aircraft and spent the first part of the journey trying to arrange myself in a comfortable way. Finally I shut my eyes and wished I didn't still feel so shaky.

"Todd?" I opened my eyes. Sarah was standing in the aisle by my seat. "Are you all right."

"Mmm."

She gave me a worried look and I assembled a few more wits. "Sarah, you were followed to the airport. You'll very likely be followed from Melbourne. Tell Jik to take a taxi, spot the tail, lose him, and take a taxi back to the airport to collect the hired car. Okay?"

"All right."

She went up front to her seat. The airplane landed at Adelaide, people got off, people got on, and we took off again for the short flight to Melbourne. Halfway there, Jik paused beside my seat.

"Here are the car keys," he said. "Sit in it and wait for us."

He went without looking back. I put the keys in my jeans pocket and thought grateful thoughts to pass the time.

I dawdled a long way behind Jik and Sarah at disembarkation. My gear attracted more scandalized attention in this solemn financial city, but I didn't care in the least. Jik and Sarah walked straight out toward the queue of taxis. The whole airport was bustling with Cup-eve arrivals, but only one person that I could see was bustling exclusively after my fast-departing friends.

I smiled briefly. Young and eel-like, he slithered through the throng and grabbed the next taxi behind Jik's. They'd sent him, I supposed, because he knew Jik by sight. He'd flung turps in his eyes at the National Gallery.

Good, I thought. The boy wasn't overintelligent, and Jik should have little trouble in losing him. I eased out to the car park.

The night was chilly after Alice Springs. I unlocked the car, climbed into the back, took off the successful hat, and settled to wait for Jik's return.

They were gone nearly two hours.

"Sorry," Sarah said breathlessly, pulling open the car door and tumbling into the front seat.

"We had the devil's own job losing him," Jik said, getting in beside me in the back. "He stuck like a bloody little leech. That boy from the National Gallery."

"Yes, I saw him."

"We thought it would be better not to let him know we'd spotted him, if we could," Sarah said. "So we set off to the Naughty Ninety."

"It was packed," Jik said. "It cost me ten dollars to get a table. Marvelous for us, though. All dark corners and psychedelic-colored lights. We ordered some drinks, then got up and danced. When we saw him last, he was standing in the queue for tables. We got out through an emergency exit past some cloakrooms. We'd dumped our bags there when we arrived, and simply collected them again on the way out."

"Great."

With Jik's help I changed my clothes. We drove back to the Hilton, and walked into the lobby as if we'd never been away.

No one took any notice of us. The place was alive with excitement. People in evening dress flooding downstairs from the ballroom to stand in loud-talking groups before dispersing home. People returning from eating out, and calling for one more nightcap. Everyone discussing the chances of the next day's race.

"Night," I said to Jik and Sarah. "Thanks for everything."

"Thank us tomorrow," Sarah said.

THE NIGHT PASSED. Well, it passed.

In the morning I did a spot of one-handed shaving. Jik came up to help with my tie. I opened the door in underpants and dressing gown, and endured his comments when I took the latter off.

"God Almighty, is there any bit of you neither blue nor patched?"

"Help me rearrange these bandages. I'm itching like mad."

With a variety of oaths he undid the expert handiwork of the Alice hospital. The outer bandages were large strong pieces of linen, fastened with clips and placed so as to hold my left arm in one position, with my hand across my chest and pointing up toward my right shoulder. There was a tight cummerbund of adhesive strapping, presumably to deal with the broken ribs. And just below my shoulder blade a large padded dressing, which, Jik kindly told me, covered a mucky-looking bit of darning. "There are four lots of stitching," he said. "Looks like Clapham Junction."

We left untouched two dressings on my thigh and one below my knee. Then Jik untied my arm. I tentatively straightened my elbow. Nothing much happened except that the hovering ache stopped hovering and came down to earth. We designed a new and simpler sling that gave my elbow support but was less of a straitjacket. When we'd finished, we had a heap of bandages and clips left over.

"That's fine," I said.

We went downstairs and met Sarah in the lobby. She was wearing a neat, tailored cream dress with gold buttons, a touch of the military.

Around us a buzzing atmosphere of anticipation pervaded the throng of would-be winners, who were filling the morning with celebratory drinks.

"Don't forget," I told Sarah. "If you think you see Wexford or Greene at the racecourse, make sure they see you."

"Give me another look at their faces," she said.

I pulled the sketchbook out of my pocket and handed it to her again, though she'd studied it the previous evening.

"As long as they look like this, maybe I'll know them," she said.

Jik laughed. "Give Todd his due, he can catch a likeness. No imagination, of course. He can only paint what he sees."

Sarah said, "Don't you mind the awful things Jik says of your work, Todd?"

I smiled. "I know exactly what he thinks of it."

"If it makes you feel any better," Jik said, "he was the star pupil of our year. The art school lacked judgment, of course."

"You're both crazy."

I glanced at the clock. "Back a winner for me," I said to Sarah, kissing her cheek. "Number eleven."

Her eyes were dark with apprehension.

"Off you go," I said cheerfully. "See you later."

I watched them through the door and wished strongly that we were all going for a simple day out to the Melbourne Cup. The effort ahead was something I would have been pleased to avoid. The beginning, I supposed, was the worst. Once you were in, you were committed. But before, when there was still time to turn back, the temptation to retreat was demoralizing.

Sighing, I went to the reception desk and cashed a good many traveler's checks. Maisie's generosity had been farsighted.

Four hours to wait. I spent them in my room calming my nerves by drawing the view from the window. Black clouds hung around the sky like cobwebs. I hoped it would stay dry for the Cup.

Half an hour before it was due to be run, I left the Hilton, walking unhurriedly toward Swanston Street. I had taken my left arm out of its sling and threaded it gingerly through the sleeves of my shirt and jacket. A man with his jacket hunched over one shoulder was too memorable for sense.

Swanston Street was far from its usual bustling self. All the shops were shut, of course, because of the national holiday. People still strode along with the breakneck speed that seemed to characterize all Melbourne pedestrians, but they strode in tens, not thousands. Trams had vacant seats. Cars sped along with the drivers, eyes down, fiddling with radio dials. Fifteen minutes to the race that annually stopped Australia in its tracks.

Jik arrived exactly on time, driving up in the hired gray car and turning smoothly round the corner where I stood waiting. He stopped outside the Yarra River Fine Arts gallery, got out and opened the boot, and put on brown overalls.

I walked quietly along toward him. He brought out a small radio, switched it on, and stood it on top of the car. The commentator's voice emerged tinnily, giving details of the runners currently walking round the parade ring.

"All set?" Jik asked when I reached him. I nodded. He dived again into the boot, which held further fruits of his second shopping expedition in Alice Springs.

"Gloves," he said, handing me some and putting some on himself. "Handles and impact adhesive."

He gave me the two handles to hold. They were chromium-plated, with flattened pieces at each end, pierced by screw holes. I held each one steady while Jik covered the screw-plate areas with adhesive. We couldn't screw these handles where we wanted them. They had to be stuck.

The front of the gallery was recessed at the right-hand end to form a doorway. Between the front-facing display window and the front-facing glass door was a joining window at right angles to the street. To this sheet of glass Jik firmly stuck the handles at waist height. We returned to the car. We were not supposed to park there, but no one told us to move.

One or two people passed, turning their heads to listen to the radio on the car roof, smiling at the universal national interest.

*"Vinery carries the colors of Mr. Hudson Taylor, of Adelaide, and has a good outside chance. Fourth in the Caulfield Cup, and before that, second at Randwick against Brain-Teaser . . ."*

We walked back to the gallery, Jik carrying a glass cutter, the sort used in framing pictures. He applied the diamond cutting edge and pushed the tool round the outside of the pane. I stood behind him to block any passing curious glances.

"Hold the right-hand handle," he said as he started on the last of the four sides, the left-hand vertical.

I stepped past him and slotted my hand through the grip.

"When it goes," Jik said, "for God's sake don't drop it. Put your knee against the glass. Gently." He finished the fourth long cut. "Press smoothly."

I did. Jik's knee, too, was firmly against the glass. With his left hand he gripped the handle, and with the palm of his right he began jolting the top perimeter of the heavy pane. The big sheet cracked away evenly all round under our pressure and parted with hardly a splinter. The weight fell suddenly onto the handle I held in my right hand, and Jik steadied the now free sheet of glass.

"Don't let go."

The heavy vibrations set up in the glass by the breaking process subsided, and Jik took over the right-hand handle from me. He pivoted the sheet of glass so that it opened like a door. He stepped through the hole, lifted the glass up by the two handles, carried it several feet, and propped it against an inside wall.

He came out, and we went to the car. From there one could not see that the gallery was not still securely shut.

*"The horses will soon be going out onto the course. . . ."*

I picked up the radio. Jik exchanged the glass cutter for a metal saw, a hammer, and a chisel, and we walked through the unorthodox entrance as if it were all in the day's work. Often only the furtive manner gave away the crook.

We walked to the back. There was a bank of switches at the top of the stairs; we pressed those lighting the basement.

Heart-thumping time, I thought. It would take only a policeman to walk along and start fussing about a car parked in the wrong place to set Cassavetes and Todd on the road to jail.

*"Horses are now going out onto the course. . . ."*

We reached the foot of the stairs. I turned toward the office, but Jik took off fast down the corridor.

"Come back," I said urgently. "If that steel gate shuts down . . ."

"Relax," Jik said. "You told me." He stopped before reaching the threshold of the farthest room. Looked. Came back rapidly. "Okay. The Munningses are all there. Three of them. Also something else which will stun you. Go and look while I get this door open."

*"Cantering down to the start . . ."*

I trekked down the passage and looked into the Munnings room. The three paintings were still there. But there was something that, as Jik had said, stunned me. Chestnut horse with head raised, listening. Stately home in the background. The Raoul Millais picture we'd seen in Alice.

I went back to Jik, who with hammer and chisel had bypassed the lock on the office door.

"Which is it?" he said. "Original or copy?"

"Can't tell from that distance. Looks like real."

He nodded. We went into the office and started work.

*"Derriby and Special Bet coming down to the start now. . . ."*

I put the radio on Wexford's desk, where it sat like an hourglass ticking away the minutes as the sands ran out.

The desk drawers were all unlocked. One of the filing cabinets, however, proved to be secure. Jik's strength soon ensured that it didn't remain that way. In it we found a gold mine.

Not that I realized it at first. The contents looked merely like ordinary files with ordinary headings.

*"Moved very freely coming down to the start and is prime fit to run for that hundred-and-ten-thousand-dollar prize . . ."*

While I looked through the files, Jik began flicking through the many framed pictures standing in a row on the floor.

"Look at this," he said.

*"More than a hundred thousand people here today to see the twenty-three runners fight it out over the three thousand two hundred meters . . ."*

Jik was looking at the foremost of three canvases tacked onto wooden stretchers, which were tied loosely together with string. I peered over his shoulder. The picture had "Alfred Munnings" written large and clear in the right-hand bottom corner. It was a picture of four horses with jockeys cantering on a racecourse.

Jik ripped off the string. The two other pictures were exactly the same. "God Almighty," he said in awe.

*"Vinery has a good position, so it's not impossible . . ."*

"Keep looking," I said, and went back to the files. We needed more than those Munnings copies, and I couldn't find a thing.

"Look at this," Jik said. He was peering inside a large flat two-by-three-foot folder, the sort used in galleries to store prints.

I picked up a file. My eyes flicked over the heading. OVERSEAS CUSTOMERS. I opened the file. Lists of people, sorted into countries. Pages of them. A good many names crossed out.

*"They're running! And Special Bet is out in front. . . ."*

"Look at this," Jik said again, insistently.

Donald Stuart, Wrenstone House, Shropshire, England. Crossed out. I practically stopped breathing.

*"As they pass the stands for the first time, it's Special Bet, Foursquare, Newshound, Derriby, Wonderbug, Vinery. . . ."*

"Bring it," I said. "And the copies. We've got less than three minutes before the race ends and Melbourne comes back to life."

I shoved the file drawer shut. "Put this file in the print folder and let's get out."

I picked up the radio and Jik's tools.

*"Down the backstretch by the river it's still Special Bet with Vinery second. . . ."*

We went up the stairs. Switched off the lights. Eased round into a view of the car. Just as we'd left it. No policemen.

*"Here comes Ringwood very fast on the stands side."*

We walked steadily down the gallery. I went through our hole in the glass and stood once more, with a great feeling of relief, on the outside. Jik stacked everything in the boot.

We climbed into the car. The commentator was yelling.

*"Coming to the line, it's Ringwood by a length from Wonderbug, with Newshound third, then Derriby, then Vinery. . . ."*

The cheers echoed inside the car as we drove away.

*"Might be a record time. Just listen to the cheers. The results of the Melbourne Cup. In the frame . . . first, Ringwood, owned by Mr. Robert Khami . . . second, Wonderbug . . ."*

Jik parked at the Hilton, and we carried the folder and pictures up to my room. He moved with his sailing speed, economically and fast, to lose as little time as possible before returning to Sarah on the racecourse and acting as if he'd never been away.

"We'll be back here as soon as we can," he promised.

Two seconds after he'd shut my door, there was a knock on it. I opened it. "Which horse won the Cup?" Jik asked.

When he'd gone, I looked closely at the spoils. I became certain that we had hit the jackpot. I began to wish that we hadn't wasted time in establishing that Jik and Sarah were at the races. It made me nervous, waiting for them in the hotel with so much dynamite in my hands.

The list of overseas customers would to any other eyes have seemed harmless. Each page had three columns, a narrow one at each side with a broad one in the center. The left-hand column was for dates and the center for names and addresses. In the right-hand column was a short line of apparently random letters and numbers. Those against Donald's entry were MM3109T; and these figures had not been crossed out with his name. Maybe a stock list, I thought, identifying the picture he'd bought.

I searched rapidly down all the other crossed-out names in the England sector. Maisie Matthews's name was not among them. Damn, I thought. Why wasn't it?

I turned all the papers over rapidly. As far as I could see, all the overseas customers came from English-speaking countries, and the proportion of crossed-out names was about one in three. If every crossing out represented a robbery, there had been hundreds since the scheme began.

At the back of the file I found a shorter section, again divided into pages for each country.

England. Halfway down. My eyes leaped at it. Mrs. Matthews, Treasure Holme, Worthing, Sussex. Crossed out.

I trembled. The date in the left-hand column looked like the date on which Maisie had bought her picture. The uncrossed-out numbers in the right-hand column were SMC29R.

I had a great deal to do before Jik and Sarah came back.

The large print folder, which had so excited Jik, lay on my bed. I inspected the contents. It contained a number of line drawings like the one the boy artist had been coloring in the National Gallery. Full-sized outlines on white canvas, as accurate as tracings.

There were seven of them, all basically of horses. I guessed that three were Munningses, two Raoul Millaises, and the other two . . . I stared at the old-fashioned shapes of the horses. Herring, I thought, nodding. The last two had a look of Herring. Clipped to one of the canvases was a memo: "Don't forget to send the original. Also find out what palette he used, if different from usual."

I looked again at the three identical finished paintings that we had also brought away. They looked very much as if they might have started out themselves as the same sort of outlines.

The technical standard of the work couldn't be faulted. The paintings looked very much like Munnings's own. The paint was at the same stage of drying on all of them. They must have all been painted at once, in a row, like a production line. Red hat, red hat, red hat . . . It would have saved time and paint. The brushwork was painstaking and controlled. Nothing slapdash. The care was the same as in the Millais copy at Alice.

I was looking, I knew, at the true worth of Harley Renbo.

All three paintings were perfectly legal. It was never illegal to copy; only to attempt to sell the copy as real.

I set rapidly to work. First I used the hotel's photocopying machine. Then I paid my bill and Jik and Sarah's, telling the clerk we would leave later. Upstairs again, I packed all my things. That done, I did my best at rigging the spare bandages and clips back into something like the Alice shape, with my hand inside across my chest. No use pretending that it wasn't a good deal more comfortable that way.

The telephone rang and I picked up the receiver. Jik's voice, sounding hard and dictatorial. "Charles, will you please come down to our room at once?"

"Well . . ." I said, "is it important?"

"Bloody chromic oxide!" he exploded. "Can't you do anything without arguing?"

God. I took a breath. "Give me ten minutes. I'm . . . er . . . I've just had a shower. I'm in my underpants."

"Thank you, Charles," he said. The telephone clicked.

If ever we needed divine help, it was now. I picked up the telephone and made a series of internal calls.

"Please could you send a porter up right away to room seventeen eighteen to collect Mr. Cassavetes's bags?"

"Housekeeper? Please send someone along urgently to seventeen eighteen to clean the room, as Mr. Cassavetes has been sick."

"Please will you send the nurse along to seventeen eighteen at once, as Mr. Cassavetes has a severe pain?"

"Please will you send four bottles of your best champagne and ten glasses up to seventeen eighteen immediately?"

"Electrician? All the electrics have fused in room seventeen eighteen; please come at once."

"The water is overflowing in the bathroom; please send the plumber urgently."

"Please would you see to the television in room seventeen eighteen? There is smoke coming from the back."

That should do it, I thought. I made one final call, for a porter to collect my bags. Ten-dollar tip if they could be down at the entrance in five minutes. No sweat, an Australian voice assured me.

I left my door ajar for the porter and rode down to Jik's floor. The corridor was empty. The ten minutes had gone.

I fretted.

The first to arrive was the waiter with the champagne. He came with a trolley, complete with ice buckets and spotless linens. It couldn't possibly have been better. As he slowed to a stop outside Jik's door, three other figures hurried into the corridor, and behind them, distantly, came a cleaner pushing another trolley, with buckets and brooms.

I gave the waiter a ten-dollar note, which surprised him. "Please serve the champagne straightaway."

He grinned, and knocked on Jik's door.

After a pause, Jik opened it. He looked tense and strained.

"Your champagne, sir," said the waiter.

"But I didn't—" Jik began. He caught sight of me suddenly, where I stood a little back from his door. I made waving-in motions with my hand, and a faint grin appeared on his face. He retreated into the room, followed by trolley and waiter.

Then, in quick succession, came the electrician, the plumber, and the television man. I gave them each ten dollars and thanked them for their promptness. "I had a winner," I said.

Jik looked across to me in rising comprehension. He flung wide his door and invited them in.

"Give them some champagne," I said.

After that came the porter and the nurse. I invited them all to join the party. Finally came the cleaner, pushing her heavy-looking load. She entered the crowded and noisy fray.

Jik and Sarah suddenly popped out like the corks from the gold-topped bottles. I gripped Sarah's wrist and tugged her toward me.

"Push the cleaning trolley through the door and turn it over," I said to Jik.

He wasted no time deliberating. The brooms crashed to the carpet inside the room, and Jik pulled the door shut after him. We ran to the lifts. One never had to wait more than a few seconds for one to arrive, but the seconds this time seemed like hours. The welcoming doors slid open, and we leaped inside and pushed the DOORS CLOSED button like maniacs.

The doors closed. The lift descended, smooth and fast.

"Where's the car?" I said to Jik.

"Car park."

"Get it and come round to the side door."

We erupted into the lobby, which had filled with people returning from the Cup. My suitcase and satchel stood waiting near the front entrance, guarded by a porter.

I parted with the ten dollars. "Thank you very much," I said.

"No sweat," he said cheerfully.

I picked up the suitcase, and Sarah the satchel, and we headed out the door. Turned right. Hurried. Turned right again, round to the side where I'd told Jik we'd meet him.

"He's not here," Sarah said with rising panic.

"He'll come," I said encouragingly. "We'll walk to meet him."

We walked. I kept looking back nervously for signs of pursuit, but there were none. Jik came round the corner on two wheels and tore millimeters off the tires, stopping beside us. We scrambled in. Jik made a hair-raising U-turn and sped us away.

"Wowee," he said, laughing. "Whatever gave you that idea?"

"The Marx Brothers."

"Where are we going?" Sarah said.

"Have you noticed," Jik said, "how my wife always brings us back to basics?"

THE city of Melbourne covered a great deal of land.

We drove randomly north and east through seemingly endless suburban developments of houses, shops, garages.

"Where are we?" Jik said.

"Somewhere called Box Hill," I said, reading it on shop fronts.

We drove a few miles farther and stopped at a motel which had strings of bright-colored flags fluttering across the forecourt. A far cry from the Hilton, though the rooms were clean and the hot tap ran hot in the shower.

There were plain daybeds, a square of nailed-down carpet, and a lamp screwed to an immovable table. The mirror was stuck to the wall and the swiveling armchair was bolted to the floor.

We sat in my room. "You do realize we skipped out of the Hilton without paying," Sarah said.

"No, we didn't," Jik said. "According to our clothes, we are still resident. I'll ring them up later."

"I paid," I said. "Before you got back."

She looked slightly happier.

"How did Greene find you?" I said.

"God knows," Jik said gloomily.

Sarah was astonished. "How did you know Greene was in our room? How did you know we were in trouble?"

"Jik told me," I said. "First, he called me Charles, which he never does, so I knew something was wrong. Second, he was rude to me, and I know you think he is most of the time, but he isn't, not like that. And third, he told me who was in your room. He mentioned chromic oxide, which is the pigment in green paint."

"Green paint! You really are both extraordinary," she said.

"Long practice," Jik said cheerfully.

"Tell me what happened," I said.

"We went back to the hotel after the last race. We'd only been in our room about a minute when there was this knock on the door, and when I opened it they just pushed in. Three of them. One was Greene. We knew him straightaway, from your drawing. Another was the boy from the National Gallery. The third was all biceps and beetle brows, with his brains in his fists."

He absentmindedly rubbed an area south of his heart.

"He punched you?" I said.

"It was all so quick," he said apologetically. "They just crammed in . . . and biff bang. The next thing I knew, they'd got hold of Sarah and were twisting her arm and saying that she wouldn't just get turps in her eyes if I didn't get you to come at once."

"Did they have a gun?" I asked.

"No, a cigarette lighter. Look, I'm sorry, mate. I guess it sounds pretty feeble, but Beetle Brows had her in a pretty rough grasp, and Greene said they'd burn her if I didn't get you. And I couldn't fight them all at once."

"Stop apologizing," I said.

"Yeah. Well, so I rang you. I told Greene you'd be ten minutes because you were in your underpants. I hoped to God you'd cottoned on. You should have seen their faces when the waiter pushed the trolley in. Beetle Brows let go of Sarah, and the boy stood there with his mouth open."

"Greene said he didn't want the champagne," Sarah said. "But Jik asked the waiter to open it at once."

"Before he got the first cork out, the others all began coming, and then they were all picking up glasses, and Greene and the boy and Beetle Brows were all on the window side of the room, pinned in by the trolley and all those people, and I just grabbed Sarah and we ducked round the edge. The last I saw, Greene and the others were trying to push through, but our guests were keen to get their champagne."

"How did Greene know I was in the Hilton?" I asked.

There was a tangible silence.

"I told him," Sarah said finally. "At first he said they'd burn my face if Jik didn't tell them where you were. He didn't want to, but he had to. So I told them, so that it wouldn't be him. I suppose that sounds stupid."

I thought it sounded extraordinarily moving. I smiled. "So they didn't know I was there, to begin with?"

Jik shook his head. "I don't think they knew you were even in Melbourne. They seemed surprised when Sarah said you were upstairs. I think all they knew was that you weren't still in hospital in Alice Springs."

"Did they know about our robbery?"

"I'm sure they didn't."

I grinned. "They'll be schizophrenic when they find out."

Jik and I both shied away from what would have happened if I'd gone to their room. With Sarah held hostage, I would have had to leave with Greene and take my chance. The uncomfortably slim chance that they would have let me off again with my life.

"I'm hungry," I said.

Sarah smiled. "Whenever are you not?"

WE ATE in a small restaurant nearby, with people at tables all around us talking about what they'd backed in the Cup.

"Good heavens!" Sarah exclaimed. "I'd forgotten your winnings. On Ringwood. It was number eleven!"

"I don't believe it."

She opened her handbag and produced a fat wad of notes. Somehow, in all the melee in the Hilton, she had managed to emerge from fiery danger with her leather pouch swinging from her arm.

"It was forty to one," she said. "I put twenty dollars on for you, so you've got eight hundred dollars. It's disgusting."

"Share it," I said, laughing. "I owe most of it to Jik, anyway."

"Keep it," he said. "We'll add and subtract later. Let me cut your steak." He sliced away neatly at my plate, and pushed it back with the fork placed ready.

"What else happened at the races?" I said, spearing the first succulent piece. "Who did you see?" The steak tasted good, and I realized that I had at last lost the overall feeling of shaky sickness. Things were on the mend.

"We didn't see Greene," Jik said. "Or the boy, or Beetle Brows."

"I'd guess they saw you at the races and simply followed you back to the hotel."

"I'm bloody sorry, Todd."

"Don't be silly. And no harm done."

"We talked to a lot of people," Jik said. "To everyone Sarah knew even slightly. It would be easy to prove I was at the races all afternoon."

"We even talked to that man you met on Saturday," Sarah agreed, nodding. "Or, rather, he came over and talked to us."

"Hudson Taylor?" I asked.

"The one you saw with Wexford," Jik said. "He asked if you were at the Cup. He wanted to invite you for a drink."

"Another commission down the drain," I said. "He would have had his horse painted if he'd won."

"You hire yourself out like a prostitute," Jik said.

"And anyway," added Sarah cheerfully, "you won more on Ringwood than you'd've got for the painting."

I looked pained, and Jik laughed.

We drank coffee, went back to the motel, and divided to our rooms. Five minutes later Jik knocked on my door.

"Come in," I said, opening it. "Thought you might come."

He sat in the armchair. His gaze fell on my open suitcase. "What did you do with all the stuff we took from the gallery?"

I told him.

"You don't mess about, do you?" he said eventually.

"A few days from now," I said, "I'm going home. Until then, I aim to stay one jump ahead of Wexford, Greene, Beetle Brows, the National Gallery boy, and the toughs who met me on the balcony at Alice. Not to mention our copy artist, Harley Renbo."

"Do you think we can?"

"No. Not from here on. This is where you take Sarah home."

He shook his head. "I don't reckon it would be any safer than staying with you. We're too easy to find. We're in the Sydney phone book. What's to stop Wexford from marching onto the boat with a bigger threat than a cigarette lighter?"

"You could tell him what I've just told you."

"And waste all your efforts."

"Retreat is sometimes necessary."

"If we stay with you, retreat may never be necessary. And anyway"—the old fire gleamed in his eye—"it will be a great game. Cat and mouse. With cats who don't know they are mice chasing a mouse who knows he's a cat."

More like a bullfight, I thought, with myself waving the cape. Or a conjurer, attracting attention to one hand while he did the trick with the other. On the whole, I preferred the notion of the conjurer. There seemed less likelihood of being gored.

# CHAPTER SEVEN

I SPENT a good deal of the night studying the list of overseas customers. It was fine in its way, but would have been doubly useful with a stock list to match the letters and numbers. On the other hand, all stock numbers were a form of code, and if I looked at them long enough, maybe a pattern would emerge.

The majority began with the letter *M*, particularly in the first and much larger section. In the smaller section, the *M* prefixes were few, and *S*, *A*, *W*, and *B* were much commoner. Donald's number began with *M*. Maisie's began with *S*. Suppose *M* simply stood for Melbourne, and the *S* for Sydney. Then *A*, *W*, and *B*. Adelaide, Wagga Wagga, and Brisbane? Alice?

In the first section, letters and numbers following the initial *M* had no clear pattern. In the second section, though, the third letter was always *C*, the last letter always *R*, and the numbers, though divided among different countries, progressed more or less consecutively. The highest number was fifty-four, sold to a Mr. Norman Updike, of Auckland, New Zealand. The stock number against his name was WHC54R. The date in the left-hand column was only a week old, and Mr. Updike had not been crossed out.

All the pictures in the shorter section had been sold within the past three years. The early dates in the longer section were five and a half years old.

I wondered which had come first five and a half years ago, the gallery or the idea. Had Wexford originally been a crook setting up a front, or a formerly honest art dealer struck by criminal possibilities? From the respectable air of the gallery and what I'd seen of Wexford, I would have guessed the latter. But the violence lying just below the surface didn't match.

I sighed, put down the lists, and switched off the light. I thought of the telephone call I'd made after Jik had left. The line had been loud and clear. "You got my cable?" I said.

"Yes. I've been waiting for your call for half an hour. What do you want?"

"I've sent you a letter. I want to tell you what's in it." I spoke for a long time to a response of grunts from the far end.

"Are you sure of all this?"

"Positive about most," I said. "Some of it's a guess."

"What do you intend doing now?"

"I'm going home soon. Before that, I think I'll keep looking into things that aren't my business."

"I don't approve of that."

I grinned. "I suppose you don't, but if I'd stayed in England, we wouldn't have got this far. Can I reach you quickly by telex?"

"Yes." A number followed. I wrote it down. "Head it urgent."

"Right," I said. "And could you get an answer to some questions for me?" He listened, and said he could. "Thank you very much," I said. "And good night."

IN THE morning we checked out of the motel and sat in the car to plan the day.

"*Can't* we get our clothes from the Hilton?" Sarah asked.

Jik and I said "No" together.

"I'll ring them now," Jik said. "I'll get them to pack all our things and keep them safe for us, and I'll tell them I'll send a check for the champagne." He went off to phone.

"I wish all this were over," Sarah said.

"It will be soon," I said neutrally. She sighed heavily. "What's your idea of a perfect life?" I asked.

She seemed surprised. "I suppose right now I just want to be with Jik on the boat and have fun, like before you came."

"And forever?"

She looked at me broodingly. "You may think that I don't know Jik is a complicated character, but you've only got to look at his paintings. They make me shudder. They're a side of Jik I don't know, because he hasn't painted anything since we met. But I know that in the end whatever it is that drives him to paint like that will come back again. . . . I think these first few months together are precious. And it isn't just the dangers you've dragged us into that I hate, but the feeling that I've lost the rest of that golden time, that you remind him of his painting, and that after you've gone he'll go straight back to it . . . weeks and weeks before he might have. But you don't care, do you?"

I looked straight into her clouded brown eyes. "I care for you both, very much."

"Then God help the people you hate."

And God help me, I thought, if I became any fonder of my oldest friend's wife. I looked away from her, out the window.

Jik came back. "All fixed. They said there's a letter for you, Todd, delivered by hand a few minutes ago. They asked me for a forwarding address. I said you'd call them yourself."

"Right. Let's get going."

"Where to?"

"New Zealand, don't you think?"

"That should be far enough," Jik said dryly.

He drove us to the airport, which was packed with people going home from the Cup.

"If Wexford and Greene are looking for us," Sarah said, "they will surely be watching at the airport."

If they weren't, I thought, we'd have to lay a trail; but Jik, who knew that, didn't tell her.

"They can't do much in public," he said comfortingly.

We bought tickets and found we could fly to Auckland at lunchtime. "Let's see if the restaurant's still open for breakfast," I said.

We squeezed in under the waitresses' pointed consultation of clocks and watches, and ordered bacon and eggs.

"Why are we going to New Zealand?" Sarah asked.

"To see a man about a painting."

"I don't see why we have to go so far, when Jik said you found enough in the gallery to blow the whole thing wide open."

"Um . . ." I said. "Because we don't want to blow it wide open." Because we want to hand it to the police in full working order."

She studied my face. "You are very devious."

"Not on canvas," Jik said.

After we'd eaten, we wandered around the airport shops, buying toothbrushes and so on for Jik and Sarah, and another airline bag. There was no sign of a tail.

I rang the Hilton. "I'm calling about a forwarding address," I told the reception desk. "I can't give you one. I'm flying to Auckland in an hour or two."

They asked for instructions about the hand-delivered letter.

"Er . . . would you mind opening it and reading it to me?"

Certainly, they said. The letter was from Hudson Taylor, saying he was sorry to have missed me at the races, and that if I would like to see a vineyard, he would be pleased to show me his.

Thanks, I said. If anyone asked for me, would they please mention where I'd gone.

During the next hour, Jik called the car-hire firm about settling their account and leaving the car in the airport car park, and I checked my suitcase through. Passports were no problem; I had mine with me, but for Jik and Sarah they were unnecessary, as passage between New Zealand and Australia was unrestricted.

Still no sign of Wexford or Greene. We sat in the departure bay thinking private thoughts.

It was only when our flight was called that I spotted a spotter. The prickles rose again on my skin. I'd been blind, I thought.

A neat dress, neat hair. A calm face. She was standing outside the departure bay, staring at Sarah. The woman who had welcomed me into the Yarra River Fine Arts, and given me a catalogue, and let me out again afterward. As if she felt my eyes upon her, she switched her gaze abruptly to my face. I looked away instantly, blankly, hoping she wouldn't know I'd seen her.

Jik, Sarah, and I stood up and drifted with everyone else to the departure doors. In their glass I could see the woman's reflection, watching us. I walked to the plane and didn't look back.

Mrs. Norman Updike stood in her doorway, shook her head, and said that her husband would not be home until six. She was sharp-featured and talked with tight New Zealand vowels. She looked us over: Jik with his rakish beard, Sarah in her slightly crumpled dress, I with my arm in a sling. She watched us retreat down her front path with a turned-down mouth.

"Dear gentle soul," murmured Jik.

We drove away in the car we had hired at the airport.

"Where now?" Jik said.

"Shops." Sarah was adamant. "I must have some clothes."

The shops, it appeared, were in Queen Street, and still open. Jik and I sat in the car while Sarah went in. She returned wearing a light olive skirt with a pink shirt, and reminded me of pistachio ice cream. "That's better," she said, tossing two well-filled shopping bags onto the backseat. "Off we go, then."

The therapeutic value of the new clothes amazed me. She seemed to feel safer if she looked fresh and clean, her spirits rising accordingly.

We dawdled back to the hill overlooking the bay, where Norman Updike's house stood in a crowded suburban street. The residence was large, and Norman Updike proved as expansive as his wife was closed in. He had a round shiny bald head on a round body, and he called his spouse Chuckles, without apparently intending satire.

We said, Jik and I, that we were professional artists who would be grateful if we could admire the noted picture he had just bought.

"Did the gallery send you?" he asked, beaming.

"Sort of," Jik said. "My friend here is a well-known painter of horses and has been hung often at the Royal Academy."

I thought he was laying it on a bit too thick, but Norman Updike was impressed and pulled wide his door. "Come in. Come in."

He showed us into a large overstuffed room with ankle-deep carpet, big dark cupboards, and a glorious view of sunlit water.

Chuckles, sitting solidly in front of a television busy with a moronic British comic show, gave us a sour look and no greeting.

"Over here." Norman Updike beamed, threading his way round a battery of fat armchairs. "What do you think?"

We looked at the painting. A black horse, with an elongated neck curving against a blue and white sky; the grass in the foreground yellow; and the whole covered with an old-looking varnish.

"Herring," I murmured. "May I look at the brushwork?"

"Go right ahead."

I looked closely. It was very good. It did look like Herring, dead since 1865. It also looked like the meticulous Renbo.

"Beautiful," I said. "You'd better beware of burglars."

He laughed. "We've got alarms all over this house."

We looked round the room and saw nothing much worth stealing. Updike watched us looking, and his beam grew wider.

"Shall I show these young people our treasures, Chuckles?"

Chuckles didn't even reply.

"We'd be most interested," I said.

He walked to one of the big cupboards that seemed built into the walls, and pulled open the double doors with a flourish.

Inside, there were six deep shelves, each bearing several complicated pieces of carved jade. Pale pink, creamy white, and pale green, smooth, polished, expensive. We made appreciative noises, and Norman Updike smiled even wider.

"Hong Kong," he said. "I worked there for years." He opened another cupboard. Inside, more shelves, more carvings.

"I'm afraid I don't know much about jade," I said.

He told us a good deal more about the ornate goodies than we actually wanted to know.

"You used to be able to pick them up very cheap in Hong Kong," he said.

Jik and I exchanged glances. I nodded slightly.

Jik immediately shook Norman Updike by the hand and said we must be leaving. Updike came with us to his front door.

"Mr. Updike," I said. "At the gallery, which man was it who sold you the Herring?"

"Mr. Grey," he said promptly. "Such a pleasant man. I told him I knew very little about pictures, but he assured me I would get as much pleasure from my little Herring as from all my jade."

"You did tell him about your jade, then?"

"Naturally. If you don't know anything about one thing, well, you try and show you do know about something else. Only human, isn't it?"

"Only human," I agreed, smiling. "What was the name of Mr. Grey's gallery?"

"Eh?" He looked puzzled. "I thought you said he sent you?"

"I go to so many galleries, I've forgotten which one it was."

"Ruapehu Fine Arts," he said. "I was down there last week."

"Down?"

"In Wellington." His smile was slipping. "Look here, what is all this? I don't think Mr. Grey sent you at all."

"No," I said. "Mr. Updike, we mean you no harm. We really are painters. But now that we've seen your jade collection, we think we must warn you. We've heard of several people who've bought paintings and had their houses burgled soon after. If I were you, I'd make sure the burglar alarms are working properly."

"But . . . good gracious . . ."

"There's a bunch of thieves about," I said, "who follow up the sales of paintings and burgle the houses of those who buy. I suppose they reckon that if anyone can afford, say, a Herring, they have other things worth stealing."

He looked at me with awakening shrewdness. "You mean, young man, that when I told Mr. Grey about my jade . . ."

"Let's just say that it would be sensible to take more precautions."

His round jolly face looked troubled. "Why did you bother to come and tell me all this?" he said.

"I'd do a great deal more to break up this bunch."

He asked "Why?" again, so I told him. "My cousin bought a painting. My cousin's house was burgled. My cousin's wife disturbed the burglars, and they killed her."

Norman Updike took a long slow look at my angry face and shivered convulsively.

I managed a smile. "Mr. Updike, please take care. And one day, perhaps, the police may come to see your picture and ask where you bought it. Anyway, they will if I have anything to do with it."

The round smile returned with understanding and conviction. "I'll expect them," he said.

WE DROVE from Auckland to Wellington—eight hours in the car—stopping overnight in Hamilton. No one followed us. I was sure that no one had picked us up in the northern city and no one knew we had called at the Updikes'.

Wexford must know, all the same, that I had the overseas customers list, and he knew there were several New Zealand addresses on it. He couldn't guess which one I'd pick to visit, but he would guess that any I picked with the prefix letter *W* would steer me straight to the gallery in Wellington. So, in the gallery in Wellington, he'd be ready.

We passed the turning to Rotorua and the land of hot springs. Anyone for a boiling mudpack? Jik asked. There was a power station farther on run by steam jets from underground, Sarah said, and horrid craters stinking of sulfur, and the earth's crust was so thin that it sounded hollow. She had been taken round a place called Waiotapu when she was a child, she told us, and had had terrible nightmares afterward, and she didn't want to go back.

"Somebody told me they have so many earthquakes in Wellington that all the new office blocks are built in cradles," Sarah said.

"Rock-a-bye, skyscraper," sang Jik, in fine voice.

The sun shone bravely, and the countryside was green with leaves. There were fierce bright patches and deep mysterious shadows; gorges and rocks and heaven-stretching tree trunks; feathery waving grasses, shoulder-high. An alien land, wild and beautiful.

"Get that chiaroscuro," Jik said as we sped into one particularly spectacular curving valley.

"What's chiaroscuro?" Sarah asked.

"Light and shade," Jik said. "Contrast and balance."

"Every life's a chiaroscuro," I said.

"And every soul."

"The enemy," I said, "is gray."

"No one," Sarah said, sighing, "would ever call you two gray."

"Grey!" I said suddenly. "Of course! Grey was the name of the man I wrote to about hiring the suburban art gallery in Sydney. And Grey is the name of the man who sold Updike his 'Herring.'"

"Oh, dear." Sarah's sigh took the dazzle from the day.

"Sorry," I said. There were so many of them, I thought. Wexford and Greene. The boy. The woman. Harley Renbo. Two toughs at Alice Springs, one of whom might, or might not, be Beetle Brows. And now Grey. And another one, somewhere. Nine at least. Maybe ten. Every time I moved, the serpent grew another head.

I wondered who did the actual robberies. Did they send their own toughs overseas, or did they contract out to local labor, so to speak? Had I already met Regina's killer? Had he thrown me over the balcony at Alice?

I pondered uselessly, and added one more twist: Was he waiting ahead in Wellington?

WE REACHED the capital in the afternoon and booked into the Townhouse Hotel because of its splendid view over the harbor. I looked up the Ruapehu Fine Arts in the telephone directory, and bought a local map at the reception desk.

I carried the map to Jik and Sarah's room. "Let's go and look at the gallery," I said. "They won't see us in the car if we simply drive past."

"And, after all," Jik said incautiously, "we do want them to know we're here."

"Why?" asked Sarah in amazement.

"Because," I said, "I want them to spend all their energies looking for us over here and not clearing away every vestige of evidence in Melbourne. We do want the police to deal with them finally, don't we, because we can't exactly arrest them ourselves. Well, when the police start moving, it would be hopeless if there was no one left for them to find."

She nodded. "That's what you meant by leaving it all in working order. But . . . you didn't say anything about deliberately enticing them to follow us."

"Todd's got that list, and the pictures we took," Jik said, "and they'll want them back. Todd wants them to concentrate exclusively on getting them back, because if they think they can get them back and shut us up—"

"Jik," I interrupted. "You do go on a bit."

"If they think they can get everything back and shut us up," Sarah said, "they will be actively searching for us in order to kill us. And you intend to give them every encouragement. Is that right?"

"No," I said. "Or, rather, yes."

"God give me strength," she said. "I see what you're doing, and I see why you didn't tell me. And I think you're a louse. But you've been more successful than I thought you'd be, and here we all are, safe and moderately sound, so all right, we'll let them know we're here. On the strict understanding that we then keep our heads down until you've alerted the police in Melbourne."

I kissed her cheek. "Done," I said.

"So how do we do it?"

I grinned at her. "We address ourselves to the telephone."

In the end, Sarah herself made the call, on the basis that her Australian voice would be less remarkable than Jik's Englishness or mine. "Is that the Ruapehu Fine Arts gallery? It is? I would like to speak to whoever is in charge. Yes, I'll wait. Oh . . . Hello? Could you tell me your name, please?" Her eyes suddenly opened wide. "*Wexford*. Oh. Mr. Wexford, I've just had a visit from three people who wanted to see a painting I bought from you some time ago. They said you'd sent them. I didn't believe them. I wouldn't let them in. But I thought perhaps I'd better check with you. Did you send them to see my painting?"

There was some agitated squawking from the receiver.

"Describe them? A young man with a beard, and another young man with an injured arm, and a bedraggled-looking girl."

She grimaced over the phone and listened to some more squawks.

"No, of course I didn't give them any information. Where do I live? Why, right here in Wellington. Well, thank you so much, Mr. Wexford; I am so pleased I called you."

She put the receiver down while it was still squawking.

Wexford himself. It had *worked*. I raised a small internal cheer.

"So now that they know we're here," I said, "would you like to go off somewhere else?"

"Oh, no," Sarah said instinctively. She looked out at the busy harbor. "It's lovely here, and we've been traveling all day."

I didn't argue. I thought it might take more than a single telephone call to keep the enemy interested in Wellington, and it had only been for Sarah's sake that I would have moved on.

"They won't find us just by checking the hotels by telephone," Jik pointed out, "and they'd be asking for Cassavetes and Todd, not Andrews and Peel."

"Are we Andrews and Peel?" Sarah asked.

"We're Andrews. Todd's Peel."

Mr. and Mrs. Andrews and Mr. Peel took dinner in the hotel restaurant without mishap, Mr. Peel having discarded his sling for the evening, on the ground that it was in general a bit too easy to notice. Mr. Andrews, however, had declined, on the same consideration, to remove his beard.

We went in time to our separate rooms, and so to bed. I spent a jolly hour unsticking the Alice bandages from my leg. The tree had made jagged tears, and I admired the long curving railway lines of stitching. In four days, during which time I hadn't been exactly inactive, none of the doctors' handiwork had come adrift.

I covered the mementos with fresh adhesive plaster and found a way of lying in bed that drew no strike action from mending bones. Things, I thought complacently, were altogether looking up.

I suppose one could say that I underestimated on too many counts. I underestimated the desperation with which Wexford had come to New Zealand. Underestimated the rage and the thoroughness with which he searched for us. Underestimated the fury our amateur robbery had unleashed in the professional thieves.

My picture of Wexford tearing his remaining hair in almost comic frustration was all wrong. He was pursuing us with a determination bordering on obsession, grimly, ruthlessly, and fast.

In the morning I woke late to a day of warm windy spring sunshine. Jik rang through on the telephone. "Sarah says she *must* wash her hair today. She wants me to drive her to the shops to buy some shampoo."

I said uneasily, "You will be careful?"

"Oh, sure. I'll call you as soon as we get back."

He disconnected cheerfully, and five minutes later the bell rang again. It was the girl from the reception desk. "Your friends say would you join them downstairs in the car."

"Okay," I said. I went jacketless down in the lift, left my key at the desk, and walked out. I looked round for Jik and Sarah, but they were not, as it happened, the friends who were waiting.

It might have been better if I hadn't had my left arm slung up inside my shirt. As it was, they simply clutched my clothes, lifted me off my feet, and bundled me into the back of their car.

Wexford was sitting inside. The eyes behind the heavy spectacles were as hostile as forty below, and there was no indecision this time in his manner. This time he as good as had me again behind his steel door, and he was intent on not making mistakes.

He still wore a bow tie. The jaunty polka dots went oddly with the unfunny matter in hand.

The muscles propelling me toward him turned out to belong to Greene and to a thug who answered the general description of Beetle Brows.

I ended up sitting between Beetle Brows and Wexford, with Greene climbing in front into the driving seat.

"How did you find me?" I said.

Greene, with a wolfish smile, took a Polaroid photograph from his pocket and held it for me to see. It was a picture of Jik, Sarah, and me, standing by the shops in Melbourne airport. The woman from the gallery, I guessed, had not been wasting time.

"We went round asking the hotels," Greene said. "It was easy." He started the car and drove out into the traffic. Wexford stared at me with a mixture of anger and satisfaction, and Beetle Brows began twisting my free right arm behind my back in an excruciating grip that forced my head practically down to my knees.

Wexford said finally, "We want our list back."

I'd been such a bloody fool, I thought miserably, just walking into it like that.

"Do you hear? We want our list back, and everything else you took."

I didn't answer. Too busy suffering.

After some time the car turned sharply left and ground uphill for what seemed like miles. Then the road began to descend.

Almost nothing was said on the journey. My thoughts about what very likely lay at the end of it were so unwelcome that I did my best not to allow them houseroom. I could give Wexford his list back, but what then? What then, indeed.

After a long descent the car halted briefly and then turned to the right. We had exchanged city sounds for those of the sea. We seemed to be on an infrequently used side road. The car stopped with a jerk. Beetle Brows removed his hands. I sat up stiffly.

They could hardly have picked a lonelier place. The road ran closely beside the sea, which was a jungle of rough black rocks with frothy white waves slapping among them, a far cry from the gentle beaches of home. On the right rose towering cliffs. Ahead, the road ended blindly in a sort of quarry. Slabs had been cut from the cliffs, and there were heaps of small jagged rocks and graded stones. All raw and harsh and blackly volcanic.

"Where's the list?" Wexford said.

Greene twisted round in the driving seat. "You'll tell us," he said. "With or without a beating. And we won't hit you with our fists, but with pieces of rock."

"What if I tell you?" I said.

The surprise on their faces was flattering, in a way. There was also a furtiveness in their expressions that boded no good at all. Regina, I thought. Regina, with her head bashed in.

I looked at the cliffs, the quarry, the sea. No easy exit. Behind us the road. If I ran that way, they would drive after me and mow me down. If I could run.

"I'll tell you . . ." I said. "Out of the car."

There was a small silence while they considered it; they weren't going to have room for much crashing around with rocks in that crowded interior.

Greene opened the glove compartment and drew out a pistol. He handled it with a great deal more respect than familiarity. He showed it to me silently and returned it to the glove compartment, leaving the flap door open so that it was in clear view.

We all got out, and I made sure that I ended up on the side of the sea. The wind was chilling in the bright sunshine. It lifted the thin hair away from Wexford's crown and left him straggly bald, and intensified the stupid look of Beetle Brows. Greene's eyes stayed watchful and sharp.

"All right," Wexford said roughly. "Where's the list?"

I whirled away toward the sea. I thrust my right hand inside my shirt and tugged at the sling. Wexford, Greene, and Beetle Brows shouted furiously and almost trampled on my heels.

I pulled the lists of overseas customers out of the sling, whirled again with them in my hand, and flung them as far into the water as I could. The pages fluttered apart in midair, but the offshore winds caught most of them beautifully and blew them like great leaves out to sea.

I didn't stop at the shoreline. I went straight on into the cold battlefield of shark's-tooth rocks and foaming waves. Slipping, falling, getting up, staggering on, finding the current much stronger than I'd expected, and the rocks more abrasive, and the footing more treacherous. Finding I'd fled from one deadly danger to embrace another. For one second I looked back.

Wexford had followed me a step or two into the sea, but only, it seemed, to reach one of the pages, which had fallen shorter than the others. He was standing there peering at the sodden paper.

Greene was leaning into the car. Beetle Brows had his mouth open.

I reapplied myself to the problem of survival. The shore shelved. Every step led into a stronger current, which shoved me around like a piece of flotsam. Hip-deep between waves, I found it difficult to stay on my feet, and every time I didn't, I was in dire trouble because of the needle-sharp rocks above and below the surface.

The rocks were the raw stuff of volcanoes, as scratchy as pumice. One's skin stuck to them and tore off. Clothes fared no better. Before I'd gone thirty yards, I was running with blood from a dozen superficial grazes. My left arm was still tangled inside the sling, which had housed the list since Cup Day as an insurance against having my room robbed. The wet bandages clung like leeches. I rolled around a lot from not having two hands free.

I scraped my shin on a submerged rock, fell forward, tried to save myself with my hand, failed, crashed chest first against a small jagged peak dead ahead, and jerked my head sharply sideways.

The rock beside my cheek splintered suddenly, as if exploding. Slivers prickled my face. I looked back to the shore with foreboding. Greene was standing there with the pistol, aiming to kill.

# CHAPTER EIGHT

THIRTY to thirty-five yards is a long way for a pistol, but Greene seemed so close. I could see his drooping mustache, and the lanky hair blowing in the wind. I could see his eyes and the concentration in his body. He was standing with his legs straddled and his arms out straight ahead, aiming the pistol with both hands.

I couldn't hear the shots or see him squeeze the trigger. But I did see the upward jerk of the arms at the recoil. I turned and stumbled a yard or two onward, though the going became even rougher and the relentless fight against current and waves and rocks was draining me to rags.

There would have to be an end to it. I slipped and fell on a jagged edge and gashed the inside of my right forearm, and out poured more good red life. God, I thought, I must be scarlet all over, leaking from a hundred tiny nicks. It gave me an idea.

I was waist-deep in dangerous water, with most of the shoreline rocks submerged beneath the surface. Close to one side, a row of bigger rock teeth ran out from the shore like a nightmarish breakwater, and I'd shied away from it. But it represented the only cover in sight. Three stumbling efforts took me nearer.

I looked back at Greene. He had reloaded the gun and was raising it again in my direction.

I took a frightful chance. I held my bleeding forearm close across my chest, and I stood up, visible to him from the waist up.

I watched him aim. It would take a marksman, I believed, to hit me with that pistol from that distance. A marksman whose arms didn't jerk upward when he fired.

All the same, I felt sick. The gun was pointing straight at me. I saw the jerk as he squeezed the trigger.

For a petrifying second I was convinced he had shot accurately, but I didn't feel or hear the passing of the flying death.

I flung my right arm high and paused there, facing him for a frozen second, letting him see that my shirt was scarlet with blood. Then I twisted artistically and fell flat, into the water, and hoped to God he would think he had killed me.

THE sea wasn't much better than bullets. Only extreme fear of the alternative kept me down in it, tumbling against the submerged razor edges like a piece of cheese in a grater. I couldn't struggle too visibly. If Wexford or Greene saw me threshing about, all my histrionics would have been in vain.

As much by luck as by trying, I found the sea shoving me into a wedge-shaped crevice between the breakwater rocks, from where I was unable to see the shore. I clutched for a handhold and then with bent knees found a good foothold, and clung there precariously while the sea tried to drag me out again. Every time a wave rolled in, it tended to float my foot out of the niche it was lodged in, and every time it receded, it tried to suck me with it. I clung in the chest-high water and grew progressively more exhausted.

I wondered forlornly how long Wexford and Greene would stay there, staring out to sea for signs of life. I didn't dare to look, in case they spotted my moving head. The water was cold, and the grazes gradually stopped bleeding. Absolutely nothing, I thought, like having a young strong healthy body. Absolutely nothing like having a young strong healthy body on dry land with a paintbrush in one hand and a beer in the other.

Fatigue, in the end, made me look. To look, I had to let go. The first outgoing wave took me with it in no uncertain terms, and its incoming fellow threw me back. In the tumbling interval I caught a glimpse of the shore. The road, the cliffs, as before. Also the car. Also people. Damn, I thought.

My hand scrambled for its former hold. My fingers were cramped, bleeding again, and cold. And then I realized that it wasn't Wexford's car, and it wasn't Wexford standing on the road. I rode the wave, then stood up gingerly and took a longer look.

A gray car. A couple beside it, standing close, the man with his arms round the girl. A nice spot for it, I thought.

They moved apart and stared out to sea. I stared back. For an instant it seemed impossible. Then they waved their arms furiously. It was Sarah and Jik.

Throwing off his jacket, Jik plowed into the waves, and came to a halt as the realities of the situation scraped his legs. All the same, he came on, after a pause, toward me, taking care. I made my slow way back. By the time we met, we were both streaked with red.

Jik put his arm round my waist and I held on to his shoulders, and together we stumbled to land. He let go when we reached the road. I sat down on the edge of it and positively drooped.

"Todd," Sarah said anxiously. She came nearer. "*Todd.*" Her voice was incredulous. "Are you *laughing?*"

"Sure." I looked up at her, grinning. "Why ever not?"

Jik's shirt was torn, and mine was in tatters. We took them off and used them to mop up the grazes that were still oozing.

"Your Alice Springs dressing has come off," Jik said.

"How're the stitches?"

"Intact."

I took off the remnants of sling. All in all, I thought, it had served me pretty well. I pulled off the adhesive rib-supporting cummerbund. That only left the plasters on my leg, and they, too, I found, had floated off in the melee.

"Quite a dustup," Jik observed, pouring water out of his shoes.

"We need a telephone," I said, doing the same.

"Give me strength," Sarah said. "What you need is hot baths, warm clothes, and half a dozen psychiatrists."

"How did you get here?" I asked.

"I came out of the shop where I'd bought the shampoo," Sarah said, "and I saw Greene drive past. I nearly died on the spot. I just stood still, hoping he wouldn't look my way, and he didn't. The car turned to the left, and I could see there were two other people in the back . . . and I went back to our car and told Jik."

"We thought it damn lucky he hadn't spotted her," Jik said. "We

went back to the hotel and you weren't there, so we asked the girl at
the desk if you'd left a message, and she said you'd gone off in a car
with some friends, with a man with a droopy mustache. So, choking down our rage, sorrow, indignation, and whatnot, we thought
we'd better look for your body."

"Jik!" Sarah protested.

"Sarah hadn't seen any sign of you in Greene's car, but we
thought you might be in the boot or something, so we got out the
map and set off in pursuit. Turned left where Greene had gone, and
found ourselves climbing a ruddy mountain."

I could hear Jik's teeth chattering even above the din of my
own.

"Let's get out of this wind," I said. "And bleed in the car."

We crawled stiffly into the seats.

"We drove for miles," Jik said. "Growing, I may say, a little frantic. Over the top of the mountain and down this side. At the bottom
of the hill the road swings round to the left, and we could see from
the map that it follows the coastline round a whole lot of bays and
eventually ends up right back in Wellington."

He started the car and rolled gently ahead. Naked to the waist,
wet from there down, and still with beads of blood forming, he
looked an unorthodox chauffeur. The beard, above, was undaunted.

"We went that way," Sarah said. "There was nothing but miles
of craggy rocks and sea."

"I'll paint those rocks," Jik said.

Sarah glanced at his face. The golden time was almost over.

"After a bit we turned back," Jik said. "There was this road saying No Through Road, so we came down it. No you. We stopped
here, and Sarah got out and started bawling her eyes out."

"You weren't exactly cheering yourself," she said.

"Huh," he said, smiling. "Anyway, I kicked a few stones about,
wondering what to do next, and there were those cartridges. On
the edge of the road."

"We should go back and pick them up," I said.

We retraced our tire treads. Jik stopped at the quarry, and
Sarah hopped out quickly to fetch the cartridge cases.

Jik shifted in his seat, wincing. "They must have gone back over the hill while we were looking for you." He glanced at Sarah, searching along the road. "Did they take the list?"

"I threw it in the sea." I smiled lopsidedly. "It seemed too tame just to hand it over, and it made a handy diversion. They salvaged enough to see that they'd got what they wanted."

"It must all have been a bugger."

"Hilarious."

Sarah picked up the six cartridge cases and came running back. "I'll put them in my handbag." She got into the car. "What now?"

"Telephone," I said.

"Like that?" She looked me over. "Have you any idea—" She stopped. "Well, I'll buy you each a shirt at the first shop we come to." She swallowed. "And don't say what if it's a grocery."

"What if it's a grocery?" Jik said.

We set off again. Near the top of the hill was a village with the sort of store that sold everything from hammers to hairpins. Also groceries. Sarah made a face at Jik and vanished inside.

I called the Townhouse from the telephone in the store. "But, Mr. Peel," said the girl, sounding bewildered, "your friend with the mustache paid your account not half an hour ago and collected all your things. . . . Yes, I suppose it is irregular, but he brought your note asking us to let him have your room key. . . . Yes, he took all your things; the room's being cleaned."

"Look," I said, "can you send a telex for me? Put it on my friend Mr. Andrews's bill."

She said she would. I dictated the message. "I'll call again soon for the reply," I said.

Sarah bought T-shirts and jeans for us, and dry socks. Jik drove out of the village to a more modest spot, and we put them on.

"Where now?" he said. "Intensive-care unit?"

"Back to the telephone."

"God Almighty."

He drove back, and I called the Townhouse again. The girl said she'd received an answer, and read it out. " 'Telephone at once, reverse charges.' " She read the number.

I gave the international exchange the number. The modern miracle. Halfway round the world, and I was talking to Inspector Frost as if he were in the next room. Eleven thirty in the morning at Wellington: eleven thirty the previous night in Shropshire.

"Your letter arrived today, sir," he said. "And action has already been started."

"Stop calling me sir. I'm used to Todd."

"All right. We telexed Melbourne to alert them, and we're checking on the people on the England list. The results are incredible. All the crossed-out names we've checked so far have been the victims of break-ins. We're alerting the police in all the other countries concerned. The only thing is, the list you sent is a photocopy. Do you have the original?"

"No. Most of it got destroyed. Does it matter?"

"Not really. How did the list come into your possession?"

"I think we'd better say it just did."

A dry laugh traveled twelve thousand miles. "All right. Now what's so urgent?"

"Two things. One is, I can save you time with the stock list numbers. But first . . ." I told him about Wexford and Greene being in Wellington and about their stealing my things. "They've got my passport and traveler's checks and also my suitcase, which contains painting equipment. They may also have a page or two of the list. They'll probably be going back to Melbourne today, and there's a good chance they'll be carrying those things with them."

"I can fix a customs search," he said. "But why should they risk stealing?"

"I think they believe I'm dead."

"Good God. Why?"

"They took a shot at me. Would cartridge cases be of any use?"

"They may be." His voice sounded faint. "What about the stock list?"

"In the shorter list, the first letter is for the city the painting was sold in: *M* for Melbourne, *S* for Sydney, *W* for Wellington. The second letter identifies the painter: *M* for Munnings, *H* for Herring, and *R* for Raoul Millais. *C* stands for copy. All the paintings on that list are copies. All the ones on the longer list are originals. Got that?"

"Yes. Go on."

"The numbers are just numbers. They'd sold Updike the fifty-fourth copy of a Herring when I . . . when the list reached me. The last letter, *R*, stands for Renbo. That's Harley Renbo, who was working at Alice Springs. If you remember, I told you about him last time."

"I remember," he said.

"Wexford and Greene have spent the last couple of days chasing around in New Zealand, so with a bit of luck they will not have destroyed anything dodgy in the Melbourne gallery. If the Melbourne police can arrange a search, there might be a harvest."

"It's their belief that the disappearance of the list from the gallery will have already led to the destruction of anything else incriminating."

"They may be wrong. Wexford and Greene don't know I photocopied the list and sent it to you. They think the list is floating safely out to sea, and me with it."

"I'll pass your message to Melbourne."

"There's also a recurring *B* on the long stock list, so there's probably another gallery. In Brisbane, maybe. There may also be another one in Sydney. I shouldn't think the suburban place I told you about had proved central enough, so they shut it."

"Stop," he said, "so I can change the tape on the recorder. . . ." Then, "You can carry on now."

"Well . . . did you get answers from Donald to my questions?"

"Yes, we did. Mr. Stuart's answers were 'Yes, of course' to the first question, and 'No, why ever should I?' to the second, and 'Yes,' to the third."

"Was he absolutely certain?"

"Absolutely."

"How is he?" I asked.

"He spends all his time looking at a picture of his wife. Every time we call at his house, we can see him through the front window, just sitting there."

"He is still . . . sane?"

"I'm no judge."

"You can at least let him know that he's no longer suspected of engineering the robbery and killing Regina."

"That's a decision for my superiors," he said.

"Well, kick them into it," I said. "Do the police positively yearn for bad publicity?"

"You were quick enough to ask our help," he said tartly.

To do your job, I thought. I didn't say it aloud. The silence spoke for itself.

"Well." His voice carried a mild apology. "Our cooperation, then." He paused. "Where are you now? When I've telexed Melbourne, I may need to talk to you again."

I read him the telephone number. "I want to come home as soon as possible," I said. "Can you do anything about my passport?"

"You'll have to find a consul."

Oh, ta, I thought. I hung up and wobbled back to the car.

"Tell you what," I said, dragging into the backseat. "I could do with a double hamburger and a bottle of brandy."

The store didn't sell liquor or hot food. Sarah bought a packet of biscuits. We ate them.

We sat in the car for two hours. "We can't stay here all day," Sarah said explosively, after a lengthy silence.

I couldn't be sure that Wexford wasn't out searching for her and Jik with murderous intent, and I didn't think she'd be happy to know it. "We're perfectly safe here," I said.

"Just quietly dying of blood poisoning," Jik agreed.

A delivery van stopped outside the shop. A man in a coverall opened the back, took out a large bakery tray, and carried it in.

Sarah went in to investigate. Jik took the opportunity to unstick his T-shirt from his healing grazes. "All these cuts didn't feel so bad when we were in the sea." He glanced at me. "Why don't you just scream or something?"

"Can't be bothered. Why don't you?"

He grinned. "I'll scream in paint."

Sarah came back with fresh doughnuts and cans of Coke. We made inroads, and I at least felt healthier.

Finally the storekeeper beckoned from the doorway.

I went stiffly to the telephone. It was Frost, clear as a bell. "Wexford, Greene, and Snell have booked a flight from Wellington to Melbourne. They will be met at Melbourne airport."

"Who's Snell?" I said.

"How do I know? He was traveling with the other two."

Beetle Brows, I thought.

"Now, listen," Frost said. "The Melbourne police want your cooperation, just to clinch things." He went on talking for a long time. "Will you do that?"

I'm tired, I thought. I've done enough. "All right."

"They want to know for sure that the three Munnings copies you . . . acquired from the gallery are still where you told me."

"Yes, they are."

"Right. Well . . . good luck."

# CHAPTER NINE

WE TOOK off for Melbourne, our passage oiled by telexes from above. A thousand miles across the Tasman Sea and an afternoon tea later, we were driven straight from the aircraft's steps to a small airport room, which contained a large Australian plainclothes policeman.

"Porter," he said, introducing himself and squeezing our bones in a blacksmith's grip. "Which of you is Charles Todd?"

"I am."

"Right on." He looked at me without favor. "Are you ill?"

"No," I said, sighing slightly.

"His clothes are sticking to him," Jik observed, giving the familiar phrase the usual meaning of being hot. It was cool in Melbourne. Porter looked at him uncertainly.

I grinned. "Did you manage what you planned?" I asked him. He decided Jik was nuts and switched his gaze back to me.

"We decided not to go ahead until you had arrived," he said, shrugging. "There's a car waiting outside."

The car had a chauffeur. Porter sat in front, talking on a radio, saying in stiltedly guarded sentences that the party had arrived and the proposals should be implemented.

"Where are we going?" Sarah said.

"To reunite you with your clothes," I said.

Her face lit up. "Are we really?"

"And what for?" Jik asked.

"To bring the mouse to the cheese." And the bull to the sword, I thought. And the moment of truth to the conjurer.

"We got your things back, Todd," Porter said with satisfaction. "Wexford, Greene, and Snell were turned over on entry, and they copped them with the lot. The locks on your suitcase were scratched and dented, but they hadn't been burst open. Everything inside should be okay. You can collect it all in the morning."

"That's great," I said. "Did they still have any of the lists?"

"Yeah. Damp but readable. Names of guys in Canada."

"Good."

"We're turning over that Yarra gallery now, and Wexford is there helping. We've let him overhear what we wanted him to, and as soon as I give the go-ahead, we'll let him take action."

We pulled up at the Hilton. Porter led us through a gate in the reception desk and into the hotel manager's office at the rear.

A member of the hotel staff offered us coffee and sandwiches. Porter looked at his watch and offered us an indeterminate wait.

It was six o'clock. After ten minutes a man brought a two-way radio for Porter, who slipped the earplug into place.

The office was a working room, with a wallpapering of charts and duty rosters. We sat, and drank coffee, and waited. Time passed. Seven o'clock.

Sarah was looking tired. So was Jik, his beard on his chest. At seven eleven, Porter clutched his ear and concentrated intently. When he relaxed, he passed to us the galvanic message.

"Wexford did what we reckoned he would, and the engine's turning over."

"What engine?" Sarah said.

Porter stared at her blankly. "What we planned," he said painstakingly, "is happening."

"Oh."

Porter listened again. "He's taken the bait."

Seven thirty came and went. The time dragged. Jik yawned, and Sarah's eyes were dark with fatigue. Outside, in the lobby, the busy life of the hotel chattered on, with guests' spirits rising toward the next day's race, the last of the carnival. No serious racegoers went home before International Day.

Porter clutched his ear again, and stiffened. "He's here."

My heart for some unaccountable reason began beating overtime. We were in no danger, yet there it was, thumping away like a calliope.

Porter went out into the foyer.

"What do we do?" Sarah said.

"Nothing much except listen."

We all three went to the door and held it six inches open. We listened to people asking for their room keys, for mail. . . . Suddenly the familiar voice, sending electric fizzes to my fingertips. Confident, not expecting trouble. "I've come to collect a package left here last Tuesday by a Mr. Charles Todd. He says he checked it into the baggage room. I have a letter here from him authorizing you to release it to me."

There was a crackle of paper as the letter was handed over.

Sarah's eyes were round. "Did you write it?" she whispered.

I shook my head. "No."

The desk clerk outside said, "Thank you, sir. If you'll just wait a moment, I'll fetch the package."

There was a long pause. My heart made a lot of noise.

The desk clerk came back. "Here you are, sir. Paintings, sir. Can you manage them?"

"Yes. Yes. Thank you." There was haste in his voice, now that he'd got his hands on the goods. "Good-bye."

Sarah had begun to say, "Is that all?" in disappointment when we heard Porter.

"I guess we'll take care of those paintings, if you don't mind," he said. "Porter, Melbourne police."

I opened the door a little more and looked out. Porter stood foursquare in the lobby, large and rough, holding out a demanding hand. At his elbows, two plainclothes policemen. At the front door, two more, in uniform.

"Why . . . er . . . Inspector . . . I'm only on an errand . . . for my young friend Charles Todd. He asked me to fetch these for him."

I walked quietly out of the office, through the gate, and round to the front. I leaned a little wearily against the reception desk. He was only six feet away.

"Mr. Charles Todd asked you to fetch them?" Porter said loudly.

"Yes, that's right."

Porter's gaze switched abruptly to my face. "Did you ask him?"

"No," I said.

The explosive effect was a good deal more than I expected. I should have remembered all my theories about the basic brutality of the directing mind.

I found myself staring straight into the eyes of the bull. He realized that he'd been tricked. The fury rose in him like a geyser and his hands reached out to grab my neck.

*"You're dead!"* he yelled. *"You're dead!"*

His plunging weight took me off-balance and down onto one knee, smothering under his choking grip, trying to beat him off with my fists and not succeeding. His anger poured over me like lava. Porter's men pulled him off before he did bloody murder on the carpet. As I got creakily to my feet, I heard the handcuffs click.

He was standing there, close to me, quivering in the restraining hands, breathing heavily, disheveled and bitter-eyed. Civilized exterior all stripped away by one instant of ungovernable rage. The violent core plain to see.

"Hello, Hudson," I said.

"Sorry," Porter said perfunctorily. "Didn't reckon he'd turn wild."

"He always was wild," I said. "Underneath."

Porter nodded to Jik and Sarah and finally to me, and hurried away after his departing prisoner.

We looked at each other a little blankly. We sat down weakly on the nearest blue velvet seat, Sarah in the middle. Jik took her hand and squeezed it. She put her fingers over mine.

It had taken nine days. It had been a long haul.

"Don't know about you," Jik said. "But I could do with a beer."

"Todd," said Sarah, "start talking."

We were upstairs in my bedroom, all of us in a relaxed mood.

I yawned. "Well . . . I was looking for Hudson Taylor, or some-one like him, before I ever met him."

"But why?"

"Because of the wine which was stolen from Donald's cellar," I said. "Whoever stole it not only knew it was there, down some stairs behind an inconspicuous door, but would have had to come prepared with proper cases to pack it in. Donald had two thousand bottles stolen. In bulk alone it would have taken a lot of shifting. And time. But also it was special wine. It needed expert handling and marketing if it was to be worth the difficulty of stealing it in the first place. And as Donald's business is wine, and the reason for his journey to Australia was wine, I started looking right away for someone who knew Donald, knew he'd bought a Munnings, and knew about good wine and how to sell it. And there, straightaway, was Hudson Taylor, who matched like a glove. But it seemed too easy; because he didn't *look* right."

"Smooth and friendly," said Sarah, nodding.

"And rich," Jik added.

"Probably a moneyholic," I said, pulling open the bed and look-ing longingly at the cool white sheets.

"A what?"

"Moneyholic. A word I've just made up to describe someone with an uncontrollable addiction to money."

"The world's full of them," Jik said, laughing.

I shook my head. "The world is full of drinkers, but alcoholics are obsessive. Moneyholics are obsessive. They never have enough. Like a drug. Moneyholics will do anything to get it. Kidnap, murder, rob banks, sell their grandmothers—you name it."

I sat on the bed with my feet up, feeling sore from too many bruises, on fire from too many cuts. They had been wicked rocks.

"Go on about Hudson," Sarah said.

"Hudson had the organizing ability. It was a huge overseas operation. It took some know-how."

Jik passed a can of beer to me, wincing as he stretched.

"But he convinced me I was wrong about him," I said, "because he was so careful." I sipped the beer. "He pretended he had to look up the name of the gallery where Donald bought his picture. He didn't think of me as a threat, of course, but just as Donald's cousin. Not until he talked to Wexford down on the Members' lawn."

"I remember," Sarah said. "When you said it had ripped the whole works apart."

"Mmm . . . I thought it was only that he had told Wexford I was Donald's cousin, but of course Wexford also told *him* that I'd met Greene in Maisie's ruins in Sussex and then turned up in the gallery, looking at the original of Maisie's burned painting."

"God," Jik said. "No wonder we beat it to Alice Springs."

"Yes, but by then I didn't think it could be Hudson. I was looking for someone brutal, and Hudson didn't look or act brutal." I paused. "Except when his gamble went down the drain at the races. He gripped his binoculars so hard that his knuckles showed white. But you can't think a man is a big-time thug just because he gets upset over losing a bet."

Jik grinned. "I'd qualify."

"I was thinking about it in the Alice Springs Hospital. There hadn't been time for the musclemen to get to Alice from Melbourne, between us buying Renbo's picture and me diving off the balcony, but there had been time for them to come from *Adelaide*, and Hudson's base was at Adelaide. It was much too flimsy, though."

"They might have been in Alice to start with," Jik said.

"They might, but what for?" I yawned. "Then on the night of the Cup you said Hudson had made a point of asking you about me, and I wondered how he knew you."

"Do you know," Sarah said, "I did wonder, too, at the time, but it didn't seem impossible that somewhere he'd seen you with us."

"The boy artist knew you," I said. "And he was at the races, because he followed you, with Greene, to the Hilton. The boy must have pointed you out to Greene."

"And Greene to Wexford, and Wexford to Hudson?" Jik asked.

"Quite likely."

"And by then," he said, "they all knew they wanted to silence you pretty badly, and they'd had a chance and muffed it. I'd love to have heard what happened when they found we'd robbed the gallery." He chuckled.

"On the morning after," I said, "a letter from Hudson was delivered by hand to the Hilton. How did he know we were there?"

They stared. "Greene must have told him," Jik said.

"That letter offered to show me around a vineyard," I said. "Well, if I hadn't been so doubtful of him, I might have gone. He was a friend of Donald's, and a vineyard would be interesting. From his point of view, anyway, it was worth a try.

"On the night of the Cup, when we were in that motel near Box Hill, I telephoned Inspector Frost in England. I asked him to ask Donald some questions, and this morning I got the answers."

"What questions and what answers?" Jik said.

"The questions were, Did Donald tell Hudson about the wine in his cellar? and Did Donald tell *Wexford* about the wine in the cellar? and Was it Hudson who had suggested to Donald that he and Regina go and look at the Munnings in the National Gallery? And the answers were 'Yes, of course,' and 'No, why ever should I?' and 'Yes.' "

They thought about it in silence. "So what then?" Sarah said.

"So the Melbourne police said that if they could tie Hudson in definitely with the gallery, they might believe it. So they dangled in front of Hudson the pictures and stuff we stole from the gallery, and along he came to collect them."

"How? How did they dangle them?"

"They let Wexford overhear a fake report from several hotels about odd deposits in their baggage rooms, including the paintings at the Hilton. Then, after we got here, they gave him an opportunity to use the telephone when he thought no one was listening, and he rang Hudson at the house he's been staying in here for the races, and told him. So Hudson wrote himself a letter to the Hilton from me, and zoomed along to remove the incriminating evidence."

"He must have been crazy."

"Stupid. But he thought I was dead . . . and he'd no idea anyone suspected him."

"You'd never have thought Hudson would blaze up like that," Sarah said. She shivered. "You wouldn't think people could hide such really frightening violence under a friendly public face."

"The nice bloke next door," Jik said, standing up, "can leave a bomb to blow the legs off children." He pulled Sarah to her feet. "What do you think I paint? Flowers?" He looked at me. "Horses?"

WE PARTED the next morning at Melbourne airport, where we seemed to have spent a good deal of our lives.

"Would you do it all again?" Jik said.

I thought of wartime pilots looking back from forty years on. Had their achievements been worth the blood and sweat and risk of death? Did they regret? I smiled. Forty years on didn't matter. What the future made of the past was its own tragedy. What we ourselves did on the day was all that counted. "I guess I would."

I leaned forward and kissed Sarah.

"Hey," Jik said. "Find one of your own."

# CHAPTER TEN

MAISIE saw me before I saw her, and came sweeping down like a great scarlet bird, wings outstretched.

Monday lunchtime at Wolverhampton races, misty and cold.

"Hello, dear, I'm so glad you've come. Did you have a good trip, because it's such a long way, isn't it, with all that wretched jet lag?" She peered at my face. "You don't look awfully well, dear, and you don't seem to have collected any suntan, and those are nasty gashes on your hand, dear, aren't they."

She stopped to watch a row of jockeys canter past to the start. Bright shirts against the gray mist. A subject for Munnings.

"Have you backed anything, dear? And are you sure you're warm enough in that anorak? And how did you get on in Australia? I mean, dear, did you find out anything useful?"

"It's an awfully long story."

"Best told in the bar, then, don't you think, dear?"

She bought us immense brandies with ginger ale and settled herself at a small table, her kind eyes alert and waiting.

I told her about Hudson's organization, about the Melbourne gallery, and about the list of robbable customers.

"Was I on it?"

I nodded. "Yes, you were."

"And you gave it to the police?" she said anxiously.

I grinned. "Don't look so worried, Maisie. Your name was crossed out already. I just crossed it out more thoroughly."

She smiled broadly. "No one could call you a fool, dear."

I wasn't so sure about that. "I'm afraid, though," I said, "that you've lost your nine thousand quid."

"Oh, yes, dear," she said cheerfully. "Serves me right, doesn't it, for trying to cheat the customs, though frankly, dear, in the same circumstances I'd probably do it again. But I'm ever so glad, dear, that they won't come knocking on my door this time—or, rather, my sister Betty's—because of course I'm staying with her again up here at the moment, until my house is ready."

I blinked. "What house?"

"Well, dear, I decided not to rebuild the house at Worthing, because it wouldn't be the same without the things Archie and I bought together, so I'm selling that plot of seaside land for a fortune, dear, and I've chosen a nice place just down the road from Sandown Racecourse."

"You're not going to live in Australia?"

"Oh, no, dear, that would be too far away. From Archie, you see, dear."

I saw. I liked Maisie very much.

"I'm afraid I spent all your money," I said.

She smiled. "Never mind, dear. You can paint me *two* pictures. One of me, and one of my new house."

I left after the third race, took the train to Shrewsbury, and from there traveled by bus to Inspector Frost's office.

He was chin-deep in papers. Also present, the unblinking Superintendent Wall, who had so unnerved Donald and whom I'd not previously met. Both men shook hands with me in a cool and businesslike manner. They offered me a chair.

Frost said, faintly smiling, "You sure kicked open an anthill."

"What about Donald?" I asked.

Wall said, "We have informed Mr. Stuart that we are satisfied the break-in at his house and the death of Mrs. Stuart were the work of outside agencies, beyond his knowledge or control."

Cold-comfort words. "And what about Mrs. Stuart? Donald wants her buried."

Frost looked up with an almost human expression of compassion. "The difficulty is," he said, "that in a murder case one has to preserve the victim's body in case the defense wishes its own postmortem. In this case, we have not been able to accuse anyone of her murder, let alone get as far as their arranging a defense."

He cleared his throat. "Your cousin already owes you a lot. You can't be expected to do more."

I smiled twistedly and stood up. "I'll go and see him."

Wall shook hands again, and Frost came out to the street with me. The lights shone bright in the early winter evening. "Unofficially," he said, walking slowly with me along the pavement, "I'll tell you that the Melbourne police found a list of names in the gallery which it turns out are of known housebreakers. There were four names for England. There's a good chance Mrs. Stuart's killer may be one of them. But don't quote me."

"I won't," I said. "So the robberies were local labor?"

"It seems to have been their normal method."

Greene, I thought. With an *e*. Greene could have recruited them. And checked afterward, in burned houses, on work done.

I stopped walking. We were standing outside the flower shop where Regina had worked. I put my hand in my pocket and pulled out the six cartridge cases. Gave them to Frost.

"These came from the gun which the man called Greene fired at me," I said. "I don't imagine they're of much practical use, but they might persuade you that Greene is capable of murder."

"Well . . . what of it?"

"Greene was in England at about the time Regina died."

He stared.

"Maybe Regina knew him," I said. "She had been in the gallery in Australia. Maybe she saw him helping to rob her house. And maybe that's why she was killed, because it wouldn't have been enough just to tie her up and gag her; she could identify him."

"That's all . . . guessing," Frost said.

"I know for certain that Greene was in England two weeks after Regina's death. I know for certain he was selling paintings and stealing them back. I know for certain that he would kill someone who could get him convicted. The rest is up to you."

"My God," Frost said. "My God."

I started off again. He came with me, looking glazed. "What

everyone wants to know," he said, "is what put you on to the organization in the first place."

I smiled. "A hot tip from an informer."

"What informer?"

A smuggler in a scarlet coat, glossy hairdo, and crocodile handbag. "You can't grass on informers," I said.

He sighed, stopped walking, and pulled a piece of torn-off Telex
paper out of his jacket. "Did you meet an Australian policeman
called Porter?"

"I sure did."

"He sent you a message." He handed me the paper.

I read it. TELL THAT POMMY PAINTER THANKS.

"Will you send a message back?"

He nodded. "What is it?"

"No sweat," I said.

I STOOD in the dark outside my cousin's house, looking in.

He sat in his lighted drawing room, facing Regina, unframed
on the mantelshelf. I sighed and rang the bell.

Donald came slowly. Opened the door. "Charles!" He was mildly
surprised. "I thought you were in Australia. Come in."

We sat in the kitchen. He looked gaunt, a shell of a man.

"How's business?" I said.

"I haven't been to the office."

"If you didn't have a critical cash-flow problem before," I said,
"you'll have one soon."

"I don't really care."

"You've got stuck," I said. "Like a needle in a record. Playing the
same little bit of track over and over again."

He looked blank.

"The police know you didn't fix the robbery," I said.

He nodded slowly. "That man Wall . . . came and told me so. But
it doesn't seem to make much difference."

"You've got to stop it, Donald. Regina's dead. She's been dead
five weeks and three days. Stop thinking about her body."

"Charles!" He stood up violently, knocking over his chair.

"She's in a cold drawer," I said, "and you want her in a box in the cold ground. So where's the difference?"

"Get out," he said loudly. "I don't want to hear you."

"The bit of Regina you're obsessed about is just a collection of minerals. The real girl is in your head. The only life you can give her is to remember her. That's her immortality. You're killing her all over again with your refusal to go on living."

He turned on his heel and walked out. I heard him go across the hall, and guessed he was making for the sitting room.

After a minute I followed him.

He was sitting in his usual place. "Go away," he said.

What did it profit a man, I thought, if he got flung over balconies and shot at and mangled by rocks, if he couldn't save his cousin's soul.

"I'm taking that picture with me to London," I said.

He was alarmed. He stood up. "You're not. You gave it to me."

"It needs a frame," I said. "Or it will warp."

"You can't take it."

"You can come as well."

"I can't leave here," he said.

"Why not?"

"Don't be stupid. You know why not."

I said, "Regina will be with you wherever you are."

Nothing.

"She isn't in this room. She's in your head. You can go out of here and take her with you."

Nothing.

"She was a great girl. It must be bloody without her. But she deserves the best you can do."

Nothing.

I went over to the fireplace and picked up the picture. Donald didn't try to stop me. I put my hand on his arm.

"Let's get your car out," I said, "and drive down to my flat."

A little silence.

"Come on," I said.

He began, with difficulty, to cry.

I took a long breath and waited. "Okay," I said. "How are you off for petrol?"

"We can get some more," he said, sniffing, "on the motorway."

REFLEX

# CHAPTER 1

WINDED and coughing, I lay on one elbow and spat out a mouthful of grass and mud. The horse I'd been riding raised its weight off my ankle, scrambled untidily to its feet, and departed at an unfeeling gallop. I waited for things to settle: chest heaving, bones still rattling from the bang, sense of balance recovering from a thirty-mile-an-hour somersault and a few tumbling rolls. No harm done. Nothing broken. Just another fall.

Time and place: sixteenth fence, three-mile steeplechase, Sandown Park racecourse, Friday, November, in thin, cold, persistent rain. I stood up wearily and thought that this was a damn silly way for a grown man to be spending his life.

The thought was a jolt. Not one I'd ever thought before. Riding horses at high speed over jumps was the only way I knew to make a living, and it was a job one couldn't do if one's heart wasn't in it. The chilling flicker of disillusion nudged like the first twinge of a toothache. But I reassured myself. I loved the life. Nothing was wrong except the weather, the fall, the lost race.

Squelching uphill to the stands in my paper-thin racing boots, I thought only about the horse I'd started out on, sorting out what I might say to its trainer. Discarded "How do you expect it to jump if you don't school it properly?" in favor of "Might try him in blinkers." The trainer, anyway, would blame me for the fall and tell the owner I'd misjudged the pace. He was that sort. I thanked heaven I didn't ride often for that stable, and had been engaged on that day only because Steve Millace, its usual jockey, had gone to his father's funeral. Spare rides were not lightly to be turned down. Not if you needed the money, which I did.

The only good thing about my descent was that Steve Millace's father wasn't there to record it. George Millace, pitiless photographer of moments all jockeys preferred to ignore, was at that moment being lowered underground. And good riddance, I thought. Good-bye to the snide pleasure George got from delivering to owners the irrefutable evidence of their jockeys' failings. Good-bye to the motorized camera catching one's balance in the wrong place, one's arms in the air, one's face in the mud.

Where other photographers played fair and shot you winning from time to time, George trafficked exclusively in ignominy and humiliation. There had been little sorrow in the changing room the day Steve told us his father had driven into a tree. Out of liking for Steve himself, no one had said much. But he knew. He had been anxiously defending his father for years.

Trudging back in the rain, it seemed odd to think that we wouldn't be seeing George Millace again. His image came sharply to mind: bright clever eyes, long nose, drooping mustache, twisted mouth sourly smiling. A terrific photographer, one had to admit, with exceptional timing, always pointing his lens in the right direction at the right moment.

When I finally reached the shelter of the veranda outside the changing room, the trainer and owner were waiting.

"Misjudged things, didn't you?" said the trainer.

"He took off a stride too soon. Might try him in blinkers."

"*I'll* decide about that," he said sharply as he led the owner away from me and the danger that I might say something truthful about the horse not being schooled properly. I turned toward the changing room.

"I say," said a young man, stepping in front of me. "Are you Philip Nore?"

"That's right."

"Could I have a word with you?" He was about twenty-five, tall as a stork, and earnest, with office-colored skin. Charcoal flannel suit, striped tie.

"Sure," I said. "If you'll wait while I get into something dry."

When I went out again, warmed and in street clothes, he was still on the veranda. "I . . . er . . . my name is Jeremy Folk." He produced a card: "Folk, Langley, Son and Folk, Solicitors, Saint Albans, Hertfordshire."

"That last Folk," said Jeremy, "is me." He cleared his throat. "I've been sent to ask you to . . . er—" He stopped, looking helpless.

"To what?" I said encouragingly.

"To go and see your grandmother." The words came out in a nervous rush. "She's dying. She wants to see you."

"I'm not going."

"But you must." He looked troubled. "I mean . . . if I don't persuade you, my uncle . . . that's Son"—he pointed to the card, getting flustered—"er . . . Folk is my grandfather and Langley is my granduncle, and . . . er . . . they sent me . . ." He swallowed. "They think I'm frightfully useless, to be honest."

A glint in his eyes told me he wasn't as silly as he made out. "I don't want to see her," I said.

"But she is dying," he said.

"I'll bet she isn't. If she wants to see me, she would say she was dying just to fetch me, because nothing else would."

He looked shocked. "She's seventy-eight, after all."

I stared gloomily out at the rain. I had never met my grandmother and I didn't want to, dying or dead. I didn't approve of deathbed repentances. It was too late. "The answer is no."

He shrugged and seemed to give up. Walked a few steps out into the rain, bareheaded, vulnerable. Turned around and came back again. "Look . . . she really needs you, my uncle says."

"Where is she?"

He brightened. "In a nursing home. I'll lead you there if you'll come. It's in Saint Albans. You live in Lambourn, don't you? So it isn't so terribly far out of your way, is it?"

I sighed. The options were rotten. That she had dished out stony rejection from my birth gave me no excuse, I supposed, for doing it to her at her death.

The winter afternoon was already fading. I thought of my empty cottage; of nothing much to fill the evening; of two eggs, a piece of cheese, and black coffee for supper; of fighting the impulse to eat more. If I went, it would at least take my mind off food. "All right," I said resignedly. "Lead on."

THE old woman sat upright in bed staring at me, and if she was dying, it wasn't going to be on that evening, for sure. The life force was strong in the dark eyes. "Philip," she said, looking me up and down. "Hah." The explosive sound contained both triumph and contempt and was everything I expected. Her ramrod will had devastated my childhood and done worse damage to her own daughter, and there was to be, I was relieved to see, no maudlin plea for forgiveness.

"I knew you'd come running," she said, "when you heard about the hundred thousand pounds."

"No one mentioned any money."

"Don't lie. Why else would you come?"

"They said you were dying."

She gave me a malevolent look. "So I am. So are we all."

She was no one's idea of a sweet little pink-cheeked granny. A strong, stubborn face with disapproval lines cut deep around the mouth. Iron-gray hair. Dark, ridged veins on the backs of the hands. A thin, gaunt woman.

"I instructed Mr. Folk to make you the offer. I told him to get you here. And he did."

I turned away and sat unasked in an armchair. She stared at me steadily with no sign of affection, and I stared as steadily back. I was repelled by her contempt and mistrusted her intentions.

"I will leave you a hundred thousand pounds in my will, upon certain conditions," she said.

"No, you won't," I said. "No money. No conditions."

"You haven't heard my proposition."

I said nothing. I felt the first stirrings of curiosity, but I was not going to let her see it. The silence lengthened. Finally she said, "You're taller than I expected. And tougher. Where is your mother?"

My mother, her daughter. "I think she's dead."

"*Think!* Don't you *know?*"

"She didn't exactly write to me to say she'd died. No."

"Your flippancy is disgraceful."

"Your behavior since before my birth," I said, "gives you no right to say so."

Her mouth opened, and stayed open for fully five seconds. Then it shut tight and she stared at me darkly. I saw in that expression what my poor young mother had had to face, and felt a great up-rush of sympathy for the feckless butterfly who'd borne me.

There had been a day, when I was quite small, that I had been dressed in new clothes and told to be exceptionally good as I was going to see my grandmother. My mother had collected me from where I was living and we had traveled by car to a large house, where I was left alone in the hall to wait. Behind a white-painted closed door there had been a lot of shouting. Then my mother had come out crying, grabbed me by the hand, and pulled me after her to the car.

"Come on, Philip. We'll never ask her for anything, ever again. She wouldn't even see you. Don't you ever forget, Philip, that your grandmother's a hateful *beast.*"

I had never actually lived with my mother, except for a trau-matic week or two now and then. We had had no house, no per-manent address. Herself always on the move, she had solved the problem of what to do with me by simply dumping me for varying periods on a long succession of astonished friends.

"Do look after Philip for me for a few days, darling," she would say, giving me a push toward yet another strange lady. "Life is so unutterably *cluttered* just now and I'm at my wits' end to know what to do with him, so, darling Deborah (or Miranda or Chloe or Samantha or anyone else under the sun), do be an absolute *sweetie,* and I'll pick him up on Saturday, I promise."

Saturdays came and my mother didn't, but she always turned

up in the end, full of flutter and laughter and gushing thanks, retrieving her parcel, so to speak, from the left-luggage office.

She was deliciously pretty, to the extent that people hugged her
and indulged her and lit up when she was around. Only later, when
they were left literally holding the baby, did the doubts creep in.
I became a bewildered, silent child, forever tiptoeing about so as
not to give offense, perennially frightened that someone, one day,
would abandon me altogether out in the street.

Looking back, I knew I owed a great deal to Samantha,
Deborah, Chloe, et al. I never went hungry, was never ill treated,
nor was I ever totally rejected. But it was a disorienting existence
from which I emerged at twelve, when I was dumped in my first
long-stay home, able to do almost any job around the house and
unable to love.

She left me with two photographers, Duncan and Charlie,
standing in their big bare-floored studio, which had a darkroom, a
bathroom, a gas ring, and a bed behind a curtain.

"Just look after him until Saturday, there's a sweet pair of
lambs." And although birthday cards arrived, and presents at
Christmas, I didn't see her again for three years. During those
years, Duncan and Charlie patiently taught me all I could learn
about photography. I started by cleaning up in the darkroom and
finished by doing all of their printing. "Our lab assistant," Charlie
called me.

Then Duncan departed, and my mother swooped in one day
and took me away from Charlie. She drove me down to a racehorse
trainer and his wife in Hampshire, telling those bemused friends,
"It's only until Saturday, darlings, and he's fifteen and strong, and
he'll muck out the stables for you. . . ."

Cards and presents arrived for two years or so, always without
an address to reply to. On my eighteenth birthday there was no
card, no present the following Christmas, and I'd never heard from
her again. She must have died, I had come to understand, from
drugs. There was a great deal, as I grew older, that I'd sorted out
and understood.

The old woman glared across the room, as unforgiving and destructive as ever, and still angry at what I'd said. I stood up. "This visit is pointless. If you wanted to find your daughter, you should have looked twenty years ago. And as for me . . . I wouldn't find her for you even if I could."

"I don't want you to find Caroline. I daresay you're right, that she's dead." The idea clearly caused her no grief. "I want you to find your sister."

"My *what?*"

The hostile dark eyes assessed me shrewdly. "You didn't know you had a sister? Well, you have. I'll leave you a hundred thousand pounds in my will if you find her and bring her here to me."

I felt an intense thrust of shock, a stinging jealousy that my mother had had another child. Now I had to share her memory. I thought in confusion that it was ridiculous to be experiencing displacement emotions at thirty.

"Well?" my grandmother said sharply.

"No," I said. "And if that's all, I'll be going."

"Wait," she said. "Don't you want to see her picture? There's a photograph of your sister over there on the chest."

Without wanting to but impelled by curiosity, I walked over to the chest. There was a snapshot lying there and I picked it up. A little girl, three or four years old, on a pony, with shoulder-length brown hair, wearing a striped T-shirt and jeans. Photographed in what was evidently a stable yard, but the photographer had been standing too far away to bring out much detail in the child's face. I turned the print over, but there was nothing to indicate where it had come from.

Vaguely disappointed, I put it down and saw, with a wince of nostalgia, an envelope lying on the chest with my mother's handwriting on it. Addressed to my grandmother, Mrs. Lavinia Nore, at the old house in Northamptonshire where I'd had to wait in the hall.

In the envelope, a letter. I took it out.

"What are you doing?" said my grandmother in alarm. "That letter shouldn't be there. Put it down."

I ignored her. The letter was dated October 2, with no year:

Dear Mother,

I know I said I would never ask you for anything again, but I'm having one more try, silly me. I am sending you a photograph of my daughter, Amanda, your granddaughter. She is very sweet and she's three now, and she needs a proper home and to go to school and everything. I know you wouldn't want a child around, but if you'd just give her an allowance, she could live with some perfectly angelic people who love her and want to keep her but simply can't afford another child. She hasn't the same father as Philip, so you couldn't hate her for the same reasons. Please, Mother, look after her. Please, please, answer this letter.

Caroline

Staying at Pine Woods Lodge, Mindle Bridge, Sussex.

I looked up at the hard old woman. "You didn't reply?"

"No."

It was no good getting angry over so old a tragedy. I looked at the envelope to try to see the date of the postmark, but it was smudged and indecipherable. How long, I wondered, had my mother waited at Pine Woods Lodge, hoping and desperate?

I put the letter, the envelope, and the photograph in my jacket pocket. I felt in an obscure way that they belonged to me and not to her.

"So you'll do it," she said.

"No. If you want Amanda found, hire a private detective."

"I did. Three detectives. They were all useless."

"If three failed, there's no way I could succeed."

"You'll try harder. For that sort of money."

"You're wrong. If I took any money from you, I'd vomit." I walked over to the door and opened it without hesitation.

To my departing back she said, "Amanda shall have my money . . . if you find her."

WHEN I went back to Sandown Park the next day, the letter and photograph were still in my pocket, but the emotions they had engendered had subsided. It was the present, in the shape of Steve Millace, that claimed everyone's attention. He came steaming into the changing room half an hour before the first race with drizzle on his hair and fury in his eyes. His mother's house, he said, had been burglarized while they were out at his father's funeral.

We sat in rows on the benches, listening with shock. I looked at the scene. Jockeys in all stages of dress—in underpants, bare-chested, in silks, pulling on boots—and all of them listening with open mouths and with eyes turned toward Steve. Automatically I reached for my Nikon and took a couple of photographs. They were all so accustomed to me doing that sort of thing that no one took any notice.

"It was awful," Steve said. "Mum had made some cakes and things for the aunts and everyone, for when we got back from the cremation, and they were all thrown around the place, squashed flat, jam and such, onto the walls. And all those things taken."

He went on. "They stripped Dad's darkroom. Just ripped every-thing out. It was senseless . . . like I told the police. They didn't just take things you could sell, like the enlarger and the develop-ing stuff, but all his work—all those pictures taken over the years, they're all gone. It's such a bloody shame. Mum's just sitting there crying."

He stopped suddenly and swallowed, as if it was all too much for him too. At twenty-three, although he no longer lived with them, he was still very much his parents' child. George Millace might have been widely disliked, but he had never been belittled by his son.

Slight in build, Steve had bright dark eyes and ears that stuck out widely, giving him a slightly comic look, but he was more in-tense than humorous and apt to keep on returning obsessively to things that upset him.

"The police said that burglars do it for spite," Steve said. "Mess up people's houses and steal their photographs. They told Mum it's always happening." He went on, talking to anyone who would lis-ten. I finished changing and went out to ride in the first race.

It was a day I had been looking forward to. I was to ride Daylight in the Sandown Handicap Pattern Steeplechase. A big race, a good horse, and a great chance of winning. Such combinations came my way rarely enough to be prized. There was just the first race, a novice hurdle, to come back from unscathed, and then, perhaps, I would win the big race with Daylight, and half a dozen people would fall over themselves to offer me their horse for the Gold Cup.

Two races a day was my usual mark, and if I ended a season in the top twenty on the jockeys' list, I was happy. For years I'd been able to kid myself that the modesty of my success was due to being too tall and heavy. Even with constant semistarvation I weighed one hundred and forty-seven. Most seasons I rode in about two hundred races with forty or so winners, and knew that I was considered "strong" and "reliable" but "not first class in a close finish."

At around twenty-six I'd come to terms with knowing I wasn't going to the top, and oddly, far from depressing me, the realization had been a relief. All the same, I'd no objection to having Gold Cup winners thrust upon me, so to speak.

On that afternoon at Sandown I completed the novice hurdle fifth out of eighteen runners. Not too bad. I changed into Daylight's colors and in due course walked out to the parade ring. Daylight's trainer, for whom I rode regularly, was waiting there, and also Daylight's owner, who said without preamble, "You'll lose this one today, Philip."

I smiled. "Not if I can help it."

"Indeed you will. My money's on the other way."

I don't suppose I kept much of the dismay and anger out of my face. Victor Briggs, Daylight's owner, had done this sort of thing before, but not for about three years, and he knew I didn't like it. A sturdily built man in his forties, unsociable, secretive, he came to the races with a closed, unsmiling face. He always wore a heavy navy-blue overcoat, a black broad-brimmed hat, and thick black leather gloves. He had been, in the past, an aggressive gambler, and in riding for him I had the choice of doing what he said or losing my job with the stable. So I had lost races I might have won. I needed to eat and to pay off the mortgage on the cottage. For that I needed a good big stable to ride for.

Back at the beginning Victor Briggs had offered me a fair-size cash present for losing. I'd said I didn't want it; I would lose if I had to, but I wouldn't be paid. He said I was a pompous fool, but after I'd refused his offer a second time he'd kept his bribes in his pocket. And since I'd been free of the dilemma for three years, it was all the more infuriating to be faced with it again.

"I can't lose," I protested. "Daylight's the best of the bunch."

"Just do it," Victor Briggs said. "And lower your voice, unless you want the stewards to hear you."

I looked at Harold Osborne, Daylight's trainer. "Victor's right," he said. "The money's on the other way. You'll cost us a packet if you win, so don't."

"Us?"

He nodded. "Us. That's right. Fall off if you have to. Come in second if you like. But not first. Understood?"

I understood. Back in the old pincers.

I cantered Daylight down to the start with reality winning out over rebellion, as before. I'd been with Osborne seven years. If he chucked me out, all I'd get would be other stables' odds and ends: a one-way track to oblivion.

I was angry. I didn't want to lose the race; I hated to be dishonest. And the ten percent of the winner's purse I would lose was big enough to make me even angrier. Why had Briggs gone back to this caper after all this time?

While the starter called the roll, I looked at the four horses ranged against Daylight. There wasn't one among them that could defeat my gelding, which was why people were staking four pounds on Daylight to win one. Four to one on . . .

Far from risking his own money at those odds, Victor Briggs in some subterranean way had taken bets from other people, and would have to pay out if his horse won. And so, it seemed, would Harold. However I might feel, I did owe him some allegiance.

After seven years of a working relationship, I had come to regard Harold Osborne as a friend. He was a man of rages and charms, of tyrannical decisions and generous gifts. He could outshout anyone on the Berkshire Downs, and stable lads left his employ in droves. But he had trusted me always, and had defended me against criticism when many a trainer would not. He assumed that I would be, for my part, totally committed to him and his stable, and for the past three years that had been easy.

The starter called the horses into line, and I wheeled Daylight around to point his nose in the right direction. No starting stalls were used for jump racing. A gate of elastic tapes instead.

In misery I decided that the race, from Daylight's point of view, would have to be over as near the start as possible. Losing would be hard enough, and practically suicidal if I waited until it was clear that Daylight would win. Then, if I just fell off in the last half mile for not much reason, there would be an inquiry and I might lose my license; and it would be no comfort to know that I deserved to.

The starter put his hand on the lever, the tapes flew up, and I kicked Daylight forward. Cheat the horse. Cheat the public. Cheat. Damn it, I thought.

I did it at the third fence, on the decline from the top of the hill, around the sharpish bend, going away from the stands. It was the least visible place to the crowd and the most likely for an accident. The fence had claimed many a victim during the year. Daylight, confused by getting the wrong signals from me and perhaps feeling my turmoil in the telepathic way that horses do, put in a jerky extra stride before takeoff, where none was needed.

I'm sorry, boy, but down you go; and I kicked him at the wrong moment, and twitched hard on his bit while he was in midair, and shifted my weight forward in front of his shoulder.

He landed awkwardly and stumbled slightly, dipping his head to recover his balance. I whisked my right foot out of the stirrup and over his back, so that I was entirely on his left side, out of the saddle. I clung to his neck for about three bucking strides and then slid down his chest, losing my grip and bouncing onto the grass under his feet. A flurry of thuds from his hoofs, a roll, and the noise and the galloping horses were gone. I sat on the quiet ground and unbuckled my helmet and felt absolutely wretched.

"Bad luck," they said in the changing room. I wondered if any of them guessed, but no one nudged or winked. It was my own sense of shame that kept me staring mostly at the floor.

"Cheer up," Steve Millace said, buttoning some orange and blue colors. "It's not the end of the world." He went off to ride, and I changed gloomily back into street clothes. So much, I thought, for winning, for trainers climbing over themselves to secure my services for the Gold Cup. So much for a boost to the finances. I went out to watch the race.

Steve Millace, with more courage than sense, drove his horse at leg-tangling pace into the second-to-last fence and crashed on landing. It was the sort of hard, fast fall that cracked bones, and one could see that Steve was in trouble. He struggled up as far as his knees, then sat on his heels with his head bent forward and his arms wrapped around his body, hugging himself. Arm, shoulder, ribs . . . something had gone.

Two first-aid men helped him into an ambulance. A bad day for Steve too, I thought, on top of all his family troubles. What on earth made us do it, disregarding injury and risk and disappointment, when we could earn as much sitting in an office?

I met him later in the changing room. His shoulder was bandaged, his arm in a sling. "Collarbone," he said crossly. "Bloody nuisance."

His valet helped him dress, touching him gently. "Could you possibly drive me home?" Steve asked me. "To my mother's house? Near Ascot."

"Yes, I should think so," I said. I took a photograph of him and his valet, who was smoothly pulling off his boots.

"What do you do with all them snapshots?" the valet said.

"Put them in a drawer."

He gave a heaven-help-us jerk of the head. "Waste of time."

Steve glanced at the Nikon. "Dad said once he'd seen some of your pics. You'd put him out of business someday, he said."

"He was laughing at me."

George Millace had seen some of my pictures, catching me looking through them as I sat in my car one day waiting for a friend. "Let's have a look," he had said. "Well, well," he remarked, going through them. "Keep it up. One of these days you might take a photograph." He was the only photographer I knew with whom I didn't feel at home.

The valet helped Steve into his jacket, and we went at Steve's tender pace out to my car and drove off in the direction of Ascot.

"I can't get used to Dad's not being there," Steve said.

"What happened? You said he drove into a tree."

"Yes." He sighed. "He went to sleep. At least, that's what everyone reckons. There weren't any other cars. There was a bend, and he just drove straight ahead. He must have had his foot on the accelerator. The front of the car was smashed right in." He shivered. "He had stopped for half an hour at a friend's house. And they'd had a couple of whiskeys. It was all so stupid. Just going to sleep . . . Turn left here."

We drove for a long way in silence and came finally to a road bordered by neat houses set in shadowy gardens. There, in the middle distance, things were happening. An ambulance with its doors open, blue light flashing. A police car. People hurrying in and out of one of the houses. Every window uncurtained, spilling out light.

"No!" Steve said. "That's our house."

I pulled up outside, and he sat unmoving, staring, stricken.

"It's Mum," he said. "It must be. It's Mum."

There was something near the cracking point in his voice. His face was twisted with terrible anxiety.

"Stay here," I said practically. "I'll go and see."

# CHAPTER 2

His mum lay on the sofa in the sitting room, quivering and coughing and bleeding. Someone had attacked her pretty nastily, splitting her nose and mouth and eyelid. Her clothes were torn, her shoes were off, and her hair stuck out in straggly wisps. I had seen her at the races from time to time—a pleasant, well-dressed woman near-ing fifty, secure and happy, plainly proud of her husband and son. As the grief-stricken, burglarized, beaten-up person on the sofa, she was unrecognizable.

There was a policeman sitting on a stool beside her, and a policewoman, standing, holding a bloodstained cloth. Two ambu-lance men hovered in the background, and a neighborly-looking woman stood around with a worried expression on her face. The room was a shambles, papers and smashed furniture littering the floor. On the walls, the signs of jam and cakes, as Steve had said. The policeman turned his head. "Are you the doctor?"

"No." I explained who I was.

"Steve's hurt!" his mother said, fear for her son overshadowing everything else.

"It's not bad, I promise you," I said hastily. "He's here, outside." I went and told him, and helped him out of the car.

"Why?" he said, going up the path. "Why did it happen?"

Indoors, the policeman was asking, "There were two of them, with stockings over their faces?"

Marie Millace nodded. "Young," she said. The word came out distorted through her swollen lips. She saw Steve and held out her hand.

"What were they wearing?" the policeman said.

"Jeans."

"Gloves?"

She closed her eyes and whispered, "Yes."

"What did they want?"

"Safe," she said, mumbling. " 'We haven't got a safe,' I told them. 'Where's the safe?' they said. One smashed things. The other hit me."

"I'd like to kill them," Steve said furiously.

"Just keep quiet, sir, if you wouldn't mind," the policeman said.

"I suppose you know," I said to him, "that this house was also burgled yesterday?"

"Yes, I do, sir. I was here yesterday myself." He looked at me as-sessingly for a few seconds and turned back to Steve's mother. "Did these two young men say anything about being here yesterday? Try to remember, Mrs. Millace."

She was silent for a long interval. Poor lady, I thought. Too much pain, too much grief, too much outrage. At last she said, "They were like bulls. They shouted. I opened the front door. They shoved in, pushed me in here. Started smashing things. Shouting, 'Tell us, where is the safe?' " She paused. "I don't think they said anything . . . about yesterday."

"I'd like to *kill* them," Steve said.

"Third time burgled," mumbled his mother. "Happened two years ago."

"You can't just let her lie here," Steve said violently. "Asking all these questions. Haven't you got a doctor?"

"It's all right, Steve dear," the neighborly woman said. "I've rung Dr. Williams. He said he would come at once." Caring and bothered, she was nonetheless enjoying the drama. "I was home next door, dear, getting tea for my family, and I heard all this shouting and it seemed all wrong, so I was just coming to see, and those two dreadful young men just burst out of the house, dear, just *burst* out, so of course I came in here and rang for the police and the ambulance and Dr. Williams."

The policeman was unappreciative. He said to her, "And you still can't remember any more about the car they drove off in?"

Defensively she said, "I don't notice cars much."

I said diffidently to the policeman, "I've cameras in my car, if you want photographs of all this."

He raised his eyebrows and considered and said yes; so I fetched both cameras and took two sets of pictures, in color and black and white, with close-ups of Mrs. Millace's damaged face and wide-angle shots of the room. The policeman told me where to send them and then the doctor arrived.

"Don't go yet," Steve said to me, and I looked at the desperation in his face, and stayed with him through all the ensuing bustle.

In fact I stayed the night, because after they took Mrs. Millace to the hospital, Steve looked so exhausted that I simply couldn't leave him. I made us a couple of omelets and then picked up some of the mess: magazines, newspapers, old letters, and also the base and lid of a flat eight-by-ten-inch box that had once held photographic printing paper.

"What shall I do with all this?" I asked Steve.

He sat on the edge of the sofa, looking strained, not mentioning that his fractured collarbone was hurting quite a bit. "Oh, just pile it anywhere," he said vaguely. "Some of it came out of that rack over there by the television."

A wooden magazine rack, empty, lay on its side on the carpet.

"That old orange thing beside it is Dad's rubbish box. He kept it in that rack with the papers. Just left it there, year after year. Funny really."

I picked up a small batch of odds and ends—a transparent piece of film about three inches wide by eight long, several strips of 35-mm color negatives, developed but blank, and an otherwise pleasant picture of Mrs. Millace that had been spoiled by splashes of chemical.

"Those were in Dad's rubbish box, I think," Steve said, yawning. "You might as well throw them away."

I put them in the wastebasket, and added a nearly black black-and-white print that had been torn in half, some more color negatives covered with magenta blotches, and another very dark print in a folder, showing a shadowy man sitting at a table.

"He kept those things to remind himself of his worst mistakes," Steve said. "It doesn't seem *possible* that he isn't coming back."

The bulk of the mess on the floor was broken china, the remnants of a sewing box, and a bureau, tipped on its side, its contents falling out of the drawers. None of the damage seemed to have had any purpose: it was a rampage designed to confuse and bewilder.

"Why would they think your mother had a safe?" I asked.

"Who knows? If she'd had one, she'd have told them where it was, wouldn't she? After losing Dad like that. And yesterday's burglary, while we were at the funeral. Such dreadful shocks. She can't take any more." There were tears in his voice. It was he, I thought, who was closest to the edge.

"Time for bed," I said abruptly. "I'll help you undress."

I WOKE EARLY AFTER AN UNEASY night and lay watching the dingy November dawn creep through the window. There was a good deal about life that I didn't want to get up and face. Wouldn't it be marvelous, I thought dimly, not to have to think about mean-minded grandmothers and one's own depressing dishonesty? Normally fairly happy-go-lucky, I disliked being backed into corners from which escape meant action.

Things had just happened to me all my life. I'd never gone out looking. Like photography, because of Duncan and Charlie. And like riding, because of my mother's dumping me in a racing stable. Survival for so many years had been a matter of accepting what I was given, of making myself useful, of being quiet and agreeable and no trouble. I had made no major decisions. What I had, had simply come.

I understood why I was as I was. I knew why I was passive, but I felt no desire to change, to be master of my fate. I didn't want to look for my half sister, and I didn't want to lose my job with Harold. I could simply drift along as usual. Yet for some reason that instinctive course seemed increasingly unattractive.

Irritated, I put my clothes on and went downstairs, peering in at Steve on the way and finding him sound asleep. To pass the time, I wandered around, just looking.

George Millace's darkroom would have been the most interesting, but the burglary there had been the most thorough. All that was left was a wide bench down one side, two deep sinks down the other, and rows of empty shelves. Grubby outlines and smudges on the walls showed where the equipment had stood, and stains on the floor marked where he'd stored his chemicals.

He had, I knew, done a lot of his own color developing. Most professional photographers do not. Developing color films is difficult, and it's easier to entrust the process to commercial labs. But George Millace had been a craftsman of the first order.

From the look of things he had had two enlargers, one big and one smaller, enlargers being machines that hold a negative in what is basically a box up a stick, so that a bright light can shine through the negative onto a baseboard beneath.

The head of the enlarger, holding the light and the negative, can be wound up and down the stick. The higher one winds the head above the baseboard, the larger one sees the picture. The lower the head, the smaller the picture. An enlarger is in fact a projector, and the baseboard is the screen.

Besides the enlargers, George would have had an electric box of tricks for regulating the length of exposures, a mass of developing equipment, and a dryer for drying the finished prints. He would have had various types of photographic paper, lightproof containers to store it in, files holding all his past work, measuring cups, paper trimmers, filters. The whole lot had been stolen.

I went into the sitting room, wondering how soon I could decently wake Steve and say I was going. Having nothing else to do, I began picking up more of the mess, retrieving bits of sewing from under the chairs.

Half under the sofa lay a large black lightproof envelope. I looked inside it. It contained a piece of clear plastic about eight by eleven inches, straight cut on three sides but wavy along the fourth. More rubbish. I put it back in the envelope and threw it in the wastebasket.

George Millace's rubbish box still lay open and empty on the carpet. Impelled by photographic curiosity, I picked up the wastebasket and sorted out all of George's worst mistakes. Why, I wondered, had he bothered to keep them? I put the spoiled prints and pieces of film back in the orange box and added the large lightproof envelope. It would be instructive to learn why such an expert had found these particular things interesting.

Steve came downstairs in his pajamas, hugging his injured arm. "Hey, thanks," he said. "You've tidied the lot." He saw the rubbish box. "For a long time he kept that box in a shed out back."

"Did your father keep other things out there?"

"Masses of stuff. You know photographers, always having fits that their work might be messed up or lost. He said the only way to posterity was through the shed. He kept his best transparencies out there."

"Did the burglars go back there?"

He looked startled. "I don't know. Why should they want his films? The policeman said what they really wanted was the equipment, which they could sell."

"Your father took a lot of pictures people didn't like."

"Only as a joke." He was defending George, the same as ever.

"We might look out back," I suggested.

"Yes. All right."

He led the way into a small yard. "In there," he said, giving me a key and nodding toward the shed's green door. I went in and found a huge wooden chest standing beside a lawn mower.

I lifted the lid. Inside were three large gray metal cashboxes, each one wrapped in transparent plastic sheeting. Taped to the top one was a terse message: DO NOT REMOVE.

I shut the lid and we went back into the house. Steve looked a shade more cheerful. "One good thing, Mum still has some of his best work."

I helped him get dressed and left soon afterward, as he said he felt better, and looked it; and I took with me George Millace's box of disasters, which Steve had said to throw into the garbage.

"You don't mind if I take it?" I said.

"Of course not. I know you like messing about with films, same as he did. He liked that old rubbish. Don't know why."

WITH the rubbish box stowed in the trunk alongside my two camera bags, I drove the hour from Ascot to Lambourn and found a large dark car standing outside my front door.

My cottage was in the center of a row of seven built in the Edwardian era: two rooms upstairs, two down, with a modern kitchen stuck on at the back. A white-painted brick front, facing out onto the road, with no room for a garden. A black door, needing paint. Nothing fancy, but home.

I drove slowly past the visiting car and turned into the muddy drive at the end of the row, continuing around to the back and parking under the carport next to the kitchen. As I went I caught a glimpse of a man getting hastily out of the car, and I thought only that he had no business pursuing me on a Sunday.

I went through the house and opened the front door. Jeremy Folk stood there, tall, thin, as earnestly diffident as before.

".Don't solicitors sleep on Sundays?" I said.

"Well, I say, I'm awfully sorry."

"Yeah. Come on in, then." He stepped through the doorway with a hint of expectancy and took the immediate disappointment with a blink. What had been the front parlor I had divided into an entrance hall and darkroom. White walls, white floor tiles; uninformative.

"This way," I said.

I led him down the hall past the darkroom and bathroom toward the kitchen. To the left of the kitchen lay the narrow stairs. "Which do you want?" I said. "Coffee or talk?"

"Er . . . talk."

"Up here, then." I went upstairs, and he followed. I used one of the two original bedrooms as a sitting room, because it was the largest room in the house and had the best view of the downs; the room next to it was where I slept.

The sitting room had white walls, brown carpet, blue curtains, track lighting, bookshelves, sofa, low table, and floor cushions. My guest looked around with small flickering glances, making assessments.

"Sit down," I said, gesturing toward the sofa. I sat on a beanbag floor cushion and said, "Why didn't you mention the money when I saw you at Sandown?"

He seemed almost to wriggle. "I just . . . ah . . . thought I'd try you first on blood-stronger-than-water, don't you know?"

"And if that failed, you'd try greed?"

"Sort of."

"So that you would know what you were dealing with?"

He blinked.

"Look." I sighed. "Why don't you just . . . drop the act?"

He gave me a small smile. "It gets to be a habit," he said.

He cast a fresh look around the room, and I said, "All right, say what you're thinking."

He did so, without squirming and without apology. "You like to be alone. You're emotionally cold. You don't need props. And unless you took that photograph, you've no vanity." He nodded toward the only thing hanging on the wall, a view of pale yellow sunshine falling through some leafless silver birches onto snow.

"I took it. Now, what did you come for?"

"To persuade you to do what you don't want to."

"To try to find the half sister I didn't know I had? Why?"

"Mrs. Nore is insisting on leaving a fortune to someone who can't be found. It is unsatisfactory."

"Why is she insisting?"

"I don't know."

"Three detectives couldn't find Amanda."

"They didn't know where to look."

"Nor do I."

He considered me. "Do you know who your father is?" he said.

A measurable silence passed. I looked out the window at the bare calm line of the downs. I said, "I don't want to get tangled up in a family I don't feel I belong to. That old woman can't claw me back just because she feels like it, after all these years."

Jeremy Folk didn't answer directly. He stood up and said, "I brought the reports we received from the detectives. I can see that you don't want to be involved. But I'm afraid I'm going to plague you until you are." He pulled a long, bulging envelope out of the inside pocket of his country-tweed jacket and put it down on the table. "They're not very long." He moved toward the door, ready to leave. "By the way," he said. "Mrs. Nore really is dying. She has cancer of the spine. She'll live maybe six weeks, or six months. So . . . er . . . no time to waste, don't you know?"

I SPENT the bulk of the day in the darkroom, developing and printing my black-and-white shots of Mrs. Millace and her troubles. Jeremy Folk's envelope stayed upstairs where he'd put it, unopened, contents unread. At six o'clock I went to see the trainer, Harold Osborne, who lived up the road.

Sunday evenings from six to seven Harold and I talked over what had happened in the past week and discussed plans for the week ahead. For all his unpredictable moods, Harold was a man of method, and he hated anything to interrupt these sessions.

On that particular Sunday the sacrosanct hour had been interrupted before it could begin, because Harold had a visitor. I walked through his house from the stable entrance and went into the comfortable, cluttered sitting room/office, and there in one of the armchairs was Victor Briggs.

"Philip!" Harold said, smiling. "Pour yourself a drink. We're just going to run through the tape of yesterday's race."

Victor Briggs gave me several nods of approval and a handshake. No gloves, I thought. Without the broad-brimmed hat, he had thick, glossy black hair, which was receding slightly above the eyebrows to leave a center peak. He still wore the close-guarded expression, as if his thoughts would show, but there was overall a distinct air of satisfaction.

I opened a can of Coca-Cola and poured some into a glass.

"Don't you drink?" Victor Briggs asked.

"Champagne," Harold said. "That's what he drinks, don't you, Philip?" He was in great good humor, his voice resonant as brass.

Harold's reddish brown hair sprang in wiry curls all over his head, as untamable as his nature. He was fifty-two and looked ten years younger, a burly six feet of muscle commanded by a strong but ambiguous face, his features more rounded than hawkish. He switched on the video machine and sat back to watch Daylight's debacle, as pleased as if he'd won the Grand National.

The tape showed me on Daylight approaching the third fence, everything looking all right, then the jump in the air and the stumbling landing, and the figure in red and blue silks going over the horse's neck and down under the feet.

Harold switched off the machine. "Artistic," he said, beaming. "I've run through it twenty times. It's impossible to tell."

"No one suspected," Victor Briggs said. There was a laugh somewhere inside him. He picked up a large envelope, which had lain beside his gin and tonic, and held it out to me. "Here's my thank-you, Philip."

I said matter-of-factly, "It's kind of you, Mr. Briggs. But nothing's changed. I don't like to be paid for losing."

Victor Briggs put the envelope down again without comment, but Harold was angry. "Don't be such a prig," he said loudly, towering above me. "You're not so squeamish when it comes to committing the crime, are you? It's just the thirty pieces of silver you turn your pious nose up at. You make me sick."

"And," I said slowly, "I don't want to do it anymore."

"You'll do what you're told," Harold said.

Victor Briggs rose purposefully to his feet, and the two of them, suddenly silent, stood looking down at me. I stood up in my turn. My mouth had gone dry, but I made my voice sound as calm, as unprovoking as possible.

"Please . . . don't ask me for a repeat of yesterday. It's the losing. You know I hate it. I don't want you to ask me again. I know I used to do it, but yesterday was the last."

Harold said coldly, "You'd better go now, Philip. I'll talk to you in the morning," and I nodded and left.

What would they do? I wondered. I walked in the windy dark down the road from Harold's house to mine, as I had on hundreds of Sundays, and wondered if it would be for the last time. He was under no obligation to give me rides. I was self-employed, paid per race by the owner, not per week by the trainer.

I suppose it was too much to hope that they would let me get away with it. It was ironic. All those races I'd thrown away in the past, not liking it, but doing it. . . . Why was it so different for me now? Why was the revulsion so strong now that I *couldn't* do a Daylight again, even if to refuse meant virtually the end of being a jockey? When had I changed? I didn't know. I just had a sense of having already traveled too far to turn back.

At home, I went upstairs and read the three detectives' reports on Amanda, because it was better than thinking about Briggs and Harold.

Owing to my grandmother's vagueness about when she had received her daughter's letter, all three had scoured the General Registry Office for records of Amanda Nore, age between ten and twenty-five, possibly born in Sussex. In spite of the unusual name, they had all failed to find any trace of her birth having been registered.

I sucked my teeth, thinking that I could do better than that about her age. She couldn't have been born before I went to live with Duncan and Charlie, because I'd seen my mother fairly often before that, and I would have known if she'd had a child. That meant that I was at least twelve when Amanda was born; and consequently she couldn't at present be older than eighteen. Nor could she possibly be as young as ten. My mother, I was sure, had died sometime between Christmas and my eighteenth birthday. She might have been desperate enough before she died to write to her own mother and send her the photograph. Amanda in the photograph had been about three. So if she was still alive, she would be at least fifteen. Born during the three years when I'd lived with Duncan and Charlie.

I went back to the reports. All the detectives had been given my mother's last known address: Pine Woods Lodge, Mindle Bridge, Sussex, from her letter to my grandmother. All had trekked there "to make inquiries."

Pine Woods Lodge, they reported, was an old Georgian mansion now gone to ruin and due to be demolished. It was owned by a family that had largely died out; distant heirs, who had no wish to keep the place up, had rented the house at first to various organizations (list attached, supplied by real estate agents), but more recently it had been inhabited by squatters and vagrants.

I read through the list of tenants, none of whom had stayed long. A nursing home. A sisterhood of nuns. An artists' commune. A television film company. A musicians' cooperative. Colleagues of Supreme Grace. The Confidential Mail Order Corporation.

There were no dates attached to the tenancies, but presumably the real estate agents could still furnish some details. If I was right about when my mother had written her desperate letter, I should at least be able to find out which bunch she had been staying with. If I wanted to, of course.

Sighing, I read on. Copies of the photograph of Amanda Nore had been extensively displayed in public places in the vicinity of

Mindle Bridge, but no one had come forward to identify either the child, the stable yard, or the pony.

Advertisements had been inserted in various periodicals and newspapers stating that if Amanda Nore wished to hear something to her advantage, she should write to Jeremy's law firm.

A canvas of the schools around Mindle Bridge had produced no one called Amanda Nore on the registers, past or present. She was on no official list of any sort. No doctor or dentist had heard of her. She had not been confirmed, married, buried, or cremated within the county of Sussex.

All the reports came to the same conclusion: that she had been, or was being, brought up elsewhere (possibly under a different name), and was no longer interested in riding.

I returned the reports to the envelope. The detectives had tried, one had to admit. They had also indicated their willingness to continue to search for Amanda.

I still couldn't understand my grandmother's late interest in her long-ignored grandchildren. She'd had a son of her own, a boy my mother had called "my hateful little brother." He would have been about ten when I was born, which made him now about forty.

Uncle. Half sister. Grandmother. I didn't want them. I didn't want to know them or be drawn into their lives. I was in no way whatever going to look for Amanda.

I stood up with decision and went down to the kitchen to do something about cheese and eggs. Then, to stave off the thought of Harold a bit longer, I fetched George Millace's box of trash in from the car and opened it on the kitchen table. It still didn't seem to make much sense that George should have kept these particular photographic odds and ends.

I picked up the folder containing the dark print of a shadowy man sitting at a table and thought it was strange that Millace had put that overexposed mess into a mount.

I slid the print out onto my hand, and it was then that I found George Millace's pot of gold.

# CHAPTER 3

IT WAS not, at first sight, very exciting. Taped onto the back of the print was an envelope made of the special sort of sulfur-free paper used by professionals for the long-term storage of developed film. Inside the envelope, a negative. It was the negative from which the print had been made, but whereas the print was mostly black, the negative itself was clear and sharp, with many details and highlights.

I was curious. I went into the darkroom and made four four-by-five-inch prints, each at a different exposure, from one to eight seconds. Even the print made at the longest exposure did not look exactly like George's dark print. So I started again with the most suitable exposure, six seconds, and left the photograph in the developer too long, until the sharp outlines went dark, showing a gray man sitting at a table against a black background—a print almost exactly like George's.

Leaving a print too long in the developing fluid has to be one of the commonest mistakes on earth. If George had been distracted and left a print too long in the developer, he'd simply have cursed and thrown the ruin away. Why, then, had he kept it? And mounted it? And stuck the clear, sharp negative onto the back?

It wasn't until I switched on a bright light and looked more closely at the best of the four original prints I'd made that I understood why; and I stood utterly still, taking in the implications in disbelief.

I finally moved. I switched off the white light, and when my eyes had accustomed themselves again to the red safelight, I made another print, four times as large, to get as clear a result as possible.

What I got was a picture of two men talking together who had sworn on oath in a court of law that they had never met.

There wasn't the slightest possibility of a mistake. They were sitting at a table outside a café somewhere in France. The café had a name: Le Lapin d'Argent. There were advertisements for lottery tickets in its half-curtained window, and a waiter was standing in the doorway. A woman was sitting inside at a cash desk in front of a mirror, looking out to the street. The detail was sharp throughout. George Millace at his expert best.

Both men were facing the camera but had their heads turned toward each other, deep in conversation. A wineglass stood in front of each of them, half full, with a bottle to one side. There were coffee cups also, and an ashtray with a half-smoked cigar on the edge. All the signs of a lengthy meeting.

These two men had been involved in an affair that had shaken the racing world like a thunderclap eighteen months earlier. Elgin Yaxley, the one on the left in the photograph, had owned five expensive steeplechasers that had been trained in Lambourn. At the end of the season all five had been sent to a local farmer for a few weeks' break out at grass; and then, while in the fields, they had all been shot dead with a rifle.

Terence O'Tree, the man on the right in the photograph, had shot them. Some smart police work had tracked down O'Tree and brought him to court.

The five horses had been heavily insured. The insurance company, screeching with disbelief, had tried to prove that Elgin Yaxley himself had hired O'Tree to do the killing, but both men had consistently denied it, and no link between them had been found.

O'Tree, saying he'd shot the horses just because he'd felt like it, had been sent to jail for nine months with a recommendation that he should see a psychiatrist.

After threatening to sue the insurance company for defamation of character, Elgin Yaxley had wrung the whole insured amount out of them and had then faded from the racing scene.

The insurance company, I thought, would surely have paid George Millace a great deal for his photograph if they had known it existed. So why hadn't George asked for a reward? And why had he so carefully hidden the negative? And why had his house been burglarized three times?

For all that I'd never liked George Millace, I disliked the obvious answer to those questions even more.

IN THE morning I walked up to the stables and rode out at early exercise as usual. Harold behaved in his normal blustery fashion, raising his voice over the scouring wind. At one point he bellowed, "Breakfast. Be there."

I nodded and finished my ride.

Breakfast, in Harold's wife's view, consisted of a huge fry-up accompanied by mountains of toast served on the big kitchen table with generosity and warmth. I always fell for it.

"Another sausage, Philip?" Harold's wife said, lavishly shoveling straight from the pan and smiling at me. She thought I was too thin and that I needed a wife. She told me so, often.

"You're destroying him, woman," Harold said, then turned to me. "Last night we didn't discuss the week's plans. There's Pamphlet at Kempton on Wednesday, in the two-mile hurdle; and Tishoo and Sharpener on Thursday. . . ."

He talked about the races for some time, munching vigorously all the while. "Understood?" he said finally.

"Yes." It appeared that I had not been given the sack after all, and for that I was relieved, but it was clear all the same that the precipice wasn't far away.

Harold glanced at his wife, who was stacking things in the dishwasher, and said quietly to me, "Victor doesn't like your attitude. Owners won't stand for jockeys passing moral judgments on them."

"Owners shouldn't defraud the public, then."

"Have you finished eating?" he demanded.

I sighed regretfully. "Yes."

"Then come into my office."

He led the way into the russet-colored room. "Shut the door." I shut it. "You'll have to choose, Philip," he said, as he stood by the fireplace with one foot on the hearth, a big man in riding clothes, smelling of horses and fresh air and fried eggs. "Victor will eventually want another race lost. He says if you won't do it, we'll have to get someone else."

I shook my head. "Why does he want to start this caper again? He's won a lot of prize money playing it straight these last three years."

Harold shrugged. "I don't know. What does it matter? We've all done it before. Why not again? You just work it out, boy. Whose are the best horses in the yard? Victor's. Who owns more horses in this yard than anyone else? Victor. And which owner can I least afford to lose?"

I stared at him. I hadn't realized until then that he was in the same position as I. Do what Victor wants, or else.

"I don't want to lose you, Philip," he said. "You're prickly, but we've got on all right all these years. You won't go on forever, though. You've been racing . . . what . . . ten years? You've got three or four more, then. At the most, five. Pretty soon you won't bounce back from those falls the way you do now. So look at it straight, Philip. Who do I need most in the long term, you or Victor?"

In a sort of melancholy we walked into the yard. "Let me know," he said. "I want you to stay."

I was surprised, but also pleased. "Thanks," I said.

He gave me a clumsy buffet on the shoulder, the nearest he'd ever come to the slightest show of affection. More than all the threatening, it made me want to do what he asked—a reaction, I acknowledged flickeringly, as old as the hills. It was often kindness that finally broke the prisoner's spirit, not torture. One's defenses were always defiantly angled outward to withstand aggression; it was kindness that crept around behind and stabbed you in the back. Defenses against kindness were much harder to build.

I sought instinctively to change the subject and came up with the nearest thought to hand, which was George Millace and his photograph. "Um," I said. "Do you remember those five horses of Elgin Yaxley's that were shot?"

He looked bewildered. "What's that got to do with Victor?"

"Nothing at all. I was just thinking about them yesterday."

Irritation immediately canceled out the passing moment of emotion, which was probably a relief to us both.

"Philip," he said sharply. "I'm serious. Your career's at stake. You can bloody well go to hell. It's up to you." He started to turn away, then stopped. "If you're so interested in Elgin Yaxley's horses, why don't you ask Kenny?" He pointed to one of his stable lads, who was filling two buckets by the water tap. "He looked after them when he was working for Bart Underfield, Yaxley's trainer."

He strode away, anger thumping down with every foot. I walked over to Kenny, not sure what questions I wanted to ask.

Kenny was one of those people whose defenses were the other way around: impervious to kindness, open to fright. He watched me come with an insolent expression, his skin reddened by the wind, eyes slightly watering.

"Mr. Osborne said you used to work for Bart Underfield," I said. "And looked after some of Elgin Yaxley's horses."

"So what?"

"So were you sorry when they were shot?"

He shrugged. "Suppose so."

"What did Mr. Underfield say about it? Wasn't he angry?"

"Not as I noticed."

"He must have been," I said. "He was five horses short. No trainer with his size stable can afford that."

Kenny shrugged again. The two buckets were nearly full. He turned off the tap. "He didn't seem to care much about losing them. Something made him mad a bit later, though."

"What?"

Kenny picked up the buckets. "Don't know. He was right grumpy. Some of the owners got fed up and left."

"So did you," I said.

"Yeah." He started walking across the yard with water sloshing at each step. I went with him. "What's the point of staying when a place is going down the drain?" he said.

"Were Yaxley's horses in good shape?"

"Sure. They had the vet in court, you know, to say the horses were fine the day before they died. I read about it in *The Sporting Life*." He reached the row of stalls and put the buckets down. "Tell you something." He looked almost surprised at his own sudden helpfulness. "That Mr. Yaxley, you'd've thought he'd been pleased getting all that cash, even if he had lost his horses, but he came into Underfield's yard one day in a right proper rage. Come to think of it, it was after that that Underfield went sour. And Yaxley, of course, quit racing and we never saw no more of him. Not while I was there, we didn't."

I walked thoughtfully home, and when I got there the telephone was ringing. "Jeremy Folk," a familiar voice said.

"Oh, not again," I protested.

"Did you read those detectives' reports?"

"Yes, I did. And I'm not going looking for her. To get you off my back, I'll help you a bit. But you must do the looking."

"Well . . ." He sighed. "What sort of help?"

I told him my conclusions about Amanda's age, and also suggested he should get the dates of the various tenancies of Pine Woods Lodge from the real estate agents.

"My mother was probably there thirteen years ago," I said. "And now it's all yours."

"But I *say*," he wailed. "You simply can't stop there."

"I simply can," I said. "Now just leave me alone."

I drove into Swindon to take the color film I'd shot at Mrs. Millace's to the processors', and on the way thought about Bart Underfield.

I knew him in the way one got to know everyone in racing if one lived long enough in Lambourn. We met occasionally in the village shops and in other people's houses, as well as at the races, but I had never ridden for him.

He was a small, busy man full of importance, given to telling people confidentially what other, more successful trainers had done wrong. Strangers thought him very knowledgeable. People in Lambourn thought him an ass.

No one had suggested, however, that he was such an ass as to deliver his five best horses to the slaughter. Everyone had felt sorry for him, particularly as Elgin Yaxley had not spent the insurance money on buying new animals, but had merely departed, leaving Bart a great deal worse off.

Those horses could have been sold for high prices. It was the fact that there seemed to be little profit in killing them that had finally baffled the suspicious insurers into paying up. That and no trace of a link between Elgin Yaxley and Terence O'Tree.

In Swindon, I left my film with the processors, picked up the developed negatives a couple of hours later, and went home. In the afternoon I printed the color versions and sent them off with the black and whites to the police; and in the evening I tried— and failed—to stop thinking about Amanda and Victor Briggs and George Millace.

By far the worst thoughts concerned Victor Briggs and Harold's ultimatum: cooperate or else. The jockey life suited me fine. I'd put off for years the thought that one day I would have to do something else. The "one day" had always been in the future, not staring me brutally in the face.

The only thing I knew anything about besides horses was pho- tography, but there were thousands of photographers all over the place and very few full-time successful racing photographers. Fewer than ten, probably. If I tried to join their ranks, the others wouldn't hinder me, but they wouldn't help me, either. I'd be out there on my own, stand or fall.

I thought violent thoughts about Victor Briggs.

Inciting jockeys to throw races was a warning-off offense, but even if I could get Briggs disqualified, the person who would suffer most would be Harold. And I'd lose my job anyway, since Harold would hardly keep me on after that, even if we didn't both lose our licenses because of the races I'd thrown in the past. I couldn't prove Victor Briggs's villainy without having to admit Harold's and my own. So it was cheat or retire. A stark choice.

NOTHING much happened on Tuesday, but when I went to Kemp- ton on Wednesday to ride Pamphlet, the changing room was elec- tric with two pieces of gossip. Ivor den Relgan had been made a member of the Jockey Club, and Mrs. Millace's house had burned down.

"Ivor den Relgan?" The name was repeated in varying tones of astonishment. "A member of the Jockey Club? Incredible!"

The Jockey Club, that exclusive and gentlemanly body, had that morning voted into its fastidious ranks a man it had been holding at arm's length for years, a rich, self-important man from no one knew where. He was supposed to be from some unspecified ex-Dutch colony. He spoke with a patronizing accent that sounded like a mixture of South African, Australian, and American. He, the voice seemed to say, was a great deal more sophisticated than the stuffy British upper crust. They, he implied, would prosper if they took his advice, and he offered it freely in letters to *The Sporting Life*.

Until that morning the Jockey Club had indeed taken his advice on several occasions while steadfastly refusing to acknowledge it. I wondered fleetingly what had brought them to such a turnabout, what had caused them suddenly to embrace the anathema.

Steve Millace walked up to me, white-faced. His arm was in a black sling and his eyes were sunken, desperate.

"Have you heard?" he said. I nodded. "It happened late Monday night. By the time anyone noticed, the whole place had gone."

"Your mother wasn't there?"

"They'd kept her in the hospital. She's still there. It's too much for her." He was trembling. "Tell me what to do, Philip. You saw Mum. All bashed about . . . without Dad . . . and now the house. . . . *Please*, help me."

"When I've finished riding," I said resignedly, "we'll work something out."

He sat down on the bench as if his legs wouldn't hold him, and just stayed there staring while I changed into my colors.

Harold came in. Since Monday he'd made no reference to the life-altering decision he'd handed me. Perhaps he took my silence for tacit acceptance of a return to things past. At any rate it was in a normal manner that he said, "Did you hear who's been elected to the Jockey Club? They'll take Genghis Khan next."

He walked out to the parade ring, and in due course I joined him. Pamphlet was walking nonchalantly around while his rockstar owner bit his nails. Harold had gleaned some more news. "I hear that it was the Great White Chief who insisted on den Relgan joining the club."

"Lord White?" I was surprised.

"Old Driven Snow himself."

"Philip," said the rock star, who had come to the races that day with dark blue hair. "Bring this baby back for Daddy." He must have learned that out of old movies, I thought. Surely not even rock musicians talked like that anymore. I got up on Pamphlet and rode out to see what I could do.

Maybe Pamphlet had winning on his mind that day as much as I did. He soared around the whole course with bursting *joie de vivre*, even passing the favorite, and we came back to bear hugs from the blue hair and an offer to me of a spare ride in the fifth race from a worried-looking small-time trainer. Stable jockey hurt. . . . Would I mind? Mind? I'd be delighted.

Steve was still brooding by my locker.

"Was the shed burned?" I asked. "Your dad's films?"

"Oh well, yes it was. . . . But Dad's stuff wasn't in there."

I stripped off the rock star's orange and pink colors and went in search of the calmer green and brown of the spare ride.

"Where was it, then?" I asked, returning.

"I told Mum what you said about people maybe not liking Dad's pictures of them, and she reckoned that you thought all the burglaries were really aimed at the films, so on Monday she got me to move them next door, to her neighbor's."

I buttoned the green and brown shirt, thinking it over.

"Do you want me to visit her in the hospital?" I asked.

He fell on it with embarrassing fervor. He had come to the races, he said, with the pubkeeper from the village where he lived, and if I would visit his mother, he could go home with the pubkeeper, because otherwise he had no transport, because of his collarbone. I hadn't exactly meant I would see Mrs. Millace alone, but on reflection I didn't mind.

Having shifted his burden, Steve cheered up a bit.

"Did your father often go to France?" I said absently.

"France? Of course. Longchamps, Saint-Cloud. All the races."

"What did he spend his money on?"

"Lenses mostly. Telephotos as long as your arm. Any new equipment. . . . What do you mean, what did he spend his money on?"

"I just wondered what he liked doing away from the races."

"He just took pictures. All the time, everywhere. He wasn't interested in anything else."

In time I went out to ride the green and brown horse and it was one of those days, which happened so seldom, when absolutely everything went right. In unqualified euphoria I dismounted once again in the winners' enclosure, and thought that I couldn't possibly give up the life; I couldn't *possibly*.

STEVE's mother was in a ward, lying on her back with two flat pillows under her head and a thin blue blanket covering her. Her eyes were shut. Her face was dreadful.

The cut eyelid, stitched, was swollen and black. The lips, also swollen, looked purple. The nose was under some shaping plaster of paris, held in place by white sticky tape. All the rest showed deep signs of bruising. I'd seen people in that state before, damaged by horses' galloping hoofs, but this injury was done out of malice to an inoffensive lady in her own home. I felt not only sympathy but anger.

She opened her less battered eye a fraction. "Steve asked me to come," I said. "He can't drive for a day or two."

I put a chair by the bed and sat beside her. Her hand, which was lying on the blanket, slowly stretched out to me. I took it, and she held on fiercely, seeking reassurance, it seemed. After a while the spirit of need ebbed, and she let go.

"Did Steve tell you," she said, "about the house?"

"Yes, he did. I'm so sorry."

A sort of shudder shook her, and her breathing grew more troubled. She could get no air through her nose. "The police came here today," she said. Her chest heaved and she coughed.

I put my hand over hers and said urgently, "Don't get upset. You'll make everything hurt worse. Just take three slow deep breaths. Four or five, if you need them."

She lay silent for a while until the heavy breathing slackened. Eventually she said, "You're much older than Steve."

"Eight years," I agreed, letting go of her hand.

"No. Much . . . much older." There was a pause. "The police said it was arson. Kerosene. Five-gallon drum. They found it in the hall." Another pause. "The police asked if George had any enemies. I said of course not. And they asked if he had anything someone would want enough . . . oh . . ."

"Mrs. Millace," I said matter-of-factly. "Did they ask if George had any photographs worth burglary and burning?"

"George wouldn't . . ." she said intensely.

George had, I thought.

"If you like," I said slowly, "I could look through the transparencies and negatives you moved to your neighbor's; and I could tell you if I think there are any that could possibly come into the category we're talking about. Then if they're okay, you can tell the police they exist. If you want to."

"George isn't a blackmailer," she said. Coming from the swollen mouth, the words sounded extraordinary, distorted but passionately meant. She hadn't much left except that instinctive faith. It was beyond me entirely to tell her it was misplaced.

I COLLECTED the three metal boxes from the neighbor. The Millaces' house itself was a shell, roofless and windowless.

I drove home with George's lifework, and spent the evening projecting his slides onto the white wall of my sitting room.

His talent had been stupendous. Seeing his pictures one after the other, not scattered in books and magazines across a canvas of years, I was struck by the speed of his vision. Over and over again he had caught life at the moment when a painter would have composed it: nothing left out, nothing disruptive let in. The best of his racing pictures were there, but there were also dozens of portraits of people. Again and again he had caught the fleeting expression that exposed the soul. Collectively the shots were breathtaking.

What George had photographed was a satirical baring of the essence under the external, and I was deeply aware that I was never going to see the world in quite the same way again. But George had had no compassion. The pictures were brilliant, exciting, and revealing, but none of them were kind.

None of them could have been used as a basis for blackmail, either.

I telephoned Marie Millace in the morning and told her so. The relief in her voice betrayed that she had had small doubts, and she heard it herself and immediately began a cover-up.

"I mean," she said, "of course I knew George wouldn't . . ."

"Of course," I said. "What shall I do with the films?"

"Oh dear, I don't know. What do you think?"

"Well," I said, "you can't exactly advertise that although George's work still exists, no one needs to feel threatened. I'm sorry, but I agree with the police. That George did have something that someone desperately wanted destroyed. Please don't worry. Whatever it was has probably gone with the house . . . and it's all over." And God forgive me, I thought, and went on. "I think the best thing for now would be to put those transparencies and negatives into storage somewhere. Then when you feel better, you could get an agent to put on an exhibition of George's work. The collection is marvelous; it really is."

There was a long pause. Then she said, "I know I'm asking such a lot. But could you put the films into storage? I'd ask Steve, but you seem to know what to do."

I said that I would, and when we had disconnected, I took the three boxes along to the local butcher. He already kept a box of my unexposed film in his walk-in freezer room. He cheerfully agreed to lock away the new lodgers and suggested a reasonable rental.

Back home, I looked at the negative and the print of Elgin Yaxley talking to Terence O'Tree and wondered what I should do with them. If George had extorted from Yaxley all the profits from the murdered horses, then it had to be Yaxley who was now desperate to find the photograph before anyone else did.

If I gave the photograph to the police, Elgin Yaxley would be in line for prosecution. But I would be telling the world that George Millace had been a blackmailer.

Which would Marie Millace prefer? I thought. Never to know who had attacked her, or to know for sure that George had been a villain? There was no doubt about the answer.

I had no qualms about legal justice. I put the negative and the dark print back into the box of rubbish, and I put the clear big print I'd made into a folder in the filing cabinet in the darkroom. No one knew I had them. No one would come looking. Nothing at all would happen from now on.

I locked my doors and went to the races to ride Tishoo and Sharpener and to agonize over my other thorny problem, Victor Briggs.

# CHAPTER 4

IVOR den Relgan was again the big news, and what was more, he was there, standing outside the changing room talking to two reporters. He wore an expensive camel-colored coat, buttoned and belted, and he stood bareheaded with graying hair neatly brushed, a stocky, slightly pugnacious-looking man with an air of expecting people to notice him. I would have been happy never to have come into his focus, but as I was passing, one of the reporters fastened a hand on my arm.

"Philip," he said. "You can tell us. You're always on the business end of a camera. How do you photograph a wild horse?"

"Point and click," I said pleasantly.

"No, Philip," he said, exasperated. "You know Mr. den Relgan, don't you? Mr. den Relgan, this is Philip Nore. Jockey, of course." The reporter was unaccustomedly obsequious; den Relgan often had that effect. "Mr. den Relgan wants photographs of all his horses, but one of them rears up all the time when he sees a camera. How would you get him to stand still?"

"I know one photographer," I said, "who got a wild horse to stand still by playing a tape of a hunt in full cry. The horse just stood and listened. The pictures were great."

Den Relgan smiled superciliously, as if he didn't want to hear good ideas that weren't his own, and I nodded with about as much fervor and went on into the changing room, thinking that the Jockey Club must have been mad. The existing members were mostly forward-looking people who put goodwill and energy into running a huge industry fairly. That they were also self-electing meant that they were almost all aristocrats, but the ideal of service bred into them worked pretty well for the good of racing. Surprising that they should have beckoned to a semiphony like den Relgan.

Harold was inside the changing room with Lord White, who was telling him that there were special trophies for Sharpener's race; should we happen to win it, both Harold and I, as well as the owner, would be required to put in an appearance and receive our gifts.

"It wasn't advertised as a sponsored race," Harold said.

"No. But Mr. den Relgan has generously made this gesture." Lord White nodded, turned, and left us.

"How many trophies does it take," Harold said under his breath, "to buy your way into the Jockey Club?" And in a normal voice he added, "Win that pot if you can. It would really give Victor a buzz, taking Ivor den Relgan's cup. They can't stand each other."

"I didn't know they knew—"

"Everyone knows everyone," Harold said, shrugging. He lost interest and went out of the room, and I stood for a few moments watching Lord White talking to the other trainers.

Lord White, in his fifties, was a well-built, good-looking man with bright blue eyes and thick, light gray hair, which was progressively turning the color of his name. A widely respected man, he was the true leader of the Jockey Club, elected not by votes but by the natural force born in him. His nickname, Driven Snow (spoken only behind his back), had been coined, I thought, to poke fun at the presence of so much noticeable virtue.

I began to change into Tishoo's colors and was guiltily relieved to find Steve Millace was not present. No beseeching eyes to inveigle me into another round of visiting the sick.

In the race itself there were no great problems, but no repeat either of the previous day's joys. Tishoo galloped willingly enough into fourth place, which pleased his woman owner, and I went back to my locker and put on Victor Briggs's colors for Sharpener. Just another day's work. Each day unique in itself, but in essence the same. On two thousand days, or thereabouts, I had put on colors and ridden the races. Two thousand days of hope and sweat. More than a job: part of my fabric.

Two other races were to be run before Sharpener's, so I put on a jacket and went outside for a while to see what was happening; and what was happening was Lady White with a scowl on her thin, aristocratic face.

Lady White didn't know me especially, but I, along with most other jump jockeys, had shaken her hand at a few parties she and Lord White had given to the racing world. Now she was hugging her mink around her and glaring forth from under a wide-brimmed brown hat. I followed her gaze and found it fixed on her paragon of a husband, who was talking to a girl.

Lord White was not simply talking to the girl but reveling in it, radiating flirtatious fun from his sparkling eyes. I thought in amusement that the pure white lord would be in for a ticking off from his lady that evening.

I gradually became aware that a man near me was also intently watching Lord White and the girl. The man was average-looking, not quite middle-aged, with dark thinning hair and black-framed glasses. He was wearing gray trousers and a green suede jacket, well cut. When he realized I was looking at him, he gave me a quick annoyed glance and moved away.

I joined Victor Briggs in the parade ring before Sharpener's race. He was pleasant and made no reference to the issue hanging between us. Harold had boosted himself into a state of confidence and was standing with his long legs apart, his hat tipped back, and his binoculars swinging from one hand.

"A formality," he was saying. "Sharpener's never been better, eh, Philip? He'll run the legs off 'em today."

Sharpener himself reacted to Harold's optimism in a thoroughly positive way, and ran a faultless race with energy and courage, so that for the third time in two days my mount returned to applause. Metaphorically Harold was by this time two feet off the ground, and even Victor allowed his mouth a small smile.

Ivor den Relgan manfully shaped up to the fact that one of his fancy trophies had been won by a man he disliked, and Lord White fluttered around the girl he'd been talking to, clearing a passage for her through the throng. At the prizegiving, the scene sorted itself out. Surrounding a table with a blue cloth bearing one large silver object and two smaller ones were Lord White, Lady White, the girl, Ivor den Relgan, Victor, Harold, and I.

Lord White announced to the small crowd that Miss Dana den Relgan would present the trophies given by her father, and it cannot have been only in my mind that the cynical speculation arose. Was it the dad that Lord White wanted in the Jockey Club, or the dad's daughter? Perish the thought. Yet it was clear that Lord White was attracted to the girl beyond sober good sense.

Dana den Relgan was enough, I suppose, to excite any man. Slender and graceful, she had a lot of blond-flecked hair curling casually onto her shoulders, a curving mouth, and wide-set eyes. Her manner was more restrained than Lord White's, and she presented the trophies to Victor and Harold and me without much conversation.

She merely said, "Well done," when she gave me the small silver object (a saddle-shaped paperweight), and had the surface smile of someone who isn't really looking at you and is going to forget you within five minutes.

While Victor and Harold and I were comparing trophies, the average-looking man in spectacles reappeared, walked quietly up to Dana den Relgan, and spoke softly into her ear. She began to move off with him, smiling a little.

This apparently harmless proceeding had the most extraordinary effect upon den Relgan. He almost ran after them, gripped the inoffensive-looking man by the shoulder, and threw him away from her with such force that the man staggered and went down on one knee.

"I've told you to keep away from her," den Relgan said, looking as if kicking a man when he was down was something he had no reservations about.

"Who is that man?" I asked of no one in particular.

Victor Briggs answered, "Film director. Fellow called Lance Kinship."

"And why the fuss?"

Briggs knew. "Cocaine," he said. "Kinship supplies the stuff. Gets asked to parties for what he brings along."

Lance Kinship was on his feet, brushing dirt off his trousers and looking murderous. "If I want to talk to Dana, I'll talk to her," he said.

"Not while I'm there, you won't."

Kinship seemed unintimidated. "Little girls don't always have their daddies with them," he said nastily, and den Relgan hit him— a sharp, efficient crunch on the nose.

There was a good deal of blood, and Lord White, hating the whole thing, held out a huge white handkerchief. Kinship grabbed it without thanks.

"First-aid room, don't you think?" Lord White said, looking around. "Er . . . Nore," he said, his gaze alighting. "Take this gentleman to the first-aid room, would you? Awfully good of you." But when I put a hand out to guide Kinship, he jerked away.

"Bleed, then," I said.

Unfriendly eyes behind the black frames glared out at me.

"Follow if you want," I said, and set off. Not only did Kinship follow, but den Relgan also.

"If you come near Dana again, I'll break your neck," I heard him say.

There was a scuffle behind me and I looked around in time to see Kinship aim a karate kick at den Relgan's crotch and land deftly on target. Den Relgan doubled over, making choking noises.

Kinship turned back to me and gave me another unfriendly stare over the reddening handkerchief.

"In there," I said, jerking my head, and he gave me a final reptilian glance as the door to the first-aid room opened.

A pity George Millace had gone to his fathers, I thought. He would have been there with his lens focused, pointing the right way, and taking inexorable notes at three point five frames a second.

Later, when I left the changing room to set off for home, I was intercepted by the tall, loitering figure of Jeremy Folk. "What do you want?" I said.

"Well . . ."

"The answer's no."

"But you don't know what I'm going to ask."

"I can see that it's something I don't want to do."

There was a pause. "I went to see your grandmother. I told her you wouldn't look for your sister for money. I told her she would have to give you something else."

I was puzzled. "Give me what?"

Jeremy looked vaguely around the racecourse from his great height. "Your grandmother agreed," he said, "that she had a flaming row with Caroline—your mother—and chucked her out when she was pregnant."

"My mother," I said, "was seventeen."

He smiled. "Funny to think of one's mother being so *young*."

Poor defenseless little butterfly. "Yes," I said.

"Your grandmother says that if you will look for Amanda, she will tell you why she threw Caroline out. And also she will tell you who your father is."

I stared at him. "Is that what you said to her? 'Tell him who his father is, and he'll do what you want'?"

"You would want to know, wouldn't you?"

"No," I said.

"I don't believe you. It's human nature to want to know."

I swallowed. "Did she tell you who he is?"

He shook his head. "No. She's never told anyone. If you don't go and find out, you'll never know."

"You're a real creep, Jeremy. I thought solicitors were supposed to sit behind desks and pontificate, not go about manipulating old ladies."

"This particular old lady is a . . . a challenge."

"Why doesn't she leave her money to her son?"

"She won't say. She told my grandfather simply that she wanted to cancel her old will and leave everything to Amanda."

"Have you met her son?"

"No," he said. "Have you?"

I shook my head. Jeremy took another vague look around the racecourse and said, "Why don't we get cracking on this together? We'd turn Amanda up in no time. Then you could go back into your shell and forget the whole thing if you want."

He would persevere, I thought, with or without my help. He wanted to prove to his grandfather and uncle that when he set his mind to sorting something out, it got sorted.

As for me, the mists around my birth were there for the parting. I could know what the shouting had been about behind the door while I waited in the hall in my new clothes. I might end by detesting the man who'd fathered me. But Jeremy was right. Given the chance, one had to know.

"All right," I said.

He was pleased. "That's great. Can you go tonight? I'll just tell her you're coming." He plunged toward the telephone booth and disappeared inside. The call, however, gave him no joy.

"Blast," he said, rejoining me. "I spoke to a nurse. 'Mrs. Nore had a bad day and she's asleep. Phone tomorrow.'"

Feeling a distinct sense of relief, I set off toward the parking lot. Jeremy followed.

"About Mrs. Nore's son, James," he said. "I just thought you might visit him. Find out why he's been disinherited." He pulled a card out of his pocket. "I brought his address." He held it out. "And you've promised to help."

"A pact is a pact," I said, and took the card. "But you're still a creep."

JAMES NORE LIVED IN LONDON, and since I was more than halfway there, I drove straight to the house. The door was opened by a man of about forty, who agreed that James Nore was his name. He was astounded to find an unknown nephew standing on his doormat, and with only a slight hesitation he invited me in, leading the way into a Victorian sitting room.

"I thought Caroline had aborted you," he said baldly.

He was nothing like my memories of my mother. He was plump, soft-muscled, and small-mouthed, and had a mournful droop to his eyes. None of her giggly lightness or grace could ever have lived in his flaccid body. I felt ill at ease with him on sight.

He listened with his small lips pouted while I explained about looking for Amanda, and he showed more and more annoyance.

"The old bag's been saying for months that she's going to cut me off," he said furiously. "Ever since she came here." He glanced around the room, but nothing there seemed to me likely to alienate a mother. "Everything was all right as long as I went to visit her in Northamptonshire. Then she came *here*. Uninvited."

A brass clock on the mantelshelf sweetly chimed the half hour.

"I'd be a fool to help you find Caroline's second child, wouldn't I?" he said. "If no one can find her, the whole estate reverts to me anyway, will or no will, although I'd have to wait years for it. Mother's just being spiteful." He shrugged. "Are you going now? There's no point in your staying."

He started to the door, but before he reached it, it was opened by a man wearing a cooking apron and limply carrying a wooden spoon. He was much younger than James, and unmistakably camp.

"Oh hello, dear," he said to me. "Are you staying for supper?"

"He's just going," James said sharply.

Suddenly it all made sense, and I said to the man in the apron, "Did you meet Mrs. Nore when she came here?"

"Sure did, dear," he said ruefully, and then caught sight of James shaking his head vigorously at him and meaning shut up. I smiled halfheartedly and went to the front door.

"I wish you bad luck," James said. "That beastly Caroline. I never did like her. Always laughing at me and tripping me up. I was glad when she went."

I nodded and opened the door.

"Wait," he said suddenly, and I could see he had an idea that pleased him. "Mother would never leave *you* anything, of course," he began.

"Why not?" I said.

He frowned. "There was a terrible drama when Caroline got pregnant. Frightful scene. Lots of screaming. I remember it, but no one would ever explain. All I do know is that everything changed because of you. Caroline went and Mother turned into a bitter old bag. She hated you."

He peered at me expectantly, but in truth I felt nothing. The old woman's hatred hadn't troubled me for years.

"I'll give you some of the money, though," he said, "if you can prove that Amanda is dead."

On Saturday morning Jeremy Folk telephoned.

"Will you be at home tomorrow?" he said.

"Yes, but—"

"Good. I'll pop over." He put down his receiver without giving me a chance to say I didn't want him.

Also on Saturday I ran into Bart Underfield in the post office. In place of our usual unenthusiastic good-mornings I asked him a question. "Where is Elgin Yaxley these days, Bart?"

"He lives in Hong Kong. What's it to do with you?"

"I just thought I saw him. A week ago yesterday."

"Well, you're wrong," Bart said. "That was the day of George Millace's funeral, and Elgin sent me a cable. From Hong Kong."

"A cable of regrets, was it?"

"Are you crazy? He'd have spat on the coffin."

"Oh well," I said, shrugging. "I must say a good many people will be relieved now George is gone."

"More like down on their knees giving thanks."

"Do you ever hear anything nowadays about that chap who shot Elgin's horses? What's his name? Terence O'Tree?"

"He's still in jail. Hit a guard and lost his chance for parole."

"How do you know?"

"I . . . er . . . just heard." Bart had suddenly had too much of this conversation and began backing away.

"And did you hear that George Millace's house burned down? And that it was arson?"

He stopped in midstride. "Arson?" he said, looking surprised. "Why would anyone want—Oh!" He abruptly understood why; and I thought that he couldn't possibly have achieved that revelationary expression by art. He hadn't known.

Elgin Yaxley was in Hong Kong and Terence O'Tree was in jail, and neither they nor Underfield had burglarized, beaten, or burned.

The easy explanations were all wrong.

I had jumped, I thought penitently, to conclusions. It was only because I'd disliked George Millace that I'd been so ready to believe ill of him. He had taken that incriminating photograph, but there was really nothing to prove that he'd used it. Elgin Yaxley had gone to Hong Kong instead of plowing his insurance money back into racehorses, but that didn't make him a villain.

Yet he was a villain. He had sworn he'd never met Terence O'Tree, and he had. And it had to have been before the trial in February, since O'Tree had been in jail ever since. Not during the winter just before the trial either, because it had been sitting-outdoors weather. I now remembered that in the photo there had been a newspaper lying on an adjacent table, on which one might possibly see a date.

As soon as I arrived home, I projected my big new print onto the sitting-room wall. The newspaper lay too flat on the table. Neither the date nor a useful headline could be seen. I studied the rest of the picture, and in the background, beside Madame at her cash desk inside the café, was a calendar hanging on a hook. The letters and numbers on it could just be discerned: it was April of the previous year. Elgin Yaxley's horses had been sent out to grass late that same month, and they had been shot on the fourth of May.

I switched off the projector and drove to the races at Windsor, puzzling over the inconsistencies.

It was a moderate day's racing at Windsor, and because of the weak opposition, one of Harold's slowest old steeplechasers finally had his day; my geriatric pal loped in first. The delight of his faithful elderly lady owner made it all well worth the effort.

"I knew he'd do it one day," she said. "It's his last season, you know. I'll have to retire him." She patted his neck. "We're all getting on a bit, old boy, aren't we? Can't go on forever. Everything ends. But today it's been great."

Her words lingered with me. "Everything ends. But today it's been great." Most of my mind still rebelled against the thought of retirement, particularly one dictated by Victor Briggs, but somewhere the frail seedling of acceptance was stretching its first leaf in the dark. Life changes, everything ends. I didn't want it, but it was happening.

Outside the changing room one wouldn't have guessed it. I had uncharacteristically won four races that week. I was offered five rides for the following week by trainers other than Harold. If anyone had asked me in that moment about retiring, I would have said, Oh yes. In five years' time.

THE following morning Jeremy Folk arrived, as he'd said he would, angling his storklike figure through my front door. He followed me to the kitchen.

"Champagne?" I said.

"It's . . . er . . . only ten o'clock."

"Four winners," I said, "need celebrating."

He took his first sip as if the wickedness of it would overwhelm him. He had made an effort to be casual in his clothes: wool checked shirt, woolly tie, neat pale blue sweater. Whatever he thought of my unbuttoned collar and unshaven jaw, he didn't say.

"Did you see . . . ah . . . James Nore?"

"Yes, I did." I gestured to him to sit down at the kitchen table and joined him, with the bottle in reach. "Mrs. Nore visited his house unexpectedly one day," I explained. "She hadn't been there before. She met James's friend, and she realized, I suppose for the first time, that her son was homosexual."

"Oh," Jeremy said, understanding much.

I nodded. "No descendants."

"So she thought of Amanda." He sighed and drank some pale gold fizz. "Are you sure he's homosexual? Did he say so?"

"As good as. Anyway, you get to know, somehow. I lived with two of them for a while."

He looked slightly shocked. "Did you? I mean, are you? . . . I shouldn't ask. Sorry."

"No, I'm not," I said, and while he buried his nose and his embarrassment in his glass, I thought of Duncan and Charlie. Charlie had been older than Duncan, solid and industrious and kind; to me he had been father, uncle, guardian, all in one. Duncan had been chatty and very good company, and neither of them had tried to teach me their way.

One day Duncan fell in love with someone else and walked out. Charlie put his arm around my shoulders and hugged me, and wept. My mother had arrived within a week, blowing in like a whirlwind. Huge eyes, hollow cheeks, fluffy silk scarves.

"But you see, Charlie darling," she'd said, "that I can't leave Philip with you now that Duncan's gone." She'd looked at me, bright and more brittle than I remembered, and less beautiful. "Go and pack, Philip darling. We're going down to the country."

Charlie had come to my room and I'd said that I didn't want to leave him. "We must do what your mother says," he told me.

He'd helped me pack, and from the old life I'd been flung straight into the new. That evening I learned how to muck out a horse stall, and the next morning I started to ride.

Charlie pined miserably for Duncan and swallowed two hundred sleeping pills. He left all his possessions to me, including his cameras and darkroom equipment. He also left a letter. "Look after your mother," he wrote. "I think she's sick. Keep on taking photographs, you already have the eye. You'll be all right, boy. So long now. Charlie."

I drank some champagne and said to Jeremy, "Did you get the list of the Pine Woods Lodge tenancies from the agents?"

"Oh gosh, yes," he said, relieved to be back on firm ground. He patted several pockets. "Here we are." He spread out the sheet of paper. "If your mother was there thirteen years ago, the people she was with would have been the Boy Scouts, the television company, or the musicians. But the television people didn't live there, they just worked there during the day. The musicians did live there. They ruined the electric wiring and were supposed to be high all the time on drugs. Does any of that sound . . . er . . . like your mother?"

"Boy Scouts don't sound like her a bit. Drugs do, musicians don't. She never left me with anyone musical. I think I'd try the television company first."

Jeremy's face showed a jumble of emotions varying from incredulity to bewilderment. "What do you mean about your mother leaving you with people, and about your mother and drugs?"

I outlined the dumping procedure and what I owed to the Deborahs, Samanthas, and Chloes. Jeremy looked shattered.

"I didn't understand about the drugs," I said, "until I grew up, but certainly she was taking them for a long time. She kept me with her for a week sometimes, and there would be an acrid distinctive smell. Marijuana. She died from heroin, I think."

"Why do you think that?"

I poured refills of champagne. "Something the people at the racing stable said. Margaret and Bill. I went into the sitting room one day when they were arguing. Bill was saying, 'His place is with his mother,' and Margaret interrupted. 'She's a heroin—' Then she saw me and stopped. It's ironic, but I was so pleased they should think my mother a heroine." I smiled lopsidedly. "It was years before I realized that Margaret had really been going to say, 'She's a heroin addict.' I asked her later and she told me. She and Bill guessed, as I did, that my mother had died, and of course, long before I did, they guessed why. They didn't tell me, to save me pain. Kind people."

Jeremy shook his head. "I'm so sorry," he said.

"Don't be. I never grieved for my mother." I had grieved for Charlie, though, for a short intense time when I was fifteen and sporadically ever since. I used his legacy almost every day, not only the photographic equipment but also the knowledge he'd given me. Any photograph I took was thanks to Charlie.

"I'll try the television people," Jeremy said. "And you'll see your grandmother?"

I said without enthusiasm, "I suppose so."

"Where else can we look for Amanda? If your mother dumped you all over the place, she must have done the same with her."

"Yes, I've thought of that." All those people, so long in the past. Shadows without faces. "I might be able to find one place I stayed. But there might be different people in the house now, and they're unlikely to know anything about Amanda. . . ."

Jeremy pounced on it. "It's a chance. Well worth trying."

I drank some champagne and looked thoughtfully across the kitchen. George Millace's box of rubbish lay on the counter, and a hovering intention suddenly crystallized. "You're welcome to stay, but I want to spend the day on a different sort of puzzle," I said. "Nothing to do with Amanda. A sort of treasure hunt, but there may be no treasure." I got up and picked the piece of clear-looking film out of the box. "Look at this against the light."

He took the piece of film and held it up. "It's got smudges on it," he said. "Very faint. You can hardly see them."

"They're pictures. Three pictures on a roll of film. If I'm careful, and lucky, we might see them."

He was puzzled. "But what's the point? Why bother?"

"I found something of great interest in that box. I think maybe some more of those bits aren't the rubbish they seem."

He followed me and watched closely while I rummaged in one of the cupboards in the darkroom. "This all looks frightfully workmanlike," he said. "I'd no idea you did this sort of thing."

I explained briefly about Charlie, and finally found the bottle of negative intensifier I was looking for. I carried it to the sink, where there was a water filter fixed under the tap.

"What's that?" Jeremy asked, pointing to the filter.

"You have to use ultraclean soft water for photographic processing. And no iron pipes. Otherwise you get a lot of little black dots on the prints."

Following the instructions on the bottle, I mixed water and intensifier and poured the solution into the developing tray.

"What exactly are you going to do?" said Jeremy.

"I'm going to print this film with the faint smudges onto some photo paper and see what it looks like. Then I'm going to put the negative into this intensifying liquid, and after that I'm going to make another print to see if there's a difference."

He watched, peering into the developing tray while I worked in dim red light. "Can't see anything happening," he said.

"It's a bit trial and error," I agreed. I tried printing the clear film four times at different light exposures, but all we got on the prints was a fairly uniform black, gray, or white.

"There's nothing there," Jeremy said. "It's useless."

"Wait until we try the intensifier."

With more hope than expectation I slid the film into the intensifying liquid and sloshed it about. Then I washed it and printed it again at the same exposures as before. This time, on the light gray print there were patchy marks and on the nearly white print, swirly shapes.

"Well, that's that," Jeremy said. "Too bad."

"I think," I said reflectively, "that we might get further if I print that negative not onto paper but onto another film."

"Print it onto a film? I didn't know that was possible."

"Oh yes. You can print onto anything that has a photographic emulsion, and you can coat practically anything with photographic emulsion. Glass. Or canvas. Or wood. Or the back of your hand, I daresay."

I took a new roll of high contrast film, pulling it off its spool into a long strip and cutting it into five pieces. Onto each piece I printed the almost clear negative, exposing each one to the white light of the enlarger for different lengths of time, from one second to ten seconds. After exposure each piece went into the tray of developer.

The results, after I took each piece of film out of the developer at what looked like the best moment, then transferred it to the tray of fixer, and finally washed it, were five new positives. Taking these, I repeated the whole process, ending with negatives. Seen in bright light, all of the new negatives were much denser than the one I'd started with. On two of them there was a decipherable image. The smudges had come alive.

"What are you smiling at?" Jeremy demanded.

"Take a look," I said. "Three pictures of a girl and a man."

He held the negative strip I gave him to the light. "How can you tell? They're clearer, but they're still smudges."

"You get used to reading negatives. To be honest, I'm dead pleased with myself. Let's finish the champagne and then do the next bit: positive prints from the new negatives. Black-and-white pictures. All revealed."

"What's so funny?"

"The girl's nude, more or less."

He nearly spilled his drink. "Are you sure?"

"We'll see better soon. Are you hungry?"

"Good heavens. It's one o'clock."

We ate ham and tomatoes and brown toast, and finished the champagne. Then we returned to the darkroom.

Printing onto paper from such faint negatives was still a critical business. Again one had first to judge the exposure right and then stop the developing print at exactly the best instant and switch it to the tray of fixer. It took me several tries, but I finished with three pictures that were clear enough to reveal what George had photographed. I looked at them with a magnifying glass, and there was no chance of a mistake.

The pictures were bloody dynamite.

# CHAPTER 5

I took Jeremy and the new pictures upstairs and switched on the episcope, which hummed slightly as it warmed up.

"What's that?" Jeremy said, looking at the machine.

"A kind of projector. You put things on this baseboard and the image is projected large and bright onto a screen—or in my case, a wall."

I drew the curtains against the fading afternoon light and put in the new pictures. The first one showed the top half of a girl and the head and shoulders of a man. They were facing each other, embracing. Neither of them wore clothes.

"Good heavens," Jeremy said faintly.

"Mm," I said. I projected the second picture, which was of much the same pose, except that the camera had been at a different angle, showing less of the girl and nearly all of the man's face.

"It's just pornography," Jeremy said.

"No, it isn't."

In the third picture both their faces were visible, and there wasn't much doubt about the activity they were engaged in. I switched off the episcope and put on the lights.

"Why do you say it isn't pornography?" Jeremy asked.

"I've met them," I said. "I know who they are." He stared and I went on. "You're a lawyer, you tell me. What do you do if you find after a man's death that he may have been a blackmailer?"

He frowned. "Are you going to tell me what you're on to?"

"Yes." I told him about George Millace. About the burglaries, the attack on Marie Millace, and the burning of their house. I told him about the photograph of Elgin Yaxley and Terence O'Tree at the French café and about the five murdered horses; and I told him about the lovers.

"George very carefully kept those odds and ends in that box," I said. "What if they all are the basis for blackmail?"

"You want to find out?"

I slowly nodded. "It's not so much the blackmail angle but the photographic puzzles. I'd like to see if I can solve them. I do enjoy that sort of thing."

Jeremy stared at the floor. Then he said abruptly, "I think you should destroy the whole lot."

"That's instinct, not reason. Someone burgled and burned George Millace's house. When I found the first picture, I thought it must have been Elgin Yaxley who'd done it, but he was in Hong Kong. And now one would think the lovers did it, but it might not be them either."

Jeremy stood up and moved restlessly around the room. "Was there any doubt," he said, "about the way George Millace died?"

I felt as if he'd punched the air out of my lungs. "I don't think so. His son said he'd stopped at a friend's house for a drink. Then he drove on toward home, went to sleep, and hit a tree."

"How did anyone know he had stopped at the friend's house? And how does anyone know he went to sleep?"

"True lawyer's questions. I don't know the answers."

"Did they do an autopsy?" he said.

"I don't know. Do they usually?"

He shrugged. "Sometimes. They'd have tested his blood for the alcohol level. They might have checked for heart attack or stroke. If there were no suspicious circumstances, that would be all. But those burglaries must have made the police think a bit."

I said weakly, "The first serious burglary occurred during the funeral."

"Cremation?"

I nodded. "The police did hint very broadly to Marie Millace, and upset her considerably, about George possessing photographs people might not want found. But they don't *know* he had them."

"Like we do," he said. "Burn those pictures. Stick to looking for Amanda. You could end up like Millace. Splat on a tree."

JEREMY left at six, and I walked over to Harold's for the briefing. He had six runners planned for me that week, and with the five spare rides I'd been offered I would be having a busy time.

"Don't come crashing down on one of those hyenas you've accepted," Harold said. "What you take them for when you've got all my horses to ride I don't know." He never admitted that some of the biggest races I'd won had been for other stables.

"Next Saturday at Ascot I'm running two of Victor's horses," he said. "Chainmail. And Daylight."

I glanced at him quickly, but he didn't meet my eyes.

He paused and then said casually, "Chainmail might be the best bet. We'll see better what the prospects are on Friday."

"Prospects for winning?" I said. "Or losing? You tell me, Harold. Tell me early Saturday morning, if you've any feeling for me at all. I'll get an acute stomachache. Won't be able to go racing."

"But Victor—"

"I'll ride my guts out for Victor as long as we're trying to win. You tell him that. And don't forget, Chainmail's still pretty wayward, for all that he's fast. He pulls like a train and tries to duck out at the hurdles, and he's not above sinking his teeth into any horse that bumps him. He's a hard ride, but he's brave, and I'm not going to help you ruin him. And you *will* ruin him if you muck him about. You'll make him a real rogue."

"I agree with you," Harold said. "And I'll say it all to Victor. But in the end, it's his horse." He sighed heavily. "If necessary, I'll give you time to get sick."

I HAD an average day on Monday—a second place and a third—and Tuesday I had no racing engagements at all. I decided to placate Jeremy Folk by seeing if I could find one of the houses where my mother had left me in my childhood. A nice vague expedition, an undemanding day.

I set off for London and drove up and down a whole lot of little streets between the western boroughs of Chiswick and Hammersmith. I knew I'd once stayed in this area. All of the streets looked familiar: rows of tidy bow-fronted town houses for middle-income people. I had lived in several like that, but I couldn't even remember the name of a road.

Buses finally triggered the memory. The house I was looking for had been just around the corner from a bus stop. I had caught the bus there, going to the river for walks. The knowledge drifted quietly back across twenty-plus years. We'd often gone down to look at the houseboats and the seagulls; and we'd looked across to the gardens at Kew.

I went down to Kew Bridge and started from there, following

buses. A slow business and unproductive, because none of the stops were near corners. I gave it up after an hour and simply drove around.

It was an old pub that finally oriented me. The Willing Horse. I parked the car and walked back to the dark brown doors and simply stood there, waiting. After a while I seemed to know which way to go. Turn left, walk three hundred yards, cross the road, first turn on the right.

I walked down a street of bow-fronted row houses, three stories high, narrow and neat, hedges and shrubs by the houses. I walked slowly, but the impetus had gone. Nothing told me which house to try. I wondered what to do next.

Four houses from the end I went up the steps and rang the doorbell. A woman with a cigarette opened the door.

"Excuse me," I said. "Does Samantha live here?"

"Who?"

"Samantha?"

"No." She looked me up and down with the utmost suspicion and closed the door.

I tried six more houses. No luck. At the eighth an old lady told me I was up to no good, she'd watched me go from house to house, and if I didn't stop it, she would call the police. I walked away and she came right out into the street to watch me.

It wasn't much good, I thought. I wouldn't find Samantha. She might be out, she might have moved, she might never have lived in that street in the first place. Under the old woman's baleful gaze I tried another house where no one answered, and another where a girl of about twenty opened the door.

"Excuse me," I said. "Does anyone called Samantha live here?" I'd said it so often it now sounded ridiculous.

"Samantha what? Samantha who?"

"I'm afraid I don't know."

She pursed her lips, not quite liking it. "Wait a moment. I'll go and see." She shut the door and went away. I hovered, waiting, aware of the old woman beadily watching from the road.

The door opened. There were two people there, the girl and an older woman. The woman said, "What do you want?"

"Are you," I said slowly, "Samantha?"

She looked me up and down with the suspicion I was by now used to. A comfortably sized lady with gray-brown wavy hair.

"Would the name Nore mean anything to you? Philip Nore or Caroline Nore?"

To the girl the names meant nothing, but in the woman there was a fast sharpening of attention. "What exactly do you want?" she demanded.

"I'm Philip Nore."

The guarded expression turned to incredulity. "You'd better come in," she said. "I'm Samantha Bergen."

I stepped through the front door, and didn't have, as I'd half expected, the feeling of coming home.

"Downstairs," she said. I followed her and the girl followed me. "Sorry not to have been more welcoming," Samantha said, "but you know what it is these days. You have to be careful."

We went through a doorway into a large country kitchen. A big table, with chairs. A red-tiled floor. French doors to the garden. A basket chair hanging on a chain from the ceiling. Beams. Copper. Without thinking, I walked across the floor and sat in the hanging basket chair, tucking my feet up under me, out of sight.

Samantha Bergen stood there looking astounded. "You *are* little Philip. He always used to sit there like that, with his feet up. I'd forgotten. But seeing you do it . . . Good gracious."

"I'm sorry," I said, standing up again. "I just . . . did it."

"My dear man," she said. "It's all right. Extraordinary to see you, that's all." She turned to the girl. "This is my daughter, Clare. She wasn't born when you stayed here." To her daughter she said, "I looked after a friend's child now and then. Heavens, it must be twenty-two years since the last time."

The girl looked a good deal more friendly. They were both attractive, wearing jeans and blouses and unpainted Tuesday-afternoon faces. The girl was slimmer than her mother and had darker hair, but they both had large gray eyes, straight noses, and unaggressive chins. Both were unmistakably intelligent.

Their work lay spread out on the table. Galley proofs, the makings of a book. When I glanced at them, Clare said, "Mother's cookbook."

Samantha said, "Clare is a publisher's assistant."

We sat around the table, and I told them about looking for Amanda, and the off chance that had brought me to their door. Samantha shook her head regretfully. "I didn't even know Caroline had a daughter."

"Tell me about my mother," I said. "What was she like?"

"Caroline? So pretty you wanted to hug her. Full of light and fun. She could get anyone to do anything. But . . . she took drugs." Samantha looked at me anxiously and seemed relieved when I nodded. "She told me she didn't want you around when she and her friends were all high. She begged me to look after you. You were such a quiet little mouse. Quite good company actually."

"How often did she bring me?" I said slowly.

"Oh, half a dozen times. You were about eight at the end. I couldn't take you the last time she asked, as Clare was imminent."

I asked if my mother had ever told her anything about my father.

"No, nothing. She was supposed to have an abortion, and didn't." She made a comical face. "I suppose you wouldn't be here if she'd done what she'd promised her old dragon of a mother."

We drank some tea Clare had made, and Samantha asked what I did.

"I'm a jockey."

They were incredulous. "You're too tall," Samantha said.

"Jockeys don't have to be small."

"Extraordinary thing to be," Clare said. "Pretty pointless."

"Clare!" Samantha protested.

"If you mean," I said equably, "that being a jockey contributes nothing useful to society, I'm not so sure. Recreation gives health. I provide recreation."

"And betting?" Clare demanded. "Is that healthy?"

"Sublimates risk taking. Stake your money, not your life."

"But you yourself take the risks."

"I don't bet."

"Clare will tie you in knots," her mother said.

Clare shook her head. "I would think your little Philip is as easy to tie in knots as a stream of water."

Samantha gave her a surprised look and asked where I lived.

"In Lambourn. A village in Berkshire. Out on the downs."

Clare frowned and glanced at me with sharpened concentration. "Lambourn. Isn't that where there are a lot of racing stables?"

"That's right."

"Hm." She thought for a minute. "My boss is doing a book on villages and village life. He was saying the book's still a bit thin—asked me if I had any ideas. He's just done a chapter on a village that produces its own operas. Mind if I give him a call?"

Before I could answer she was on her feet and at the telephone. Samantha gave her a fond motherly look. "Clare will bully you into things," she said. "She bullied me into doing this cookbook. She's got more energy than a power station. She told me when she was about six that she was going to be a publisher, and she's well on her way. She's already second-in-command to the man she's talking to."

The prodigy herself finished talking on the telephone. "He's interested. He says we'll both go down and look the place over, and then if it's okay, he'll send a writer and a photographer."

"I've taken pictures of Lambourn. If you'd like to—"

"Sorry. We'd need professional work. But my boss says if you don't mind, we'll call at your apartment, or whatever, if you'd be willing to help us with directions and general information."

"Yes, I'd be willing."

"That's great." She gave me a sudden smile. She knows she's bright, I thought. But she's not as good as Jeremy Folk at concealing that she knows it. "Can we come on Friday?" she said.

# CHAPTER 6

LANCE Kinship was wandering around at the head of a retinue of cameramen and soundmen when I arrived at Newbury racecourse the next day. We heard in the changing room that with the blessing of the management he was taking background shots for a film. I slung my Nikon around my neck and took a few pictures of the men taking pictures.

Kinship was pompously telling his crew what to do, and they listened to him tensely. I took a couple of shots of their reaction—the eyes all looking toward him from averted heads. Clearly they were men obeying someone they didn't like. At one point Kinship turned his head the instant I pressed the button, and stared straight into my lens.

He strode across to me, looking annoyed. "What are you doing?" he said, though it was obvious.

"I was just interested," I said inoffensively.

He peered through his spectacles at my camera. "A Nikon." He raised his eyes to my face and frowned with half recognition.

"How's the nose?" I asked politely.

He grunted, finally placing me. "Don't get into the film," he said. "You're not a typical jockey. I don't want Nikon-toting jocks lousing up the footage." With a disapproving nod he went back to his crew, and presently they moved off to the parade ring.

They were down at the start when I lined up on a scatty novice steeplechaser for Harold. They were thankfully absent from the eighth fence, where the novice put his forefeet into the open ditch on the takeoff side and crossed the fence almost upside down. Somewhere during this wild somersault I fell out of the saddle, but by the mercy of heaven, when the half ton of horse crashed to the ground I was not underneath it.

He lay prostrate for a few moments, winded and panting. Some horses I loved, some I didn't. This was a clumsy, stubborn delinquent with a hard mouth, just starting what was likely to be a long career of bad jumping. I waited until he was on his feet, then remounted him and trotted him back to the stands.

When I was changing, someone said there was a man outside asking for the jockey with the camera. I went to see.

"Oh there you are," said Lance Kinship, as if I'd kept him waiting. "Well, what do you say? You took some photographs today. If they're any good, I'll buy them from you. How's that?"

"Well . . ." I was nonplussed. "Yes, if you like."

"Good. The crew is over by the winning post. Take some photographs of them shooting the finish of the next race. Publicity shots. Right?"

I fetched my camera and found him still waiting but definitely in a hurry. I would have to be quick, he explained, because the crew would be moving out to the parking lot presently to film the racegoers going home.

I would have thought that if he wanted publicity pictures, he would have brought a photographer of his own, and I asked him.

"Sure," he said. "I had one lined up. Then he died. Didn't get around to it again." We were walking fast, and his breathing grew shorter. "Then today, saw you. Reminded me. Some news photographers said you could do it. If your pics are no good, I don't buy, right?"

I asked him which photographer had died.

"Fellow called Millace. Died in a car crash. Here we are. Now get on with it."

He turned away to give instructions to the crew; they again listened with slightly averted heads. He wouldn't buy pictures showing that response, I thought, so I waited until he'd left, and shot the crew absorbed in their work.

The horses came out onto the course and cantered down to the start. One of the crew, a frizzy-haired boy with a clapper board who happened to be close to me, said with sudden fierceness, "You'd think this was an epic, the way he messes about. We're making commercials. A second on screen, flash off."

I half smiled. "What's the product?"

"Some sort of brandy."

Kinship came toward me and said it was important that he should be prominent in my photographs. The frizzy-haired boy surreptitiously raised his eyebrows into comical peaks, and I assured Lance Kinship that I would do my absolute best.

I did by good luck get one or two reasonable pictures. Kinship gave me a card with his address and told me again that he would buy the pictures if he liked them. He didn't say for how much, and I didn't like to ask. I would never be a salesman. Taking photographs for a living, I thought ruefully, would find me starving within a week.

When I reached home, I drew the curtains in my kitchen and once again went through George Millace's rubbish box, wondering just how much profit he had made from his deadly photographs.

I lifted out the large black lightproof envelope and removed its contents: the page-size piece of clear plastic and also, what hadn't registered before, two sheets of paper of about the same size. I looked at them briefly, then quickly replaced them, because it suddenly occurred to me that George must have stored them in a lightproof holder for a reason. That plastic and that paper might bear latent images. If they did, I didn't know how to develop them.

I sat staring vaguely at the black envelope and thinking about developers. To bring out the image on any particular type of film or paper one had to use the right type of developer, which meant that unless I knew the make and type of the plastic and of the two sheets of paper, I couldn't get any further.

I pushed the black envelope aside and took up the strips of blank negatives. They were 35-mm color negatives, some completely blank and others blank except for uneven magenta blotches. I laid the strips out end to end and made the first interesting discovery.

All the plain blank negatives had come from one roll of film, and those with magenta blotches from another, thirty-six exposures from each. I knew what make of film they were, because each manufacturer placed the frame numbers differently, but I didn't suppose that that was important. What might be important, however, was the very nature of color negatives.

While color transparencies appear to the eye in their true lifelike colors, color negatives appear in the reciprocal colors; to get back to the true colors one has to make a print from the negative. The primary colors of light are blue, green, and red. The reciprocal colors in which they appear on a negative are yellow, magenta, and cyan—a greenish blue. In order to get good whites and highlights, all manufacturers give their negatives an overall pale orange cast, which has the effect of masking the yellow sections.

George Millace's negatives were a pale clear orange throughout. Just suppose, I thought, that hidden under the orange was an image in yellow. If I made prints from those negatives, the invisible yellow image could turn into a visible printed image in reciprocal blue.

Worth trying, I thought. I went into the darkroom and mixed the developing chemicals and set up the color-print processor. I found out almost at once, by making contact prints, that under the orange masking there was indeed blue, but not blue images. Just blue.

There are so many variables in color printing that searching for an image on blank negatives is like walking blindfold through a forest, and although I tried every way I knew, I was only partially successful. I ended with thirty-six solid blue oblongs, enlarged and printed four to a sheet, and thirty-six more with greenish blotches here and there.

I knew that George Millace wouldn't have taken seventy-two pictures of a blue oblong for nothing. When it finally dawned on me what he *had* done, I was too tired to start all over again. I cleaned up and went to bed.

JEREMY Folk telephoned early the next morning and asked if I'd been to see my grandmother.

"I'll go," I said. "Saturday, after the race at Ascot."

"What have you been doing?" he asked. "You could have gone any day this week. Don't forget she really is dying."

"I've been working," I said. "And printing."

"From that box?" he said suspiciously.

"Uh-huh."

"What have you got?"

"Blue pictures. Pure deep blue. George Millace screwed a deep blue filter onto his camera and photographed a black-and-white picture through the blue filter onto color-negative film."

"You're talking Chinese."

"I'm talking Millace. Crafty Millace. As soon as I work out how to unscramble the blue, the next riveting Millace installment will fall into our hands."

"Well, be careful."

I said I would. One says things like that so easily.

I WENT to Wincanton and rode twice for Harold and three times for other people. The day was dry with a sharp wind. I rooted my way around five times in safety, and in the novice steeplechase found myself finishing in front, all alone.

There had been a time, when it was all new, that my heart had pumped madly every time I cantered to the start. Now, after ten years, my heart pumped above normal only for the big ones like the Grand National. The once fiendish excitement had turned to routine. Bad weather, long journeys, disappointments, and injuries had at first been shrugged off as part of the job. After ten years I saw that they *were* the job. The winners were the bonuses.

The tools of my trade were a liking for speed and a liking for horses. Also an ability to bounce, and to mend quickly when I didn't. None of these tools, except probably the liking for horses, would be of the slightest use to me as a photographer.

I walked irritably out to my car at the end of the afternoon. I didn't want to be a photographer. I wanted to remain a jockey. I wanted things to go on as they were, and not to change.

Early the following morning Clare Bergen appeared on my doorstep accompanied by her boss, the publisher, a dark young man

whose handshake almost tingled with energy. Clare wore a bright
woolly hat, sheepskin jacket, yellow ski pants, and huge fleece-lined
boots. Ah well, I thought, she would only frighten half the horses.
The nervous half.

I drove them up onto the downs in a Land Rover borrowed from
Harold, and we watched a few strings of horses go through their
workouts. Then I drove them back to the cottage for coffee. The
publisher said he would like to poke around a little on foot, and
walked off. Clare drank her second steaming cup and said, "Most
of the people I know despise horse people."

"Everyone likes to feel superior," I said, uninsulted.

"And you don't mind?"

"What those people feel is their problem, not mine."

She looked straight at me. "What does hurt you?"

"People saying I fell off when it was the horse that fell, and took
me with it."

"And there's a distinction?"

"Most important. What hurts you?"

"Being held to be a fool."

"That," I said, "is a piercingly truthful reply."

She looked away from me as if embarrassed, and said she liked
the cottage and the kitchen and could she see the rest. I showed her
the sitting room, the bedroom, and finally the darkroom.

She said slowly, "You mentioned that you took photographs, but
I'd no idea . . . Can I see them?"

"If you like." I opened my filing cabinet and sorted through the
folders. "Here you are, Lambourn."

"What are all those others?" she said. She read the tags on the
folders aloud. "America, France, Children, Jockey's Life. What's
Jockey's Life?"

"Just everyday living, if you're a jockey."

She eased the well-filled folder out of the drawer and carried it
to the kitchen. At the table she went through it, picture by picture.
No comments.

"Can I see the Lambourn photos?" she said. She looked through
these also in silence.

"I know they're not marvelous," I said mildly. "You don't have to rack your brains for something kind to say."

She looked up fiercely. "You know they're good." She closed the file. "I don't see why we can't use these. But it's not my decision, of course."

She lit a cigarette, and I noticed with surprise that her fingers were trembling. Something had disturbed her deeply; all the glittery extrovert surface had vanished.

"What's the matter?" I said at last.

She gave me a quick glance. "I've been looking for something like you."

"Something?" I echoed, puzzled.

"I want . . . I need to make a book that will establish my own personal reputation in publishing. I need to be known as the person who produced a very successful book. What I want is exceptional. And now . . . I've found it."

"But," I said, "Lambourn's not news, and anyway, I thought it was your boss's book."

"Not that, you fool. This." She put her hand on the Jockey's Life folder. "The pictures in here. Arranged in the right order . . . presented as a way of living . . . as an autobiography, a social comment . . . as well as how an industry works . . . it'll be spectacular. You haven't had any of these published before, have you?"

I shook my head. "Nowhere. I've never tried."

"You're amazing. You have this talent, and you don't use it."

"But everyone takes photographs."

"Sure they do. But not everyone takes a long series of photographs which illustrate a whole way of life. The hard work, the dedication, the bad weather, the humdrum, the triumphs, the pain . . . Look at this last one," she said, taking it out of the folder. This picture of a man pulling the boot off this boy with the broken shoulder. You don't need any words to say the man is doing it as gently as he can, or that it hurts. You can see it all." She replaced the picture and said seriously, "Will you give me your assurance that you won't go straight off and sell these pictures to someone else?"

"Of course," I said.

"And don't mention any of this to my boss. I want this to be my book, not his. You may have no ambition. But I have."

She thrust the folder into my hands and I put it back in the filing cabinet, so that when her boss returned, it was only the views of Lambourn that he saw. He said that they would do well enough, and shortly afterward he and Clare bore them away.

When they'd gone, I thought to myself that Clare's certainty about her book would evaporate. She would write apologetically and say that after all, on reflection . . . I had no expectations.

I went into Swindon to collect the films I'd left there for processing, and spent the rest of that Friday printing the shots of Lance Kinship and his crew. In the evening I captioned the prints and, feeling faintly foolish, added the words "Copyright Philip Nore." Charlie seemed almost to be leaning over my shoulder, reminding me to keep control of my work.

Work. The very word filled me with disquiet. It was the first time I'd actively thought of my photographs in those terms.

No, I thought. I'm a jockey.

Saturday morning at ten Harold called. I waited for him to tell me to get sick. Instead he said, "Are you well? You'd better be. I told Victor what you said. Word for word. I said you would ride your guts out for him as long as we're trying to win. And do you know what he said? He said, 'Tell that pious idiot that's just what I expect.' "

"Do you mean . . ."

"I mean," Harold bellowed, "he's changed his mind. You can win on Chainmail, if you can. In fact you'd better. See you at Ascot." He slammed the receiver down.

It seemed only too likely that Harold had promised Victor that Chainmail would win. If he had, I could be in a worse fix than ever.

As I took off my street clothes in the changing room at Ascot, someone was voicing the first rumors of a major racing upheaval.

"Is it true the Jockey Club is forming a new committee for

appointing *paid* stewards? No more working for the love of it?"

"I heard Lord White has agreed to the scheme," said someone else. "And Ivor den Relgan is to be chairman."

I turned to him. "That gives den Relgan an awful lot of power all of a sudden, doesn't it?"

He shrugged. "I don't know if it's true. I just heard it from one of the gossip writers."

During the afternoon one could almost see the onward march of the rumor as uneasy surprise spread from one Jockey Club face to the next. The only ones who seemed unaffected were Lord White, Lady White, Ivor den Relgan, and Dana den Relgan.

They stood near the course in weak November sunshine, the women both dressed in mink. Lady White looked gaunt and plain and unhappy. Dana den Relgan, laughing and glowing with health, twinkled her eyes at Lord White, who basked in the light of her smile, shedding years like snakeskins. Ivor den Relgan smirked at the world in general and smoked a cigar with proprietary gestures, as if Ascot were his own.

Harold appeared at my elbow. "Genghis Khan," he said acidly, is setting out to rule the world. What they're really doing is saying to den Relgan, 'Okay, you choose anyone you like as stewards, and we'll pay them.' It's incredible. Old Driven Snow is so besotted with that girl that he'll give her father *anything*."

"You really care," I said wonderingly.

"Of course I do. Racing is a great sport, and at the moment, free, its health guaranteed by having unpaid aristocrats who love the work. If den Relgan appoints paid stewards, for whom do you think those stewards will be working? For us? For racing? Or for the interests of Ivor den Relgan?"

We watched the group of four. Lord White was continually touching Dana—her arm, her shoulders, her cheek. Her father smiled indulgently and poor Lady White seemed to shrink even further into her mink.

"Someone," Harold said grimly, "has got to stop this."

I turned away, troubled, and found Lance Kinship coming slowly toward me, his gaze flicking rapidly from me to the den

Relgans and back again. It struck me that he wanted to talk to me without den Relgan noticing he was there.

"I've got your pictures in the car," I said to him.

"Good, good. I'll get them after the last race. I want to talk to that girl." He glanced at Dana. "Can you give her a message? Without that man hearing?"

"I might try," I said.

"Right. Tell her that I'll meet her after the third race in one of the private boxes." He told me the number.

I nodded, and he scuttled away. He was dressed for the role of country gentleman—tweed suit, brown trilby, checked shirt—except that he'd ruined the blue-blood impression with some pale green socks. A pathetic man, I thought, buying his way into the big time with little packets of white powder.

I looked from him to den Relgan, who was using Dana for much the same purpose. Nothing pathetic, though, about Ivor den Relgan. Power hungry and complacent, a trampler of little men. I went up to him and, in an ingratiating voice, thanked him again for the silver gifts he had scattered at Kempton. "The silver saddle," I said. "Great to have."

"So glad," he said, his gaze passing over me without interest. "My daughter selected it."

"Splendid taste," Lord White said fondly.

I said directly to Dana, "Please tell me, is it unique, or is it one of many?" I moved a step or two so that to answer she had to turn away from the two men, and almost before she had finished replying that it was the only one she'd seen, I said to her quietly, "Lance Kinship is here, wanting to see you."

"Oh." She glanced quickly at the two men. "Where?"

"After the third race, in a private box." I gave her the number and wandered away.

Daylight's race was third on the card, and Chainmail's fourth. When I went out for the third, I was stopped by a pleasant-mannered woman who I realized with shock was Marie Millace. Scarcely a trace showed of the devastation of her face. She was pale and ill-looking, but healed. "You look great," I told her.

"They said there wouldn't be a mark," she said, "and there isn't. Can I talk to you?"

"Well, how about after the fourth race? After I've changed?"

She mentioned a particular bar up in the stands, and we agreed on it, and I went on to the parade ring, where Harold and Victor Briggs waited. Neither of them said anything to me, nor I to them. Everything of importance had already been said.

I cantered down to the starting gate, thinking about courage, which was not normally a word I found often in my mind. The process of getting a horse to go fast over jumps seemed to me merely natural, and something I very much liked doing. I had no preoccupation with my own safety. On the other hand I'd never been reckless, as Steve Millace was, throwing his heart over a fence and letting the horse catch up if he could. It was the latter style of riding that Victor Briggs would be expecting now. And moreover I'd have to do it twice.

Daylight and I turned in what was for us a thoroughly uncharacteristic performance, leaving more to luck than judgment. He was accustomed to measuring his distance from a fence and altering his stride accordingly, but infected by my urgency, he began simply to take off when he was vaguely within striking distance of getting over. We hit the tops of three fences hard, and raced over the last as if it were but a shadow on the ground. But hard as we tried, we didn't win. A stronger, faster, fitter horse beat us into second place by three lengths.

In the unsaddling enclosure, I unbuckled the girths while Daylight panted and rocketed around in a highly excitable state. Victor Briggs watched without letting a thought surface.

"Sorry," I said to Harold as he walked in with me to the changing room.

He merely grunted, then said, "Don't kill yourself on Chainmail. It won't prove anything except that you're a bloody fool." But I noticed that he did not instruct me to return to a more sober style for his second runner. Perhaps he, too, wanted Victor to run his horses straight, and if this was the only way to achieve that, well, so be it.

With Chainmail things were different. The four-year-old hurdler was unstable to begin with, and what I was doing to him was like urging a juvenile delinquent to go mugging. He fought and surged and flew. I went with him to his ultimate speed, totally disregarding good sense. Without any reservation I rode my bloody guts out for Victor Briggs.

It wasn't enough. Chainmail finished third.

Victor Briggs unsmilingly watched me pull the saddle off his second stamping, tossing, hepped-up horse. I wrapped the girths around the saddle and paused for a moment face to face with him. He said nothing at all, nor did I. We looked with blankness into each other's eyes. I had needed two winners to save my job, and had none. Recklessness wasn't enough. He wanted winners. If he couldn't have certain winners, he wanted certain losers. Like three years ago, when I and my soul were young. With a deep feeling of weariness I went in to change and to meet Marie Millace.

SHE was sitting in an armchair, deep in conversation with another woman, whom I found to my surprise to be Lady White.

"I'll come back later," I said, preparing to retreat.

"No, no," Lady White said, standing up. "I know Marie wants to talk to you." The two women smiled and kissed cheeks, and Lady White made her way out of the bar, a thin, defeated lady trying to behave as if the whole racing world were not aware of her discomfiture.

"We were at school together," Marie Millace said. "I'm very fond of her."

"You know about . . . er . . ."

"About Dana den Relgan? Yes. Would you like a drink?"

"Let me get you one." I fetched a gin and tonic for her and some Coke for me, and sat in the armchair Lady White had left.

The bar itself, an attractive place of bamboo furniture and green and white colors, was almost empty. It was a good place for talking, and it was also warm.

Marie Millace said, "Wendy—Lady White—was asking me if I thought her husband's affair with Dana would just blow over. What could I say? I said I was sure it would." She gloomily swirled the ice around in her drink. "It's so awful. Wendy thought it was all over."

"All over? I thought it had just started."

She sighed. "Wendy says her husband fell for this creature months ago, but then the wretched girl faded off the scene and Wendy thought he'd stopped seeing her. Now she's back in full view and it's obvious to everyone. I'm so sorry for Wendy. It's all so horrid."

"Do you know Dana den Relgan yourself?" I asked.

"No, not at all. George knew her, I think. He said when we were in Saint-Tropez last summer he'd seen her there one afternoon, but I don't know; he was laughing when he said it.

"Anyway, that's not what I wanted to talk to you about. I wanted to thank you for your kindness and ask you about that exhibition you suggested. And about how I might make some money out of George's work. Because I'm going to need . . . er . . ."

"Everyone needs," I said comfortingly. "But didn't George leave things like insurance policies?"

"Some. But it won't be enough to live on."

"Did he," I asked delicately, "have any . . . well . . . savings in any separate bank accounts?"

Her friendly expression began to change to suspicion. "Are you asking me the same sort of things as the police?"

"Marie, think of the burglaries and the arson."

"George wouldn't," she said explosively. "I told you before."

I sighed and asked if she knew which friend George had stopped for a drink with on his way back from Doncaster.

"He wasn't a friend. Barely an acquaintance. A man called Lance Kinship. George phoned me in the morning and mentioned he'd be late as he was calling at this man's house. This Kinship wanted George to take some pictures of him working. He's a film director or something. George said he was a pernicious little egotist, but he'd pay well. That was almost the last thing he said to me."

She sniffed, fishing in her pocket for a handkerchief and wiping her eyes. "I'm so sorry. The very last thing he said was to ask me to buy some Ajax Window Cleaner. It's stupid, isn't it? I mean, except for saying, 'See you,' the last thing George ever said to me was, 'Get some liquid Ajax, will you?' " She gulped. "I don't even know what he wanted it for."

"Marie . . ." I held my hand out toward her and she gripped it as fiercely as in the hospital. But presently her turmoil subsided and she gave a small laugh of embarrassment. I asked her if there had been an autopsy.

"Oh . . . alcohol, do you mean? Yes, they tested his blood. They said it was below the limit. He'd only had two small whiskeys with that Kinship. The police asked Kinship about it after I told them that George had planned to stop there. Kinship wrote to me, you know, saying he was sorry. But it wasn't his fault. George often got dozy when he'd been driving a long way."

I told her how it happened that Lance Kinship had asked me to take photographs that George had been going to do. "George always said you'd wake up one day and steal his market," she said, and produced a wavery smile.

I asked for her address so that I could put her in touch with an agent, and she said she was staying with some friends who lived near Steve. She didn't know, she said, where she would be going from there. She had no furniture, nothing to make a home with. Much worse, she had no photograph of George.

BY THE time I left Marie Millace, the fifth race had been run. I went out to the car to fetch Lance Kinship's pictures, and returned toward the changing room to find Jeremy Folk standing outside the door on one leg. "You'll fall over," I said.

"Oh." He put the foot down gingerly. "I thought—"

"You thought if you weren't here, I might not do what you want. Well, you may be right."

"I came here by train," he said contentedly, "so can you take me with you to Saint Albans?"

"I guess I'll have to."

Lance Kinship, seeing me there, came over to collect his prints. I introduced him to Jeremy, and added for Jeremy's sake that it was at Lance Kinship's house that George Millace had taken his last drink. Kinship gave each of us a sharp glance followed by a sorrowful shake of the head.

"A great fellow, George," he said. "Too bad."

He pulled the pictures out of the envelope and looked through them with his eyebrows rising high above his spectacle frames. "Well, well," he said. "I like them. How much do you want?"

I mentioned an exorbitant figure, but he merely nodded, pulled out a stuffed wallet, and paid me there and then in cash.

"Reprints?" he said. "Two sets?"

"Complete sets?" I said, surprised. "All of them?"

"Sure. All of them. Very nice, they are. Want to see?" He flicked them invitingly at Jeremy, who also inspected them with eyebrows rising.

"You must be," said Jeremy, "a director of great note."

Kinship positively beamed, tucked his pictures back into the envelope, and walked away. Before he'd gone ten paces he was pulling the pictures out again to show to someone else.

"He'll get you a lot of work," Jeremy said.

I didn't know whether or not I wanted to believe him, and in any case my attention was caught by something much more extraordinary. "Do you see," I said to Jeremy, "those two men over there, talking? One of them is Bart Underfield, who's a trainer in Lambourn. And the other is one of the men in that photograph I told you about of the French café. That's Elgin Yaxley . . . come home from Hong Kong."

Three weeks after George's death, two weeks after the burning of his house, and Elgin Yaxley was back on the scene. I had jumped to conclusions before, but surely this time it was reasonable to suppose that Elgin Yaxley believed the incriminating photograph had safely gone up in smoke. Reasonable to suppose, watching him smiling expansively, that he felt free and secure.

Jeremy said, "It can't be coincidence. You've still got that photo?"

"I sure have."

"I think I was wrong," Jeremy said thoughtfully, "to say you should burn all those things in the box."

I smiled. "Tomorrow I'll have a go at the blue oblongs."

"So you've worked out how?"

"Well, I hope so. I think if I enlarge the orange negatives through blue light onto high contrast black-and-white paper, I might get a picture."

Jeremy blinked.

Later, as we drove toward Saint Albans, he told me about his researches into the television company.

"They only filmed at Pine Woods Lodge for six weeks. I got them to show me the credits, and I asked if they could put me in touch with anyone who had worked on the program. They told me where to find the director, who's still working in television. Very dour and depressing man, all grunts and a heavy mustache. He wasn't much help. Thirteen years ago? How did I expect him to remember one crummy six weeks thirteen years ago?"

"Pity."

"After that I tracked down one of the actors, who is temporarily working in an art gallery, and got much the same answer. Thirteen years? Girl with small child? Not a chance."

I sighed. "How long were the musicians there?"

"Three months, give or take a week."

"And after them?"

"The religious fanatics." He grimaced. "It's so long ago."

"Let's try something else," I said. "Why not publish Amanda's photograph in *Horse and Hound*, and ask for an identification of the stable? The buildings are probably still standing."

He sighed. "Okay, then. But I can see the final expenses of this search costing more than the inheritance."

We reached Saint Albans and the nursing home; Jeremy would read magazines in the waiting room while I talked upstairs with the dying old woman. Sitting up, supported by pillows, she watched me walk into her room. The strong, harsh face was still full of stubborn life, the eyes unrelentingly fierce. She said nothing like good evening but merely, "Have you found her?"

"No."

She compressed her mouth. "Are you trying?"

"I've spent some time looking for her but not my whole life." I sat down in an armchair. "I went to see your son," I said.

Her face melted into a revealing mixture of rage and disgust, and with surprise I saw the passion of her disappointment.

"Your genes to go on," I said. "Is that what you want?"

"Death is pointless otherwise."

I thought that life was pretty pointless, but I didn't say so. One woke up alive, and did what one could, and died. Perhaps she was right—that the point of life was for genes to survive, through generations of bodies. "Whether you like it or not," I said, "your genes may go on through me."

The idea still displeased her. Her jaw tightened. "That young solicitor thinks I should tell you who your father was."

I stood up at once, unable to stay calm. Although I had come to find out, I now didn't want to hear.

"Are you afraid?" She was scornful. Sneering.

I simply stood there, not answering, wanting to know and not wanting, afraid and not afraid. In an absolute muddle.

"I have hated your father since before you were born," she said bitterly. "I can hardly bear even now to look at you, because you're like he was at your age. Thin . . . and physical . . . and with the same eyes."

I swallowed and waited and felt numb.

"I loved him," she said, spitting the words out. "I doted on him. He was thirty and I was forty-four. I'd been a widow for five years. I was lonely. We were going to marry."

She stopped. There really was no need to go on. I knew the rest. The hatred she had felt for me all those years was finally explained. So simply explained . . . and forgiven.

I took a deep breath. "And what . . . was his name?"

She stared at me. "I'm not going to tell you. I don't want you seeking him out. He ruined my life. He bedded my seventeen-year-old daughter under my own roof and he was after my money. That's the sort of man your father was. The only favor I'll do you is not to tell you his name."

I nodded and said awkwardly, "I'm sorry."

Her scowl if anything deepened. "Now find Amanda for me." She closed her eyes. "I don't like you," she said. "So go away."

"WELL?" Jeremy said, downstairs.

I relayed to him the gist of what she had told me, and his reaction was the same as mine. "Poor old woman."

"I could do with a drink," I said.

# CHAPTER 7

IN PRINTING color photographs, one's aim is usually to produce a result that looks natural, and this is nowhere near as easy as it sounds. For one thing, the color itself comes out differently on each make of film and on each type of photographic printing paper, the reason being that the four ultrathin layers of light-sensitive emulsion that are laid onto color printing paper vary slightly from batch to batch. In the same way that it is almost impossible to dye two pieces of cloth in different dye baths and produce identical results, so it is with emulsions.

To persuade all colors to look natural, one uses color filters— pieces of colored glass or plastic inserted between the bright light on the enlarger and the negative. Get the mixture of filters right, and in the finished print blue eyes come out blue and cherry lips, cherry.

In my enlarger, as in the majority, the three filters were the same colors as the negatives: yellow, magenta, and cyan. Used in delicate balance, the yellow and magenta filters could produce skin colors that were neither too yellow nor too pink for human faces. However, if one did not balance them properly and simply put a square of magenta-colored glass on a square of cyan-colored glass and shone a light through both together, the result was a deep clear blue.

I went into my darkroom on that fateful Sunday morning and adjusted the filters in the head of the enlarger so that the light that shone through the negatives would be an unheard-of combination for normal printing—full cyan and full magenta filtration, producing a deep clear blue.

Black-and-white printing paper is sensitive only to blue light. I thought that if I printed the blank-looking negatives through heavy blue filtration onto black-and-white paper, I would get rid of the blue of the oblongs and I might then get a greater contrast between the yellow dye image on the negative and the orange mask covering it. Make the image, in fact, emerge from its surroundings.

I had a feeling that whatever was hidden by the mask would not be black and white. If it were, it would have been visible in spite of the blue. What I was looking for would be gray.

I set out trays of developer, stop bath, and fixer. Then I put the first thirty-six unblotched negatives into a contact-printing frame, which held all thirty-six negatives conveniently so that they would be printed at once onto one eight-by-ten-inch sheet.

Getting the exposure time right was the biggest difficulty, chiefly because the heavy blue filtration meant that the light getting to the negatives was far dimmer than I was used to. I wasted about six shots in tests, getting useless results ranging from gray to black, all the little oblongs still stubbornly looking as if there were nothing on them to see, whatever I did.

Finally in irritation I cut the exposure time way down and came up with a sheet of prints that was almost entirely white.

Sighing with frustration, I dipped the sheet in the stop bath, fixed it, washed it, and switched on the bright lights. The frame numbers had very palely appeared, and five of the little oblongs, scattered at random through the thirty-six prints, bore gray geometric shapes. I had found them.

I smiled. George had left a puzzle; I had almost solved it.

I wrote down the frame numbers of the five gray-patterned prints. Then I took the first one numerically and enlarged it to the full size of the eight-by-ten-inch paper. A couple more bad guesses at exposure times left me with unclear dark gray prints, but in the

end I came up with one that developed into mid-gray on white. I
carried it out to the kitchen.

Although the print was still wet, I could see exactly what it
was—a letter typed on white paper with an old grayish ribbon. It
bore no heading, date, or handwritten signature. It said:

Dear Mr. Morton,

   I am sure you will be interested in the enclosed two
photographs. As you will see, the first one is of your horse
Amber Globe running poorly at Southwell on Monday, May 12.
The second is of your horse Amber Globe winning the race at
Fontwell on Wednesday, August 27.

   If you look closely at the photographs, you will see that they
are not of the same horse. Alike but not identical.

   I am sure that the Jockey Club would be interested in this
difference. I will telephone you shortly, however, with an
alternative suggestion.

   Yours sincerely,
   George Millace

I read it through six times. I felt as though I were looking into a
pit. Presumably the other four gray geometric patterns would also
turn out to be letters. What I had found was George's idiosyncratic
filing system. If I enlarged and read the other letters, I would have
to accept the moral burden of deciding what to do about them . . .
and of doing it.

To postpone the decision, I went upstairs to the sitting room
and looked up Amber Globe's career in the form books. On average it amounted to three or four poor showings followed by an
easy win at high odds, this pattern being repeated twice a season.
Amber Globe's last win had been the one on August 27 four years
previously, and from then on he had run in no more races at all.

Dear Mr. Morton and his trainer had been running two horses
under the name Amber Globe, switching in the good one for the
big gambles, letting the poor one lengthen the odds. I wondered
how George had noticed, but there was no way of knowing, as I
hadn't found the two photographs in question.

I looked out the window at the downs for a while, waiting for the arrival of a comfortable certainty that knowledge did not involve responsibility. I waited in vain. I knew that it did.

Unsettled, fearful, I finally went down to the darkroom and printed the other four negatives one by one, and read the resulting letters in the kitchen. The sly malice of George's mind spoke out clearly. The second letter said:

Dear Bonnington Ford,

I am sure you will be interested in the enclosed series of photographs, which, as you will see, are a record of you entertaining in your training stables a person who has been disqualified. I need not remind you that the racing authorities would object strongly to this continuous association, even to the extent of reviewing your license to train.

I could of course send copies of these photographs to the Jockey Club. I will telephone shortly, however, with an alternative suggestion.

Yours sincerely,
George Millace

Bonnington Ford was a third-rate trainer who was as honest and trustworthy as a pickpocket. Again I hadn't found the photographs in question, so there was nothing I could do, even if I wanted to.

The last three letters were a different matter. The first said:

Dear Elgin Yaxley,

I am sure you will be interested in the enclosed photograph. As you will see, it clearly contradicts a statement you recently made on oath at a certain trial.

I am sure that the Jockey Club would be interested to see it, and also the police, the judge, and the insurance company. I will telephone shortly, however, with an alternative suggestion.

Yours sincerely,
George Millace

The next letter would have driven the nails right in. It said:

Dear Elgin Yaxley,

Since I wrote to you yesterday there have been further developments. I visited the farmer upon whose farm you boarded your unfortunate steeplechasers, and I showed him in confidence a copy of the photograph that I sent to you. I suggested that there might be a further inquiry, during which his own share in the tragedy might be investigated.

He responded to my promise of silence with the pleasing information that your five good horses were not after all dead. The five horses that died had been bought especially and cheaply by your farmer friend from a local auction, and it was these that were shot by Terence O'Tree at the appointed time and place. Terence O'Tree was not told of the substitution.

Your farmer friend also confirmed that you yourself arrived at the farm to supervise the good horses' removal. Your friend understood you would be shipping them out to a buyer in the Far East.

I enclose a photograph of his signed statement to this effect. I will telephone shortly with a suggestion.

> Yours sincerely,
> George Millace

The last letter had been written in pencil:

Dear Elgin Yaxley,

I bought the five horses that T. O'Tree shot. You fetched your own horses away, to export them to the East. I am satisfied with what you paid me for this service.

> Yours faithfully,
> David Parker

I thought of Elgin Yaxley as I had seen him the previous day at Ascot, smirking complacently and believing himself safe. I thought of right and wrong, and justice; of Elgin Yaxley as the victim of George Millace; and of the insurance company as the victim of Elgin Yaxley. I couldn't decide what to do.

After a while I got up stiffly and went back to the darkroom. I put all of the magenta-splashed negatives into the contact-printing frame and made a nearly white sheet of prints, as I had done with the first set. This time there were fifteen little gray oblongs. With a feeling of horror I turned off the lights, locked the doors, and walked up the road to my briefing with Harold.

"PAY ATTENTION," HAROLD SAID sharply. "What's the matter with you? I'm talking about Coral Key at Kempton on Wednesday, and you're not listening."

I dragged my attention back to the matter at hand.

"Coral Key," I said. "For Victor Briggs. Has Victor said anything about yesterday?"

Harold shook his head. "Until he tells me you're off his horses, you're still on them."

I WENT back to the quiet cottage and made enlargements from the fifteen magenta-splashed negatives. To my relief they were not all threatening letters—only the first two were.

I had expected one on the subject of the lovers, and it was there. It was the second one that left me breathless and laughing, and put me in a better frame of mind for revelations to come.

The last thirteen prints, however, turned out to be George's notes of where and when he had taken his incriminating pictures, and on what dates he had sent the frightening letters. I guessed he had kept his records in this form because it seemed safer. They were fascinating, but they all failed to say what the alternative suggestions had been. There was no record of what monies George had extorted or of where he had stashed the proceeds.

I went to bed late and couldn't sleep, and in the morning I made some telephone calls. One to the editor of *Horse and Hound*, whom I knew, begging him to include Amanda's picture in that week's issue, emphasizing that time was short. He said he would print it if I got it to his office that morning.

I said I would, and then telephoned old Driven Snow at his home in the Cotswolds.

"You want to see me?" he said. "What about?"

"About George Millace, sir."

"Photographer? Died recently?"

"Yes, sir. His wife is a friend of Lady White's."

"Yes, yes," he said impatiently. And although he wasn't overpoweringly keen on the idea, he agreed to see me the next day.

After that I telephoned Samantha and asked if I could take her and Clare out to dinner. She sounded pleased. "I can't tonight," she said. "But I'm sure Clare can. She'd like it."

"Would she?"

"Yes, you silly man. What time?"

I said I would pick her up at eight. Samantha said fine and how was the search for Amanda going, and I found myself talking to her as if I'd known her all my life. As in a way I had.

I drove to London to the *Horse and Hound* offices and arranged to have Amanda's picture run with the caption, "Where is this stable? Ten pounds' reward for the first person—particularly the first child—who can phone Philip Nore to tell him."

"Child?" said the editor, adding my telephone number. "Do they read this paper?"

"Their mothers do."

"Subtle stuff," he said.

SAMANTHA was out when I went to fetch Clare.

"Come in for a drink first," Clare said, opening the door wide. "It's such a lousy evening."

I stepped out of the cold November wind, and she led me into a long, gently lighted sitting room.

"Do you remember this room?"

I shook my head.

"Where's the bathroom?" she asked.

I answered immediately, "Upstairs, turn right, blue tub."

She laughed. "Straight from the subconscious." She handed me a glass of wine, and we sat down in a couple of pale velvet armchairs. She wore a scarlet silk shirt and black trousers, and made a bright statement against the soft coloring of the room.

"I saw you racing on Saturday," she said. "On television. You do take some frightful risks. What happens if you're really smashed up by one of those falls?"

"You've got a problem. No rides, no income."

"What happens if you're killed?"

I smiled. "The risk is less than you'd think. But if you're really unlucky, there's always the Injured Jockeys' Fund."

"What's that?"

"The racing industry's private charity. It looks after the widows and orphans of dead jockeys and gives succor to badly damaged live ones."

We went out a little later and ate in a small restaurant determinedly decorated as a French peasant kitchen with scrubbed board tables, rushes on the floor, and dripping candles stuck in wine bottles. While we ate, Clare turned to the subject of photographs and said she would like to come down to Lambourn again to go through the Jockey's Life file. "You haven't sold any to anyone else, have you? You did say you wouldn't."

"Not those." I told her about Lance Kinship and how odd I found it that all of a sudden people wanted to buy my work.

"The word is going around," she said. She finished her coffee and sat back, looking thoughtful. "What you need is an agent."

I explained about having to find one for Marie Millace anyway; she brushed that aside. "Not *any* agent," she said. "Me."

She looked at my stunned expression and smiled. "Well?" she asked. "What does any agent do? He knows the markets and sells the goods. What if I got you commissions for illustrations for other books—on any subject? Would you do them?"

"Yes, but—"

"No buts. There's no point in taking super photos if no one sees them." The candlelight shone on her intent eyes. She was a girl of decision and certainty. She looked steadily at a future I still shied away from. I wondered what she'd say if I said I wanted to kiss her, when her thoughts were clearly more practical.

"I'd like to try," she said persuasively. "Will you let me?"

She'll bully you into things, Samantha had said.

Take what comes, and hope for the best. I said, "All right," and she said, "Great." And later, when I delivered her to her doorstep and kissed her, she didn't object.

FOUR times on Tuesday morning I lifted the telephone to cancel my appointment with Lord White. Four times I put the receiver down and decided I would have to go.

Lord White's house turned out to be a weathered stone pile with more grandeur than gardeners. Noble windows raised their eyebrows above drifts of unswept leaves. A mat of dead weeds glued the gravel together. I rang the doorbell and wondered about the economics of being a baron.

Lord White received me in a small sitting room where everything was of venerable antiquity, dusted and gleaming. But there were patches on chintz chair covers. Less money than was needed, I diagnosed. He shook hands and offered me a chair. I found it an agony to begin.

"Sir," I said. "I'm very sorry, sir, but I'm afraid what I've come about may be a great shock to you."

He frowned slightly. "About George Millace?"

"Yes, about some photographs he took."

I stopped. Too late, I wished fervently that I hadn't come. I should after all have adhered to the lifetime habit of noninvolvement. But what I was there for had to be done. With foreboding I opened the large envelope I carried. I pulled out the first of the three pictures of the lovers and put it into his outstretched hand, and for all that I thought he was behaving foolishly over Dana den Relgan, I felt deeply sorry for him.

His first reaction was extreme anger. How dared I, he said, standing up and quivering, how dared I bring him anything so filthy and *disgusting*? I took the second and third photographs out of the envelope and rested them picture-side down on the arm of my chair. "As you will see," I said, "the others are worse."

I reckoned it took a lot of courage for him to pick up the other two pictures. He looked at them in desperate silence and slowly sank down again in his chair. His face told of his anguish. Of his horror. The man making love to Dana was Ivor den Relgan.

Several moments later Lord White said, "They can fake pictures of anything." His voice shook. "Cameras do lie."

"Not this one," I said regretfully. I took from the envelope a print of the letter George Millace had written, and gave it to him. The letter, which I knew by heart, read:

Dear Ivor den Relgan,

I am sure you will be interested in the enclosed photographs, which I was able to take a few days ago in Saint-Tropez. As you will see, they show you in a compromising position with the young lady who is known as your daughter. (It is surely unwise to do this sort of thing on hotel balconies where one can be seen by telephoto lenses.) There seem to be two possibilities here.

One: Dana den Relgan is your daughter, in which case this is incest. Two: Dana is not your daughter, in which case why are you pretending she is? Can it have anything to do with the ensnaring of a certain member of the Jockey Club? Are you hoping for entry to the club, and other favors?

I could of course send these photographs to the lord in question. I will telephone you shortly, however, with an alternative suggestion.

Yours sincerely,
George Millace

Lord White became older before my eyes, the glow that love had given him shrinking back into deepening wrinkles. Finally he said, "Where did you get these?"

"After George Millace died, his son gave me a box with some things of his father's in it. These photos were among them."

He suffered through another silence, then said, "Why did you bring them to me? To cause me mortification?"

I swallowed. "Sir, people are worried about how much power has been given recently to Ivor den Relgan."

"And you have taken it upon yourself to try to stop it?"

"Sir . . . yes."

He looked grim, and as if seeking refuge in anger, he said authoritatively, "It's none of your business, Nore."

I didn't answer at once. I'd had enough trouble persuading myself that it *was* my business. But in the end, diffidently, I said, "Sir, if you are certain in your own mind that Ivor den Relgan's sudden rise to power has nothing whatever to do with your affection for Dana den Relgan, then I most abjectly beg your pardon."

He merely stared. "Please leave," he said rigidly.

"Yes, sir." I stood up and walked over to the door.

"Wait, Nore. I must think. Will you please come back and sit down?" His voice was still stern, still full of accusation and judgment and defense.

I returned to the armchair, and he went and stood by the window with his back to me, looking out at straggly rosebushes and unclipped hedges. Finally he spoke, but without turning around. "How many people have seen these pictures?"

"I don't know how many George Millace showed them to. As for me, they've been seen only by one friend. He was with me when I found them. But he doesn't know the den Relgans."

"Do you intend," he said quietly, "to make jokes about this on the racecourse?"

"No." I was horrified. "I do not."

"And would you expect any reward, in service . . . or cash . . . for this silence?"

I stood up as if he had hit me. "I would not," I said. "I'm not George Millace. I think I'll go now." And go I did, impelled by a severe hurt to the vanity.

On Wednesday Harold called me with the news that Coral Key wouldn't be running that day at Kempton after all. "Bloody animal banged itself up in its stall during the night," Harold said. "It won't please Victor." So I stayed at home all day and did Lance Kinship's reprints.

Thursday I set off to Kempton with only one ride, thinking it was a very thin week on the earning front, but almost as soon as I'd stepped through the gate I was offered spare rides by a trainer whose regular jockey had called in sick.

His horses were no great shakes. I got one of them around into third place, and on the other I came down two fences from home; a bit of a crash but nothing broken in either him or me. The third horse, the one I'd originally gone to ride, wasn't much better: a clumsy baby with guts equal to his skill. We finished, not unexpectedly, in the middle of the pack.

The surprise of the afternoon was the presence of Clare. She was waiting for me outside the changing room.

"Hullo," she said. "I decided to come out by train and take a look at the real thing." She smiled. "Is today typical?"

I looked at the gray windy sky and the thin Thursday crowd and thought of my three nondescript races. "Pretty much," I said. "Would you like a cup of tea? A drink? A trip to Lambourn?"

She thought it over briefly. "Lambourn," she said. "I can get a train back from there, can't I?"

As I drove, I had an unaccustomed feeling of contentment. It felt right to have her sitting there in the car.

The cottage was cold but soon warmed. Just as I put the kettle on for tea the telephone rang. I answered it and had my eardrum half shattered by a piercing voice that shrieked, "Am I first?"

"First what?" I said, wincing and holding the receiver away.

"First!" A child's voice. Female. "I've been ringing every five minutes for *hours*. Am I first? Do say I'm first."

Realization dawned. "You're first. Have you been reading *Horse and Hound*? It isn't published until tomorrow."

"It gets to my auntie's bookshop on Thursdays. I collect it for Mummy on my way home from school. And she saw the picture, and told me to ring you. So can I have the ten pounds? Can I?"

"If you know where the stable is, yes, of course."

"Mummy knows. She'll tell you. You'd better talk to her now."

There were some background noises, and then a woman's voice, pleasant and far less excited.

"Are you the Philip Nore who rides in National Hunt races?"

"Yes," I said, and she went on without further reservation.

"I do know where that stable is, but it isn't used for horses any longer. It's in Horley, near Gatwick Airport. It's still called Zephyr Farm Stables, but the riding school has been closed for years. It's been converted into living quarters. Do you want the actual address?"

"I guess so," I said. "And your name and address too, please."

She read them out to me and I wrote them down, and then I said, "Do you happen to know the name of the people living there now?"

"Huh," she said scornfully. "You won't get far with them, I'm afraid. They've got the place practically fortified to ward off furious parents. It's one of those commune things. Religious brainwashing. They call themselves Colleagues of Supreme Grace."

I felt breathless. "Thanks very much. I'll send your daughter the money."

"What is it?" Clare said as I slowly replaced the receiver.

"The first real lead to Amanda." I explained about the advertisement, and about the tenants of Pine Woods Lodge.

Clare shook her head. "If these Supreme Grace people know where Amanda is, they won't tell you. You must have heard of them. All gentle and smiling on the surface, and like steel rattraps underneath. They lure young people with friendliness and songs and hook them into 'believing,' and once they're in, the poor slobs never get out. They're in love with their prison."

"I've heard of them. But I've never seen the point."

"Money," Clare said crisply. "All the darling little Colleagues go out with saintly faces and collection boxes, and line the pockets of their great leader."

I made the tea and we sat at the table to drink it.

Amanda in a stable yard at Horley; Caroline twenty miles away at Pine Woods Lodge. Colleagues at Pine Woods Lodge; Colleagues at Horley. Too close to be a coincidence.

"You'll go looking?"

I nodded. "Tomorrow, I think, after racing."

We finished the tea and talked of her life and mine, and later in the evening we went to a good pub for a steak.

"A great day," Clare said over coffee. "Where's the train?"

"Swindon. I'll drive you there. Or you could stay."

"Is that the sort of invitation I think it is?"

"I wouldn't be surprised."

She looked down and fiddled with her spoon, paying it a lot of attention. I knew that if it took her so long to answer, she would go. "Philip . . ."

"It's all right," I said easily. "If one never asks, one never gets." I paid the bill. "Come on."

She was quiet on the six-mile drive to the railway station, and not until I was waiting with her on the platform did she give any indication of what was in her mind.

"There's a board meeting in the office tomorrow," she said. "It will be my first. They made me a director a month ago."

I was most impressed, and said so. It couldn't be often that publishing houses put women of twenty-two on the board. I understood, also, why she wouldn't stay.

The train came in and she paused, before climbing aboard, to exchange kisses. Brief unpassionate kisses. See you soon, she said, and I said yes. About contracts, she said. A lot to discuss.

"Come on Sunday," I said.

"Let you know. Good-bye."

"Good-bye."

The impatient train ground away, and I drove home to the empty cottage with a most unaccustomed feeling of loneliness.

NEWBURY races, Friday. Harold greeted me with mischievous amusement. "Did you hear that Genghis Khan got the boot?"

"Are you sure?" I said.

Harold nodded. "They held an emergency-type meeting of the Jockey Club this morning in London. A friend of mine was there. Lord White asked the members to cancel plans for a committee chaired by Ivor den Relgan, and as it was old Driven Snow's idea in the first place, they all agreed. It's the best about-turn since the Armada."

Harold left me, had he but known it, in a state of extreme relief. My visit to Lord White had achieved its main objective. At least I hadn't caused so much havoc in a man I liked without some good coming out of it.

That afternoon I rode a novice hurdler that finished second, and later a sensitive mare that had no real heart for the job and finished fourth in a two-mile steeplechase.

After I changed, I found Lord White waiting outside the room.

"I want to talk to you," he said. "Come into the stewards' room."

I followed him and shut the door after us. He stood behind one of the chairs that surrounded the big table, grasping its back with both hands as if it gave him a shield.

"I regret," he said formally, "what I imputed to you on Tuesday. I was upset . . . but it was indefensible."

"It's all right, sir. I understand."

"I want to request den Relgan's resignation from the Jockey Club. The better to persuade him, I am of a mind to show him those photographs, which of course he has seen already. I think, however, that I need your permission to do so."

"I've no objection. Please do what you like with them."

He let go of the chair back as if no longer needing it, and walked around me to the door. "I can't exactly thank you," he said, "but I'm in your debt." He gave me a slight nod and went out of the room, dignity intact.

From Marie Millace I learned more. Steve's collarbone had mended and she had come to Newbury to see him ride, though she confessed, as I steered her off for a cup of coffee, that watching one's son race over fences was an agony. We sat at a small table in one of the bars.

"You're looking better," I said.

She nodded. "I feel it." She had been to a hairdresser, I saw, and had bought some more clothes. Still pale, with smudged, grieving eyes. Four weeks away from George's death.

She sipped the hot coffee and said, "You can forget what I told you last week about the Whites and Dana den Relgan. Wendy's very much happier now. She says that last Tuesday her husband found out something he didn't like about Dana den Relgan. He didn't tell her what. But he told her his affair with Dana was over, and that he'd been a fool, and would she forgive him."

"And will she?"

"Oh, I expect so. Wendy says his trouble was the common one among men of fifty or so, wanting to prove to themselves they're still young. She understands him, you see."

"So do you," I said.

She smiled. "Goodness, yes. You see it all the time."

When we'd finished the coffee, I gave her a list of agents that she might try, and said I'd give any help I could. After that I told her I'd brought a present for her. I fetched my bag from the changing room and handed her an eight-by-ten-inch envelope.

She opened it. Inside was a photograph I'd taken once of George. George holding his camera, looking toward me, smiling his familiar sardonic smile. George in a typical pose, one leg forward, with his weight on the other, head back, considering the world a bad joke. George as he'd lived.

Marie Millace flung her arms around me and hugged me as if she would never let go.

# CHAPTER 8

ZEPHYR Farm Stables was fortified like a stockade, surrounded by a seven-foot fence with a gate that would have done credit to Alcatraz. I sat in my car, waiting for it to open. No one went in or out, and after two fruitless hours I booked into a local hotel.

Inquiries brought a sour response. Yes, the hotel receptionist said, they did sometimes have people staying there who were hoping to persuade their children to come home from Zephyr Farm Stables. Hardly any of them ever managed it; they were never allowed to see their children alone. And the law can't do a thing about it, she said. All over eighteen, they are, see?

I spent the evening drifting around, talking about the Colleagues to a succession of locals propping up the bars.

"Do they ever come out?" I asked. "To go shopping, perhaps?"

Amid a reaction of rueful smiles I was told that yes, indeed, they did emerge, always in groups, and always collecting money.

"They'll sell you things," one man said. "Bits o' polished stone and such. Just beggin' really."

"They don't do no harm," someone else said. "Always smiling."

Would they be out collecting in the morning? I asked. And if so, where?

"Sure. Your best bet would be right here in the center of town."

I thanked them all and went to bed, and at ten in the morning I parked in a lot near the center of town and wandered about on foot. I had to leave by eleven thirty to get back to Newbury, where I was riding in the third race.

I saw no groups of collecting Colleagues. No chanting people with shaven heads and bells. All that happened was that a smiling girl touched my arm and asked if I would like to buy a pretty paperweight. The polished stone lay in the palm of her hand.

"Yes," I said. "How much?"

"It's for charity. As much as you like." She produced a plain wooden box with a slit in the top.

"What charity?" I asked pleasantly, pushing a pound note through the slit.

"Lots of good causes," she said, and smiled.

"What's your name?" I asked.

She broadened the smile as if that were answer enough, and gave me the stone. "Thank you very much," she said. "Your gift will do so much good."

I watched her move on down the street, pulling another stone from a pocket in her swirling skirt and accosting someone else. She was too old to be Amanda, I thought.

"Would you like to buy a paperweight?" asked another stone seller in my path.

"Yes."

Within half an hour I bought four paperweights. To the fourth girl I said, "Is Amanda out here this morning?"

"Amanda? We haven't got . . ." Her eyes went to a girl across the street.

"Never mind," I said. "Thanks for the stone."

She smiled a bright empty smile and moved on, and I waited

a short while before drifting in front of the girl she'd suddenly glanced at. She was young, short, smooth-faced, blank about the eyes, and dressed in a parka and long, full skirt. Her hair was medium brown, like mine, but straight. There was no resemblance between our faces. She might or might not be my mother's child. "Amanda," I said.

She jumped, looked at me doubtfully. "My name's not Amanda."

"What, then?"

"Mandy."

"Mandy what?"

"Mandy North."

I breathed very slowly, and smiled, and asked her how long she had lived at Zephyr Farm Stables.

"All my life," she said limpidly.

"And you're happy?"

"Yes, of course. We do God's work."

"How old are you?"

"Eighteen. . . . But I'm not supposed to talk about myself."

The childlike quality was very marked. She seemed not exactly mentally retarded, but simple. There was no life in her, no fun. Beside the average teenager she was like a sleepwalker. "What was your mother's name, Mandy?"

She looked scared. "You mustn't ask such things."

"When you were little, did you have a pony?"

For an instant her blank eyes lit with an uncrushable memory, and then she glanced over my shoulder at someone, and her simple pleasure turned to red-faced shame. I half turned. A tough-looking man stood there. Very clean, very neatly dressed, and very annoyed.

"No conversations, Mandy," he said to her severely. "Remember the rule. You'll be back on housework, after this. Go along; the girls will take you home." He nodded to a group of girls, and watched as she walked leaden-footed to join them. Poor Mandy. Poor Amanda. Poor little sister.

"What's your game?" the man said to me. "The girls say you've bought stones from all of them. What are you after?"

"Nothing," I said. "They're pretty stones."

He glared at me doubtfully, and he was joined by another man, who had been talking to the now departing girls.

"This guy was asking the girls their names," the second man said. "Looking for Mandy. He talked to her."

They both looked at me with narrowed eyes, and I decided it was time to leave. I headed off in the general direction of the parking lot, but they followed along in my wake. There were five more loitering around the parking lot entrance, and all seven of them encircled me. "What do you want?" I said.

"Why were you asking for Mandy?" one of them said.

"She's my sister."

It confounded the men. They looked at each other. Then one said, "She's got no family. Her mother died years ago. You're lying."

Another one said, "If you ask me, he's a reporter."

The word stung them all into reconciling violence with their strange religion. They banged me up against a brick wall and shoved and kicked a bit hard, but no one wanted to go too far. They were just delivering a warning, so I pushed against their close bodies and that was that.

I didn't tell them the one thing that would have saved me the drubbing—that if Mandy was indeed my sister, she would inherit a fortune.


HAROLD watched my arrival at the track with a scowl of disfavor. "You're late. Why are you limping?"

"Twisted my ankle."

"I hope you're fit to ride. Sharpener's out to win, and you can ride him in your usual way. None of those crazy fool heroics. Understood?"

I nodded, walked inside, and changed into Victor Briggs's colors, feeling an overall ache. Not enough, I hoped, to make any difference in my riding.

When I went outside I saw Elgin Yaxley and Bart Underfield, who were slapping each other on the shoulder and looking faintly drunk. Yaxley peeled off, and Bart, turning with an extravagant lack of coordination, bumped into me.

"Hullo," he said, giving a spirits-laden cough. "You'll be the first to know. Elgin's getting some more horses. They're coming to my stable, of course. We'll make the whole of racing sit up. Elgin's a man of ideas."

"He is indeed," I said dryly.

Bart took his good news off to other ears. I stood watching him, thinking that I didn't like the sound of it. Elgin Yaxley believed himself undetected . . . and people didn't change. If their minds ran to fraud once, they would again.

The old dilemma remained. If I gave the proof of Elgin Yaxley's fraud to the police, I would have to say how I came by the photograph. From George Millace, who wrote threatening letters. George Millace, husband of Marie, who was climbing back with frail hand-holds from the wreck of her life. If justice depended on smashing her deeper into soul-wrecking misery, justice would have to wait.

Sharpener's race was not the biggest event of the day, but he was the favorite. With real *joie de vivre* he sailed around Newbury's long oval, and I thought, I could do with the muscle power I'd lost in the parking lot.

Sharpener won and I was exhausted, which was ridiculous. Harold, beaming, watched me fumble feebly with the girth buckles. The horse, stamping around, almost knocked me over.

"You only went two miles," Harold said. "What's the matter with you?"

I got the buckles undone and pulled off the saddle, and began to feel a trickle of strength flow again through my arms. I grinned and said, "Nothing. It was a good race."

I went in, and while I was sitting on the bench waiting to get my strength back, I decided what to do about Elgin Yaxley.

I HAD grown a habit, over the past two weeks, of taking with me in the car the photographs I might be needing. Lance Kinship's reprints were there, and so were the four concerning Yaxley. I went out and fetched them.

Then I found Yaxley and persuaded him to come with me to the entrance gate, away from the crowd. "You won't want anyone hearing," I said.

"What the devil *is* this?" he said crossly.

"A message from George Millace," I replied.

His sharp features grew rigid and his small mustache bristled. Complacency vanished in a furious concentration of fear.

"I have some photographs you might like to see," I said, and handed him the cardboard envelope.

Yaxley first went pale, then red. He found the whole story there— the café meeting, George's two letters, the note from the farmer, David Parker. The eyes he raised to me were sick and incredulous.

"Any number of copies," I said, "could go off to the insurance company and the police and so on."

He managed a strangled groan.

"There's another way," I said. "George Millace's way."

I'd never seen anyone look at me with total hatred before, and I found it unnerving. But I wanted to find out just what George had extracted from at least one of his victims, and this was my best chance.

I said flatly, "I want the same as George Millace."

"No." It was more a wail than a shout. Full of horror, empty of hope.

"Yes, indeed," I said.

"I can't afford it. Not ten. I haven't got it."

I stared at him. He mistook my silence and gabbled on, finding his voice in a flood of begging, beseeching, cajoling words.

"I've had expenses. It hasn't been easy. Can't you let me alone? George said once and for all . . . and now *you*. . . . Five, then," he said in the face of my continued silence. "Will five do? That's enough. I haven't got any more. I haven't."

I stared once more, and waited.

"All right, then. All *right*." He was shaking with worry and fury. "Seven and a half. It's all I've got, you bloodsucking leech. . . . You're worse than George Millace."

He fumbled in his pockets and brought out a checkbook and

pen. Clumsily supporting the checkbook on the photograph envelope, he wrote the date and a sum of money and signed his name. Then with shaking fingers he tore the slip of paper out of the book and stood holding it. "Not Hong Kong again," he said. "I don't like it."

"Anywhere out of Britain." I stretched out my hand for the check. He gave it to me, his hand trembling. "Thank you," I said.

"Rot in hell."

He turned and stumbled away, utterly in pieces. Serves him right, I thought callously. Let him suffer. It wouldn't be for long. I would tear up his check after I'd seen how much he'd paid George.

I meant to, but I didn't. When I looked at that check, something like a huge burst of sunlight happened in my head, a bright expanding delight of awe and comprehension. The alternative suggestion! Elgin Yaxley's check for seven thousand five hundred pounds was made out not to me, or to Bearer, or even to the Estate of George Millace, but to the Injured Jockeys' Fund.

I walked around, trying to find the ex-jockey who was now administrator of the fund, and tracked him down in the box of one of the television companies. There was a crowd in there, but I beckoned to him and gave him the check.

"Phew," he said, looking at it. "And likewise *wow*."

"Is this the first time Elgin Yaxley's been so generous?"

"No, it isn't. He gave us ten thousand a few months ago, just before he went abroad."

"Have you had any other huge checks like this?" I inquired.

"Not many."

"Would Ivor den Relgan be a generous supporter?"

"Well, yes, he gave us a thousand at the beginning of the season. Sometime in September."

I thanked him and returned to the changing room to get ready for the last race.

In the parade ring, Harold said sharply, "You're looking pleased with yourself."

"Just with life in general."

I *was* pleased with myself. I'd ridden a winner. I'd almost certainly found Amanda. I'd discovered a lot more about George Millace. Sundry kicks and punches on the debit side, but who cared? Overall, not a bad day.

"This hurdler," Harold said severely, "needs a good clear view of what he's got to jump. Understand? Go to the front. I don't want him being jostled in the pack early on."

I nodded. There were twenty-three runners, almost the maximum allowed in this type of race. Harold's hurdler was already sweating with nervous excitement.

"Jockeys, please mount," came the announcement, and when the tapes went up, off we set. Over the first, leading as ordered; good jump, no trouble. Over the second, just out in front; passable jump, no trouble. Over the third—disastrous jump, all four feet seeming to tangle in the hurdle.

We crashed to the turf together, and twenty-two horses came over the hurdle after us.

Horses do their best to avoid a man or a horse on the ground, but with so many, so close, it would have been a miracle if I hadn't been touched. One could never tell how many galloping hoofs connected—it always happened too fast. It felt like being rolled like a rag doll under a stampede. I lay painfully on my side looking at a close bunch of grass, and thought it was a damn silly way to be earning one's living. I almost laughed. I knew I'd thought that before.

A lot of first-aid hands arrived to help me up. Nothing seemed to be broken. I rode back to the stands in an ambulance, demonstrated to the doctor that I was basically in one piece, and winced my slow way into ordinary clothes.

Harold met me outside. "I'll drive you home," he said. "One of the stable lads will take your car."

I didn't argue. We drove in companionable silence toward Lambourn. I felt beaten up and shivery, but it would pass. It always passed. Always would, until I got too old for it.

Harold stopped at my front door. "Sure you're all right?"

"I'll have a hot bath, get the stiffness out. Thanks."

It was already getting dark. I went around drawing the

curtains, switching on lights. Bath, food, aspirin, bed, I thought.

Mrs. Jackson, the woman next door, came to tell me the tax assessor had come by the day before.

"Hope I did right, letting him in. Mind you, I went around with him. He didn't touch a thing. Just counted the rooms."

"I'm sure it's fine, Mrs. Jackson."

"And your telephone," she said as she departed. "It's been ringing and ringing. I can hear it through the wall, you know."

I called Jeremy Folk. He was out. Would I care to leave a message? Tell him I found what we were looking for, I said.

The instant I put the receiver down the phone rang. I picked it up again and heard a child's breathless voice. "I can tell you where that stable is. Am I the first?"

I regretfully said no. I also passed on the same bad news to ten more children within the next two hours. I began asking if they knew how the Colleagues had chanced to buy the stables, and eventually came across a father who did.

"Us and the people who kept the riding school," he said, "were pretty close friends. They wanted to move to Devon and were looking for a buyer for the place, and these fanatics just turned up one day with suitcases full of cash and bought it on the spot."

"How did the fanatics hear of it? Was it advertised?"

"No." He paused, thinking. "Oh, I remember. It was because of one of the children who used to ride the ponies. Sweet little girl. Mandy something. She used to stay with our friends for weeks on end. There was something about her mother being on the point of death, and the religious people looking after her. It was through the mother that they heard the stables were for sale. They were in some ruin of a house at the time, I think, and wanted somewhere better."

"You don't remember the mother's name, I suppose?"

"Sorry, no."

"You've been tremendously helpful," I said. "I'll send your son the ten pounds, even though he wasn't first."

After I'd bathed and eaten, I unplugged the telephone from the kitchen and carried it up to the sitting room, where for another hour it interrupted the television. By nine o'clock I was thoroughly tired of it. I unplugged the phone again and went down to the bathroom for a scratch around the teeth; and the front doorbell rang.

Cursing, I went to see who it was. Opened the door.

Ivor den Relgan stood there, holding a gun.

"Back up," he said. "I'm coming in."

I was certain he was going to kill me. For the second time that day I looked into the eyes of hatred, and the power behind den Relgan's paled Elgin Yaxley's into petulance. He jerked the lethal black weapon toward me. I took two or three steps backward. He stepped through my door and kicked it shut. "You're going to pay," he said, "for what you've done to me. George Millace was bad. You're worse."

I wasn't sure I was actually going to be able to speak, but I did. My voice sounded squeaky. "Did you burn his house?"

His eyes flickered. "Burgled, ransacked, burned," he said furiously. "And you had the stuff all the time."

I had destroyed his power base. Left him metaphorically as naked as on his Saint-Tropez balcony. George must have used the threat of those photographs to stop den Relgan from angling to be let into the Jockey Club. I'd used them to get him thrown out. He'd had some standing before, in racing men's eyes. Now he had none. Never to be in was one thing. To be in, then out, quite another.

"Get back," he said. "Back there. Go on."

He made a small waving movement with the pistol.

"My neighbors'll hear the shot," I said hopelessly.

He sneered and didn't answer. "Back past that door."

It was the door to the darkroom, solidly shut. No sanctuary there, no lock. I'd have to run, I thought wildly. Had at least to try. I was already turning on the ball of one foot when the kitchen door was smashed open. I thought for a split second that somehow den Relgan had missed me and the bullet had splintered some glass, but then I realized he hadn't fired. People had come into the house from the back. Two burly young men with nylon-stocking masks over their faces.

"Take him," den Relgan said, pointing with his gun.

Marie's battered face lit in my memory, and her description: like bulls . . . young . . . stockings over their faces—

They were rushing, banging against each other, eager, infinitely destructive. I tried to fight them. God Almighty, I thought. Not three times in one day.

I couldn't see, couldn't yell, could hardly breathe. They wore roughened leather gloves, which tore my skin. The punches to my face knocked me silly. When I fell on the ground they used their boots. I drifted off altogether.

When I came back it was quiet. I was lying on the white-tiled floor with my cheek in a pool of blood. In a dim way I wondered whose blood it was. Tried to open my eyes. Something wrong with the eyelids. Oh well, I thought, I'm alive.

Did he shoot me? I tried to move, to find out. Bad mistake. My whole body went into a sort of rigid spasm. Locked tight in a monstrous cramp from head to foot, I gasped with the crushing, unexpected agony of it. Worse than fractures, worse than dislocations, worse than anything . . .

Screaming nerves, I thought. Saying too much was injured, nothing must move. I daresay it was the body's best line of defense, but I could hardly bear it. I won't move, I promised. Just . . . let me go. It lasted too long, and went away slowly, tentatively.

I lay in relief in a flaccid heap. Too weak to do anything but pray that the cramp wouldn't come back. Too shattered to think much at all. Except of den Relgan, returning to finish the job. Thoughts that I was dying. Bleeding to death.

Ages passed.

The lights in the cottage were on, but the heating was off. I grew very cold. Cold stopped things bleeding, I thought. I lay quiet for hours, waiting. Sore but alive. Increasingly certain of staying alive. Increasingly certain I'd been lucky. If nothing fatal had ruptured, I could deal with the rest.

I lay on the floor all night and well into the morning. There were splits in my mouth, and I could feel with my tongue the jagged edges of broken teeth. Eventually I lifted my head off the floor. No spasm.

I was lying in the back part of the hall, not far from the bottom of the stairs. The telephone was upstairs. I might get some help if I could get to it. Gingerly I tried to sit up. Couldn't do it. I moved a few inches across the floor, still half lying down. Got as far as the stairs. Hip on the hall floor, shoulder and head on the stairs. In another hour I'd got my haunch up three steps and was again rigid with cramp. Far enough, I thought numbly. I stayed still. For ages.

Somebody rang the front doorbell. Whoever it was, I didn't want him. Whoever it was would make me move. I no longer wanted help. Peace would mend me, given time.

The bell rang again. Then someone came in through the broken back door. Don't let it be den Relgan, I thought.

It wasn't, of course. It was Jeremy Folk, standing still with shock when he reached the hall. *"Philip,"* he said blankly. He leaned over me. "Your face . . ."

"Yeah."

"What happened? Did you have a fall at the races?"

"Yeah," I said. "A fall."

"But the blood. You've got blood everywhere."

"Leave it," I said. "It's dry."

"Can you see? Your eyes are—" He stopped.

"I can see out of one of them," I said. "It's enough."

He wanted to move me, wash the blood off. I wanted to stay just where I was, without having to argue. I persuaded him to leave me alone only by confessing to the cramps.

His horror intensified. "I'll get you a doctor."

"I'm all right. Just don't *do* anything."

"Well . . ." He gave in. "Do you want tea or anything?"

"Find some champagne. Kitchen cupboard."

He looked as if he thought I was mad, but champagne was the best tonic I knew for practically all ills. I heard the cork pop and presently he returned with two tumblers. He put mine on the stair by my left hand, near my head. Oh well, I thought. Might as well find out. The cramps would have to stop sometime. I stiffly moved the arm and fastened the hand around the chunky glass, and I got at least three reasonable gulps before everything seized up. But the spasm wasn't so long or so bad that time. Things were getting better.

The front doorbell rang yet again, and Jeremy went to answer it. The visitor was Clare, come because I'd invited her.

She knelt beside me and said, "This isn't a fall. Someone's done this to you, haven't they?"

"Have some champagne," I said.

"Yes. All right." She stood up and argued on my behalf with Jeremy. "If he wants to lie on the stairs, let him. He's been injured countless times. He knows what's best."

My God, I thought. A girl who understands. Incredible.

She and Jeremy sat in the kitchen, introducing themselves and drinking my booze, and on the stairs things improved. I drank some more champagne. Felt that sometime soon I'd sit up.

The front doorbell rang. An epidemic.

Clare went to answer it. I was sure she intended to keep whoever it was at bay, but she found it impossible. The girl who was there wasn't going to be stopped at the door. She pushed past Clare, and I heard her heels clicking speedily toward me. "I must see," she said frantically. "I must know if he's alive."

I knew her voice. I didn't need to see the distraught beautiful face staring at me, frozen with shock. Dana den Relgan.

# CHAPTER 9

"Oh no!" she said.

"I am," I said in my swollen way, "alive."

"He said it would be a toss-up. He didn't seem to care if they'd killed you. . . . Didn't seem to realize what it would mean."

Clare demanded, "Do you mean you know who did this?"

Dana gave her a distracted look. "I have to talk to him. Alone. Do you mind?"

"But he's—" Clare stopped. "We'll be in the kitchen, Philip."

Dana perched beside me on the stairs. I regarded her through the slit of my vision, seeing her frantic anxiety and not knowing its cause. The gold-flecked hair fell softly forward, almost touching me. The silk of her blouse brushed my hand. The voice was soft . . . and beseeching.

"Please," she said. *"Please . . ."*

"Please, what?" Even in trouble she had a powerful attraction. I found myself wanting to help her if I could.

"Please give me what I wrote for George Millace."

I lay without answering. She misread my inaction, which was born of ignorance, and rushed into a flood of impassioned begging.

"I know you're thinking how can I ask you for the slightest favor when Ivor's done this to you. But please, I beg of you, give it back."

"Is den Relgan your father?" I said.

"No." A whisper, a sigh. "We have . . . a relationship. Please, please give me the cigarettes."

The what? I had no idea what she meant. Trying to make my slow tongue lucid, I said, "Tell me about your relationship with den Relgan, and with Lord White."

"If I tell you, will you give it to me? Please, will you?"

She took my silence to mean that at least she could hope. She scurried into explanations, all of them self-excusing, a distinct flavor of "poor little me, I've been used, it's not my fault."

"I've been with him two years. . . . Not married. . . . Last summer he came up with a brilliant idea. So pleased with himself. If I'd cooperate, he'd see I didn't suffer. I mean, financially." A neat euphemism for hefty bribe.

"He said there was a man at the races wanting to flirt. He said would I pretend to be his daughter and see if I could get the man to flirt with *me*. Ivor said this man had a reputation like snow, and he wanted to play a joke on him."

"So you did," I said.

She nodded. "He was a sweetie. John White. It was easy. I mean, I liked him. I just smiled and he, well, it was true, he was on the lookout for a pretty girl. And there I was."

Poor Lord White, I thought. Hooked because of his nostalgia for youth.

"Ivor wanted to use John, of course. I didn't see that much harm in it. Everything was going fine until Ivor and I went to Saint-Tropez for a week. Then that beastly photographer wrote to Ivor saying lay off Lord White, or else he'd show him those pictures of Ivor and me. Ivor was livid."

"Does he know you're here?"

"No!" She looked horrified. "He hates drugs. It's all we have rows about. George Millace made me write that list, said he'd show the pictures to John if I didn't. I *hated* George Millace. But you'll give it back to me, won't you? Please, you must see. It would ruin me with anyone who matters. I'll pay you if you'll give it to me."

Crunch time, I thought. "What do you expect me to give you?"

"The packet of cigarettes, of course. With the writing on it."

"Yes. Why did you write on a cigarette packet?"

"George Millace said write the list and I said I wouldn't whatever he did, and he said write it then with this red felt-tip pen on the cellophane wrapper of this cigarette pack. He said no one would take seriously a scrawl on cellophane wrapping paper." She stopped suddenly and said with awakening suspicion, "You have got it, haven't you? George Millace gave it to you with the pictures, didn't he?"

"What did you write?"

"You haven't got it! You haven't and I've told you . . . all for nothing." She stood up abruptly, beauty vanishing in fury. "You creep. Ivor should have killed you." She whisked down the hall and slammed out the front door.

Clare and Jeremy came out of the kitchen.

"What did she want?" Clare said.

"Something I haven't got."

They began asking what was happening, but I said, "Tell you tomorrow," and they went back to the kitchen and left me alone.

I still ached all over, incessantly, but movement was becoming possible. Movement soon, I thought, would be imperative. I needed increasingly to go to the bathroom. I sat up on the stairs, my back against the wall. Not so bad. No spasms. I could stand up, if I tried.

Clare and Jeremy appeared inquiringly, and I used their offered hands to pull myself upright. Tottery, but upright. Jeremy helped me across the hall to the bathroom, said something about washing the blood off the floor, and left me.

I hung on to a towel rail in the bathroom and looked at my face in the mirror. Unrecognizable. Hair spiky with blood. One eye lost in puffy folds, one showing a slit. Purple mouth. Two chipped front teeth. Give it a week, I thought, sighing. I ran some warm water into the washbasin, sponged off some of the dried blood, and gingerly patted the washed parts dry with a tissue. Leave the rest, I thought.

There was a heavy crash somewhere out in the hall.

I pulled open the bathroom door to find Clare coming from the kitchen. "You're all right?" she said. "You didn't fall?"

"No. Must be Jeremy."

Unhurriedly we went toward the front of the house to see what he'd dropped, and found Jeremy himself face down on the floor, half in and half out of the darkroom. The bowl of water he'd been carrying was spilled all around him, and there was a strong smell of bad eggs. A smell I knew. Dear God, I thought, and it was a prayer, not a blasphemy. I caught Clare around the waist and dragged her to the front door. Opened it. Pushed her outside. "Stay outside," I said. "It's gas."

I took a deep lungful of the dark wintry night air and turned back. Felt so feeble, so desperate. Bent over Jeremy, grabbed his wrists, and dragged him over the white tiles, feeling the deadly tremors in my weak arms and legs. Out of the darkroom, through the hall, to the front door. Not more than ten feet. My lungs were bursting for air.

Clare took one of Jeremy's arms and between us we dragged him outside. I shut the door, then knelt on the cold road, retching and gasping and feeling utterly useless. Clare was already banging on the house next door.

She returned with the schoolmaster who lived there. "Breathe into him," I said.

"Right." He knelt down beside Jeremy, turned him over, and began mouth-to-mouth resuscitation, knowing the drill. Clare ran back into the schoolmaster's house to call the ambulance.

Jeremy didn't stir. Dear God, I thought, let him live. The gas in my darkroom had been meant for me, not for him. Must have been in there waiting for me all the hours I'd spent lying outside in the hall. I thought incoherently, Jeremy, *don't die*. It's my fault. I should have burned George Millace's rubbish . . . not used it . . . not brought us so near to death.

People came out from all the cottages, bringing blankets, looking shocked. The schoolmaster went on with his task, though I saw from his face that he thought it was useless.

*Don't die.*

Clare felt Jeremy's pulse. "A flutter," she said.

The schoolmaster took heart.

The ambulance arrived, and a police car and Harold and a doctor. Expert hands took over from the schoolmaster and pumped air in and out of Jeremy's lungs. Jeremy himself lay like a log while he was lifted onto a stretcher and loaded into the ambulance. He had a pulse. That was all they would say. They shut the doors on him and drove him to the hospital at Swindon. *Don't die,* I prayed. It's my fault.

A fire engine arrived with men in breathing apparatus. They went around to the back of the cottage carrying equipment with dials, and eventually came out through my front door. They told the police that there should be no investigation inside the cottage until the toxic level was within limits.

"What gas is it?" one of the policemen asked them.

"Hydrogen sulfide. Lethal. Paralyzes the breathing. There's some source in there still generating gas."

The policeman turned to me. "What is it?" he said.

I shook my head. "I don't know."

He asked about my face. "Fell in a horse race," I replied.

The whole circus moved up the road to Harold's house, and events became jumbled. Harold got through to Jeremy's father. A police inspector came, asking questions. I told him I didn't know how hydrogen sulfide had got into my darkroom. I didn't know why anyone would want to put gas in my darkroom. I'd tell him, I thought, if Jeremy died. Otherwise not.

The inspector said he didn't believe me. How had I known so quickly that there was gas? he asked. My reaction had been instantaneous, Clare had said. Why was that?

"Because of the smell. Sodium sulfide used to be used in photographic studios. But I didn't have any."

"Is it a gas?" the inspector asked, puzzled.

"No. Comes in crystals. Very poisonous."

"But you knew it *was* a gas."

"Because I breathed it. It felt wrong. You can make hydrogen sulfide gas using sodium sulfide, but I don't know how." Truthfully I didn't.

Now, sir, he said, about your injuries. Are you sure, sir, that these were the result of a fall in a horse race? Because they looked to him, he had to say, more like the result of a severe human attack.

A fall, I said.

The inspector shrugged. When he'd gone, Harold said, "Hope you know what you're doing. Your face was okay when I left you, wasn't it?"

"Tell you one day," I said, mumbling.

Harold's wife gave Clare and me comfort and food and eventually beds. And Jeremy at midnight was still alive.

IN THE morning Harold came into the little room where I sat in bed, still aching all over. My young lady, he said, had gone off to London to work. The police wanted to see me. And Jeremy was still unconscious.

The whole day continued wretchedly. The police went into my cottage, and the inspector came to Harold's house to tell me the results. "There's a water filter on the tap in your darkroom," he said. "What do you use it for?"

"All water for photographs," I said, "has to be clean."

Some of the worst swelling around my eyes and mouth was subsiding and I could see better, talk better, which was some relief.

"Your water filter," the inspector said, "is a hydrogen sulfide generator."

"It can't be. I use it all the time. It's only a water softener. It couldn't possibly make gas."

He gave me a long, considering stare. Then he went away. He returned with a box and a young man in jeans and a sweater.

"Now, sir," the inspector said to me with the studied politeness of the suspicious cop. "Is this your water filter?" He opened the box. One Durst filter. Screwed onto its top was the short rubber attachment that was normally pushed onto the tap.

"It looks like it," I said.

The inspector gestured to the young man, who put on a pair of plastic gloves and picked up the filter. It was a black plastic globe about the size of a grapefruit, with clear sections top and bottom. He unscrewed it around the middle.

"Inside here," he said, "there's usually just a filter cartridge. But inside this particular object there are two containers, one above the other. They're both empty now, but the lower one contained sodium sulfide crystals, and the upper one contained sulfuric acid. There must have been some kind of membrane holding the contents of the two containers apart. But when the tap was turned on, the water pressure broke or dissolved the membrane, and the two chemicals mixed. Sulfuric acid and sodium sulfide, propelled by water. A highly effective sulfide generator."

There was a long, depressing silence.

"So you can see, sir," the inspector said, "it couldn't in any way have been an accident."

"No," I said dully. "But I truthfully don't know who could have put such a thing there. They would have to have known what sort of filter I had, wouldn't they?"

Another silence. They seemed to be waiting for me to tell them who, but I didn't know. It couldn't have been den Relgan. Why should he bother with such a device when one or two more kicks would have finished me? It couldn't have been Elgin Yaxley; he hadn't had time. It couldn't have been any of the other people George Millace had written his letters to. Two of them were old history. One was still current, but I'd done nothing about it, and hadn't told the man concerned that the letter existed.

All of which left one most uncomfortable explanation: that somebody thought I had something I didn't have. Someone who knew I'd inherited George Millace's blackmailing package and that I'd used some of it, and who wanted to stop me from using any more of it. George Millace had definitely had more in that box than I'd inherited. I didn't have, for instance, the cigarette packet on which Dana den Relgan had written her drugs list. And I didn't have . . . What else?

"Well, sir," the inspector said.

"No one's been into my cottage since I was using the dark-room on Wednesday. Only my neighbor, and the tax assessor—" I stopped, and they pounced.

"What tax assessor?"

Ask Mrs. Jackson, I said, and they replied yes, they would.

"She told me he didn't touch anything."

"But he could have seen the type and size of the filter," the younger man said. "Then he could have come back. It would take about thirty seconds, I'd reckon, to take the filter cartridge out and put the packets of chemicals in. Pretty neat job."

They went away after a while, taking the filter.

I rang the hospital. No change.

Later in the afternoon Harold's wife drove me to the hospital. I didn't see Jeremy. I saw his parents. They were too upset to be angry. Not my fault, they said, though I thought they would change their minds later.

I returned to Harold's house and stayed there until the inspector telephoned to say I could go back to my cottage, but not into the darkroom—the police had sealed it.

I wandered around my home, feeling neck-deep in guilt. There were signs everywhere that the police had searched, but they hadn't found the few prints I still had of George Millace's letters, which were locked in the car. And they had left the box with the blank-looking negatives undisturbed in the kitchen.

I opened it. It still contained the one puzzle I hadn't solved: the black lightproof envelope containing what looked like a piece of clear plastic and two sheets of typing paper.

Perhaps, I thought, it's because I have these that the gas trap was set. But *what* did I have? I needed to find out, and pretty fast, before whoever it was had another go at killing me, and succeeded.

I begged a bed again from Harold's wife, and in the morning had a call from Jeremy's father. "We want you to know he's awake," he informed me. "He's still on the respirator. But they say he'll recover."

"Thank you," I said, and felt an incredible sense of release. I had been freed. Let off a life sentence of guilt.

Later Clare telephoned.

"He's all right. He's awake," I said.

"I'm so glad."

"Can I ask you for a favor? Can I dump myself on Samantha for a night or two?"

"As in the old days? Why not? We'll expect you for supper."

Harold wanted to know when I thought I'd be fit to race. I said I would get some physiotherapy and be ready by Saturday.

I still felt distinctly unfit, but I did some packing, collected George's rubbish box from the kitchen, and set off for Samantha's house, where I got a horrified reception when she and Clare saw my black bruises, cuts, and three days' growth of beard.

"But it's *worse*," Clare said, staring closely.

"Looks worse, feels better."

Samantha was troubled. "Clare said someone had punched you, but I never thought—"

"Look," I said. "I can go somewhere else."

"Don't be silly. Sit down. Supper's ready."

They didn't talk much or seem to expect me to. With the coffee Samantha said calmly, "If you're tired, go to bed."

They both followed me upstairs. I walked automatically, without thinking, into the small bedroom next to the bathroom.

They laughed. "We wondered if you would remember," Samantha said.

The next morning Clare went to work and I dozed in the swinging basket chair in the kitchen. Thursday I took myself to the Clinic for Injuries for massage and exercises. Between sessions I telephoned four photographers, and found no one who knew how to raise pictures from plastic or typing paper.

When I got back to Samantha's, the winter sun was low and Samantha was cleaning the panes of the French doors to the garden. "Sorry if it's cold in here, but I won't be long," she said.

I watched her. She finished the outsides of the doors and came in, bolting them after her. A plastic bottle stood on a table. AJAX, it said in big letters. I frowned at it, trying to remember. Where had I heard the word Ajax? I walked over for a closer look; AJAX WINDOW CLEANER, it said in smaller letters; WITH AMMONIA. I shook the bottle, then opened it. Soapy. I smelled it. Less pungent than straight ammonia.

"Why would a man ask his wife to buy him some liquid Ajax?" I asked.

"What a question," Samantha said. "I've no idea."

"Nor did she have," I said. "She didn't know why."

Samantha took the bottle out of my hands and continued with her task. I went back to the basket chair and swung in it gently.

She cast me a sideways glance, smiling. "Who punched you?" Her voice sounded casual, but it was a serious question. If I didn't tell her, she wouldn't persist, but we would have gone as far as we ever would in our relationship.

What did I want, I thought, in that house that now increasingly felt like home? I had never wanted a family. No suffocating emotional ties. If I nested comfortably into the lives lived in that house, wouldn't I feel impelled in a short while to break out with freedom-seeking wings? Did anyone ever fundamentally change?

Samantha read my silence as I expected, and her manner altered subtly, not to one of unfriendliness but to a cutoff of intimacy. Before she'd finished the window, I'd become her guest, not her . . . what? Her son, brother . . . part of her. She gave me a bright smile and put the kettle on for tea.

Clare returned from work, and she, too, though not asking, was waiting.

So, halfway through supper I found myself quite naturally telling them about George Millace. "You see," I said at the end, "that it isn't finished yet. There's no going back or wishing I hadn't started. I asked to come here for a few days because I didn't feel safe in the cottage. And I'm not going back there to live until I know who tried to kill me."

Clare said, "You might never know."

"Don't say that," Samantha said. "If he doesn't find out—"

I finished it for her. "I'll have no defense."

We passed the rest of the evening more in thoughtfulness than depression, and the news from the Swindon hospital was good. Jeremy was still on the respirator, but his lungs were significantly improved.

I SPENT a long time in the bathroom on Friday morning scraping off beard. The cuts had all healed and the swelling had gone, although there were still the chipped teeth.

"You need caps," Samantha said, and insisted on telephoning her dentist. And caps I had, late that afternoon. Temporaries, until porcelain jobs could be made.

After another exercise session in the clinic I drove north to Essex, to visit a firm that manufactured photographic printing paper. I went in person instead of telephoning, because I thought they would find it less easy to say they had no information if I was actually there; and so it proved.

They did not, the front office said politely, know of any photographic materials that looked like plastic or typing paper. Had I brought the specimens with me?

No, I had not. Could I see someone else?

Difficult, they said.

I showed no signs of leaving. Perhaps Mr. Christopher could help me, they suggested at length, if he wasn't too busy.

Mr. Christopher turned out to be about nineteen, with an antisocial haircut and a chronic cough. He listened, however, very attentively.

"This paper and this plastic have got no emulsion on them?"

"No, I don't think so."

He shrugged. "There you are, then. You got no pictures."

I sucked at the still broken teeth and asked him what seemed to be a nonsensical question. "Why would a photographer want ammonia?"

"Well, he wouldn't. Not for photographs. No straight ammonia in any developer or bleach or fix that I know of."

"Would anyone here know?" I asked.

He gave me a pitying stare, implying that if he didn't know, no one else would.

"You could ask," I said persuasively. "Because if there's a process that does use ammonia, you'd like to know, wouldn't you?"

"Yeah. I reckon I would."

He nodded briskly at me and vanished, returning a few minutes later with an elderly man in glasses.

"Ammonia," he said, "is used in the photographic sections of engineering industries. It develops what the public calls blueprints. More accurately, it's the diazo process. What's the matter with your face?"

"Lost an argument. Please, the diazo process. What is it?"

"You get a line drawing from a designer. Say of a component in a machine. The industry will need several copies of the master drawing. So they make blueprints of it."

"Please go on."

"From the beginning?" he said. "The master drawing, which is on translucent paper, is pressed tightly by glass over a sheet of diazo paper. Diazo paper is white on the back, and yellow or greenish on the side covered with ammonia-sensitive dye. Bright light is shone onto the master drawing for a measured length of time. This light bleaches out all the dye on the diazo paper underneath except for the parts under the lines on the master drawing. The diazo paper is then developed in hot ammonia fumes, and the lines of dye emerge, turning dark. Is that what you want?"

"Indeed it is. Does diazo paper look like typing paper?"

"Certainly it can, if it's cut down to that size."

"And how about a piece of clear-looking plastic?"

"Sounds like diazo film," he said calmly. "You don't need hot ammonia fumes for developing that. Any form of cold liquid ammonia will do. But be careful. If your piece of film looks clear, it means that most of the yellow-looking dye has already been bleached out. If there is a drawing on it, you must be careful not to expose it to too much more light."

"How much more light is too much?" I said anxiously.

"In sunlight, you'd have lost any trace of dye forever in thirty seconds. In normal room light, five to ten minutes."

"It's in a lightproof envelope."

"Then you might be lucky."

"And the sheets of paper? They look white on both sides."

"The same applies," he said. "They've been exposed to light. You might have a drawing there, or you might not."

"How do I make hot ammonia fumes, to find out?"

"Simple," he said. "Put some ammonia in a saucepan and heat it. Hold the paper over the top and steam it."

"Would you," I said, "like some champagne for lunch?"

I RETURNED to Samantha's house at about six o'clock with a cheap saucepan and two bottles of Ajax. I felt dead tired. Samantha had gone out and Clare was working at the kitchen table. She scrutinized me and suggested a large brandy. "And pour me some too, would you?" she added.

I sat at the table with her for a while, sipping my drink. Her dark head was bent over the book she was working on.

"Would you live with me?" I said.

She looked up, abstracted, faintly frowning. "Is that an academic question or a positive invitation?"

"Invitation."

"I couldn't live in Lambourn," she said. "Too far to commute. You couldn't live here. Too far from the horses."

"Somewhere in between."

She looked at me wonderingly. "Well . . ." She took refuge with sips from her glass. I waited for what seemed an age. "I think," she said finally, "why not give it a try?"

I smiled with intense satisfaction.

"Don't look so smug." She bent her head down again but didn't read. "It's no good. How can I work? Let's get supper."

Cooking frozen fish fillets took ages, because she was trying to do it with my arms around her waist and my chin in her hair. I didn't taste the food when we ate it. I felt extraordinarily light-headed. I hadn't deeply hoped she would say yes, and still less had I expected the incredible sense of adventure I felt since she had. To have someone to care about no longer seemed a burden to be avoided, but a positive privilege.

After supper, while she tried again to finish her work, I fetched the black lightproof envelope from George Millace's rubbish box. I borrowed a flat glass dish from a cupboard. Put the plastic film from the envelope into the dish. Poured Ajax Window Cleaner over it. Held my breath.

Almost instantly dark brownish red lines became visible. I sloshed the liquid across the plastic surface, knowing that all of the remaining dye had to be covered with ammonia before the light bleached it away.

It was no engineering drawing, but handwriting. As more and more developed, I read the revealed words. They had to be what Dana den Relgan had written on the cigarette packet: heroin, cocaine, marijuana. Quantities, dates, prices paid, suppliers. No wonder she had wanted it back.

Clare looked up from her work. "What have you found?"

"What that Dana girl was wanting."

She looked into the dish, reading. "That's pretty damning. But how did it turn up like this?"

"Crafty George Millace. He got her to write on cellophane wrapping with a red felt-tip pen. She felt safer that way, because cigarette wrapping is so fragile, so destructible. But all George wanted was solid lines on transparent material, to make a diazo print. And he got it."

I explained what I'd learned in Essex. "With the list recorded, it didn't matter if the wrapping came to pieces. And the list was safely hidden from angry burglars, like everything else."

"He was an extraordinary man."

I nodded. "Extraordinary. Though, mind you, he didn't mean anyone else to have to solve his puzzles."

"What about all your photographs?" she said in sudden alarm. "All the ones in the filing cabinet. Suppose . . ."

"Calm down. The butcher down the road has all the negatives and transparencies."

"Maybe all photographers," she said, "are obsessed."

It wasn't until much later that I realized I hadn't disputed her classification. I hadn't even thought, I'm a jockey.

She went to wash her hair. I drained the Ajax out of the dish into the saucepan and opened the French doors while it heated, so as not to become asphyxiated. Then I held the sheets of what looked like typing paper over the simmering Ajax and watched George's words come alive, as if they'd been written in secret ink. Together the sheets constituted one handwritten letter. He must have written it on some transparent material—a plastic bag, tracing paper, a piece of glass, film with the emulsion bleached off, anything. He had then put his letter over diazo paper and exposed it to light, and immediately stored the exposed paper in the lightproof envelope.

And then what? Had he sent his transparent original? Had he typed a copy? One thing was certain. In some form or other he had dispatched his letter. I knew the results of its arrival.

And I could guess who wanted me dead.

# CHAPTER 10

HAROLD found me on the veranda at Sandown. "You at least look better. Have you passed the doctor?"

"He signed my card." By the doctor's standards, a jockey who took a week off because he'd been kicked was acting more self-indulgently than usual.

"Victor's here," Harold said.

"Did you tell him?"

"I did. He says he's coming to see his horses work on the downs on Monday. He'll talk to you then."

"How about today? Is Coral Key running straight?"

"Victor hasn't said anything."

"Because I am," I said. "If I'm riding it, I'm riding it straight. Whatever Victor says."

"You've got bloody aggressive all of a sudden."

"Just saving you money. Don't back me to lose, like you did on Daylight."

He said he wouldn't. He also said there was no point in holding the Sunday briefing if I was talking to Victor on Monday. . . . I wondered, after Monday, would there be any need for a briefing?

As I walked toward the parade ring, I saw Bart Underfield. He was lecturing to a reporter on the subject of unusual nutrients. "It's rubbish giving horses beer and eggs. I never do it."

The reporter refrained from saying—or perhaps he didn't know—that the trainers addicted to eggs and beer were on the whole more successful than Bart.

Bart's face, when he saw me, changed from bossy know-it-all to tight-lipped spite. He took two decisive steps forward to stand in my path, but when he'd stopped me he didn't speak.

"Do you want something, Bart?" Likely he couldn't find words intense enough to convey his hatred.

"You wait," he said with bitter quiet. "I'll get you." If he'd had a dagger and privacy, I wouldn't have turned my back on him, as I did, to walk away.

Victor Briggs was waiting in the parade ring. A heavy, brooding figure—unsmiling, untalkative, gloomy. When I touched my cap to him politely, there was only an expressionless stare.

Coral Key was an oddity among Victor Briggs's horses, a six-year-old novice steeplechaser brought out of the hunting field when he had begun to show promise. Great horses in the past had started that way, and Coral Key, too, had the feel of good things to come. There was no way that I was going to mess up his early career. In my mind and very likely in my attitude I was daring Victor Briggs to say he didn't want him to try to win.

Briggs said nothing at all. He simply watched me.

Harold bustled about as if movement itself could dispel the atmosphere existing between his owner and his jockey; and I mounted and rode out to the course feeling as if I'd been in a strong field of undischarged electricity. A spark, an explosion might lie ahead. Harold had sensed it.

I lined up at the start. Good ground underfoot. Seven other runners, none brilliant. Coral Key should have a good chance. I settled my goggles over my eyes and gathered the reins.

"Come in now, jockeys," the starter said. The horses advanced toward the tapes in a slow line. Thirteen fences, two miles. Important, I thought, to get him to jump well. It was what I was best at.

There were two fences at the start, then the uphill stretch past the stands, then the top bend, then the downhill fence where I'd stepped off Daylight. No problems on Coral Key. He cleared all of them. Then the sweep around to seven fences in quick succession. I lost one length getting Coral Key set right for the first one, but by the seventh I'd stolen ten. Still, it was too soon for satisfaction. Around the long bottom curve Coral Key lay second, taking a breather. Three fences to go. Between the last two I caught up with the leader. We jumped the last fence alongside and raced up the hill toward home, stretching, flying. I did everything I could.

The other horse won by two lengths.

In the unsaddling enclosure, Harold said a shade apprehensively, "He ran well," and patted Coral Key. Victor Briggs said nothing.

I pulled the saddle off. There was no way I could think of that I could have won the race. The other horse had been stronger and faster. I hadn't felt weak. I hadn't thrown anything away in jumping mistakes. I just hadn't won. I needed a strong hand for talking to Victor Briggs, and I didn't have it.

I won the other steeplechase, the one that didn't matter much except to the owners, four businessmen. "Bloody good show," they said. Victor Briggs watched from ten paces away, balefully staring.

Clare, who had come to the races with me, said later, "I suppose the wrong one won?"

"Yeah."

I looked at the trim dark coat, the long polished boots, at the large gray eyes and the friendly mouth. Incredible, I thought, to have someone like Clare waiting for me outside the changing room. Like a fire in a cold house. "Would you mind," I said, "if we made a detour for me to call on my grandmother?"

THE old woman was markedly worse. No longer propped upright, she sagged back on the pillows. Even her eyes seemed to be losing the struggle, with none of their usual aggressiveness.

"Did you bring her?" she asked. Still no salutation, no preliminaries. Her hatred for me remained immutable.

"No," I said. "I didn't bring her. She's lost."

She gave a feeble cough, the thin chest jerking. Her eyelids closed for a few seconds and opened again. A weak hand twitched at the sheet.

"Leave your money to James," I said.

She shook her head.

"Leave some to charity, then. Medical research?"

"Hasn't done me much good, has it?"

"Well," I said slowly, "how about a religious order?"

"You must be mad. I hate religion. Cause of trouble. Cause of wars. Wouldn't give them a penny."

I sat down unbidden in the armchair.

Amanda was lost within her religion. Indoctrinated, cared for, perhaps loved; and fourteen formative years couldn't be undone. Wrenching her out forcibly would inflict incalculable psychological damage. For her own sake one would have to leave her in peace, however strange that peace might seem. If one day she sought change of her own accord, so much the better. Meanwhile, she just had to be provided for.

"Can I do anything for you?" I asked. "Besides, of course, finding Amanda. Can I fetch anything? Is there anything you want?"

My grandmother sneered. "Don't think you can soft-soap me into leaving any money to you."

"I'd give water to a dying cat. Even if it spat in my face."

Her mouth opened and stiffened with affront. "How dare you?"

"How dare you think I'd shift a speck of dust for your money?"

The mouth closed into a thin line. Then she said, "Go away."

"I will, but I want to suggest something else. In case Amanda is ever found, why don't you set up a trust for her? Tie up the capital tight with masses of trustees. Make it so that no one who was perhaps after her fortune could get hold of it. Make it impossible for anyone but Amanda herself to benefit, with an income paid out only at the direction of the trustees. Leave it to her with strings like steel hawsers."

She lay quiet. I waited. I had waited all my life for something other than malevolence from my grandmother.

"Go away," she said.

"Very well." I stood up and walked to the door.

"Send me some roses," my grandmother said.

Clare and I found a flower shop still open. All they had were fifteen small pink buds on very long thin stems. We drove back to the nursing home and gave them to a nurse to deliver, with a card enclosed saying I'd get some better ones next week.

"She doesn't deserve it," Clare said.

"Poor old woman."

NEXT AFTERNOON WE WENT TO see Jeremy. He was lying in a high bed with a mass of breathing equipment to one side, but breathing for himself. He looked thin and pale, yet the eyes were as intelligent as ever.

I tried to apologize for what he'd suffered. He wouldn't have it. "I was there because I wanted to be," he said. He gave me an inspection. "Your face looks okay. How do you heal so fast?"

"Always do."

He gave a weak laugh. "Funny life you lead. Always healing."

"How long will you be in here?"

"Three or four days. Once there's no danger the nerves will pack up again, I can go. There's nothing else wrong."

We didn't stay very long because talking clearly tired him, but just before we went he said, "You know, that gas was so quick, I'd no time to do anything. It was like breathing a brick wall."

Into a short reflective silence Clare said, "No one would have lived if they'd been there alone."

After we left she said, "You didn't tell Jeremy about Amanda."

"Plenty of time."

"He came down last Sunday because he'd got your message that you'd found her. He told me while we were in the kitchen. He said your telephone was out of order, so he came."

"I'd unplugged it."

"Odd how things happen."

I drove her to the train and went on to Lambourn. When I got to my cottage it seemed strangely unfamiliar, no longer the embracing refuge a home should be. I saw for the first time the bareness, the emotional chill that had been so apparent to Jeremy on his first visit. It no longer seemed to fit me. The maturing change had gone too far.

In the morning I spread out on the kitchen table a variety of photographs of different people, and then I asked my neighbor Mrs. Jackson to come in and look at them.

"What am I looking for, Mr. Nore?" she asked.

"Anyone you've seen before."

Obligingly she studied them carefully one by one and stopped

without hesitation at a certain face. "How extraordinary!" she exclaimed. "That's the tax assessor. The one I let in here. Ever so
sarcastic the police were about that, but you don't *expect* people to
say they're tax assessors if they aren't."

"You're sure he's the one?"

"Positive. He had that same hat on, and all."

"Then would you write on the back of the photo for me, Mrs.
Jackson?" I gave her a felt-tip pen and dictated the words, saying
that this man had called at the house of Philip Nore posing as a
tax assessor on Friday, November 27. "Now sign your name, Mrs.
Jackson. And would you mind repeating the message on the back
of this other photograph?"

With concentration she did so. "Are you giving these to
the police?" she asked. "Will they come back again with their
questions?"

"I shouldn't think so," I said.


Victor Briggs had come in his Mercedes, but he went up to the
downs with Harold in the Land Rover. I rode up on a horse. The
morning's workout got done to everyone's satisfaction, and we all
returned to the stable the way we had come.

When I rode into the yard, Victor Briggs was standing by his
car, waiting. "Get in the car," he said. No waster of words, ever. He
stood there in his usual clothes, gloved as always against the chilly
wind, darkening the day. If I could see auras, I thought, his would
be black.

I sat in the front, and he slid in behind the wheel and drove
back out to the downs. He stopped on a wide grass shoulder, from
where one could see half of Berkshire. He switched off the engine,
leaned back in his seat, and said, "Well?"

"Do you know what I'm going to say?" I asked.

"I hear things. I heard that den Relgan set his goons on you."

I looked at him with interest. "Where did you hear that?"

He made a small, tight movement of his mouth, but he did answer. "Gambling club."

"Did you hear any reasons?"

He produced the twitch that went for a smothered smile. "I heard that you got den Relgan chucked out of the Jockey Club a great deal faster than he got in."

"Did you hear how?"

He said with faint regret, "No. Just that you'd done it. The goons were talking. Stupid boneheads. Den Relgan's heading for trouble, using them. They never keep their mouths shut."

"They beat up George Millace's wife. Did you hear that too?"

After a pause he nodded, but offered no comment. A secretive, solid, slow-moving man, with a tap into a world I knew little of. Gambling clubs, hired bullyboys, underworld gossip.

"The goons said they left you for dead," he said. "One of them was scared. Said they'd gone too far with the boots."

There was another pause, then I said, "George Millace sent you a letter."

He seemed almost to relax, breathing out in a long sigh. He'd been waiting to know for sure, I thought.

"How long have you had it?" he said.

"Three weeks."

"You can't use it. You'd be in trouble yourself."

"How did you know I'd got it?"

He said slowly, "I heard you had George Millace's . . . files."

"Ah. Nice anonymous word, files. How did you hear I had them? Who from?"

He thought it over, and then said grudgingly, "Ivor. And Dana. Separately. Ivor was too angry to be discreet. He said you were fifty times worse than George Millace. And Dana, another night, said did I know you had copies of some blackmailing letters George Millace had sent, and were using them. She asked if I could help her get hers back. I said I couldn't."

"When you talked to them, was it in gambling clubs?"

"It was."

"Are they your gambling clubs?"

He said after a pause, "I have two partners. The clientele in general don't know I'm a proprietor. I move around. I play. I listen. Does that answer your question?"

I nodded. "Yes, thank you. Are those goons yours?"

"I employ them," he said austerely, "as bouncers. Not to smash up women and jockeys."

"A little moonlighting, was it? On the side?"

He didn't answer directly. "I have been expecting," he said, "that you would demand something from me if you had that letter."

I thought of the letter, which I knew word for word:

Dear Victor Briggs,

I am sure you will be interested to know that I have the following information. You did on five separate occasions during the past six months conspire with a bookmaker to defraud the betting public by arranging that your odds-on favorites should not win their races.

I hold a signed affidavit from the bookmaker in question. As you see, all five of these horses were ridden by Philip Nore, who certainly knew what he was doing.

I could send this affidavit to the Jockey Club. I will telephone you soon, however, with an alternative suggestion.

The letter had been sent more than three years earlier. For three years Victor Briggs had run his horses straight. When George Millace died, Victor had gone back to the old game, only to find that his vulnerable jockey was no longer reliable.

"I didn't mean to tell you I had the letter," I said.

"Why not? You wanted to ride to win. You could have used it to make me agree."

"I wanted to make you run the horses straight for their own sakes."

He gave me a long, uninformative stare. "I'll tell you," he said finally. "Yesterday I added up all the prize money I'd won since Daylight's race at Sandown. All those seconds and thirds, as well as Sharpener's wins. And it turned out I made more money in the past month with you riding straight than I did with you stepping off Daylight."

He paused, waiting for a reaction, but I simply stared back. "I've seen," he went on, "that you weren't going to ride any more crooked races. You're older. Stronger. If you go on riding for me, I won't ask you to lose a race again. Is that enough? Is that what you want to hear?"

I looked out across the windy landscape. "Yes."

After a bit he said, "George Millace didn't demand money."

"A donation to the Injured Jockeys'?"

"You know the lot, don't you?"

"I've learned," I said. "George wasn't interested in extorting money for himself. He extorted"—I searched for the word—"frustration. He enjoyed making people cringe. He did it to everybody in a mild way. To people he could catch out doing wrong, he did it with gusto. He had alternative suggestions for everyone. Disclosure, or do what George wanted. And what George wanted was to stop Ivor den Relgan's power play. To stop Dana taking drugs. To stop other people doing other things."

"To stop me," Victor said with a hint of dry humor, "from being disqualified. You're right, of course. When George Millace telephoned, he said all I had to do was behave myself. Those were his words. 'As long as you behave, Victor,' he told me, 'nothing will happen.' He called me Victor, as if I were a little pet dog. 'If I suspect anything, Victor,' he said, 'I'll follow Philip Nore around with my motorized telephotos until I catch him, and then, Victor, you'll both be finished.'"

"And was that all? Forever?"

"Besides suggesting that I give a thousand pounds to the Injured Jockeys' Fund, he used to wink at me at the races."

I laughed.

"Yes, very funny. Is that the lot?"

"Not really. There's something you could do for me in the future. Hearing things, as you do. It's about Dana's drugs."

"Stupid girl. She won't listen."

"She will soon. She's still savable. And in addition to her . . ." I told him what I wanted.

He listened acutely. When I'd finished I got the twitch of a smile. "Beside you," he said, "George Millace was a beginner."

VICTOR DROVE OFF, AND I walked back to Lambourn over the downs.

An odd man, I thought. I'd learned more about him in half an hour than I had in seven years, and still knew next to nothing. He had given me what I'd wanted, though. Given it freely—my job without strings for as long as I liked, and help in another matter just as important. It hadn't all been, I thought, because of my having that letter.

Out on the bare hills, I thought of the way things had happened during the past few weeks. Because of Jeremy's persistence I'd looked for Amanda, and because of looking for Amanda I had now met a grandmother, an uncle, a sister. I knew something at least of my father. I had a feeling of origin that I hadn't had before. I had people, like everyone else had. Not necessarily loving or praiseworthy, but *there*. I hadn't wanted them, but now that I had them they sat quietly in the mind like foundation stones.

I reached the point on the hill from where I could see down to my cottage. I could see most of Lambourn, stretched out. Could see Harold's house and the yard. Could see the whole row of cottages, with mine in the center. I'd belonged in that village, breathed its intrigues for seven years. Been happy, miserable, normal. It was what I'd called home. But now I was leaving that place, in mind and spirit as well as body. I would live somewhere else, with Clare. I would be a photographer. The future lay inside me, waiting, accepted.

I would race until the end of the season. Six more months. Then I'd hang up my boots. I still had the appetite, still had the physique. Better to go, I supposed, before both of them crumbled.

I went on down the hill without any regrets.

# CHAPTER 11

CLARE arrived on the train two days later to sort out the photographs she wanted from the filing cabinet. Now that she was my agent, she said, she'd be rustling up business.

I had no races that day. I'd arranged to fetch Jeremy from the hospital and take him home, and to have Clare come with me. I'd also telephoned Lance Kinship to say I had his reprints ready and would he like me to drop them off, as I was practically going past his house. That would be fine, he said.

"And I'd like to ask you something," I said.

"Oh? All right. Anything you like."

Jeremy looked a great deal better, without the gray clammy skin of Sunday. We helped him into the back of my car and tucked a lap robe around him, which he plucked off indignantly, saying he was no aged invalid but a perfectly viable solicitor. "And incidentally," he said, "my uncle came down here yesterday. Bad news, I'm afraid. Old Mrs. Nore died Monday night."

"Oh, no," I said.

"Well, you knew. Only a matter of time. My uncle brought two letters for me to give to you. They're in my suitcase somewhere."

I fished them out, and we sat in the hospital parking lot while I read them. The first was a copy of her will.

Jeremy said, "My uncle told me he was called out urgently to the nursing home on Monday morning. Your grandmother wanted to make her will. Stubborn old woman to the last."

I unfolded the typewritten sheets. "I, Lavinia Nore, being of sound mind, do hereby revoke all previous wills."

There was a good deal of legal guff and some complicated

pension arrangements for an old cook and gardener, and then two final paragraphs:

> Half the residue of my estate to my son, James Nore.
> Half the residue of my estate to my grandson, Philip Nore, to be his absolutely, with no strings or steel hawsers attached.

The old witch had defeated me.

I opened the other envelope and found a scribbled note:

> I think you did find Amanda, and didn't tell me because it would have given me no pleasure. Is she a nun?
> You can do what you like with my money. If it makes you vomit, as you once said, then *vomit*.
> Or give it to my genes.
> Rotten roses.

I handed the will and the note to Clare and Jeremy, who read them in silence. "What will you do?" Clare said.

"I don't know. See that Amanda never starves, I suppose. Apart from that . . ."

"Enjoy it," Jeremy said. "The old woman loved you."

I wondered if it was true. Love or hate. Perhaps she'd felt both at once when she'd made that will.

I started the car and we drove toward Saint Albans, detouring to Lance Kinship's house. "Sorry," I said. "Won't take long."

They didn't seem to mind. The house was typical Kinship—fake Georgian, grandiose front, pillared gateway. I took the photographs from the trunk of the car and rang the doorbell.

Lance opened the door, dressed in white jeans, espadrilles, and a red-and-white striped T-shirt. Film director gear. All he needed was the megaphone.

"Come inside," he said. "I'll pay you for these."

"Okay. Can't be long, though, with my friends waiting."

He looked toward my car, where Clare's and Jeremy's interested faces showed in the windows, and then led the way into a large sitting room with expanses of parquet and too much black lacquered furniture. Chrome-and-glass tables. Art deco lamps.

I gave him the packet of pictures. "You'd better make sure they're all right."

He shrugged. "Why shouldn't they be?" All the same, he opened the envelope and pulled out the top picture. It showed him looking straight at the camera in his country-gent clothes—glasses, trilby hat, air of bossy authority.

"Turn it over," I said.

He did so. And read what Mrs. Jackson had written. "This is the tax assessor. . . ." The change in him from one instant to the next was like one person leaving and another entering the same skin. I saw the Lance Kinship I'd only suspected existed. Not the faintly ridiculous poseur, but the tangled psychotic who would do any-thing to preserve the outward show. It was in his very inadequacy, I supposed, that the true danger lay. In his estrangement from reality and in his theatrical turn of mind, which allowed him to see murder as a solution to problems.

"Before you say anything," I said, "you'd better look at the other things in that envelope."

He let the picture of the great film producer fall to the floor. Angrily he sorted out the regular reprints and let them drop too. Then he found the reproduction of Dana den Relgan's drug list. He stood holding it in visible horror. "She swore you didn't know what she was talking about," he said hoarsely.

"She was talking about the list of drugs you supplied her with. Complete with dates and prices. As you see, your name appears on it liberally."

"I'll kill you," he said.

"No, you won't. You've missed your chance. If the gas had killed me, you would have been all right, but it didn't."

He didn't say, What gas? He said, "It all went wrong. But I thought it wouldn't matter."

"You thought it wouldn't matter because you heard from Dana den Relgan that I didn't have the list. And if I didn't have the list, I didn't have George Millace's letter, and there was no more need to kill me. Well, it's too late to do it now, because there are extra prints of those things all over the place. Another copy of that picture of you, identified by Mrs. Jackson. Bank, solicitors, several friends—all have instructions to take everything to the police if an accidental death befalls me. You've a positive interest in keeping me alive from now on."

The implication of what I was saying slowly sank in. He looked at the drug list, then back at me. "George Millace's letter—"

I nodded. George's letter, handwritten, read:

Dear Lance Kinship,

I have received from Dana den Relgan a most interesting list of drugs supplied to her by you over the past few months. It appears to be well known in certain circles that in return for being invited to places, you will, so to speak, pay for your pleasure with gifts of marijuana, heroin, and cocaine.

I could of course place Dana den Relgan's candid list before the proper authorities. I will telephone you shortly, however, with an alternative suggestion.

"I burned it when I got it," Lance Kinship said dully.

"Did George telephone and tell you to stop supplying drugs and donate to the Injured Jockeys' Fund?" His mouth opened and snapped shut viciously. "Or did he tell you his terms when he came here?"

"I'm telling you nothing."

"Did you put something into his whiskey?"

"Prove it!" he said with sick triumph.

One couldn't, of course. George had been cremated, with his blood tested only for alcohol, not for tranquilizers, which in sufficient quantity would have put a driver to sleep.

George, I thought regretfully, had stepped on one victim too many. Had stepped on what he'd considered a worm and never recognized the cobra. He must have enjoyed seeing Lance Kinship's fury. Must have driven off laughing. Poor George.

"Didn't you think," I said, "that perhaps George had left a copy of his letter behind him?" From his expression, he hadn't.

"When did you begin thinking I might have your letter?"

He said furiously, "I heard in the clubs that you had some letters. That you'd ruined den Relgan, got him sacked from the Jockey

Club. Did you think that, once I knew, I'd wait for you to come around to *me?*"

"Unfortunately," I said slowly, "I have now come around to you. And like George Millace I'm not asking for money. You see, it's your bad luck that my mother died from addiction to heroin."

He said wildly, "But I didn't know your mother."

"No, of course not. There's no question of your ever having supplied her yourself. It's just that I have a certain long-standing prejudice against drug pushers."

He took a compulsive step toward me. I thought of the brisk karate kick he had delivered to den Relgan at Kempton and wondered if in his rope-soled sandals on parquet he could be as effective. He looked incongruous, not dangerous. A man not young, hair thinning on top, wearing glasses, and beach clothes indoors in December. A man who would kill if pushed too far.

He never reached me to deliver the blow. He stepped on the fallen photographs, slid, and went down hard on one knee. The indignity of it seemed to break up whatever remained of his confidence, for when he looked up at me, I saw not hatred but fear.

I said, "I don't want what George did. I don't ask you to stop peddling drugs. I want you to tell me who supplies you with heroin. You must have a regular supplier."

He staggered to his feet, aghast. "I *can't*. It's impossible. I'd be dead."

"He's the one I want," I said mildly. The source, I thought. One source supplying several pushers. The drug business was like some monstrous tentacly creature: cut off one tentacle and another grew in its place. The war against drugs would never be won, but it had to be fought, if only for the sake of silly girls who were sniffing their way to perdition. For the sake of Dana. For Caroline, my lost butterfly mother.

"It will be between the two of us," I said. "No one will ever know you told me, unless you yourself talk, as den Relgan did in the gambling clubs. If you don't tell me, I will tell the police investigating an attempted murder in my house that my neighbor positively identifies you as having posed as a tax assessor. This isn't enough to get you charged, but it could certainly get you *investigated* for access to chemicals, and so on."

He looked sick.

"Then I'll see that it gets known all over the place that people would be unwise to ask you to their parties, despite your little goodies, because they might at any time be raided. I know where you go, to whose houses. I've been told." And would be kept posted in future, I might have added, thanks to Victor Briggs. "A word in the ear of the drugs squad and you'd be the least welcome guest in Britain."

"I . . . I . . ."

"Yes, I know," I said. "Going to these places is what makes your life worth living. I don't ask you not to go or to stop your gifts. Just to tell me where the stuff comes from. What you tell me will go to the drugs squad. But don't worry. By such a roundabout route that no one will ever connect it with you. Your present supplier, however, may very likely be put out of business. If that happens, you might have to look around for another. In a year or so, I might ask you for *his* name."

His face was sweating and full of disbelief. "You mean it will go on and on?"

"You killed George Millace. You tried to kill me. You very nearly killed my friend. You think I don't want retribution?"

He stared.

"I ask very little," I said. "A few words written down now and then. Don't worry, you'll be safe. I promise you. Neither my name nor yours will ever be mentioned." Secretive, close-mouthed Victor would see to that.

"You . . . you're *sure?*"

"Sure." I produced a small notebook and a felt-tip pen. "Write now," I said. "Your supplier."

He sat down by one of his glass-and-chrome coffee tables and, looking totally dazed, wrote a name and an address. One tentacle under the axe.

"And sign it," I said casually.

He began to protest, but then wrote, "Lance Kinship." And underneath, with a flourish, "Film Director."

"That's great," I said without emphasis. I picked up the notebook and stored away in a pocket the small document that would make him sweat next year and the next and the next. The document that I would photograph and keep safe.

He didn't stand up when I left him. Just sat in his T-shirt and white trousers, stunned into silence. He'd recover his bumptiousness, I thought. Phonies always do.

I WENT out to where Clare and Jeremy were still waiting, and paused briefly in the winter air before getting into the car.

Most people's lives, I thought, weren't a matter of world affairs, but of the problems right beside them. Not concerned with saving mankind, but with creating local order, in small checks and balances. Neither my life nor George Millace's would ever sway the fate of nations, but our actions could change the lives of individuals; and they had done that.

The dislike I'd felt for George alive was irrelevant to the intimacy I felt with him dead. I knew his mind, his intentions, his beliefs. I'd solved his puzzles. I'd fired his guns.

I got into the car.

"Everything all right?" Clare asked.

"Yes," I said.

RICHARD Stanley Francis was born on October 31, 1920, in Pembrokeshire, Wales, and grew up in Berkshire, England. Both his father and grandfather were jockeys, and young Dick learned to ride when he was five years old. He left school at fifteen with the intention of becoming a jockey himself; instead, he wound up becoming a trainer. During World War II, he served in the Royal Air Force, piloting fighters and bombers. He met his future wife, Mary Margaret Brenchley, in October 1945. They were married in June 1947 in London, and eventually had two sons, Merrick and Felix.

Dick Francis finally became a professional rider in 1948, and went on to become one of the most successful post-war National Hunt jockeys, riding for HM Queen Elizabeth—the Queen Mother—among others. It wasn't always easy, and he suffered his share of broken collarbones, skull fractures,

and dislocated shoulders. "You don't count broken ribs," he joked.

Despite his success—he won over 350 races and was champion jockey in 1953/1954—he might be best known as the man who *didn't* win the prestigious Grand National. In 1956, he was riding the Queen Mother's horse, Devon Loch, in that famous steeplechase, and had landed first by several lengths over the last fence. Winning seemed a certainty, but fifty yards from the finish, Devon Loch collapsed and was unable to continue the race. The reason the horse fell was never determined, and the loss went down in racing history.

It was a particularly bad fall in 1957 that convinced Francis that it was time to give up the sport. On his retirement, he published his autobiography, *The Sport of Queens*, following which he became the racing correspondent for London's *Sunday Express*, a job he kept for sixteen years. But he found it difficult to support his wife and two sons on his journalist's salary and decided to try his hand at a mystery thriller set in the world he knew best—steeplechasing—with the rites of the changing room and the wet, gray chill of its winter racing season. That first thriller, published in 1962, was *Dead Cert*. The classic *Nerve* came next, marking the beginning of a long relationship between *Reader's Digest* and Dick Francis, a relationship that continues to this day now that his son Felix has taken over the family writing franchise.

During his career, Dick Francis averaged a book a year, starting a new one each January and finishing it by the end of April. Then he and his wife would spend the rest of the year researching the next book. "Mary works out a lot of the crimes for the novels," Francis once told us. "My colleagues say she has a crooked mind!"

There was a certain trademark quality to Francis's novels that readers came to expect and love. They all had a racing background of some sort, although some were a little more on the track than others. Francis and his wife loved finding new subject areas in their research, with Dick carefully working the details of industries like wine merchant, artist, pilot, lawyer, etc., into a given plot. As for style, each of the novels is narrated in the first person by someone who at first appears average and just seems to get drawn into things before not only solving the crime but also facing great personal danger. It is the heroes' resourcefulness that readers came to depend on more than anything.

Over the course of his career Francis wrote forty-three best-selling novels, a volume of short stories (*Field of 13*), and a biography of jockey Lester Piggott. He was the winner of the prestigious Crime Writers' Association's Cartier Diamond Dagger and the only three-time recipient of the Edgar Award for Best Novel from the Mystery Writers of America, winning for *Forfeit* in 1970, *Whip Hand* in 1981, and *Come to Grief* in 1996, the same year he was made a Grand Master for a lifetime's achievement. He was created an Officer of the British Empire (OBE) in 1983 and promoted to Commander of the British Empire (CBE) in 2000.

In the 1980s, Francis and his wife moved to Florida; in 1992, they moved to the Cayman Islands, where Mary died of a heart attack in 2000. Francis's last four novels—*Dead Heat, Silks, Even Money*, and *Crossfire*—were written in collaboration with his younger son, Felix, a former teacher who, over the past forty years, helped research many of the Dick Francis novels. *Crossfire*, published in September 2010, was the book that he and Felix were working on before Dick's death in February 2010.

Since his father's death, Felix has taken over the Francis franchise, and Dick's legacy lives on through the "Dick Francis" novels in his son's more than capable hands.